WENDY
DARLING

WENDY DARLING

Volume One: STARS

COLLEEN OAKES

SPARKPRESS, A BOOKSPARKS IMPRINT
A DIVISION OF SPARKPOINT STUDIO, LLC

Published by SparkPress, a BookSparks imprint,
A division of SparkPoint Studio, LLC
Tempe, Arizona, USA, 85281
www.gosparkpress.com

Published 2015
Printed in the United States of America
ISBN: 978-1-940716-95-4 (pbk)
ISBN: 978-1-940716-94-7 (e-bk)

Library of Congress Control Number: 2015940086

Cover design © Julie Metz, Ltd./metzdesign.com
Author photo © Colleen Oakes

For Maine, who is the sun and the moon and everything in between.

"Can anything harm us, Mother, after the night-lights are lit?"

"Nothing, precious," she said. "They are the eyes a mother leaves behind to guard her children."

She went from bed to bed, and little Michael threw his arms around her. "Mother," he cried, "I love you!" They were the last words she was to hear from him for a long time.

—*Peter Pan* by J. M. Barrie

PROLOGUE

IT WAS COMING.

They had called it, and now, it came. They could feel it in the thrumming quarter seconds that reverberated through the tips of their wings and down their bodies, each second playing out like a lifetime in their minds. The wind had changed as it wrapped around them; there was a funnel structure now in the way the breeze blew their wispy hair. Dust streamed down from the tips of their wings, and they could feel it leaving their veins, the power and the love, a constant pouring in and back out, power and love, power and love, more with each tiny breath.

The ground beneath their feet shimmered, its crystalline properties shaming the diamonds the humans needlessly worshipped. Their toes were covered in the dust as they raised their arms and voices together, their many bodies pulsing and breathing as one mind as they lifted their tired sister up in song. They sang of her body cradled forever in the stars, that her wings would rest after her long journey into the great night sky. She rose above them, the years trailing from her fingertips like water off a leaf, her body spiraling and convulsing at the beauty of their pitch. Oaks and bluebells bowed their heads to the melody, and even the sky seemed to curl in on itself, so great was their song.

It was coming, they could feel it, could feel its gentle breath, its arrival like the inky darkness that comes before slumber. The song swept through the trees, causing the souls in Neverland to let peaceful smiles drape across their faces, unsure of why, but grateful for this unexpected pinprick of contentment, their ears turning to hear this melodic song that came from their own hearts, yet from somewhere else as well. Their voices carved out the lullaby as she rose up in front of them, a life so lived, a surrender so sweet.

So entranced were they in their song that they did not hear the soft crunch of twigs underfoot, nor did they see the eyes that watched from the trees. They did not sense the ears that turned curiously toward their heavenly dirge.

CHAPTER ONE

London, August 1911

"SEE THAT STAR RIGHT THERE? Second star to the right."

Wendy Darling squinted her light hazel eyes, straining to see the star, the lavender flecks of her irises illuminated by the bright moon.

"Papa, I still don't see it."

Mr. Darling was practically leaning out of Wendy's bedroom window now, his red robe flapping around his worn flannel pajamas in the cold London air. He sighed exasperatedly.

"Here. Here, Wendy, sit here. You're not looking right. You're just not looking in the correct manner." He pulled his daughter close to his side, taking her pale hand and curling it within his weathered own, pointing it to the sky. "If you squint, if you really squint, you can see it there, just over Cygnus, straight over from Lyra."

Wendy placed her hands on the window frame and leaned out as far as she dared, her eyes trained on the dotted stars rising out above Big Ben, just barely visible in the distance. The dark streets of London lay out before her, bedroom lights glimmering in the shadows, the streetlights rising out of a hazy evening like the masts of ships.

"Careful . . ." her father muttered, his eyes trained on his only daughter, who had always leaned a little too far out her bedroom window. "Careful, child."

Wendy closed her eyes, feeling the bitter evening air ripple across her lips and chin, making its way through her thin nightgown.

"We wouldn't want your mother to . . ."

"WENDY MOIRA ANGELA DARLING!" A shrill shriek filled the room, and Wendy cringed, her hands clenching. Her mother tended to enter a room in hysterics, and it seemed the older Wendy became, the more it rattled her. Her mother barreled through the nursery like a storm, picking up clothing as she walked, kicking drawers shut, throwing toys into bins, and pulling curtains. "Get away from that window right now! You'll catch your death!"

Sadly, Wendy pulled herself back from the sill, her father rubbing his head anxiously, as he always did when her mother was near.

"George Darling, how dare you let our daughter run wild, hanging from windows?"

"She was hardly hanging, Mary. We were simply looking for . . ."

"I know, *the* star. No one minds it, George. It's simply a figment of your imagination." She pushed past her husband and pulled the window shut with a huff, her ample chest bouncing with the effort. Once the window was shut, she straightened the beds before turning back to her daughter and husband. Wendy curled to the floor with disappointment and folded her arms.

"He was just showing me, Mother. I wasn't leaning over."

George, always the peacemaker, reached for his wife, who always seemed to be in a tizzy. "Mary, we were just looking. Poor Mary, always working. My darling, I love you. Have you taken anything for your nerves today?"

Mary Darling looked at her husband for a long time before pressing her pillowy body against his. Even though Wendy's father was a bit aloof and her mother a bit of a nag, the love shared between them had always felt sincere, and Wendy couldn't help but smile as they wrapped their arms around each other. Her father ran his hands through her mother's hair. Aside from the lustrous light brown and honeyed locks that fell on either side of her face, there was nothing terribly beautiful about Mary Darling . . . except for the fact that she had very beautiful children. Wendy considered this now as she stared up at her mother.

"Mother, I wasn't leaning. I was looking. And I believe in Papa's star. He said he saw it last year as well."

"Yes, yes, we all saw it the year before."

Her mother was lying, and Wendy had a sneaking feeling that perhaps as she grew older, lying about her father's star would become harder. But she had seen it last year—hadn't she? Tucked against her husband, Mary Darling continued warning him about the dangers of windows. Wendy looked over at him as her mother railed on, seeing his shaking hands and the slight quiver in his step. Feeling protective, Wendy pushed herself off the floor and wrapped her arms around her mother's waist, hoping to be a distraction.

"Mother, I'm sorry I was leaning out the window. You were right; I was leaning out too far." Mary Darling dropped her lips to her daughter's head, and Wendy smelled the lye and lemon soap on her mother's skin.

"Thank you, my dear. I'm glad someone has some semblance of sense in this room." With a hard look at her husband, Mary kissed Wendy's head again before retreating. "I'll have Liza put on the tea downstairs, and she'll be up in a few minutes. It's time for bed, Wendy. The boys will be up in a moment, and your father has work to do tonight. He doesn't have time to play." She gave George *the look,* clarifying, "Work that doesn't have to do with stars."

Wendy resisted the strong urge to stick her tongue out at her mother, and she gave a submissive nod, always the good daughter. "And you. You are sixteen years old. You should be focusing on your studies and etiquette so that we may find you an appropriate match when the time comes. Your head should be in your books, not the stars."

With that, Wendy's mother stomped out of the bedroom, and they could hear her steps echo down the stairs to the kitchen below. Wendy's hazel eyes found her father's blue ones, already sparkling with mischief.

"We really shouldn't . . ."

"No, we shouldn't."

Without another word, they both scampered back to the window, flinging open the wide panels, each pane ribbed with decorative iron swirls. This time Wendy was more mindful of the steep drop down to their small garden below, a drop that could easily kill a child, impaling her on the fence posts encircling the yard. Wendy shook her head as a blush rose up her cheeks. *What a terrible thought!* Her father took her hand and pointed it back at the dark sky.

"Okay, Wendy. Now really look. There's Cygnus. Look over half an inch, and then an inch upward and then again to the right. You see the first star and then . . ."

"I SEE IT, PAPA!" Her mother's words completely forgotten, Wendy was leaning out the window again, her father loosely holding onto the ribbons around her waist. "I SEE IT!" Past her trembling finger, she could see something. A glimmer, a moving shadow of light. It winked at her and then was gone, a sleight of the magician's hand. *She had seen it, hadn't she?* There was certainly something in the void there, in that dark corner where no stars lingered night after night. It was the same thing that she had seen last year, and she had spent a year wondering if she had actually seen it. Now it was gone again.

"But . . . how? I saw it. I know I did . . ."

George Darling stroked his long chin. "I'm not sure, but I've documented it once every year for the past three years, as long as I've been studying it. This star, Wendy, it reveals itself for only a few days every year, and never for very long. The clouds have to be *just* right. It can't be explained in any of the astrological books I've read, or any of the maps I've consulted. I'm preparing a paper for Reid, my colleague at Oxford." He sighed and rubbed his head. "Well, at least I should begin preparing it. In any case, it's an astrological phenomenon, and I am determined to stake my scientific career on it."

"But what about the firm?" she asked quizzically. Her father wasn't a scientist, much to his disappointment. He was an accountant at the bustling law practice down the street. A good job, as her mother was constantly reminding him. George Darling gazed sadly out at the rooftops of their London neighborhood.

"Yes. The firm. That is right. The firm matters." He said it in such a way that Wendy was sure that the firm didn't matter one bit. She looked at the ground shyly, making small taps with her tiny black slippers on the window ledge.

"How quickly did John see it?"

She hoped her father would say that John didn't, that it was something he only shared with her—his eldest daughter, their relationship so special—but of course that wasn't the case.

"Oh yes, so quickly! John saw it early this morning, before you got up, before the sun came up. He actually didn't need my help to find it!"

A familiar disappointment rose in her chest. John, always at her father's heels; John, so prized, so brazenly intelligent, her father's eyes lighting up at the very sound of his name.

"Say, where is John?"

"He's giving Michael a bath. It was his turn."

"Hmm . . ." Her father stepped back, tucking his flannel shirt into his pajama pants. "Well, I should find your mother. She's probably lying in bed right this moment having nightmares about children falling out nursery windows."

Wendy stepped back into the nursery, pulling the windows closed. "Thanks for showing me, Papa."

He gave Wendy an absentminded smile. "Of course, my dear!

When John comes in, will you send him to my study? I'm going to have him help me with some star charting."

By "study," her father meant the cluttered extra bedroom stuffed with navigation charts and star illustrations, with socks drying and mobiles of the planets circling overhead, with science textbooks overturned, their ripped-out pages dripping with scribbled notes.

"Yes, Papa."

George Darling turned and patted Wendy's head, tucking a strand of her hair behind her ear.

"Night then, Wendy bird."

He left the nursery door cracked open a few inches, so the light from the hallway could filter through the bedroom, illuminating her brothers' double beds, stripped down to the blue sheets and thick wool blankets. Their beds were always messy, despite the fact that Liza made them each morning. Wendy's bed, moved across the room last year by her annoyed father, sat closest to the window. Now she could watch the stars from her bed, see them whirling in the bright night sky. She could watch the snow fall down in endless whorls, or see the occasional blowing autumn leaf dance across the frame. In the winter it had proved to be bitterly cold, and she found herself often climbing into bed with Michael, snuggling against his warm, round body, pushing aside his teddy bear, Giles, and tucking her freezing feet under his warm blankets. His bed always smelled like little boy—like dirt and cookies and worms—but Wendy never slept as soundly as she did when he was tucked securely under her chin, his breath on her neck, her baby brother. Before John woke every morning, she would try to sneak back into her own bed, not wanting to see his judgmental face as she headed across the room.

"Scared, Wendy?"

"No. Just cold."

"Of course."

Not that his snide comments would ever make her pull her bed away from the window. That would be taking the stars from her, and that she could not abide. Also, it wasn't just the stars that she could see from her window. It was a tiny shop, down the street, and the bedroom that she knew sat in the attic of that building . . . Looking over her shoulder, seeing no one, she started to reach under her bed for the letter that she had read four times already today; but figured once more couldn't hurt. Her hands curled around the paper, folded so gently, the thin papyrus crumpling under her fingers. She hoped that it would still smell like him as she brought it up to her nose . . .

"OWW!" Now there were little boy knees in her stomach, on her chest, feet in her face, a tumble of blond hair.

"Michael! Get off me!"

Michael giggled and jumped on her again, his head buried in her armpit, his chubby legs kicking everywhere, destroying her neatly made bed.

"Michael, I mean it!" With a big laugh, he rolled off Wendy, but not before sticking a foot into her face.

"Smell! All clean!"

"Michael," she said calmly, pushing his foot away. "No, thank you. I would not like to smell your feet right now or anytime, even if you have just had a bath."

Michael gazed up at her before sticking his foot out again, wiggling his pudgy toes around. His tousled, wet blond hair hung over his eyebrows, and his mischievous blue eyes gazed up at her with adoration that bordered on worship. "Kiss them!"

"No."

"Please, Wendy?" She looked at his chubby cheeks, always reddened and raw, and his full pouty lips, and she gave a sigh of surrender before planting one kiss on the sole of his foot.

"There. No more." That seemed to be enough for the five-year-old.

"Whatcha looking at? What is that letter?"

Wendy felt her face burning and tucked the envelope back underneath her bed. "It's nothing, Michael. It's for grown-ups."

Michael turned his head. "But you're not a grown-up."

The nursery door bounced open, and John stalked into the room, wearing, as he always did, his long cotton nightshirt and sensible brown slippers, looking much older than his fourteen years. His messy straight brown hair was tousled on his head, his heavy eyebrows hiding hazel eyes. From behind his perfectly round spectacles, he peered at Wendy with that infuriating, studious look before grabbing a book down from the bookshelf and curling himself into the rocking chair.

"It's from Booth. It's probably a misguided declaration of love."

"John!" Wendy felt the blush rise to her cheeks. "You don't know what you are talking about."

Michael was standing beside her bed now. "Booth? Booth sent you a letter?" He narrowed his eyes. "Booth?"

John pulled his father's top hat from the rocking chair arm and placed it cockeyed on his head. "Yes. Booth is in love with Wendy, the fool." He continued reading as if nothing had happened. Wendy felt her heart go cold, and her skin suddenly seemed too tight.

"You don't . . . you shouldn't talk about that."

John raised an eyebrow at her. "Don't worry, I won't tell Mother. You know how women can be. Hysterical."

"John, you don't know anything."

A wide grin stretched across his thin face, a lock of dark brown hair falling out of the hat and onto his forehead. "I know that you like to meet at the bookshop. I know that you are gone for several hours in that attic before anyone comes looking for you. And I know you have lots of books that you pretend to read, so that you have an excuse to go there, when you really only read about two novels a week, though usually they're quite sizeable."

Wendy stood up to face John. "You don't know anything about Booth and me. We are just friends. He is my dearest friend."

John rubbed his glasses absentmindedly, something their father always did, and Wendy realized with a shock how much he was beginning to look like George Darling. "Your friend who wants to kiss you."

Wendy quickly closed the three steps between them and hit him hard on the shoulder.

"OW! Wendy!" Her troubled eyes met his narrow, cynical face.

"At least I have friends, John."

His face collapsed. Wendy knew very well that John had no friends at St. Mary's School, that he spent their recess reading adventure books in the library. She saw his mouth curl with betrayal before he spun the rocking chair around to face the wall.

"You should be very careful about those letters, Wendy. You wouldn't want Mother to find them. You know what she would do. Booth is hardly the suitor she imagines for you." He gave a loud sigh, as though giving her advice was exhausting him. "Liza's likely to find them sooner or later, and she will surely give them to Mother. I would try a better hiding spot, perhaps tucked in a book."

"John . . ."

He raised his hand to shush her and went back to reading *The Time Machine*. Michael watched them both with wide blue eyes as he sucked on the arm of his teddy bear.

"Michael, that is disgusting. Please stop." He dropped the teddy bear out of his mouth and reached for Wendy's hand. She sighed.

"Hold on."

Taking the letter from under her bed, she walked carefully over to the bookshelf, an elaborate piece of wood carved to look like an enchanted forest. Wendy ran her fingers along the spines of the books, making sure to put the letter in between the right books so that it would be pressed between two things she loved. She glanced back at John, who was still sitting in the rocking chair, facing away from her, the creaks of the chair matching the bounces of his top hat as he rocked hard, no doubt lost in another world. She looked toward the door and then quickly tucked the letter between *Alice in Wonderland* and *Jane Eyre*. Michael raised his eyes to hers, and Wendy brought her finger to her lips, making the gesture that meant the same thing to all three of the Darling children: secrets of the Darling children were not to be shared. Michael made the motion as well. Wendy crawled into bed with him, and Michael buried his sleepy head in her neck, mumbling, "Sleep now."

She tucked Giles in beside him. Michael's eyes were already drooping; he had always fallen asleep quickly.

"Wendy?"

"Yes?"

"You have letters from Booth?"

"Yes."

"You kiss Booth?" His tone was concerned.

She kissed Michael's cheeks. "Only you, Michael," she whispered. He gave her a sleepy grin and then closed his eyes, happily surrendering to his dreams, which she imagined consisted of puppies, play swords, and a towering pile of cakes. She pulled the wool blanket over the sheet and tucked it around his feet.

"Goodnight, Michael."

She made her way over to her bed near the window. John continued to rock, and Wendy looked back at the bookshelf. Unfortunately, John had been correct; the bookshelf was a much safer place to store her letter.

The letter.

She settled into her sheets and closed her eyes, seeing Booth's elegant scrawl climbing across the thin pages:

Wendy,
It is plain to me that because of
our families' respective social
statuses — I am, as you may have
noticed, somewhat poor — that we can

never dream of being together, but if I am allowed to dream, then I see myself carrying you in a field of wildflowers . . . . Our great God above seems to have carved out my feelings for you, feelings that I can no more hold inside of me . . . Should I even dare to hope that one day it will only be us on all the earth, and that we will be able to love each other freely and with an abandon that will make the heavens shake? . . . If the stars above saw what I felt for you, they would pour out their wonders . . .

She heard the sound of the nursery door opening, and her parents appeared in the sliver of gaslight, followed by Liza, their waifish brunette servant, carrying a tray with two cups of tea, their nightly ritual. Michael, to his dismay, was still too young for tea.

"Miss Wendy?"

Wendy gently took her cup off the tray, taking in the delicate lines of pink that etched the outer rim. The tea was too warm to drink, but Wendy let the calming vapors of vanilla and chamomile waft over her face and warm her soul.

"Thank you, Liza."

Liza gave a nod and bustled over to John, who simply reached out his hand from the rocking chair. Liza put the cup in his outstretched palm, and he went back to rocking and reading without a word. Wendy hated how John treated Liza.

"Now, John, don't be rude. Into bed with you," George Darling chided, pulling off his son's top hat and placing it on the bedpost.

"Thank you, Liza," John muttered in the deadest voice possible as he crawled into bed with his tea.

"You're welcome, Mr. John." Liza bustled out of the room, leaving the parents alone to say goodnight to the Darling children. Wendy sat on the edge of her bed, kicking off her slippers and tucking her feet into the cold sheets. She held her warm cup of tea against her chest, trying to calm the flush on her face that crept up when she thought about tomorrow. *Tomorrow with Booth.*

"Goodnight, my darling girl." Her father kissed her forehead and took a sip of her tea. "Oh, still hot. I would wait a bit on that, Wendy."

"I will, Father."

Her father leaned forward and whispered in her ear. "Thanks for stargazing with me. We'll see it together next year. Is it a date?"

"Yes, Papa."

George Darling headed over to Michael's bed to tuck some blankets around his slumbering form. Her mother sat down beside her, tracing Wendy's cheek with her hand.

"How was your day, lovie?"

"Fine, Mother."

"I'm glad."

"Mother? Tomorrow after Mass, may I go to the bookseller's for more books?"

"Of course. Tell Mr. Whitfield that the Darlings send their love."

"I will."

"But be home early. Your father and I have the Midsummer Night's Ball tomorrow night."

"Yes, Mama."

Her mother kissed her forehead and tucked the sheets around Wendy's legs. "That's my good girl. I love you so." Mrs. Darling glanced around and then gave a low whistle. Nana, their massive Newfoundland, trotted into the room, her plumy tail knocking against the dressers. Nana went to each bed, checking that each child was there. She licked Michael's elbow before her huge paws clumped across the floor to Wendy's bed. Nana rested her enormous head on the side of the bed, and Wendy buried her face in her soft black fur. Nana gave her a single lick on her cheek, and Wendy kissed her nose.

"Goodnight, Nana." Nana gave a huff and made her way over to her bed—which was John's bed. Of all the things that John did that drove Wendy mad, this fact made her feel the most small: Nana loved John best. She watched as the gigantic dog leapt onto John's bed and snuggled against his side. *How nice, to have that warmth, that comfort.* As she shifted her head against her feathery pillow, her mind made its way back to Booth, and she fell asleep replaying his words in her head, her eyes ever watchful through the windowpanes for her father's star.

If the stars above saw what I felt for you, they would pour out their wonders . . .

She slept.

CHAPTER TWO

AFTER A LONG MASS THAT MORNING, Wendy tucked her hands deeper into her dress pockets. It was summer, but when the bitter London winds snaked through her thin dress, Wendy was glad that she had listened to her mother and brought a shawl. Today was unseasonably cool for the summer months, with the gray skies and chilly rains that would mark autumn plunging all of London into dreary waiting. Her boots clicked on the cobblestones as she passed the butcher's that Liza bought meat from every other day and the bakery that always smelled heavenly, their windows full of lovely treats in pinks and creams. Hordes of businessmen, their hats pulled hard over their ears, swarmed around her, all vying for a spot at the restaurant her parents frequented. Most of them worked at her father's firm and treated Sunday like any other workday once church was over. She passed the tailor, who regularly shook his head at Wendy's quickly lengthening torso and Michael's wiggly body, and the medicinal dispensary, which provided her mother with her many tonics, which John insisted didn't actually cure anything.

Two horse-drawn carriages rumbled past Wendy, and she stepped aside to make sure that water didn't splash over her pretty cream dress and maroon stockings. She tried to make sure that her gait was calm and normal and that any number of her parents' friends milling around wouldn't be able to tell that it was taking everything inside of her not to sprint toward the bookseller's, the wind flush on her face, her hair ribbons blowing about behind her. Instead, she kept her walk steady and controlled, her hands clutching inside her white gloves.

Whitfield's Bookshop appeared ahead, and Wendy quickened her pace. The gray brick building wrapped around the corner, its curled sides the cause of much speculation amongst the neighbors who wondered how the Whitfield family, so many years ago, had afforded such impressive architecture. The gold lettering above the bookseller's was rusty and weatherworn, and the *f* in *Whitfield* was hanging cockeyed from its last nail. A worn rack of discounted books sat outside, each for sale for a shilling. The neighborhood boys regularly stole the books from the rack, but Mr. Whitfield would just smile whenever he was told about it.

"At least they are reading," he would mutter, before getting back to work. It made Wendy adore the old man even more. As she approached the shop, her mouth became very dry, her palms now sweaty when they had been cold before. This familiar place, as comfortable and comforting as her own house, now seemed to loom large overhead, much larger than she remembered. Her heart pressed against the inside of her chest, and she had to stop for a moment to take a deep breath and remind herself that Booth was her best friend. He knew her. Today would be no different. So she had gotten a letter, so what? It didn't change anything. She pulled open the door to Whitfield's, the brass bells on the door giving a familiar clink. She stepped inside, hanging her shawl on a coatrack by the door. The bookstore was almost as chilly as it was outside. Wendy decided to keep her gloves on.

"Hello? Mr. Whitfield?"

"WENDY!" There was a loud clatter of books falling to the floor, and the smiling bookseller emerged from behind a shelf. His white eyebrows leapt crazily, like two wiggling caterpillars.

A neatly trimmed beard etched out the corners of his weathered face. Vivid blue eyes—the same exact shade as Booth's, something she had never noticed before—looked out from behind gold-rimmed glasses. Wendy found herself gazing at his eyes for a second too long and turned away with a blush.

"Good afternoon, sir."

Mr. Whitfield knocked over a pile of books with his leg as he reached out to pat her head. "I'm so glad to see you today! How was Mass? You're the only Catholics on the whole street!"

Wendy shrugged. It had been the same as always, the rhythm and the music service awakening the deep peace inside of her, while at the same time she was terribly bored. John had fallen asleep, twice, only to be shaken awake by her father, and Michael had yelled out once in the service, "But I don't want to be quiet!" which drew the judgmental eyes of the priest and the faithful gathered in the pew in front of them. Wendy had been quiet, though she felt ashamed that through almost the entire service, her mind had been lingering on Booth.

"Mass was fine."

"Glad to hear it. Tell your parents I said hello when you head home." His eyes fell to the bundle in her hand. "What have you brought with you today?"

Wendy reached into her bag and pulled out two books in perfect condition that she had snatched from her father's expansive library. He would never miss them. Mr. Whitfield took them from her, turning the books over in his wrinkled hands. He opened the books and let the pages fall, inspected the spines, and finally, smelled the books. "Yes, yes . . . these would be perfect for our window shelf. I'll give you eight pounds for both of them."

Wendy gave him a smile. "Can we do a trade instead?"

"Well, I suppose. Let me guess, you want a *new* book."

She grinned in spite of her nervousness.

"I have just the book." He disappeared into the folds of the shop, a whimsical warehouse of books and papers, all overshadowed by the giant printing press in the middle of the store. It wasn't used, of course, but Mr. Whitfield had turned it into a desk of sorts. Wendy closed her eyes and took a deep breath, inhaling the scent of worn, musty pages, the knowledge and adventure that lay between them, the fresh ink, and the old baguette that lay uneaten on a typewriter nearby.

It triggered her first memory of Booth.

She had first discovered the bookstore when she was ten years old, when her mother sent her down the street to get a school-book for John. Wendy had been nervous on her first solo errand outside of the home, and so her mother had sent Nana with her, then much smaller and wilder than the gentle dog she was today. Wendy remembered pushing open the door and letting her mouth drop open. Books! More books than she had ever seen in her life, all waiting to be read! These weren't the books from school, with their endless pages and lessons; these were adventures! Mr. Whitfield, who unlike Wendy and Nana looked exactly the same as he did then, had insisted that Nana come inside with Wendy and had given her a tour of the store.

"Usually it's your mother who comes; is she well?"

"Yes, but she is very busy preparing for her Valentine's Day party," Wendy had answered with a shy smile.

"Well, I am glad, for even though I've been sending your mother home with textbooks for you and your brother for years, I've never met the famous Wendy until now."

When she had first seen Booth, he was in the foreign-language section, a small, dusty corner of the store, sitting on a pile of books, which Wendy remembered thinking was so disobedi-ent and wild. His very long legs had stretched out from the pile, his wheat-colored pants held tight by brown suspenders that stretched over a clean white shirt. Still, he wore no jacket, no undershirt, and Wendy remembered thinking, *This boy must be poor.* He slammed *The Adventures of Huckleberry Finn* shut and jumped to his feet, looking at her from underneath his pageboy hat, his bright blue eyes widening when he took in this well-dressed girl, her hair falling in short brown ringlets.

"Can I help you find something, miss?"

Wendy had been confused. *Was he teasing her?* Then Mr. Whitfield had come around the corner.

"Oh! Wendy Darling, this is Booth, my son. He's twelve going on thirty." Booth stuck out his hand, and Wendy shook it with a blush, feeling suddenly so insecure.

Booth looked down at the books stacked in Wendy's arms and said, "So. What are you reading?" He circled around her, asking rapid-fire questions, his tone polite but insistent as he looked at the books, his fingers brushing one spine and then the next. "*Les Miserables.* Very sad, but very good. That's one for the ages. Are you going to read it in the original French? *Black Beauty,* very good. You're a girl, so you will enjoy it. Lots of hair blowing in the wind. *The Crossing*—good. But Churchill can write better, don't you believe? *The Golden Bowl*—didn't like it. *The Call of the Wild,* excellent choice. Have you read *The Wizard of Oz* yet?"

Wendy nodded, her tongue tied in her mouth, realizing that this boy was possibly, besides John, the smartest person she had ever met.

Finally she stuttered, "Yes. Yes. It was quite good."

Booth laughed, a reassuring deep sound, as he clasped her kindly on the back. "Quite good. That's one way to describe it. I like you, Wendy. Would you like to see the rest of the store?"

She smiled. "Yes."

Booth carefully took the books from her arms and set them on a shelf behind him. "Don't worry; no one will steal them here. No one ever comes back to this corner of the store." Then he took her hand, curling his fingers around her small palm. "C'mon!"

Looking around the store now, almost a woman, Wendy remembered that long-ago moment when Booth had taken her hand. Maybe she was just imagining it, but even then, she had felt her senses shudder, as if someone had turned a key inside of her.

Mr. Whitfield returned to her now, dragging one leg behind him slightly. Wendy frowned. "Is your leg bothering you again?"

"Ah. It's nothing. It's just the autumn coming nearer; it always gets stiff this time of year."

Wendy knew from Booth that Mr. Whitfield's leg was prone to infection and spasms. "I'll have Mama send you over some ointment."

"Nonsense, child! I'm fine. Here, take this book." He put the novel into Wendy's palms. "Well, knowing you, you will need to have a long conversation with Booth about what book he recommends, although may I remind you that your parents are probably missing you." Wendy heard the slightest bit of reprimand in his voice.

"I'd like to see Booth if that's all right, sir."

Mr. Whitfield shook his head. "You two spend too much time together. I tell you, that boy. He insists on taking over the accounting for the store, even though I'm perfectly capable, and just this week he reorganized the travel atlases without asking me. I've had it, I tell you!"

Wendy couldn't hide her smile. Mr. Whitfield had probably never been cross with Booth in his life. Both father and son were loving and bighearted, and their arguments tended to last seconds, unlike the time Wendy had pulled out a clump of John's hair, or John had bit Wendy on her upper arm. Wendy longed to belong to both Whitfields, but in very different ways.

"I'll see myself up. Is he in his room?"

The bookseller stared at her for a long moment before nodding and heading over to greet another customer. Wendy squinted toward the door, making sure it wasn't her parents, or any of her parents' many friends, before making her way to the steep staircase in the middle of the store. Gripping the wood railings on both sides, she climbed the precipitous ladder that vaulted her up into the storage area of the bookstore, a dusty attic that housed crates of books, journals, and the bookkeeping records. Wendy ducked her way past the cobwebs, their location so familiar to her now, past the cutouts of Father Christmas and his woodland creatures that decorated the store every Christmas, past bins of unused journals and fountain pens, their ostrich feathers caked in dust. She stopped when she came to his door, willing herself to breathe, the words of his letter echoing in her head. She knew that once she crossed this threshold, everything would be different. Beyond that door was something so unfamiliar to her, a desire, something that she had always wanted but never dared to express, for how could she? Booth looking at her with those knowing eyes made her heart race. When had he turned from a boy who chased her through stacks of books into this, a man who seemed to peer right through her? Who was this boy to make her feel such desperation to be near him? Wendy was sure she knew who she was—she was a Darling, proud and privileged, a good girl and a good Catholic, Michael's older sister, her father's second-favorite child, a lover of the stars. She raised her gloved palms and laid them against the door, centering herself for just a second more . . .

The door flew open, and Booth stood before her.

A long exhale escaped his full lips as he looked at her with surprise. "You came."

"I did."

Wendy had to duck her head down to enter his room, which was little more than a bed between two slanted eaves of the roof. She looked down at his unmade bed and felt a blush rise to her face. "Booth, I . . ."

"Wait."

He paced around the room, and she watched the way his long strides made the muscles in his lean shoulders flex with each step. His tweed trousers hugged his lean frame, topped with a clean white button-down shirt and gray suspenders that dotted his shoulders with red tips. He had removed his hat when she came through the door, and his shaggy brown hair was pressed down across his forehead; it took everything within her not to reach out and brush it away from his face, his perfect face. He had full pink lips that stretched into a wide, trusting grin, the kind of endearing smile that let the receiver know that everything was going to be fine. His face was still now, though, as his bright blue eyes bore into her face, his cheeks ruddy. He pulled a chair out from behind his bed, his hands shaking ever so slightly.

"Please sit."

Wendy sat obediently, her eyes never leaving his face. His mouth opened and poured out a great jumble of words. "I'm guessing that you found the letter tucked into *The Woman in White*. Before you send me crashing down to earth, please just let me explain. I understand that we are not of the same social standing. Your family is rich, and while my father and I are not extremely poor, I am certainly not a suitable suitor in your parents' eyes. However, I have a plan."

Wendy stayed silent, watching Booth pace around the room.

"If you share my affections, I will take an internship at your father's firm. My father can find someone to help with the store in exchange for food and a warm place to sleep, I'm sure of it. I will take an internship, and in a few years, I will become one of them. I'm sure of it. I'm smart. I'm a fast learner, and I'm good with numbers. I will begin attending Mass with your family. At first they will take me out of pity, but if I work on them long enough, surely I can win your parents over as a man worthy of your hand. My father will eventually leave me the bookstore, but hopefully by then I will be so successful in my own right that I can hire someone to run the store, and perhaps branch out into other stores. Surely owning a number of stores would be quite a legacy for our children, no? That is . . ."

Wendy was trying not to smile now, as she watched Booth, always so collected, tie himself into knots.

"Of course, if you reject this proposal, I will absolutely understand, for God knows that there are some holes that could possibly arise in each projected outcome, but in each plan, if one depends on . . ." Finally, his blue eyes met Wendy's. "Oh, Wendy, I'm sorry. I haven't even asked you if you feel, if you share . . ."

Wendy looked at the ground for a moment before raising her eyes to meet his, family and class long forgotten.

"Booth." She struggled to find the right words. Finally, she let a smile creep across her face. "I feel . . . yes."

Booth crossed the room in a few steps and knelt in front of her. "Oh, Wendy, my darling . . ." He reached for her hands. She extended them toward him and he grasped them gently, her fingers curling into his, the exact same way they had six years ago, when they had just been children together. Moving very slowly, he began to peel the glove off her left hand first.

"Wendy, the way I feel about you, it's pure, you must know. I'm not talking about having a secret affair in my attic. I'm talking about a proper, public courtship, because if I may confess, my feelings for you have been suppressed for years, and I refuse to waste those years trying to hide what we've known for certain."

Wendy was having a hard time breathing as Booth pulled the white glove from her hand.

"You must know . . ." he murmured. "That you are a beauty divine, and though the lines of your face have driven this man to madness, that I love you most for what lies inside of you, for you are a good soul, Wendy, a loving sister and kind friend, and you have a wondrous mind."

"Booth."

"Shhh . . ." With that murmur, he bent his head and gave her the softest of kisses on her open palm. It was as if her skin had been set on fire. Desire raced through her palm and through her body, so taking her by surprise that she practically leapt up and out of the chair. Booth stepped backward.

"Wendy! Dear, have I offended you? That was too forward. I should have known, I'm sorry. Here, I will help you put your glove back on. I have been presumptuous and improper."

He didn't have a chance to finish, because Wendy stepped up in front of him, her heart hammering. The glove fell to the floor. Booth, never a person comfortable with silence, went still, his blue eyes widening as her face came closer to his. Wendy looked at his face, so close now. Then she raised her ungloved hand and traced her fingers over the places that she had so longed to touch, longed to touch for years, her desire unleashed with the kiss of her hand. Her fingertips ran over his lips, over his stubbly cheeks, over the small scar that dotted the side of his mouth, the result of a fall from a bookshelf two years ago. She touched his long black eyelashes, his strong Roman nose, traced his jaw to the curve of his neck. This boy that she knew so well, as close to her heart as her own family, was now a man, and with each beat of her heart, Wendy found herself pulling more and more away from her childhood. Finally, her hand found a place on his shoulder, and she raised her eyes to meet his.

He looked down at her face with amazement before murmuring, "Wendy." He lowered his lips to hers and with a brush as soft as a feather, dashed them against her own.

It was her first kiss, and he tasted of whipping cream and books.

She sighed.

Booth pulled back from her, his eyes wide with shock, his cheeks flushed.

"Wendy . . . I . . ." She stepped back from him, raising both hands to her face. She was suddenly so ashamed. What if he hadn't wanted to kiss her? What if his opinion of her had suddenly changed? What if he thought she was of loose moral character? What—

Booth pulled her close and pressed his lips against hers for the second time. They fell hard against the bookshelf behind Wendy, and a shower of loose notebooks fell around them. His lips traced the corners of her mouth.

"My light soul . . ."

With each kiss, Wendy was falling deeper into him, realizing that she would never again be able to live without his touch. She traced her fingers through his messy hair, and he smiled, tugging carefully on the light blue ribbon in her hair.

"We mustn't go much further, otherwise, I'm not sure . . ."

"We couldn't stop," Wendy whispered.

"Exactly." Booth turned away from her then and sat on the corner of his bed, pushing aside a pile of clean laundry to make room for her beside him. They both sat in silence for a moment, Booth wrapping his hand around her own.

"What do we do now?" she asked. Booth squinted in the dusty attic, his eyes trained on the ceiling. She could see that he was thinking, calculating.

"We should tell your parents that I would like to court you."

Wendy shook her head. "No. Booth, they will never let us be together."

"What other option do we have?"

She struggled to find a solution that wouldn't involve her mother screaming and wailing, tugging at her own hair until Wendy acquiesced. She suddenly saw herself climbing into a black carriage, a suitcase at her side.

"Booth, they would send me away. To a boarding school. We can't tell them. Even John said that they never would allow it."

"John knows?"

She turned her head away from him. "John knows everything."

"That nosy little prat."

Booth stood and crouched in front of her, his hands resting gently on her knees.

"Wendy, even if they won't allow it, I feel the right thing would be to tell your parents. I am fond of your family, and I will not sneak around behind their backs. That would be dishonest. I want ours to be a public love, not something we hide in the shadows." Wendy buried her face in her hands. In her mind, she saw her mother's reaction to Booth's advances, the disappointment in her father's face as he realized that his second-favorite child would fall from her rightful social status. It couldn't happen, not now. Not until she could figure out a way to raise Booth from his status as a bookseller's son . . .

"I can see the wheels in your head turning, Wendy. But there is no other way if we want to be together now."

Wendy found her voice, which had been pressed back against her throat. "Booth, if we can just wait, wait until you become an accountant, wait until you have the chance to . . ."

He stood up. "To what, Wendy? How long should I wait for you? Until I am thirty and you have been betrothed to one of your father's older colleagues? Or perhaps until you get sent off to a girls' college? Perhaps I can climb a vine up to your window . . ."

His voice had turned cold. Wendy stood up and reached for him. He pulled her against his warm chest, and Wendy felt herself curling into him, fading into the smell of him, the intoxication of the bookseller's son being so near. His lips traced her brow.

"I can't wait that long for you, Wendy. You are going to have to be brave. Can you do that for me?"

Her lips opened just slightly. "I need time, Booth."

A door slammed from below the attic, and they leapt apart from each other, Booth's feet skittering on an empty lantern. He looked up at Wendy, annoyed.

"This is what we have to look forward to if we decide not to tell your parents."

"Booth?" The shopkeeper's voice echoed sharply up through the attic. "Booth, what are you doing up there? I need you to carry some books for Miss Rochester!"

Booth leapt up, snapping his suspenders and pulling on his pageboy cap. He spun back toward Wendy, putting his hands over her warm cheeks.

"Let me look at you, just as you are now, so that later I can remember the moment you became mine." Time seemed to slow as she fixed her eyes on his perfect face, golden fragments of dust circling around it, the face that she longed to see above all others. Booth leaned his cheek against hers, and Wendy closed her long eyelashes, taking in the feel and the smell of him. A peace she had hardly known in her life welled up inside of her.

"I will remember always," she promised. "I will remember for both of us."

Booth's blue eyes met hers. "We will finish this conversation later."

And then he was gone, and she was left alone in his bedroom, her mind a whirling storm, filled with both passion and dread. She brushed off her dress and spent a few minutes straightening her hair bow and her tights and pushing back the stray hairs that had crept forward. Even when picking the woolly lint specks off her tights, Wendy could not keep the smile off her face. Finally satisfied that she looked completely like nothing had happened in Booth's bedroom, Wendy stepped out from behind his door and made her way to the ladder and back down to the store. Her hands wrapping around the wood, so warped by Booth's hands that it was smooth, she climbed down, mindful of her dress with each chaste step. She had almost reached the bottom when she heard her name screeched, a sound that made her hairs stand on end.

"Wendy Darling?" Mrs. Tatterley, her mother's favorite gossip partner, was standing at the register, where Mr. Whitfield was dutifully ringing up cookbooks. She bounced over to Wendy, her large bosom traveling first, followed by the swaying of a dozen pearl necklaces, all real. Wendy knew this because Mrs. Tatterley always made it a point to tell others about her wealth. A buttoned-up silk gray dress flared out in double layers around her feet, and the collar stretched wide over her pink corseted bodice. On her head sat an enormous hat of peach silk roses, greenery, and a black and white striped bow.

"Wendy Darling! I didn't know you would be here! Is your dear mother here?"

"Mama is not here today. She had a ladies' meeting after Mass."

Mrs. Tatterley bustled around her. "Oh, of course, of course, she mentioned that last week. A meeting about the new parchments for the altar, is that correct?"

"Yes, ma'am."

Mrs. Tatterley bent over Wendy and squinted. "Good Lord, child, your cheeks are so flushed. I don't think I've ever seen you so red. Are you sure you are not feverish?" Wendy politely sidestepped her touch, not wanting this woman's perfume-drenched hands to touch anywhere Booth had kissed. Her mother's friend eyed the ladder. "Did you come from upstairs? Why on earth would you want to go into that musty attic? I've told Mr. Whitfield here several times that if he wants to continue getting my business that he will clean up this store to a more sanitary level! He can't expect people of our stature to shop amongst such dust. And some of the books he carries! Did you know that I saw a copy of Ibsen's *Ghosts* in the back the other day? Obviously someone had been reading it! The filth of that novel! Good Christians truly should not even shop here."

Wendy knew she should bite her tongue, and yet her defensiveness over Booth and his father rose up instead. "Then why do you?"

Mrs. Tatterley's mouth dropped open. "Wendy Darling! Well, I never. Wait until your mother hears of how rude you have been! That is no way to talk to an adult. And for your information, we come to Whitfield's because it is the only bookstore within walking distance of our home. You know that. I never . . ." She turned and walked back to the register, grabbing the books roughly from Mr. Whitfield. "That will be all. Thank you," she snapped. With a toss of her head and a whiff of overpowering freesia, she exited the store, the bells clanking loudly after her. Wendy turned back to Mr. Whitfield.

"You shouldn't have angered her," he said quietly.

"She was insulting! Also, she'll forgive me. She comes over every week to eat all of Liza's pound cake. I'll apologize then."

Mr. Whitfield shook his head. "You have no idea what you are doing, do you?"

Wendy bent over to pick up some of the books that Mrs. Tatterley's large behind had knocked over. "I don't know what you are speaking of, sir."

"Don't think I don't know," he said coldly, the first time she had ever heard that tone come out of his mouth. "You could ruin him, my son."

Wendy jerked her head up. "Ruin? How?"

"Your family could ruin our business."

"My family would never—"

"They would. The Darlings and the Tatterleys and the Muchsens and the Browns, if they ever found out that one of their precious daughters was in love with the bookseller's son . . ."

"I'm not in love with Booth!" she protested weakly, trying to hide the blush rising in her cheeks. "Booth is my friend."

His voice softened. "I know that you care dearly for Booth, and for me. Wendy, you are like my own daughter. But if you truly love my family, you will stay away from my son. Think of what your parents would say. Think of what they would do. To us. Booth has everything to lose, while you only risk your heart." The bookseller shook his head. "I should have seen this coming a long time ago. I indulged you both for too long. The Mrs. Tatterleys of the world do not look lightly upon adoration between the classes."

Wendy felt her world unraveling, thread by tiny thread. "Mr. Whitfield . . ."

"Away with you now. Your face is already breaking my heart as it is. I'll tell Booth that you went home. Please don't forget the books for your brothers."

Her movements stiff and mechanical, Wendy picked up the pile of books from the table, one of them slipping out of the twine binding and hitting the floor with a loud thud. "Tell Booth that I . . ." She tried to maintain control over her voice, which was cracking, her lower lip trembling. Mr. Whitfield looked away from her with red eyes behind his glasses.

"Wendy, I'm sorry for this misfortune. It isn't fair. But please think about Booth's future before you consider your own needs. Good day, child." He waved his arm toward the door. Wendy moved toward it, unsteadily gathering her shawl and stepping outside onto the dusty street. Her skin, still warmed by Booth's touch, seemed to steam in the cool London air, and the world suddenly seemed strange and unfriendly.

CHAPTER THREE

WENDY DIDN'T REMEMBER THE WALK HOME, only that she had been numb, her hands wrapped tightly around her books, her heart strangely empty and sad. People moved around her in a blur: men with black hats, boys in wool shorts, babies pushed in their prams with bright red cheeks and curious eyes. She stepped into Number 14, and before she even had a chance to breathe, Liza was on her, fussing about her missing gloves.

"Miss Wendy! Why are you so pale? Where are your gloves?"

Wendy looked down at her hands, remembering Booth's lips on her palm. "Sorry, I must have lost them."

Liza sighed. "Those were expensive, child! A gift from your mama! Are you feeling okay?" She was pressing her hands against Wendy's cheeks now, feeling her forehead and lips. "You feel clammy. Go put on your nightgown and lie down. I'll be up with some tea in a few minutes for you. Tell those boys to vacate the nursery so that you may rest." She tsk-tsked. "Between you and your brothers, I get no rest . . ."

Wendy slowly climbed the stairs up to the nursery, pushing open the champagne double doors that her mother had spent weeks fussing over. When she walked into the room, a wave of sound pushed its way out toward her. John, his eye covered with a black eye patch, leapt down from her dresser, a long stick in his hand. Michael, running as fast as he could on short little legs, careened into her waist.

"WENDY! We are pirates! Now you can be our captive!"

"Michael, not now," she mumbled, pushing her way past him before thinking better of it and rustling his hair affectionately. "I'm sorry, Michael. I'm not feeling well. Could you play pirates in the sitting room perhaps, or maybe the library?" John looked up at her, his hazel eyes, the exact shade of hers, simmering with annoyance.

"We were here first. Maybe you can go lie down in the library instead."

"John, please." Wendy wandered over to the dresser that had just been a pirate ship and gently pushed John's display of tiny wooden soldiers to the side. "I need to get dressed. Please, can you play somewhere else?"

Michael stomped across the room and plopped heavily down on his bed, pulling Giles, adorned with a red scarf around his neck, with him.

"But we were playing here, Wendy."

She needed desperately to be alone, thoughts of Booth and Mr. Whitfield spinning through her mind. She was nauseated and elated all at once, thinking of her first kiss and Mrs. Tatterley's judgmental expression. "I'm exhausted, Michael. I'm not asking again."

John walked over to Wendy and, with a cold look, slapped the books out of her hands. "She's not even sick. She's sad." He tilted his head so that he could peer at her face. "Are you sad about Booth? Does he have a little crush on someone else?" His voice was so cruel that Wendy recoiled. Before she realized what she was doing, her hand slapped his cheek with a sharp crack. John stepped back in shock, his hand on his face.

"You hit me!"

Wendy was mortified. What kind of girl slapped her brother? "John, I'm sorry, forgive me . . ."

A cruel sneer crossed his face, but she saw the tears clouding his eyes. "Poor Wendy. It's not like it would have worked out. He's a bookseller's son. You might as well have fallen in love with a gutter rat."

Unable to hold back her emotions anymore, Wendy let out a cry. "Get out! Get out right now! Please! Go away!" John's face was smug as she turned away from him.

Michael wrapped himself around her leg. "Stop being mean, John! I don't want to play with you anymore!"

"Fine." John threw his eye patch to the ground. "I'm going to find Father. Perhaps he would like some enlightened conversation from *one* of his children." With a final glance over his shoulder, John exited the nursery. Wendy threw herself onto the bed, laying her forehead against her arm as a single tear ran down her face. Michael climbed up into the bed and snuggled beside her. With a cry, she curled him against her side. His small hands reached for her face.

"Wendy, why you crying?"

"It's nothing, Michael." She wiped her face. "It's nothing you've done. I promise." Raising her head, she took in her youngest brother's kind face, every inch lacking the sharpness that clouded John's. "I will be perfectly fine, Michael. May I have just a few minutes alone? "

Michael eyed her with suspicion. "Okaaay, Wendy. But Giles will stay with you. For comfort." He ripped the red scarf off the teddy bear's head. "See, now he's just a teddy bear. He's not a pirate, so you don't have to be afraid."

Wendy ran her hand over Giles's worn fur. "Thank you, Michael." She gave him a soft kiss on his satin cheek. He turned and scampered out the door, no doubt in search of brighter adventures, or to go annoy John. Arms shaking, she pulled her cream lace dress over her shoulders and untied her corset. She let her maroon stockings fall to the ground and slipped off her church shoes. She searched in her drawer for her favorite nightgown—a worn, light blue cotton one with a simple lace hem and a darker ribbon under the bust. She pulled her hair back into a ponytail, using the same blue ribbon that Booth had tugged on earlier, and climbed into bed. With a sigh, she pulled the covers over her head, wanting to disappear, wanting to forget the touch of his skin on her own, the look on Mr. Whitfield's face, his dire warnings, the cruelty in John's gaze. She wanted to forget all of it. She pulled out a book from under her mattress, losing herself in a tale of a girl and her secret garden. Eventually, her eyes pressed shut, and she dipped her head against the book pages. Wendy Darling fell asleep, her dreams crushing all around, pressing her into slumber.

Early evening had arrived. She awoke to the sound of rain clattering against the window. Rubbing her eyes, she stared at the ceiling, clutching her blanket to her chest. The rain pounded hard on the window, echoing through the entire room. She could hear her parents bustling around downstairs, probably having dinner with the boys. Perhaps . . . she paused. No, that sound wasn't rain. She rushed over to the window, her nightgown swirling behind her. Pushing open the double windows, she looked down at the street, where Booth stood in the pouring rain, his hat in his hands. Wendy clutched the window latch, afraid of falling at the sight of his devastated face.

"Wendy! Can you come down?"

She shook her head. "I can't. I just, I can't. Not now while my parents are home."

Booth's eyes widened. "Wendy, why didn't you wait for me? Have I done something to offend you? Was I too forward? Have I been improper? Tell me, and whatever it is, I'll rectify it!" His long shadow cast itself out onto the street, pacing back and forth. She stared out at this boy who had kissed her hours ago, the boy who made her see stars. "Wendy, come down! I just need a minute, please!"

Wendy stared down at Booth, her heart hammering uncontrollably in her chest. She longed to throw herself into his arms, to disappear into the rainy night together, to tumble unburdened into his small, poor bed. Through the blur of her tears, she saw his handsome face, and in his face she saw the weathered lines of Mr. Whitfield's brow, the concern on his face for his son, a lifetime of work, generations of Whitfields. *Would she take his future? Would she tell her parents, something that terrified her?* She shrank back a step.

"I . . . Booth, I can't."

Booth's face seemed to dissolve in the rain. "I don't understand. Why not? Wendy, I've come here to speak with your parents."

"Booth, no! Please don't." The rain pelted down on his shoulders, his wide blue eyes looking up at her with suspicion.

"And why not?"

Wendy felt the shame of cowardice deep in her chest. Booth was everything to her, and yet, she couldn't have him tell her parents, not yet. She wanted what he detested: a hushed love affair, kisses in attics and behind bookshelves, nothing public for now. She wanted him, more than a person had any right to desire another, and yet, she wouldn't do this to her parents. Nor to him. She cared for Booth too much to have his name dragged through the mud by Mrs. Tatterley and the low likes of her. She leaned on the windowsill, her nightgown brushing her ankles.

"Booth! My parents will hear you! Please go!"

"I DON'T CARE IF THE WORLD HEARS ME!" he shouted back, and Wendy heard a sudden silence from downstairs, followed by the sound of a heavy chair moving.

"Go away! Get out of here! Go!"

"I won't!"

"I will come to you later, but please leave! Go!" Even from the pavement, Wendy saw the disappointment in Booth's face as he gazed up at her.

"You will come later?"

She nodded. "I'll sneak out while my parents are at the party and meet you at the bookstore. Now go!" He slowly shook his head before clenching his pageboy hat angrily in his hands.

"Oh, Wendy," he said quietly, just loud enough for her to hear, loud enough to shatter her heart, "I thought you so much braver than this."

Wendy backed away from the window, her hands jerking back from the windowsill as if it had singed her skin. She watched in the growing dusk as Booth stared up at the window for another moment before walking up the cobblestone street with a shake of his head. He had just passed the gaslight when a sliver of light beamed out from the doorway; Mr. Darling was poking his head out, seeing what all that silly noise was about. Wendy ducked behind the curtains. George Darling paused for a moment; she could hear his curt breaths before he headed back inside. Wendy slowly stepped back toward the window, but Booth was gone. She brushed a tear away from her eye. Was she forever ruined in his eyes? She looked around the nursery. Was she so weak that she would give him up for a few comforts? A warm bed, a stately house? Her hands ran over the bookcase near the window, searching for his letter. She pulled it out and unfolded it before her. At the sight of his scrawled letters, Wendy came undone, a sensible girl unraveled by the bookseller's son.

"Oh, Booth," she murmured. "Forgive me." She clutched the letter to her chest, pretending it was him, remembering the way he had pulled her body against his, the sound of his heart through his thin shirt. She heard the thud of footsteps on the stairs and turned to climb back into bed. Her feet hit the tray of soup that Liza had left for her—*When had she come in?*—and Wendy tripped forward, her ankles snapping against the floor, her letter fluttering to the ground. The bedroom door flew open.

"Wendy, daughter, did you hear a ruckus out—" Her father stopped short, looking debonair in his black tuxedo and white cummerbund. "Wendy, what on earth are you doing?"

Wendy looked up at him with fear as his eyes came to rest on the letter lying face up on the rug. "Father, no . . ." Walking quickly, Mr. Darling scooped up the letter from the ground. His eyes went wide with concern as he read the words, Wendy slowly getting to her feet. The look of disappointment she had so feared crossed his drawn features as he looked over at his eldest child, next to an overturned tray with cold lemon soup seeping out from underneath. Then, to her surprise, a gentle smile crept across his face.

"Oh, my dear. Come with me."

Wendy followed her father down the hallway, past the bathroom where Liza was giving Michael a bath, past her father's study and her parents' expansive bedroom, decorated in rich greens and filigree golds, their elaborate colors frozen under a crystal chandelier. George Darling made a right turn into the drawing room at the end of the hall, and once Wendy had entered, he clicked the small gold lock on the door. Wendy felt her body tense. She had never known her father to lock a door. The Darlings' drawing room was lined in oak panels that made the small space feel even more closed in. The gold-framed paintings of horses hanging around the room had always been a source of amusement for John, who liked to point out that not one single member of the family knew anything about horses or particularly enjoyed them. Wendy took a step past one of the paintings and sat down on a hard blue velvet loveseat, her eyes trained on an antique Dutch vase of pink flowers. With a sigh, Mr. Darling sat down beside her on the loveseat, gently resting his hand upon her head. They sat in silence for a few moments, his hand absentmindedly stroking her light brown hair. His eyes came to rest on the small windows in the room, no doubt focused on the emerging stars outside.

"I remember my first heartbreak," he said quietly. Wendy stayed silent, daring to hope that perhaps this would not be the lecture she was expecting. "Her name was Clara, and she was the most delicate creature I had ever seen."

Wendy's mouth dropped open. Her father had never spoken of his life before her mother. Mr. Darling looked over at her and laughed. "Don't look so shocked, my dear. Your parents had rich lives long before you came along. Clara was a teacher. I loved her dearly, the true match for my soul. She shared my curiosity for the cosmos, and I saw a life with her stretch out before me, a beautiful existence filled with knowledge and compassionate listening. Our passion for learning was only outmatched by our passion for each other."

"What happened to her, Papa?"

He looked away from his daughter, but not before she saw tears in his eyes. "She died of pneumonia. Too many afternoons in a cold classroom with no fire to warm her."

Wendy looked down, thankful that Booth had a warm place to sleep. "I'm sorry, Papa."

"So was I, my love. So was I. But, life marches cruelly on, even if you don't think it will. I am sorry for her death, but I am also thankful that I met your mother. While she wasn't a perfect match for me, my union with her brought us both to prosperity, both in income and many other ways. Without your mother, I wouldn't have you, or John, or Michael. And what would my life be like without my children? It is something I daren't think about. It is unfathomable."

He tipped her face up to his, and Wendy saw a hardness in his eyes. "Booth is a good boy, a young man that I like very much, and by the sounds of this letter, he is very much in love with you."

Wendy blushed. "Yes, Papa."

"And you—do you love him as well?"

Wendy nodded, thinking of Booth's incredible mind and the way he seemed to understand her with just a glance. "I do, Papa."

His mouth gave a painful twist. Wendy's stomach dropped.

"Ah, my poor girl." He stood up abruptly. "Cry for him tonight. Mourn that love. And tomorrow, never see him again."

Wendy let out a loud cry. "No!"

"You know it must be this way, dearest girl. I'm sorry for it, but this match cannot be. It would be disastrous for our family. Your mother and I have worked too hard to see this family brought low by a marriage to a bookseller's son. You are never to see that boy again."

"No! NO!"

Her father unlocked the door. "I will leave you to your grief. I will not share this with your mother, because God knows we would never hear the end of it. She would ship you off to boarding school by tomorrow, and I rather enjoy your company. I insist on just one sane woman residing somewhere in this house. But see him again, and I will tell her without hesitancy. This relationship is highly inappropriate for a woman of your standing." He gave a tired sigh. "Your mother and I will be leaving soon for this blasted ball. Please be ready to put your brothers to bed in about an hour." He looked down at his daughter, silently crying into her hands. "Tonight is the last night that our star is visible. Perhaps you and the boys could look for it later. John can usually find it. He's good that way."

Wendy turned away from her father, not wanting to see his face. He planted a quick kiss on her head before walking out of the drawing room. "I'm so sorry, my dear. You must believe that we have your best interest at heart. I know how the fire of young love can consume, and I ache for what you must be going through. Still, it's time to be a grown-up, Wendy."

"Please go away," Wendy murmured softly.

"Indeed I will. Goodnight, my child."

Wendy was left staring at the floor in the silent drawing room, feeling all her hope siphoned into this still vault of puffy furniture and equestrian art.

A few minutes later, when her mother crept into the nursery with Nana at her heels, Wendy could barely look at her. Mary Darling hustled around the room, her elegant black dress draped with white fox fur and her ears dripping with diamonds.

"Oh, clothes everywhere, soup on the floor, what have you been doing in here?"

"Nothing, Mother." Wendy was staring out the window, her eyes trained on the dark summer night. The light afternoon rain had tapered off, and the resulting sky was as clear and sharp as glass. Starlight beamed through the window, casting light on her ruddy, tear-stained features.

"Oh my dear, have you been crying?"

Wendy sniffled. "No, mother. My nose has been running. I have a cold."

"Well, it's a good night to turn in early then." John and Michael shuffled into the nursery, rifling through their dressers for nightshirts. After dressing, John picked a book off the bookshelf, put on his father's top hat, and settled himself in the rocking chair.

"Oh, John, I do wish you would leave that silly hat off."

"Oh, Mother, I do wish you would be quiet and let me read," he imitated her in a mocking tone.

"John!"

"Sorry," he mumbled without meaning it, and he turned away. With a whine, Nana settled herself near John, his long fingers affectionately rubbing her chin. Michael climbed into his bed, already sleepy. Wendy handed him Giles, and he turned over in his bed.

"Are you sad still, Wendy bird? About the boy?"

Mrs. Darling's eyes widened. "He means about the pirates," Wendy said quickly, making her way over to the reading seat near the door.

"Oh. Well, then, that is something to be sad about." Wendy looked at Michael and raised her finger to her lips. He shut his eyes with a sleepy smile. Her mother drew the curtains over the large nursery window and turned down the lanterns. She kissed Michael and John, and patted Wendy's head.

"Don't stay up reading too late. Especially if you aren't feeling well. Shall I have Liza bring up some tea with herbs and honey?"

Wendy shook her head, trying not to meet her mother's eyes as she climbed into bed.

"All right then, but don't be short tomorrow when you don't feel better."

Wendy tried her hardest not to look at her mother's face, for she knew that if she did, she wouldn't be able to hold back her tears.

"You look lovely, Mother," she said in a flat voice, her face buried in the opening pages of *North and South*.

"Thank you, my dear. Do try and cheer up." Her mother took a step toward the nursery door, and suddenly Michael bolted up from a dead sleep with a scream, his eyes wide and confused. The entire Darling family jumped at the sound. He let out another long scream and then began pawing at his blankets.

"Mama, don't leave!" he screamed.

"What do you mean, my dear? We have the Midsummer Night's Ball at the Brown's mansion tonight."

Michael let out a whimper and clutched Giles with desperation. "I have a bad feeling about tonight. Don't go, Mummy; stay."

"Oh, you must have had a quick dream when you were falling asleep, like when you dream of tripping down the stairs! A little nightmare. Don't worry. Liza and John and Wendy and Nana will be here to protect you. Everyone is here to keep you safe, especially Wendy."

Michael gave a quiet sob, his eyes clouding over with something unseen. "Please, please stay. I don't like tonight. It's dark! I'll never see you again!"

Mrs. Darling looked at her youngest with adoration. "Oh, Michael, what a thing to say! John must have been whispering things in your ear! There's nothing to be afraid of, my dear. The window is locked up tight, and Liza will be awake until we return."

Michael continued to cry. "Something bad is waiting in the dark, Mummy!"

"Oh, sweet boy! What a dream you must have had." Mrs. Darling looked over with concern at her youngest son. Her face alarmed Wendy—the last thing she wanted was for her mother to stay or for her father to come into the room. The thought of his face telling her to never see Booth again made her stomach turn.

"Mother, we will be fine. Michael can sleep with me tonight."

Michael sat up in his bed, rubbing his red eyes. "Really, Wendy? Really?"

She nodded. He bounced across the room and buried himself in Wendy's bed, his warm and pudgy body curling against her chest.

"I still wish they would stay, Wendy."

"I know, little one."

Wendy's mother gave her children one last, loving gaze.

"It's settled then. Be good tonight, children. If you need anything, call Liza up from the servants' quarters. We shan't be later than midnight. Don't forget to say your prayers." She shut the door behind her, praying to herself and dimming the lanterns as she walked: "Holy Father, watch over my children tonight. Keep them safe from all harm and danger and the evil foe. Let the stars above guard their sleeping forms, and the Holy Virgin grant her mercy from afar."

With the door to the nursery shut tight, the room was plunged into quite twilight. Michael gave a whimper but soon fell asleep nestled up against Wendy's hip. John, too, eventually made his way from the rocking chair over to his bed, Nana at his heels. He collapsed into bed, Nana plopping herself next to him with a happy sigh. He wrapped one arm around the giant dog, turned down his lantern, and fell asleep, soon filling the room with his loud snoring. Wendy, however, lay wide awake, her eyes focused on the ceiling, her mind churning, weighing love and family and loyalty. She watched as the loudly ticking clock hit nine, and then ten.

At ten on the dot, Liza poked her head in and looked in on the children, as she always did when their parents were gone. Wendy knew that she would now don her nightgown and retire for good to the cozy servants' quarters. She heard the loud click of Liza locking the nursery door from the outside, securing the children inside. When her parents returned, they would check the door, and finding it still locked, retire to bed. No use in waking sleeping children. At the sound of Liza's footsteps fading in the distance, Wendy let herself breathe out for the first time in what seemed like hours. Moving ever so gently, she pulled herself away from Michael's sticky forehead and rested him against a pillow where her form had been. He didn't stir, a happy sleep smile stretching across his face. Wendy crouched behind her bed and looked over at John's bed. He didn't move.

She tiptoed over to the wardrobe, the mirrors reflecting back a flushed girl with terrified eyes that burned like coals. She pulled out a fitted black ankle-length coat and quickly buttoned it up over her blue nightgown. The wool pressed snug against her chin, the buttons tangling in her ponytail. She crossed to the window, stopping at the bookcase to grab Booth's note, and looked back at the quiet nursery before hopping up on the window ledge. Wendy Darling had never done something like this, but she had known Booth's lips on hers. She had failed him once already today, and she wasn't about to repeat the pattern, her father be damned.

When she had sat in that drawing room, she saw her future without Booth, a still room without love, her years wasted to the ticking of a quiet clock, tick-tock, tick-tock, as she wished for her youth. No. Within an hour, she would be entwined in his strong arms, and that was all that mattered. They would figure out a plan. They would tell her parents and hold fast to each other until a compromise was made. This was her life, not theirs. She chose Booth *and* her family. Her slim fingers trembling, she straightened herself in front of the window and reached for the latch.

"How exactly do you plan on getting down?" She spun around.

John was standing behind her, his glasses sitting crooked on his long nose.

"Go back to bed, John," she hissed. "This is none of your concern."

"It is my concern when you fall to your death outside our window and I'm the only one left to care for Michael. You know how he taxes my nerves."

Wendy shooed him back with her hand. "John, I am going. You can't stop me. Please go back to sleep and don't worry."

"I can't stop you? What if I scream for Liza right now? Or tell Papa that you tried to sneak out to see Booth in the middle of the night? What would happen then?" He tilted his head. "They would blame me for not stopping you, and that's truly not in my best interest." An honest curiosity crossed his face. "What do you see in him anyway? He's poor. A bookseller's son."

Wendy shook her head. "I love him because he's the book-seller's son. Because he's witty and kind and smart. Booth is even smarter than you, and you know that, which is why you've always been threatened by him. How could I ever expect you to under-stand? Your love is always conditional and only when it suits your needs. I pity you, John."

The words were tumbling out of her mouth with a surprising cruelty, but Wendy felt relieved. John's eyes narrowed with anger. "I'm leaving. You can yell for Liza if you wish." She cinched her coat tight around her and reached for the latch again. Then, as if God's breath had blown through the room, all the lanterns in the nursery were extinguished.

"Wendy?" John asked, his voice peaking at the curve of her name. "Did you do that?" She barely had time to open her mouth before the chaos began.

Suddenly there was a loud slam against the window, and Wendy tumbled backward off the sill. The sound rang like a shot through the room. Another slam followed, as if a carriage were being thrown against the glass. Wendy leapt backward, her arm reaching for John. His hand was clammy as she curled her fingers around his.

"Is that Booth?" he whispered hopefully. Another slam echoed out from the panes, which were flexing outward, the glass bending as if it were fabric blowing in the wind.

"What the devil?" John cursed. With a wicked snarl, Nana leapt up from his bed and crouched in front of the window, growling ferociously, her hair standing on end. As if pulled by an invisible hand, the curtains were yanked down from the window on their own accord, and the room filled with Wendy's screams. She rushed back to her bed and picked up Michael, cradling him against her body. John stood paralyzed in the middle of the nursery, his body shaking as he watched the window pulse in and out again, his feet frozen to the floor. The slams continued as the glass began melting, its transparent rivulets running down from the top as if it were made of water. It puddled into a silver mess on the window seat and dripped onto the floor. The violent thudding continued, and with each crash, Michael shuddered against Wendy's body, his face buried in her neck.

"What is it, Wendy? What is it?" She stayed silent, because not even in her wildest and most terrible imaginings could she guess at what this might be. Then, as quickly as they began, the crashes against the window stopped, and the remaining panes of glass melted to the floor. John ran for Wendy and climbed behind her on the bed, putting her body between the window and himself, his thin arms wrapped around her neck. There was a moment of silence as the Darling children waited in terror. Then an earsplitting whine filled the nursery as Michael began screaming. The pooled glass rippled and then exploded outward, a thousand tiny rounded drops falling into the room. The curtains were whisked out the open window and sent spiraling up into the night sky, where the stars were shining so brightly that Wendy could barely look at them. Chilly London air rushed into the room as the children sobbed. With a whooshing sound, a potent darkness spiraled into the nursery, and then everything was silent, even Nana.

"Wendy, are we dead?" John whispered, a sob climbing up his throat.

"I don't know," she whispered back, her arms still firm around a trembling Michael. The children watched in silence as a tiny shadow floated toward them, like a black feather. It lingered over the children for a minute before suddenly zipping out the window and into the starry sky, which exploded into a fragmented whirling blue and purple spiral of light. All three children were struck silent by its beauty, and for reasons she couldn't fully explain, Wendy stopped being afraid. Nana gave a groan and lay down on the floor, rolling over to show the window her belly.

"Hold Michael," Wendy ordered John, who, for once, didn't argue with her. He wrapped the trembling little boy against his thin chest and pulled the blankets around them both. Wendy rose and walked toward the window.

"Be careful!" John hissed. "Wendy!"

The blue nightgown swirled around her legs as Wendy approached the window, a curious ecstasy filling her chest as she reached her fingers out to touch the turbulent light. When her fingers met the translucent rays of color, the light gave a shudder, as if she had dipped her fingers in a pond. With her touch, the spiral began closing in on itself, and as it shrunk, Wendy began seeing familiar glimpses of the London streets below. There was a musical tinkling of notes, a most enchanting melody gracing her ears, and she watched in shock as a dark shape began coming up through the light. The figure moved fluidly, as if it were swimming up toward the nursery. The shape was undoubtedly human. A tiny sliver of dread blinked in her mind as the shape grew larger, and she ran back to the boys. She had barely made it to the bed when she saw a hand emerge from the tunnel of light. Wendy let out a scream and pressed herself in front of her brothers.

The hand opened slowly, as if feeling the air around it, and then, almost pulling itself out hand over hand, the figure rose upward. Two arms followed, then the shadow of a head, then a body. It was a boy. The boy, silhouetted in black against the swirling light, rose up out of the tunnel, his feet not touching the ground. The tunnel pulsed once more, lighting the entire nursery up as if it were dawn. The rocking horse threw its shadow over the terrified children as it was rocked wildly by an unseen hand. Nana held her submissive position, looking terrified as she declined confronting the unseen force that rose up in front of the window. The boy snapped his fingers twice. The tunnel quickly faded, pulling into itself until it was only the size of an apple. It floated over to his outstretched hand. The boy hovered in front of the window, gazing at the tiny swirling light for just a moment before stuffing it into his pocket.

At that, all the lanterns in the nursery lit back up, and when Wendy raised her head, the glass and the rest of the nursery had returned to its original form, down to the small wooden soldier that stood by itself in the middle of the nursery. Nana gave a whimper and closed her eyes.

The boy turned to look at them. Closing her eyes against this terrifying creature, Wendy pressed both boys against her tight, and John repeated the Lord's Prayer over and over again in convulsing sobs. Wendy raised her trembling voice.

"Leave us, please! Please! Go back to whatever hell you came from! Please! We are just children here!"

Through the darkness, an unexpected sound rose up, a low chuckle that grew into the laugh of a maniacal child.

"Oh, my, have I frightened you?"

Chapter Four

Wendy didn't look up, afraid to see the face that possessed that voice, that voice that rang with male confidence through the nursery. She felt air push over her hands, her body, and she knew without a doubt that the boy had moved much closer to them. The boy gave a sigh.

"I see I have frightened you. You have no reason to be afraid of me, I promise."

Wendy pressed both boys' heads down and with hesitancy raised her own, her wide hazel eyes taking in a sight that she could not believe. Floating over her bed was a boy who looked to be about sixteen years old. What struck Wendy first was not actually that he was floating—which was an unbelievable sight; it was that he was simply the most beautiful boy she had ever seen. His radiant winsomeness beamed out from his grin as he looked down at Nana with a pitying smirk. She snarled in his direction. The boy had blazing red hair, its color the same shade as a lick of flame, which flew out from all sides of his head, curly in some parts, straight in others. He had golden freckled skin, freshly sun-kissed, and peachy pink lips. He was muscular, with tan calves that appeared carved from stone, slender hips, strong forearms, and a strapping, confident chin.

He turned his face to her and smiled, and she felt her heart skip a beat. His lips curled backward to reveal small but blinding white teeth. The smile unnerved her—it was a cocky, cunning grin, the kind that John gave her when he had hid all her underthings or put a worm in her bed. Staring at him from under her raised hand, the boy's eyes were what brought her back from the uneasy place that the smile had taken her. Wide set and brushed with impossibly long dark lashes, the boy's bright green eyes, a shade that she had never seen before—like glittering emeralds!—fixed on hers. She lowered her hand and raised her chin into the light. She saw his eyes widen a bit at the sight of her, saw his lips part in confusion. He dropped out of the air, quickly, just for a moment, before flying (flying!) up toward the ceiling again.

"I . . . I'm sorry, I thought you were their mother."

Wendy found it impossible not to stare at his face, his green eyes holding her captive as he fluttered around the room.

"No, I am not their mother. I am their sister. My name is Wendy."

"Weendee." The boy seemed to weigh this on his tongue for a moment before laughing. "Wendy. Yes. You are beautiful! How old are you, Wendy?"

"I'm sixteen." Wendy tried to calm the heaving of her chest, searching for a clear breath, the fear from his arrival still pulsing through her body. "And your name?" she gasped.

"Peter. I'm Peter Pan."

"And how old are you?"

"Guess."

"Are you sixteen as well?"

"You could say that."

Wendy could feel John pulling away from her, but she wasn't ready, not yet. She pulled him back against her chest. Michael remained trembling against her lap. Wendy didn't know how to phrase the question without sounding terribly rude, but she dared anyway.

"How did you . . . how are you . . . ?"

"Flying?"

"Yes!"

With a wicked grin, he turned in a circle, like the Christmas ornaments that her mother hung every year. Then he took off, dashing from one corner of the room to another, sailing up and back down. With a sharp tug, Wendy felt John pull away from her and stand beside her.

"Say! How are you doing that?"

"Well, hello, young man!" Peter lazily circled back down and landed beside John, shaking his hand, his luminous eyes sizing up her brother. "And what might your name be?"

John blushed and stammered. "John. John Darling, sir."

"Well, John Darling, how would you like to go on an adventure?"

John looked up at Peter with silent awe. The redheaded boy gave a curt laugh and swooped up toward the ceiling once again, this time flying backward, as though he were standing up. Wendy couldn't stop staring with amazement, and to her dismay, she felt Michael uncurl from her side and stand atop the bed.

"Hey, mister! You are flying!" He pointed at Peter. Peter flew down quickly and hovered above Michael for a moment before lazily floating down and sitting in front of him cross-legged.

"What is your name, little boy?"

Michael puffed up his chest. "I'm Michael!" He dangled his teddy bear by the leg up in front of Peter's face. "And this is Giles!"

Peter tilted his head and looked for a long moment at Michael's face before bursting out with a strange crow. "Welcome, Giles!"

The boys laughed, but Wendy stayed silent, still wondering if she was dreaming.

"So, the Darling family is Wendy, John, and Michael."

"And our parents," Wendy said softly.

"Oh, yes, parents." Peter gave a soft laugh, as if they were something so ridiculous that he couldn't even comprehend the thought. With a sigh, he settled onto the foot of Wendy's bed, just inches away from her. Wendy blushed and sat back against the headboard, wary of having a boy on her bed. Peter tossed his beautiful red hair out of his eyes.

"So, Wendy, please tell me about where you live."

"Where I live?" she stammered. "Well, we live in London . . ."

"We live in London, and we live here with our mother and father and Nana and Liza! Our parents are at a ball tonight!" Michael exclaimed, climbing up beside Peter.

The flying boy rested his hands on his chin. "How intriguing! And what do you do here in this . . . this London?"

Michael considered for a moment. "We go to school and Mass and sometimes we have friends over to play with us."

Peter rubbed his chin. "Hmm. How interesting. And then your friends leave and you play no more? Does that make you sad?"

Michael nodded, a lock of his blond hair falling into his eyes. "It does, flying sir."

John strode up beside them, his face betraying his jealousy that Peter was talking to his siblings and not to him. He pushed his glasses up. "We live just outside Kensington Gardens, which is on the west end of London. Our father is an accountant and an amateur astronomer, and our mother is a lady of society."

Peter laughed, unfolding his legs. "And what does a lady of society do?" His green eyes rested on Wendy with amusement, and she found it impossible to look away.

"She reads, and sews, and writes a column for the daily paper, and goes to balls and parties," muttered John, disdainfully. Wendy raised her voice to weakly defend her mother: "She also does a lot of charity work for disadvantaged children and sometimes treats the illnesses of the poor."

John frowned. "Really, she does nothing."

"Does she now?" Peter shook his head. "What a sad life that must be!"

Michael was now running in gleeful circles around the bed. "Mr. Peter, can you fly again?"

"There are no misters where I come from, Michael."

John scampered up closer to Peter. "And where is that? You must be from some strange continent not yet discovered."

"Hardly." Peter leapt up from the bed and rose up in the air, unfolding his long arms with a grin. "I come from a place called Neverland."

"Neverland?" asked Wendy, tucking a loose strand of hair behind her ear. "Is that near the Pacific Islands?"

The boy gave her a wide grin, curling his lips back to show his very white teeth. "Hardly." His eyes widened, and the lights in the nursery dimmed just a flicker. "Neverland is an island of dreams."

Wendy watched as he ran his hands through his hair absent-mindedly, floating idly around the room as Michael followed him from below. She had never seen anyone dressed like Peter before. He wore dark mahogany cropped pants that were so tight they could almost be called stockings—stockings on a boy!—with a hunter green wool-like tunic that belted around the middle. His sleeves were a lighter, almost tweed pattern, interwoven with what looked like the vines of tree roots, running up and down the sleeves. High leather boots were etched with green leaves that her eyes followed upwards, and then . . . Wendy turned and looked away. The pants didn't leave much to the imagination. Boys in London didn't dress like him. Her mind darted to Booth for a moment, but then she caught Peter staring at her.

"Do you like my clothing, Wendy?"

She felt a blush rise up her cheeks and turned away. "No. Yes. I mean, it's perfectly suitable."

"What are you wearing? What do the lovely women of London wear?"

"Wendy isn't very fashionable," John muttered, annoyed by Peter's interest in her. "She just wears what our mother gives her."

Peter's inquisitive eyes never left Wendy's face. "Well, let's see it."

Wendy climbed out of her bed, standing slowly as Peter floated closer and closer to her.

"Why are you wearing a coat over that pretty dress, Wendy Darling?"

"That's not a *dress*," John groaned. "It's just a nightgown. And she's wearing a coat because she was sneaking out to see—"

"Be quiet, John! For once, hold your tongue!" Wendy snapped.

Peter moved toward her, covering the distance between them an inch at a time. The control in his flying was incredible. With a ravishing smile, Peter reached out gently and unsnapped the top button of her coat. The wool fell open and revealed the blue nightgown underneath, slipping from her shoulders.

Wendy's mouth fell open at his forwardness.

"Now that is a lovely nightgown, Wendy." He steadily backed up as Wendy's heart hammered against her chest. The buttons on her chest burned.

"Tell us more about Neverland, Mr. Peter!" Michael was now jumping on the bed. Peter seemed to have unleashed some sort of wildness in him.

"Michael!" Wendy admonished. "Calm yourself!"

Peter winked at Wendy quickly before flying over to Michael's bed. He began bouncing up and down on the mattress, each time getting higher and higher, until his red hair was brushing the ceiling.

"Well, children, what shall I tell you? Neverland is magical! Anything you see there has been kissed by magic! The trees and the soil and the water! It's a place where boys play endlessly, and we eat whatever we like every day!"

"Like chocolate?" Michael's eyes were as big as saucers.

"Like chocolate! And cheese! And meat pies!"

"Can everyone fly there?"

Peter's eyes clouded over for a moment, and Wendy swore she saw them turn from a bright green to a deep navy. He blinked, and they were green again—she must have imagined it. Peter smiled gently at Michael.

"Well, Michael, only the really special people can fly there. But you seem pretty special to me. But don't let the flying distract you from the mermaids."

"There are mermaids there?"

"Tons of them. They can be a bit mean though, so we try and stay away from them."

"What else? What else?" Michael was jumping up and down now on the bed like a deranged child, and John was mesmerized by every word that came out of Peter's mouth, standing rapt by his side.

"Well, there are pirates and . . ."

John's ears perked up. "Pirates, you say? What kind of pirates?"

"The best kind!" Peter replied, flying to the windowsill. "The kind that have lots of goodies to steal, and then there is the infamous Captain Hook!"

Michael stepped down off the bed to get closer to Peter. "Can we go? Can we visit? Can we come with you? I want to fight Captain Hook!"

"Of course," he murmured, stroking Michael's blond hair. "Of course you can visit."

"But if there are no grown-ups there . . ." John looked confused and excited at the same time as he rubbed his glasses. "Then who is in charge?"

The room seemed to darken as Peter's eyes lit up. "We are."

Wendy frowned. "No grown-ups?"

"Oh, there are grown-ups there, but they don't decide what we do. Pan Island is home to the free. There are no rules, and if there are, we BREAK them!" With that, Peter gave an excited bounce off the windowsill and spiraled through the air toward Michael. He stretched out his hand to the little boy, his earth-stained palm scarred with a dozen tiny cuts. He saw Wendy looking at them and shrugged.

"There are lots of trees in Neverland." Then he scooped Michael up into his arms. "Do you want to see what it feels like to fly?"

Wendy lurched toward the bed, tripping over an overturned wooden cat. "No! Michael, perhaps this isn't the best idea."

"You fret like a mother," Peter teased. "But don't worry, Wendy Darling. I won't hurt him."

John put his hands on his hips. "Why does he get to fly and I don't?"

"Well, you can fly too. Come grab his hand!"

John reluctantly walked toward Peter and then grabbed Michael's hand.

"Yuck! John, you're sweaty!"

"Shut up, Michael."

Peter gave a laugh. "Ah, brothers. What a delightful family this is! Okay, boys, are you ready?"

The boys nodded, their faces flushed with excitement. *Is this really happening right now?* Wendy wondered as she clutched her headboard. *Am I dreaming?*

"Now! The first rule of flying, at least if you are flying with me, is that you never, ever, let go of my hand or the hand of the person who is holding onto my hand. Do you understand? It's like a chain, and if you let go of your connection to me, you will fall."

The boys nodded.

"Okay! Let's try!" Peter took Michael's hand in his own. A ripple of air passed through the room, blowing Wendy's hair back from her face. Then all three rose up inches off the floor. Michael began laughing crazily, and a huge smile, one that Wendy had never seen, cracked the hardened scowl that was John's face. Peter then flew upward, the boys a second behind him, a miraculous wave. Wendy remained speechless.

"Are we heavy?" John asked, wiggling his legs. "Can you feel our mass against your own?"

Peter gave a grin. "I'm not sure exactly what mass means, John, but I feel no heavier than I did before I grabbed Michael's hand. I am not carrying you, rather, my gift of flying is passing through my hands to yours."

Peter maneuvered both of the boys over a massive pile of stuffed animals, towered over by a stuffed white horse.

"Just so you understand . . . John, I want you to let go."

John looked down. It was a fall of only about eight feet. "But . . ."

"It'll be fine, John. You aren't a coward, are you?"

John's brow furrowed. "No."

He let go of Michael's hand and fell promptly into the pile of fluff. With a giggle, he rolled out of it.

"That was actually quite enjoyable."

"My turn," Michael crowed.

Peter moved over the bed. "All right, Michael, let go."

Michael let go of Peter's hand and tumbled down onto his soft bed.

"Again!" he shrieked, kicking his legs. "Again!"

"It's Wendy's turn." Peter turned his green eyes onto her, and Wendy felt her heart thud fast against the inside wall of her chest.

"No, I couldn't. What if Liza hears?"

"Liza can't hear us," he said, grinning. "Only children can hear the magic of Neverland. For all she knows, you are happily asleep in your beds."

Wendy wrung her slender hands. "Well, I suppose."

Peter flew over to her bed and landed gently beside her. She reached out her hand, and he shook his head, his eyes flashing mischievously in the lamplight.

"That's no way to treat a possible lady of society, now, is it? Especially not for her first time flying."

Michael giggled, tossing Giles in the air. "But that's Wendy. She's not a lady!"

"Doesn't seem that way to me." Peter grinned.

"If I'm not to hold your hand—"

With a laugh, Peter scooped Wendy up into his arms and floated quickly up in the air. With a shriek, Wendy wrapped her arms around his neck as they rose up, much faster than he had done with the boys. Peter's strong arms held her curled up against him. He smelled like earth and berries, like adventure, and she found herself intoxicated with his warm, glistening skin. They rose up in the cool air of the nursery, so close that Wendy could have brushed it with her fingertips, seeing the view that only the creeping tiny creatures of the world saw, the view of the ceiling and its cobwebs, its dusty secrets. As Peter circled around the room with her, swooping up and down, Michael reaching for her hand and then laughing as she was pulled away from him, Wendy let the smile she was holding in burst free through her pink lips. Then she was laughing, and she knew without a doubt that she wanted to fly forever. As Peter neared the window, the glass panes burst open, and the curtains billowed out into the night sky. The damp air rushed in, and Wendy looked out at London before her, in all its gray stone glory.

"Beautiful, isn't it?" Peter asked, his eyes on Wendy's face. She looked out at the streetlights, at the winding streets, all so romantic.

"Yes. It is." Her eyes flitted down the street to Whitfield's. "Beautiful . . ." The window shrunk back as they flew backwards into the heart of the nursery.

"Then come with me."

She turned to him, her face inches from his. "Come where?"

"To Neverland." He turned and returned Wendy to the ground beside her bed. When his touch left her, Wendy felt her practical nature return. She laughed.

"We can't go to Neverland. We live here, in London. With our parents."

"Yes, but do your parents give you adventures?"

"No," Michael said glumly, collapsing onto the rocking horse. "They don't!"

"Can your parents fly?"

"Nope."

John looked very interested. It made Wendy uneasy.

"They might not give us adventures, but they are our parents," she protested weakly, but then in her mind she saw her father's face as he told her she could never see Booth again, the way his eyes became hard and unforgiving. She saw her mother, who would faint at the very mention of him. And then she saw Booth in her mind, waiting for her in the rain, the disappointment in his eyes as he understood that she wasn't brave, not like him. If she went to him now, would he reject her? The thought was almost too painful to bear. She suddenly felt very trapped, and a cold sweat broke out on her brow.

"We can't just . . . leave."

"Yes, you can!" Peter swooped down and trailed his fingers along the floor. "You can just visit Neverland, and then I'll return you here, safe to your parents, whenever you want. They won't even know you have gone. Time goes faster in Neverland. You'll be back before they return from the Ball!"

"Do you promise?"

Peter's eyes focused in on hers, turning that same shade of navy blue that she had seen before.

"Would I lie?"

He raised his eyebrows at her, and Wendy felt that same thrilling feeling that she had when they had been flying. She did want to fly again, desperately. She had had a sip of wine once at one of her parents' dinner parties, when her mother stated flatly that she should try it in the presence of responsible adults. After drinking it, Wendy had felt grown-up and full of possibility. That's what flying had felt like, and Wendy needed to feel it at least once more before this very strange and handsome bird flew their coop. She eyed him skeptically.

"Fine. We will come for just a quick visit. But we'll need a few things."

Peter rolled his eyes and laughed.

"You don't need things from this world in Neverland. Everything you need will be provided for you."

John turned his head. "What about books?"

"You don't have need for magical stories in Neverland. There, you'll create your own." His eyes rested on Wendy. "There are very big adventures waiting for us."

Swallowing the uncomfortable feeling churning its way up her chest, Wendy tucked her hair behind her ear.

"How do we get there?"

"Come up here, and I'll show you." Wendy and the boys climbed up on the windowsill, each of them clutching an earthly possession: Wendy with her note from Booth tucked into her nightgown, John with their father's top hat ("Are you really bringing that?" she asked, to which he ignored her completely), and Michael with Giles. Peter swung his body up onto the ledge using the bookcase edge and then proceeded to linger inches above the ground in front of them.

"Well, Darling family, this is it—no turning back. Are you ready to have an adventure?"

Wendy nodded, unsure of what strange intoxication led her to do so. This was so dangerous! This was so exciting! The quieted flame in her mind whispered Booth's name, and Wendy suddenly understood exactly why she was doing this. Just for a night, she could have a distracting adventure, just for a few hours, before she must decide between the family that she loved, and the boy that she loved. Yes, that was it. Just a tiny escape. Peter reached deep into his pocket and pulled out the swirling ball of lavender light. The children's eyes went wide as they stared at it.

"Peter, what is that?" John whispered. They clustered around his hand. The light ebbed with each breath from Peter's mouth. It seemed connected to his skin, to his being. Lavender lights reflected in his eyes as he gazed at it with adoration.

"This, my friends, is a celestial gate to every star cluster and constellation in the universe. It can take you wherever you desire to go." He grinned and tossed it in the air, catching it lightly in his outstretched palm in front of Wendy's face.

"I call it the doorway." He looked proud of himself for

explaining it with such clarity. A satisfied look crossed over his charming features. "And it belongs to me."

Peter pursed his lips together and let out a low whistle, a series of notes that rose and fell. The doorway rose slowly out of his hand and circled in the light, growing larger and larger. Peter flung his hand out, and the doorway flew out the window, climbing up and up until it disappeared into the night sky.

"But Peter . . ." Michael whined.

"Just wait, my little friend. Just wait."

Wendy held her breath as a great cracking sound erupted through the sky, as if God were crumbling the world in his large hands. A pair of tuxedoed men drunkenly staggered beneath the window, not even looking up as the world shook with such a great sound that the children covered their ears. The cracking sound eventually subsided into a low hum, and Wendy watched in wonder as the stars exploded into a thousand brilliant whirling shades of blue and purple, pulled into the whirlpool of the doorway's vortex, constellations becoming streams of heavenly light. Peter took her hand lightly and raised it to the sky, her fingers tracing what seemed like ink. She pulled her hand back out of shyness, before realizing that her fingertips glowed.

"Pieces of star," he murmured. Then he took her fingertips and ran them along his cheeks in two lines. When Wendy jerked her hands away, Peter looked as if he were a warrior, streaked with glowing white light.

"That's the doorway. We'll fly up to it, second star to the right and straight on till morning!" he crowed. Reaching down, he took Wendy's hand in his own, and she began to float off the windowsill.

"John!" John reached out and took her hand and then reached down for Michael. Michael squealed with delight and grabbed John's hand. All of the children were floating now, rising higher with each second. Wendy felt a rush of fear and delight, equally excited and terrified of what came next. Surely, this was still a dream, so what was the danger? Then she saw Peter's eyes bearing down into her own, felt the sweat of his palm and the firm way he cradled her fingers within his own, and she knew it was not a dream, for her subconscious could never create someone so beautiful and complex and so completely free. She raised her head to look at him, this strangely childlike man, his eyes focused on the glowing vortex in the sky. She was struck by the sudden need to kiss his chin. She shook her head. Booth! What was wrong with her?

"Remember that you cannot let go of my hand, Wendy, and boys—you cannot let go of each other, or of Wendy. Do you understand? If you do, your parents will have to scrape you off the sidewalk."

A tremor of fear ran through Wendy as she realized the implications of his warning. John's hand tightened within her own.

"Now, I'll ask you once more—are you ready for an adventure?" Intoxicated by the power of flight, all the children screamed their consent, and Peter launched them up off the windowsill and into the London night sky, leaving Nana howling and pacing back in the nursery.

Had they waited five more minutes, they would have seen their parents returning and breaking down the nursery door, convinced by some divine intuition that their children were not safe; they would have heard their frantic cries as they pulled back their bed sheets one by one, and they would have seen their panicked movements as they searched under every bed and inside every wardrobe, desperate to be angry with their children for worrying them so. Alas, it was not meant to be, for since the children were flying away through the night, they would never see their father fall to his knees in front of the window or hear their mother screaming at Liza. Adventure had beckoned, but in the same way, an unfathomable grief had arrived for the Darling parents.

Chapter Five

As Wendy left the confines of her nursery, she felt the humid London air whipping around her face and felt the incredible power coming down through Peter's hand, clutched so tightly around her own that it gave the semblance of safety, though they were hundreds of feet in the air. She was afraid to look down at her own dangling feet, so instead she kept her eyes on the brilliant city that unfolded itself underneath her like a lover. To the east she could see the slums, their dark, wet corridors sending a shiver of terror down her spine. From here, the mangled streets looked like twisted roots, each one playing into each other, winding and leaping around dilapidated buildings, which she had heard were filled with hungry orphans and serpentine men of the night. The Isle of Dogs was sparsely lit, but even in the darkness, Wendy could make out its famous lawns and ancient trees. Peter squeezed her hand even harder.

"Incredible, isn't it?"

Michael was screaming with delight below, while John had been shocked into an awed silence. Wendy's heart felt like it might burst with the joy of it all. Peter led them east, crossing over the great expanse of Buckingham Palace, past dark gardens that appeared now as a black spot from above. In the distance, Wendy could make out the upward spires of Westminster Abbey;

below her feet was Victoria Station, bustling even now. Peter took them lower toward the House of Parliament, nodding down at her briefly before she gave a gasp of delight at the appearance of the massive River Thames, so thick it appeared like an enormous snake curling its way through London, wanting to devour everything in its path. The National Gallery came into view, and Peter gave a burst of speed, pulling them along behind him.

"Wanna do something fun?" he whispered. Then they were diving, Wendy trying her best to hold John's and Peter's hands as the air pushed hard around them, whipping them behind Peter like a ribbon in the wind. Peter pulled them down, farther and farther, until Wendy was sure they were going to hit the ground at an incredible speed.

"Say, Peter, I dare say that we should pull up!" John yelled cautiously. His tone betrayed that while he had spoken politely, he was absolutely terrified.

"Nonsense!" Peter shouted back. "Trust me!"

They sank lower, until they were level with some ancient three-story buildings, their peaked windows and gargoyles growing closer every second. Peter turned his body, rotating his arm slowly so that Wendy might turn as well and so on down the line. He banked a hard right, the children following him into a wide alley. The flying boy gave a yell and increased his speed, and the lights around them became a blur. Wendy felt a smile erupt upon her face as they soared between the buildings, up and down with the rolling cobblestone pavement, one time even sinking so low that John almost tangled himself in some hanging laundry. Their pace slowed, and Wendy turned her head to peer into the lighted windows around her, seeing glimpses of life that she never dreamed of: a small Indian child staring out the window, his eyes lighting up when he saw Peter, as his parents danced and laughed in the background; a couple screaming at each other while playing cards; a group of dock workers standing around drinking; a man who simply sat in a chair and stared at a wall while mumbling to himself, puppets on both his hands; a woman with impossibly dark eyes reading on a dangerous ledge, a thin blanket wrapped around her shoulders. As she flew past them, Wendy was struck by how small and insignificant her own life was; everyone was trying to get by, and even if she had never met them, they existed to her now.

Peter was pulling them lower now, so that they could smell the life in the streets below them: the day-old fish sitting out, the warm bread from the bakery, the stench of waste and liquor. Someone yelled out from an alley, and Wendy saw two forms converge, saw a knife flash in the light. Then they were climbing upward again, up and out of the city, and flying over the Thames, taking a moment to circle over the golden glowing House of Parliament, passing the stern face of Big Ben, so close that Wendy could see the tiny russet sparrows nesting in its golden etchings. Diving low, they flew upward on the river, Peter heading toward Tower Bridge, a beacon of light in the dark night. The children dipped down low, so close to the water that Wendy could see her own shadow in the inky liquid. She heard giggling behind her, and when she looked back at Michael, he was trailing his foot in the river, laughing as water splashed up his thigh.

Wendy let out a laugh of pure happiness, followed by a hysterical one. She had never felt so free or light. This was what being alive felt like! For too long she had been trapped in drawing rooms and stuffy classrooms. Here, in the air, with this strange boy, she was free, even if only for a moment. She grinned and looked straight up the river to Tower Bridge, which grew impossibly large, a behemoth of beams and light climbing its way out of the water, pointing its ridges straight to the sky. Wendy had only seen the bridge from a distance while riding in a carriage, tuning out as her father had rambled on about the bascules, the hydraulics, and the glory of architects. Now, soaring below it, she marveled at its steel beams and crisp lines of wires, at its sheer impassive glimpse into the future.

Peter looked down at Wendy, and again she was taken aback by the allure of his charm: the hard line of his jaw, the way his bright red hair blew in the wind, his boyish cheeks on a man's face. The joy that radiated from his eyes as he flew was contagious. He saw her looking his way and gave a happy grin.

"I bet your parents have never shown you anything like this!"

Wendy felt light-headed as she shook her head. *No, no, of course not, how could they?* Peter looked back at the boys, who were giggling together as they rounded out the bottom of the bridge and began climbing upward, their bodies dangerously close to one of the massive pillars. John was pointing out the various features of the bridge to Michael as they flew.

"Look there, Michael, do you see how the suspension wires anchor to the pillars? Father told me that this is the first bascule bridge of its kind!" Of course, their father had told John about the bridge as well. Wendy gave a smile. Well, she knew that the Prince and Princess of Wales had been at the naming of the bridge and that was very exciting. Peter pulled them through the middle of the bridge, and then up the side of one of the piers, circling around the gray stonework.

"This is Cornish granite and concrete!" John yelled to Michael, who was just helplessly laughing, so delighted he was beyond himself.

"John, be quiet," he shrieked. John shook his head, obviously disappointed.

Peter looked back at John. "I find it very interesting, John; Cornish granite, do you say?" John flushed with happiness as they made their final lap around the gothic buttresses that topped the east tower. Wendy could see inside the walkways of the Tower, could see the faint outlines of *women of the night*—as her mother called them—sad creatures who trolled for lustful men, theirs a marriage of desperation.

"Children, are you ready?" The children looked up toward Peter as he trailed them up and away from the bridge. "Shall we pay Neverland a little visit? Shall we see what fantastic adventures await us?"

The boys erupted in loud cheers, and Wendy gave a girlish tilt of her head to show her approval. Michael smiled up at Wendy with a toothy grin and then looked down at his bear.

"Shall we go, Giles? Shall we go to Neverland?"

Then Michael reached down with his other hand to pat his teddy bear's head.

"Michael, NO!" John yelled as his little brother fell from his hand. Michael let out a piercing scream as he tumbled down into the darkness. Wendy began screaming his name. With a jerk, Peter's hand left her own and then she and John were also falling, so quickly that she didn't even understand what was happening. Peter was gone in a flash of light, and then there was just the sky above her and the dark water below. Her body turned as she fell, her hands out in front of her, as if she could break her fall, John tumbling beside her, calling "Papa!" as he fell. Falling was even faster than flying, Wendy thought with horror, as they plummeted down toward the Thames. Suddenly Peter was above her and then beside her, Michael's body up over his shoulder.

"Take my hand," Peter shouted to Wendy, his hand reaching for hers. She flailed her arms, hoping to catch his hand. Finally, their fingers connected, and her fall simply stopped, as if the momentum of falling just failed to exist, and then she was moving with intent, with Peter, toward John's tumbling form, twisting as it fell. The note from Booth fluttered out of her pocket and lazily flapped down towards the Thames. Wendy's heart twisted at the sight of it, but her focus, for the moment, was on saving her brother.

"Grab him!" Peter shouted.

Wendy lunged for John's leg and wrapped her hand firmly around his ankle, and then they were motionless in the air, a family hovering. John's sobs faded quickly, and he turned to hide his face from Peter.

"I'm sorry," Peter breathed heavily. "I couldn't catch Michael and still hold you both. Better to catch him first and then grab you on my way up."

John wrenched himself upward and traded his foot for his hand, finally righted. Michael was sobbing.

"I'm sorry, John! I forgot! I wanted to touch Giles."

"It's all right, Michael. It was an accident," Wendy soothed him.

"It is certainly NOT all right!" John yelled. "Michael, you could have killed us all! Do you understand? What were you thinking? What is wrong with you?"

"John, leave him be! You're being quite terrible!" Wendy admonished.

"No! He needs to understand. You could have killed us because you were worried about your stupid teddy bear." John reached out and grabbed Giles out of Michael's hand.

"John, stop it, right now!" Michael wailed.

"No. You need to learn. You aren't a baby anymore." With that, John dropped Giles. The teddy bear fell swiftly and silently into the dark night.

"Giles! NO!" Michael turned his body into Peter's chest.

"John!" Wendy turned her hazel eyes on him, righteous anger curling up her chest. "I know you are scared, but try not to take out your anger on Michael. He is five."

"He needs to grow up," John snapped. "We're going somewhere to have adventures, not play with stuffed toys."

Peter silently watched the family bicker before clearing his throat. Gently, he uncurled Michael from his arm and took his hand in his own. Michael and Wendy were now on either side of Peter, with John at the end of the line. Peter tucked in his chin and peered into Michael's tear-streaked face.

"John is right, Michael. You shouldn't have let go of John's hand. That was very dangerous." But then he grinned, his eyes lighting up with delight. "But how would you like to go to a place where you don't need to grow up—ever? Where you can have all the teddy bears you want?"

Michael nodded. Peter then circled around until he was face to face with John. "And John, how would you like to go somewhere where you aren't in charge of a five-year-old boy, but an army?"

John looked intrigued. "Yes, sir."

"Yes, *Peter.*"

"Yes, Peter," John corrected himself.

Finally, Peter leveled his gaze on Wendy. "And you?" Wendy was lost for a moment, looking back the way they had come. What was Booth doing right now? Was he still waiting for her? Did it even matter? If Peter was telling the truth, then Booth wouldn't even notice her absence, and yet . . . Then Peter was in front of her, his green eyes looking into hers with a ferocious intensity, and her thoughts about Booth disappeared. "Do you want to go somewhere where your parents' opinions and rules don't matter?" He leaned in toward her and then brought his lips to her ear, so close they brushed her cheek. "Do you want to go somewhere where you can have anything you desire?"

Peter's warm breath washed over her, smelling like leaves and honey, and then she was gone, caught up in him, caught up in the night, in the wind that whistled around them.

"Yes," she whispered. "Take us there."

"I will." Peter raised his face to the night, to where the passage had climbed earlier, now a small white light twinkling in the last corner of the sky. "Open," he whispered quietly.

He began pulling the children upward, upward, until they were flying through cold and wet clouds, upward as a hard rain pelted their faces, upward through thick fog, so thick that if it weren't for Peter's warm hand and John's cold one, Wendy would have been drifting alone in a sea of gray. Upward they climbed, past the cloud cover and the strange, thin air around it, crackling with energy and a strangely magnetic current that made Wendy's arm hair stand on edge. The temperature began steadily dropping. Frost formed on her lips and eyelashes. Higher and higher they climbed, until the air was too thin to breathe and there was nothing to fill her lungs with, nothing at all, and then her chest began painfully seizing as she struggled for air. She heard John gasping below her and tried to yell to Peter that he couldn't breathe, that she couldn't breathe, but there was no voice, no air, only the burning in her lungs.

"Almost there!" Peter yelled.

Wendy felt her throat close up, and her lungs felt like they were bursting against her chest, beating against her ribs, desperate to breathe. She felt John jerking his hand violently in hers, choosing between breathing and falling. Black stars exploded in her vision, and she tried to pull her hand out of Peter's to grab at her throat, to grab anything that would make her breathe; even if she fell, it would be better than this because she would have air . . . and then it was over. The night sky exploded into a thousand fractured lights before them, bursting open like a doorway. The protective sky itself curled and tucked around the children, as lavender and blue light began leaking out of the hole in the stars. It reflected upon itself like a puddle of glass that then began to swirl clockwise, a whirling star made up of hazy colors. Out of the star poured air, sweet, glorious warm and wet air, delicious and life-giving, and Wendy gulped it into her lungs greedily, each breath making her feel more alive. John and Michael were doing the same.

"You made it!" Peter grinned. "It's difficult the first time. The air gets thin when you're this high. It can be unpleasant. "

Wendy looked up at him accusingly, her politeness worn away by the lack of air. "Unpleasant? We have almost died twice tonight! Are you sure that this is safe?"

His eyes narrowed before he gave a scoff. "You have never been in any real danger. I would never put you in harm's way, Wendy Darling. Neverland is the safest place in the world. No one ever wants to leave Neverland!" He shook his head with a laugh. "You beautiful, proper girl! You'll understand when we get there."

Wendy flushed at his compliment, ducking her head. Peter turned now to the doorway opening up before them, the buzzing spiral in the sky that churned and winked its treasures. Looking through the doorway was like looking into a cosmic hallway. Inside the room were three other wavy windows, shuddering and changing shape in the drifting light: one window was a world where the stars moved and shifted, one featured a pink and orange sky that radiated with light and life, and the last one had two bright moons that blazed like the sun. Peter pulled them up to the last window: a world with a faultless blue sky, a blue that burned the eyes.

"Open," Peter whispered, for the second time. The window with the blue sky blinked and grew larger. The center of swirling light expanded and swallowed Peter's window, the light reaching outward, growing into the same tunnel formation that Wendy had seen in the nursery. There was a moment of silence as the Darling children looked down the tunnel into another world, into this Neverland.

"Well," John muttered, "we've come this far. We might as well go on."

Peter let out a delightfully deep laugh and flew into the tunnel, pulling the Darling children with him. Wendy gave one momentary glance back, taking in the gray cloudy skies of London, but soon the window faded and all she could see were swirling lights. She faced forward, tumbling through a vortex, tumbling down, Peter's hand strongly wrapped around her own, and before she knew it, it was daytime and all three children were floating in a cloudless blue sky, bright and clean as pool water. A thousand feet below them, a gigantic green island rose out of the water. The warm, wet air of the island enveloped them. A question pressed against her heart at the sight of it. *What is . . .* Peter let himself explode into a greedy and consuming laughter.

"Welcome! Welcome to Neverland, Darling family!" He pulled Wendy closer to him as they lazily drifted down into a bright new world. London faded from her mind like the minute details of a discombobulated dream.

CHAPTER SIX

NEVERLAND SPILLED OUT UNDERNEATH THEM, a gigantic garden isle drenched with emerald valleys, jagged white cliffs, and a towering mountain spire that watched over the island like an impassive guardian. An unnaturally turquoise sea battered at the coasts. It was such an enchanting sight that it made Wendy's chest ache. She took a deep breath of air that was very different than London's thin, smoke-clogged offerings; here the air was heavy and warm, like the draping of a blanket. The smells of sweet flowers, a salty sea, and honey overtook her nostrils. Neverland smelled like life. *Flying must be easier in this atmosphere*, she thought, noticing that the wind wasn't pushing up against her body the way it had before.

John was pulling ahead at the end of their chain excitedly, his top hat close to falling off.

"Peter! Say, how big is this island we're seeing?"

Peter looked back at him, his red hair settling messily on his forehead. His skin flushed in the sun. He was home.

"It's about five hundred miles by your London measurements! By my measurements, it takes about two hours to fly from end to end!"

Wendy looked down at the island, unable to control the hungry excitement bubbling up in her chest. Life in London was filled with gray skies and gray buildings, the clopping of horse hooves at all hours of the night, buildings upon alleys upon shops; this was untouched lushness, the wild. It was like nothing she had ever seen, more exciting than she had imagined possible! To think, only two hours ago, she had been lying in the nursery, covers tucked up to her chin. Wendy turned her head back to look at the doorway. In the few moments that they had been free from it, it was already churning in on itself, the lights dimming with each passing second. She watched silently as their way home became smaller and smaller until it simply folded into one small burst of lavender light, which then dissolved into a thousand tiny pieces in the sky. All that was left was the prick of shadow, no bigger than a marble. Peter nodded his head, and the light flew silently into his pocket.

"Well!" he declared with a boyish grin. "That wasn't terribly complicated, was it?"

From the air, Wendy could make out that the island was entirely consumed with lush greenery. With the exception of the east side of the island, which was covered in a craggy white rock face that looked uninhabitable, the rest of the island was a verdant spread of a thousand different greens, like mosaics of flora and fauna, none of it familiar. A range of tree-covered mountains cut the middle of the island in half, a zipper of such immense size that Wendy found herself tempted to reach out for them. The lower peaks rose up to meet one towering peak, its very tip free of greenery; it was sharp and black, and it shimmered in the sunlight.

"Shadow Mountain!" Peter shouted down to her when he saw her looking at it. "The highest peak in Neverland, and one of the most dangerous places around. See that black tip?" Wendy nodded, spellbound. "It's made of a flaky shale, as thin as a wafer! If you step on it, you'll find yourself sliding down the sides with a terrible tinkling, and you'll be impaled on a tree below."

Mist trailed off the tip of Shadow Mountain, the white clouds wheeling down into the rolling hills of green like waves of fog, cascading down from one peak to the next. Wendy had never seen anything like it. Of course, she had seen mountains in picture books, and grainy photos of the impressive peaks of the Americas or Switzerland, but here was a real mountain, and its power, its immovable mass, caused something deep inside of her to tremble, as if she were kneeling before an indifferent god. Peter grinned.

"When Shadow Mountain blows smoke, the natives used to believe it was a sign of fertility, a time to fall in love, a time to make children."

Wendy blushed. "The natives?"

Peter rolled his eyes. "The Pilvi Indians, a silly people, through and through."

"Will we meet them?"

"No. Unfortunately you will not." Peter shrugged, suddenly seeming uninterested in the conversation. Wendy looked back to the large island, growing closer with every minute, her eyes trying desperately to take it all in and failing. At the southern end of the island, resting at the bottom of the sharp green peaks, there was a small town, a long collection of rickety buildings, a few roads edging the top of a gigantic bay. The bay bristled with life—three ships rocked in the turquoise waters, anchored by a long stretch of beach with white sand. It wasn't the sandy color of the dilapidated and litter-strewn beaches of London—no, this sand was a pure white, untainted by color, like a new lamb. Light shimmied and danced across the sand, reflecting on the faces of a half dozen gigantic ships that were overturned on the beach, their rotting hulls made beautiful by the contrast. Peter bit his lip as they flew to the east of the bay.

"The sand . . . it's made of naturally crushed pearls that the waves deposit there! That's why it's called the Bay of Treasures." Peter started laughing. "The Lost Boys call it 'Booty Bay.'"

"And above it?" Wendy trained her eye on the collection of

wooden buildings that looked to be about a mile long, all leaning against each other as if exhausted. Some were large and ornate, others crumbling.

"Port Duette," he replied. "A place that you will see for yourself one day, but never without me . . ." He turned and looked at her, his vivid green eyes burying deep into her consciousness, his face etched with worry. "Only I can protect you here."

She flushed, a tiny trickle of pleasure crawling over her skin. Wendy let her eyes run upward to the west side of the island, where a dozen thin waterfalls rushed down from the peaks above, disappearing into the depths of towering green trees. When she looked at them, the air shimmered and jumped, like watching a rock under a river. She blinked. There was something beneath the trees—something that winked in the sunlight and then concealed itself again. Shades of gray flowered from underneath the leaves, but then, with a breath of warm wind, they concealed themselves again. When she squinted, she thought perhaps she could make out dilapidated pearled archways—maybe?—and black fog winding itself between them.

"Peter, is that a city?"

"It was, at one time. That's the Forsaken Garden. It used to be the fairy city, until they all died. It's rumored to be haunted by all sorts of wicked creatures. We don't go there because it's too dangerous."

"We?"

Peter unleashed his hypnotizing smile upon her. "The Boys. You'll see. Any other questions?"

Wendy couldn't help herself and burst out laughing. "Yes! About a thousand thousand!"

Peter squeezed her hand, and she felt a familiar warmth spread through her limbs. He had quite the effect on her. "I promise I'll answer all of them. But for now, just take in the view." A softness crossed his features. "Why, Neverland from above is my favorite sight in all the world."

"And there?" John asked. "That wild forest beyond the Forsaken Garden?"

"Empty," Peter shouted. "Abandoned, like the Forsaken Garden, abandoned by the natives who should have guarded it! I'll take you flying there someday, John, the flying through the trees—well, there's nothing quite like it!"

Wendy reluctantly forced herself to bite back her inquiries and focus on the incredible scene unfolding underneath her feet, teetering now directly above the massive island below. Without warning, Peter banked a hard right, and they were flying directly to the east of the island. Soon, the sharp white cliffs gave way to the endless turquoise sea. There was nothing below them but water and the occasional arching back of some flitting sea creature that lingered just below the surface.

"Peter . . . ?" Michael had finally found his voice. "Where are we going, Peter?"

Peter squeezed their hands before flying them in a dizzying upside-down loop. All the children squealed and laughed with delight. "Here's the best surprise of all: We don't live on the main island. We live in an even more magical place."

"And where's that, mate?" John laughed nervously.

"Just wait a moment," Peter shouted. "Be patient, Darling children, and we will soon be there."

The waves underneath their feet changed directions and began getting more violent as they flew away from the shore.

"Pan Island."

"You have an island named after you?" John shook his head. "Brilliant! Do you live there alone?"

Peter laughed. "Ah, John, my friend, you have no idea what awaits you!"

John was unable to keep the joy off his face at being called someone's friend. Without warning, Peter began spiraling downward in an ever-widening circle with the children trailing behind him, reminding Wendy of the birds of prey that she occasionally spotted soaring over the parks in London.

"There it is!" John cried.

At first glance, Wendy thought she was looking at another mountain, but as the children covered the distance between the islands, she saw that it was a . . .

"A tree!" she shouted. "Pan Island is a tree?" As long as her block in London and just as wide, the tree seemed to burst forth from the ground with a certain violence. Pan Island rose almost vertically out of the ocean. It was indeed a tree, a tree that could swallow all other trees and the sea and sky around it. From above, it reminded Wendy of the bonsai that her father kept in his office. Levels upon levels layered the tree, wooden beams and walkways visible from the air. From above, the round, flat huts that dotted the tree's branches looked like ants on a log. Sunlight filtered down on its thousands of leafy branches, each one its own unique hue of green. Choked vines and variegated leaves as big as horses provided the massive tree with shade and protection. At the base of the great tree, pale beige roots rose out of the ocean, the tree's main trunk not even beginning until thirty or so feet up in the air. Beyond that, a green maze of bamboo that surrounded the base peacefully swayed in the wind, brushing its tips to wave to the children above. From there, the great branches, some as wide as buildings, curled out, contorted, gnarly and thick, their upward-facing surfaces worn with the sun. As they flew closer and closer to the island, Wendy thought she saw a boy scampering down a branch before he disappeared into the green leaves of the tree.

"It's, it's . . . incredible," John gasped.

The humid Neverland air seemed to beckon Wendy ever nearer as Peter began leading their descent to the topmost point of the tree. As they dropped swiftly, Wendy saw a flag emerge out of the dense foliage. As they grew closer to the tree itself, she could see that it wasn't so much a tower as a wide, circular thatched roof that loomed above all the others. Peeking out from a jumble of overlapping dried palms and leaves was a thick branch, and at the end of the branch, a handmade flag snapped in the wind. It had once been a shirt, Wendy observed, a black threaded shirt, sized for an adult. Someone had painted a crude yellow moon on the back of the shirt, the fingerprints still visible where they wiped the paint off on the side of the flag. Silhouetted in the middle of the rising, messy moon was a black figure, his arms outstretched in flight.

Peter Pan.

CHAPTER SEVEN

"I'M SLOWING NOW!" Peter shouted, and he pulled back so that the children trailed feet behind him, their arms all stretched beyond being comfortable. As light as a feather, Peter landed gently on the thatched roof, his feet barely making a sound as they brushed its scratchy surface, at which point he let go of their hands.

The Darling children were not so graceful. Michael went tumbling, almost pitching off the edge of the roof before Peter grabbed his arm roughly to catch him. John ended up on his knees first and then skidded face-first into the roof, leaving his burning face marked with tiny red slivers. Wendy landed hard on her side and rolled a few times before coming to an abrupt stop, her nightgown hiked up just over her thighs. Mortified at both her landing and her white legs, she yanked it down with a cry, Peter looking away quickly to pretend he hadn't noticed. All three children staggered to their feet, and Wendy felt her stomach give a heave of nausea. She turned away just in time to miss Michael getting sick off the side of the roof, but she heard it. It took all her willpower to force the nausea down. Peter came to her side, concern etched across his impossibly beautiful face.

"Are you feeling all right, Wendy?"

She held out her hand. "We're . . ." She laughed. "We're just not used to flying. We might need a few minutes before our stomachs settle."

To her great annoyance, besides the rough landing, John seemed perfectly fine. He walked swiftly to the edge of the roof and was looking out at Pan Island with a huge smile across his face. Wendy pushed herself up to her knees and laid her hands firmly against the strange roof, unlike anything she had ever seen. Even the smallest palms were woven, and not in a simple cross-pattern, but rather in an ever-widening circle of elaborate designs. Her fingers traced the design upward until she reached the center of the roof, where a gorgeously sewn night sky was pierced through by the branch holding Peter's flag.

"Why, this is amazing work," she stuttered. "Who made this?"

Peter shrugged nonchalantly. "Magic. Probably. But wait until you see the rest!" Wendy stood, shakily, and Peter reached out to steady her. His green eyes met hers, and he reached down and, without warning, he unlatched the two navy buttons holding her coat on. The coat fell to her feet, and Wendy felt like she was shedding a skin.

"I thought you might be warm. Here, I'll help you down." Peter gestured to her brother. "Aye, John, do you see that bell?"

Peter pointed to the farthest point of the roof, where a perfect silver bell was perched upon an outlying branch. "Ring it!"

As John scampered over, Wendy took note of how out of place the silver bell looked amongst the tree branches and the natural, woven roof.

"That bell is so lovely."

Peter turned to her, his naughty grin at once so enticing that Wendy had to clench her hands to keep from caressing his face.

"I stole it. From Hook."

Michael, wiping his mouth on his sleeve, looked up from where he was finished getting sick on the roof, and Wendy made a note to clean his face as soon as she had access to water.

"Captain Hook?" Michael asked, eagerly.

Peter wagged his long finger. "Later. That is a tale for later. I'm assuming that you could probably use a good meal and perhaps a nap?"

At the mention of a nap, Wendy felt all the energy drain from her body. Peter was right—she was exhausted. It had been night when they had left . . . where was it that they lived? London, yes. How silly that she forgot! When they had left London, it had been night. Now it was midday. Her senses were out of whack and the strange question that had leapt into her chest when they arrived whispered once more before settling into the folds of her subconscious: *what is . . . what is . . .*

"Yes. That sounds quite lovely, Peter." With that, John began ringing the bell. Its harsh clang sounded out over the roof and echoed down into the tree below, out over the island.

"Thank you, John."

John's hand slipped, and the bell gave an extra clang. Peter laughed. There was a moment of deafening silence in the absence of that harsh, sharp sound, and then Wendy heard a rising wave of whooping. Whooping and cheering, banal and animalistic in its nature, as if the tree itself were calling back to Peter its happy reply. It was the joyful cries of boys, boys calling like wolves to the moon, scampering and yipping toward them. Peter flew to the side of the roof, where a clumsy ladder made of branches was attached.

"Come, Darlings! Let's go meet my boys." He gave Wendy a naughty grin before leaping off the side of the roof, while Wendy self-consciously tucked her blue nightgown underneath her, climbing down one rung at a time until her feet met a boarded platform. She turned her face upward and reached her arms out to catch Michael, who, to her dismay, simply jumped.

"I'm Peter!" he cried, before landing heavily in her arms, his foot pushing roughly into her hip.

"Oof, Michael, you are getting so heavy! You can't jump like that."

He giggled, and Wendy curled him up for a kiss. His fat hand pushed her face away.

"No, Wendy! Not in front of Peter!" With a shake of her head, she put her little brother down and turned around. A sudden, sharp silence filled the air. Finally, a brave boy's voice rose up through the silence, cutting through it like a blade.

"What the bloody hells 'tis a GURL doing here?"

The Darlings and Peter were now standing on a high platform that overlooked several descending levels of a dizzyingly large tree house. Staggered down from their spot on the platform were several more very wide and flat circular thatched roofs, each gorgeously patterned. The manzinita-esque tree wrapped and clung to the different buildings, leaping in and out of windows, its fingers splaying and supporting each of the levels, which were connected by endless mazes of rope walkways, tattered pieces of rope that ran from hut to hut. Each rope walkway was strung with perhaps a dozen hanging lanterns. There were probably about thirty huts in all, some larger than others, some shaped like tents, others like round bowls, still others like tiny versions of rickety square buildings. The tree groaned and creaked in the wind, and Wendy was struck that Pan Island, this fortress of nature, was somehow alive. A raw bustling energy ran through its veins, something she could feel in the air, sense on her skin. It was the feeling of boys, a crackling and fervent energy, and as she looked out from the platform, she understood why. About two hundred boys of every shape, color, and nationality stared up at her. There were pale white skinny boys with red hair and dashes of freckles; black-skinned boys with dark, beautiful eyes; black-haired lads with icy blue eyes; tanned boys with curly brown hair, their skin the color of cocoa; blond boys with strong chins; and Asian boys with long black hair and tanned skin.

Dirty boys all of them, wearing similar outfits to Peter: leggings and loose tunics decorated with leaves and visible stitching, and a variety of random leather pieces that didn't seem to really fit them. Across their chests, some of them wore a haphazardly painted moon, drawn with the same messy yellow paint that had marked the flag. They stared at Wendy, and she felt the eyes of each boy: piercing, judgmental, and foreign. Their faces contorted between fascination, anger, and confusion as they looked at the strange girl standing in pajamas in their midst. Wendy suddenly felt very naked.

"I said," yelled the boy in the front, small but bulky, with a tangle of red hair. "What's SHE doing hyah?"

Wendy instinctively took a step backward, so that John stood in front of her. John looked amused at her discomfort. Peter stepped up to the front of the platform and raised his hands. The rumbling crowd of dirty boys below fell into a reverent silence. He grinned and spoke.

"Boy oh boy, I missed my boys!" The boys erupted into cheers, several of them crowing into their hands. "And I have good news for you boys! I have found two more brave soldiers to join our ranks, two more men to stand at our side when we knock on Hook's door!" He grabbed John's hand and raised it up. "This is John! He's very smart. In fact, he's so smart that I have decided to make him a General!" There was an audible whisper that ran through the crowd. Many of the smaller boys jumped up and down with excitement, but Wendy noted that several did not, most noticeably three older boys who stood at the front, arms crossed at the chest, two of them staring at John with sneers of contempt.

"And this . . ." Peter swept Michael out of Wendy's arms and held him up in front of the crowd. "Is baby Michael!" Michael scowled at being called a baby, but he obviously loved the roaring of the crowd at his name. He wiggled and waggled in Peter's arms.

Peter put him down gently and reached his palm out to Wendy. "And now I have one more person to introduce to you." Tentatively, Wendy put her hand in his, feeling the warmth of him and the tingle of power that came with it. Peter pulled her closer, and as she neared his side, she could hear the confused grumbling of several boys. "Peter?" "A girl?" "This was unacceptable." Peter turned his brilliant green eyes on the crowd, daring those voices to continue their dissent. They didn't. He waited a moment before smiling again.

"Generals, Lost Boys, and Pips: May I introduce to you, Wendy Darling. She is here to share with us in our adventures. She is our friend, and when she is here, on Pan Island, she is under my protection. No one is allowed to touch her or hurt her. She is our honored guest, sister to John and Michael, and we will treat her with respect. We protect who?"

"Our own . . ." echoed back the dull voices of bored boys. Peter jumped up, taking to the air and flying low over the crowd, reaching out his hands to touch some of their heads, patting them with affection, tugging on their ears.

"I said, *we protect who?*"

"Our own!" they screamed back, leaping and reaching for his hand. He laughed joyfully.

"And to celebrate their arrival, I've just made the decision that in two days, we shall help relieve Hook of his generous bounty of alcohol. A raid is needed! What do you think? Are you ready for an adventure?" The boys were frenzied now, hugging each other and clapping. Peter rose up above them, his feet dangling near their heads. "And tell me, whose name shall he cry to the skies when we take it?"

The throng of boys fell silent and then a whisper pierced the group. "The Lost Boys." The whisper grew among them until it had grown into a scream. Peter sailed above them, his face aglow with pride. Wendy felt a flare light inside of her chest as she watched him. He was dynamic.

"That's right! Hook will cry for the Lost Boys. Not Pan, not you, but us, the Lost Boys. For it is all due to your courage, and let's not forget, your quick swords and arrows!"

The boys erupted in laughter. Peter flew back up to the overhang, where Wendy and the boys stood perfectly still, mesmerized by this God-child who obviously commanded the worship of hundreds. The yearning eyes of the Lost Boys looked to Peter in that the same worshipful way that the faithful looked toward their God. Except that this was a different kind of church, a sanctuary of leaves and branches, their stained glass remnants of tattered fabric that hung and blew in the breeze. And Peter, well . . .

Without warning, he grasped a young boy from the crowd and pulled him into the air with him, the boy granted the power to fly, just as the Darlings had been.

"Do you all know who this is?"

The boys cheered.

"This is Thomas. Even though he is just a Pip, I have decided that Thomas will be a companion to Michael, but if he does his job well, he will be joining the Lost Boys and the Generals when we borrow from Hooky!"

The crowd erupted with cheers of encouragement that concealed a simmering jealousy at Peter's attention. Thomas, who looked to be about seven, was beside himself with happiness, the blush rising from his sallow cheeks a complement to the curly blond hair that cascaded down his back in a ponytail. Aside from the occasional street urchin, Wendy had never seen a boy with curls quite like that. Peter flew back up to the platform, taking Thomas with him and placing him down beside Wendy.

"Hallo," Thomas whispered to Wendy, the joy in his voice touching something deep within her. She placed her hand on the back of his head and smiled, and the mass of dirty boys seemed to relax a bit. Without warning, Thomas took her hand and squeezed it. Michael narrowed his eyes before Wendy giggled and poked him. Peter flew up to rest upon the dilapidated wooden banister that separated the Darlings from the rest of the boys below, his hands upon his hips.

"Now, the Darlings have had a very long night of flying, and they are probably tired. Tomorrow night we will celebrate their arrival with a grand feast, but today . . ." His eyes rested on Wendy. "We'll let them sleep."

Wendy found herself beyond thankful, for nothing sounded more terrible at the moment than feasting with hundreds of loud and curious boys. Her eyes were barely staying open as it was, and she found that moving her head too quickly resulted in a lingering light-headedness. Peter waved his arms out over the boys, their eyes rapt on his figure.

"Now, go about your day and do whatever you please! That's the freedom of Pan Island! Generals, stay—we have an adventure to talk about!" He turned his head to the three older boys who were still staring at John. "Abbott, Oxley, and Kitoko—join me in a one clock turn? John will be joining us as well—unless he's too tired." He gave John a tempting grin, one eyebrow cocked.

John shook his head. "No—no, sir. I'm not tired at all."

"Sir?" All the Generals laughed. John did look raggedly tired— the bags under his eyes spoke to his lie, but Wendy was secretly pleased to see him included. Michael gave a huge yawn, throwing his arms up.

"Peter, I'm *very* tired."

Peter laughed and rubbed his towhead. "Indeed you are!" The boys had begun to disperse silently into the gentle folds of the tree that cradled the buildings around them.

Peter turned to Wendy. "Shall I show you to your private hut?"

Wendy nodded. "That would be lovely, Peter, thank you," she said, taking Michael's hand.

"First I'll show you the basics of Pan Island so that when you wake, you'll know where to find everything you need!" Alternating between flying, leaping, and walking, Peter led the Darlings down several descending levels of branches until they reached a very wide and large rope walkway that linked two large structures together at the very heart of the tree. Peter gestured to the space.

"We call this the Centermost. It's the heart of Pan Island."

Wendy nodded, taking in the shower of petite yellow flowers that dotted the canopy overhead and the elaborate nautilus carved into the trunks that arched above their heads. Peter touched her arm with a tender brush of his fingers before pointing.

"These are the two main gathering rooms: the Table and the Teepee. One is for eating, and the other is for storytelling. Ox will show you those tomorrow." Peter's tone implied that the purpose of these rooms was obvious.

Wendy nodded. She felt swallowed by the tree, by its branchy folds and twisty corners. They walked down several more walkways, Peter leading Wendy by the hand, his skin warm and soft against her own. This little adventure so far had been nothing if not improper, through and through, but strangely enough, Wendy found herself not caring.

"I think," he said, running his hands though his thick red hair, "that we will head down to where the Pips sleep at the base of the tree. Michael can sleep there. John will take his rest here." He pointed to a group of hammocks that swayed just underneath the Teepee, each strung with red and purple nets, the beds swaying ever so slightly of their own accord, strung between two smaller branches. Michael looked at Peter and then back again at Wendy before shaking his head no and clinging to Wendy's leg. Wendy laughed and looked back at Peter.

"I would much prefer Michael to sleep with me, if that is all right. He's had a long night and is in a strange place. You understand."

Peter's quizzical look told her that he didn't, and for just a moment, he looked almost disappointed, but then the look disappeared, and Wendy wasn't sure if she was hallucinating in her exhaustion.

"Of course. You're . . ." He looked at Michael and searched for the words. "Little."

Michael stuck out his bottom lip. "I'm not little." He paused. "But I'm maybe a little little."

Peter laughed. "That's fine, Michael. I have a very special place in mind for Wendy. Hold on tight to her!"

Wendy gripped Michael's hand tightly, her other hand still holding Peter's, and suddenly they were soaring up through the tree, upward to the tips of Pan Island. Wendy watched as the light brightened as they rose, washing its sea tone all over the thrusting branch tips as Peter pulled them closer to the light. At the tip of the tree were two small huts, separate from the rest, a tree branch snaking through the middle of them, both invasive and supportive. Peter pointed.

"That's yours, Wendy, and that one there is mine!" They landed with a bump on a wooden platform that ran around Wendy's charming little bungalow. The small but perfectly round room was bordered on all sides by open archways that let the warm breeze float in and out. Dyed fabrics shuttered the archways, blowing and curling in the breeze. The tree ran through the center of the room, a silent but benevolent giant, a strip of trunk so impassable that it took Wendy ten steps to walk around it. Tethered from the tree to the wall was a single large hammock, bright blue, with hundreds of brightly colored ribbons tied on the bottom. The hammock rocked endlessly as if moved by an invisible hand, the ribbons brushing the floor back and forth with a soothing *whoosh* sound that made Wendy long to plunge heedlessly into sleep right then and there. In the corner sat a clear bowl made of some sort of translucent shell and filled with water, and next to it sat a small wooden bowl. Wendy curled her lip when she realized its purpose. Peter saw her expression and giggled.

"It's surely not as nice as your previous home, but there will be a Pip sent up to clean it every morning and evening."

Wendy didn't know what to say to that, so instead she reached out and ran her fingers down the hammock, feeling the impossibly soft fibers. She closed her eyes, afraid to wake from this enchanting dream. When she turned back to Peter, his eyes fixated hard on her face, and she felt her skin come alive under his gaze, something inside of her pulling toward his touch. She blushed and turned back to the hammock.

"It's perfect, Peter. Thank you. We shall see you when we wake, I suppose."

Peter smiled at her. "And when you wake, we will have a welcome celebration!" Peter saluted them both and began making his way out to the platform. Wendy splashed some water on her face, and when she looked back, he was gone, his absence marked by the sudden longing to see him again. Although—she truly was very tired. Wendy lay down in the hammock, pulling her nightgown tightly around her body. Michael leapt up onto the hammock, his little body causing it to rock wildly.

"Shhhh . . ." Michael immediately curled next to Wendy, his soft breath on her cheek.

"Wendy?"

"Yes?"

"Do you remember my teddy bear's name?"

Wendy had to think about it for a minute. "Miles, wasn't it?"

"I think so. I miss him, I think."

"I know you do. But I'm here with you, and I'll keep you safe."

There was a moment of silence. Wendy struggled to keep her eyes open.

"Wendy?"

She groaned. "Yes, Michael?"

"I like Peter."

"I do as well. Now go to sleep." She heard the shushed whispers of the ribbons as they dragged on the floor below her, and she felt her consciousness fading into a blissful blackness.

"Wendy?"

"*What*, Michael?"

"We didn't say our prayers."

"You're right." She took his little hand in her own and there, in Neverland, they repeated their prayers to the bright afternoon sky, though she struggled to remember the words. Michael was already asleep by the middle of the Lord's Prayer, and so Wendy was left alone with her own sleepy thoughts, marveling that just that previous evening, she had climbed into her own bed. How could that be? That was a lifetime ago. A lifetime ago . . . she felt Booth's name was just on the tips of her lips like a hot coal. Her mind whirled on the memory of his face, shutting down, turning in. Just before Wendy fell swiftly into the void, she thought she heard a slight wail carried in on the wind. Faint as it was, she heard it clearly: an unearthly, distinctly female voice crying with a heartbreaking abandon. Who could that be? The cry wove its way deep into her dreams, where stars fell from the sky, each one burning bright with longing.

CHAPTER EIGHT

WHAT A FANTASTIC DREAM.

Wendy woke slowly, her body putting up a mighty struggle to return to slumber. She felt as though she could sleep for a thousand years. Her body was sore, her wrists cramped, and her legs tender and numb. Why was she sore? It couldn't be real—the flying boy who made her heart race, the emerald island, the face of Big Ben. With a groan, Wendy opened her eyes, a scream catching in her throat. Twelve boys stared down at her, their bedraggled faces all rapt with fascination. Wendy swallowed and let her eyes sweep over the round hut, the open archways letting in the late morning light. One of the boys grinned, a high-pitched voice making its way through a mouth of scattered and grimy teeth.

"MORNING!"

Not wanting to move too quickly, Wendy slowly reached down and pulled the ratty blanket at her feet up over herself. Her body screamed at her for what she had done to it, and she knew it would be a long day of trying to coax it back into its normal state. The boys continued to stare at her as she cleared her throat.

"Hello, boys—may I ask, where is my little brother?"

"I'm over here, Wendy!" a voice in the corner chimed, and Wendy let herself exhale. The boys stood silent and still, watching her like a frozen group of deer.

"If you wouldn't mind just backing up so I may get out of bed, yes?"

The boys looked at one another and then took a few steps back, perfectly in sync with each other, as if they were of one mind. Wendy found herself unnerved by it, but she still sat up, rubbing her sleepy eyes. The boys clustered in the corner, whispering to each other as she delicately climbed out of the hammock, trying all the while to be ladylike about it, which in the end didn't happen. She ended up on the floor on her knees, with her night-gown piled up around her thighs. With a blush, she yanked it back down and stood up, her body wobbling back and forth as it readjusted to Neverland's strange gravitational pull. A chocolate-haired boy scampered over with some sort of rubbery flower in his hands.

"Here, Wendy. This is for you. I'm Brock!"

Another one followed him with a small cup of water.

Wendy nodded her head. "Thank you."

A tiny boy with toffee skin and impossibly big, dark eyes crept up beside her. "I'm Naji!" Suddenly, she was swarmed again, with boys all around her, handing her gifts. They placed a dark green crown of leaves upon her head and looped vines around her wrists. The boy Brock was touching her hair, lifting and watching it fall, while an adorable ginger-haired boy named Tally stuck his finger curiously between her toes. Two small boys were trying to climb her arms, and another had wrapped himself around her leg. The names bounced off the room like the patter of rain: "Paran!" "Marcus!" "Alfonso!" "Lok!" "Vasha!" Collectively they smelled like earth and sweat. Wendy squirmed, suddenly feeling very uncomfortable, a normal feeling when being buried in a pile of small boys. To her relief, an authoritative voice rang out through the tiny hut.

"Oy! Boys! Get off her!" The boys scampered away like mice, out the door and into the tree or up onto the open window arches. Wendy looked up and saw one of the three Generals poking his head through the door. The boy shook his head.

"Sorry about the Pips. They're young and usually quite bored."

She stared at him intensely, but then she was aware that he noticed her staring, and she ducked her head down, ashamed. He laughed.

"It's okay to stare. I'm guessing you've never seen anyone who looks like me."

"No, I'm sorry, I haven't."

He grinned. "Well, take a good look. Not everyone on this island is this handsome. You might as well get your fill now."

Wendy smiled as she raised her eyes to look at his face with fascination. Michael had scampered over as well.

"What are those lines on your face, Mr. . . . . Mr. . . . . what's your name?"

The General laughed. "I'm Oxley. You can call me Ox. And these lines on my face are the markings of my tribe where I grew up. I got them when I was very young, about your age."

"Did it hurt?"

Oxley gave Michael a patient smile. "Yes. It did. But I barely remember it. These marks, where I came from, they told strangers things about me that they wouldn't know right away." He bent down, and Michael cautiously ran his hands over them.

"They are bumpy!"

Wendy couldn't tear her eyes from his face. His skin was so dark that it was almost black. She had seen the Africans in London, the telltale packs of foreigners across their strong backs, their brown skin like cocoa shining in the sun. But she had never seen one that was this dark, like ebony. The scars stretched up from the corners of his mouth, hundreds of tiny dots that spread out like constellations across his cheekbones and up toward his ears. Across his forehead were several variations of dotted lines, stretching from one temple to the other. Down his chin was a single line of the dots.

He was stunningly regal.

"What do the lines mean?" Wendy asked. Her eyes never left

Oxley's magnificent face as he sat by Michael, though she did begin pulling the leaves out of her hair. Oxley ran his fingers across his forehead.

"These show which tribe I'm from. It's a way of telling people who you are without having to tell them everything about yourself. The lines passed down from family to family, identifying our royal lineage."

Michael was still running his fingers over the man's scars.

"Michael," Wendy warned.

"It's all right," Oxley said, laughing.

"I don't know what lineage means, but I LIKE your dots," Michael mumbled.

"These were from my tribe, and these . . ." he touched the pattern on his cheek, "are my tribal markings for my tribe here, in Neverland. Peter gave me these."

"WOW!" Michael's eyes were as big as saucers. "And now you are a part of Peter's tribe!"

"That I am!" Oxley jumped up and offered his hand to Wendy. "It's nice to meet you, Darling family."

"Thank you." Wendy looked over at two boys watching through her open window, dangling upside down from a tree branch. "Are they always like this?"

Oxley smiled. "It's been a long time since any of us have seen a girl. They are just curious. I'm sure it will wear off." One of the boys scampered forward and ripped a ribbon off of Wendy's nightgown and then launched himself out into the treetops. "LOK!" Oxley bellowed, before shaking his head. "Sorry. They are a little, well—wild. We all are. Go on, get out!" The boys swiftly disappeared. "Sorry about that. Here's your breakfast."

He put down a plate filled with fruit and what looked like misshapen biscuits. The Darlings grabbed at the food, even Wendy, who wolfed down two biscuits faster than a proper lady should. She had no idea she was starving until the food touched her lips, but then it was gone, and she wished she had more.

Michael had done the same. "Are there any more biscuits, Mister Oxley?"

"No, sir. Food is a precious commodity here. Everyone else only got one biscuit." Oxley stretched, his body short but stocky and strong. Wendy noticed that he had scars on his hands as well, lines of black dots that curved up his palms. The more she looked at them, the more beautiful they became. What would her parents think of her admiring the scars of an African?

"Wendy and Michael, if you wouldn't mind getting dressed, then I can start your tour."

"The tour?"

"Oh, yes. Peter had some business to attend to this afternoon, so he ordered me to give you an informal tour of Pan Island. After that, we will celebrate your arrival!"

"That sounds wonderful."

Oxley opened up the ratty bag that was slung across his shoulders, right under a bow and quiver of arrows.

"Is that real?" Michael whispered.

"Yes. So be careful."

Michael ran a finger over an arrow tip. "Wow."

"Here are some clothes for you both." Oxley raised his dark brown pupils to look at Wendy. "Unless of course you want to wear a dress for climbing a tree."

"No, thank you," she politely replied.

He laid out a brown pair of pants for her and a long white lacy shirt with a strange fluttery neck. She looked at it quizzically. "This is interesting—where did you get this?"

He shrugged. "Peter probably stole it from a pirate. I'll be waiting outside."

As he turned his back, Wendy picked up the pants and the shirt, as well as a belt that had tumbled out of the bag. Michael was already practically naked, pulling on a long brown tunic adorned with maroon leaves.

"I look just like Peter now, Wendy!"

"You do."

Wendy was pulling on pants. Pants. She frowned, immediately missing her dresses back at home. Pants were so boyish. They pulled uncomfortably at her hips. The lacy shirt fit better, and cinching it with a belt made it less revealing at the neck. She slipped her feet back into her black shoes and tied her hair up with a blue ribbon. "What do you think?"

Michael was prancing around the room, pretending he was Peter. "I'm Peter Pan! I can fly!"

"You two Darlings coming?" Oxley called from outside.

"Yes!" Wendy and Michael ran to one of the many openings of Wendy's hut and peered out. Huge branches snaked down from the room, some as wide as a man. Wendy looked helplessly down. She had very little experience climbing trees aside from one time in the park, when she made it about halfway up the tree before ripping her pinafore. Her mother had been furious. Wendy paused, resting her hand on one of the cool greenish branches. Her mother, what had she looked like? Before she could focus in on that thought, she saw Oxley strapping Michael to his back with a leather strap. Michael was laughing, sticking his feet in Oxley's face.

"What are you . . .?" Wendy began to ask.

"Follow me!" he cried with a smile. "Do what I do!" The Lost Boy put his hands on either side of the branch and then wrapped his body around it. Without warning, he pushed away from the small platform outside Wendy's door and quickly slid down the branch, disappearing without a breath into the leaves below. Wendy gasped. With shaking hands, she reached out for the branch. It was cool beneath her clean fingernails. She hugged herself against the tree and then reached out with one leg, instantly pulling back when her balance shifted. Hesitating, she looked down at the ground, so far below her, and then back at the branch in front of her.

"Be brave," she whispered to herself. "Be brave." That reminded her of someone . . . who?

Wendy reached for the tree, and with determination and a small cry of terror, she leapt into the air, wrapping herself around the branch, her feet leaving the secure, safe wooden platform. She screamed out loud as her body slid down the tree, ever gaining speed as her tiny hut disappeared above her into a quilt of leaves. Faster and faster, she was sliding, her hands becoming lacerated with tiny slivers. *I'm going to hit the ground*, she thought with a rush of fear. *Oh dear, how does one stop?* But then she was yanked off the tree by a strong arm and set on her feet. She took a breath and burst out laughing before turning to Oxley.

"Well, that was terrifying." She paused. "And fun!"

Wendy heard padded steps approaching behind her.

"Ah, your brother is here, so we can start the tour!"

Wendy spun around and saw John standing silently behind her, arms crossed. He looked angry, as always.

"JOHN!" Michael squealed, launching himself at his brother. "Where did you sleep? Why didn't you sleep with Wendy and me?"

Wendy watched her brother's face as it finally bowed to the unleashing of love from Michael. Oxley cracked a sly smile.

"John was up with the Generals, going over the beginning plans for a raid!"

"A raid?" Wendy asked. Her eyes narrowed. "John will be participating in a raid? But he doesn't know anything about that."

"Shut up!" John snapped.

"John! What's gotten into you?"

Oxley frowned. "John, be nice to your sister."

John moaned. "Fine." He turned to Michael. "I was up late with Oxley here, Abbott, and Kitoko. We were talking battle strategies for a pirate raid."

"And what exactly would you know about pirates, or raids, or battles?" Wendy voiced, her tone growing more aggressive than she would like.

"More than you," he muttered.

"All right, children," Oxley said in a calm voice, which was amusing considering Oxley was younger than Wendy. "Shall we take the tour?" Oxley stepped back. "You'll see the Teepee and the Table tonight, so, Darlings, why don't you pick? What would you like to see?"

John cleared his throat. "I . . . I would like to see the base of the tree. I want to understand the physics of how it holds everything up."

Wendy almost laughed out loud. "Oh, John," she said. Here they were, on a magical island, and John wanted to understand the science of it. She reached out to ruffle his hair, but he stepped away, annoyed.

"You're not our mother," he snapped. She recoiled, stung by his words, remembering how he had looked at her with such hatred the night before.

Wendy turned away from him. "I'd like to see the water, I think—the beach?"

"I can show you that!" With a wide grin, Ox loped over a few feet to the largest branch that Wendy had ever seen. Several thick ropes dangled down from its upper branches, and Ox began tying one around himself and Michael.

"There are, of course, several ways to get anywhere in Pan Island, but this is probably the fastest."

Wendy looked at the ropes, frayed at the ends, thinking that a longer way down would probably be fine with her. He looped one around Wendy's waist, and John's, and gave the ropes a tug. Then he turned his face upward.

"DARBY, MATE! TAKE US ALL THE WAY DOWN!"

"Yes, sir!" came the reply from one of the branches above. Oxley laughed.

"Darby will be a General soon, we hope. He's a good chap. Getting old enough now."

Wendy hadn't been aware that anyone was near them, but as she looked up into the tree, she could see the subtle movements of dozens of boys, watching them. Boys everywhere. Where was

Peter? For reasons that she wouldn't let herself linger on, she was desperate to see him. Ox took her outstretched hand in his own and gave a tug on the ropes that pulled them up on their tippy toes. Then he leapt off the tree, off the platform that held him, and disappeared into the canopy below. Wendy followed with an unladylike screech, John with a cry of pure joy. At first they were free-falling, or so it seemed, but then there was a gradual tightening of the rope around her waist, and it seemed that they were in a controlled fall. Wendy dangled helplessly in the air, her feet circling above Oxley's head, eternally thankful that she wasn't wearing a dress at the moment. She leaned forward and looked down at the ground, still hundreds of feet below her.

"What do we do now?"

"Watch!" Oxley grinned. He swung forward toward the largest nearby tree branch and placed his feet up against the trunk, leaning backward on his rope belt. Soon, he was horizontal to the ground, and began steadily walking backward down the trunk. It was astonishing.

"Say! That's pretty great! You are using your weight to balance against the . . ." John squinted his eyes above. "Pulley system. Is that right?"

Oxley nodded and began taking longer, graceful leaps down the tree as the two clumsy Darling children attempted to do the same. Michael giggled the entire way down, happily strapped to Ox's back, oblivious to anything else but the wind on his face. Wendy crept down, step by tiny step. John had passed her up a long time ago, but with each step she seemed to grow a bit bolder, and each step grew longer than the next. It seemed to be an eternity before she reached the ground. Finally, her shoes met solid ground, and she quickly untied the rope around her waist, letting it fall into the pale sand that lined the base of the roots. She knelt down and ran her fingers through it. It was so fine that she was able to carve tiny lines with her fingertips, little circles and swirls by barely moving her fingers, so fine that it barely left any stain on her nails. She picked some up and held it up to the wind, where it disappeared in the slightest lukewarm breeze.

"Neverland soil," Oxley said, laughing, "is very fertile." He gestured to Pan Island. "As you can see."

Wendy dusted off her hands and leaned back, way back, to take in Pan Island.

"Brilliant," John said breathlessly.

Michael silently appeared by Wendy's side. "That is one big tree." She pulled him close to her. To call it an island was almost a stretch. There was the tree, and the tree was the island. There was very little beach—ten feet maybe—between the tree and the water. It was as if the island solely existed to support the great tree, and the tree itself was the source of life for the island.

"It's wonderful, isn't it?"

She turned around to look behind her. A thatch of branches dotted with tiny blackberries ran around them, but if she closed her eyes, she could smell that it was very close: the turquoise sea. She let Michael's hand drop and walked forward, ducking under the thicket of pink flowers that bordered the berries, brushing branch after branch out of her hair. Within a few steps, she was there. It stirred something in her heart, each gentle curve of the waves whispering its joy into her ear. Wendy wiped away a tear. She had never seen anything so superb. The ocean lapped silently near her feet, the brilliant blue green stretching out as far as she could see. The sun blazed overhead, warm but never hot. John was running back and forth at the base of the tree, knocking on its wood, measuring out its distance by walking carefully, foot by foot, around its perimeter. Michael was playing happily in the sand with Ox, building small castles and rivers.

The turquoise water beckoned Wendy, its lulling sound too peaceful to ignore. She slipped off her shoes and waded in, her toes playfully splashing. She took a deep breath in, tasting the sweet air of Neverland on her tongue, wondering how she could ever return to normal life again. She felt so *alive* here. The water pulled tenderly at her ankles, its white foam lapping over her bare feet. She had only stood in the ocean once before, and the freezing cold shores of . . . of—Wendy couldn't remember the name of it, but it didn't matter!—had so little in common with the water licking her shins that they might have been from different worlds. She smiled quietly to herself. As indeed they were. She took another step forward, listening to Michael babble pleasantly back on the beach. That's when she heard the voice, at first so faint that she wondered if it was the wind.

"Wendy. . ." She turned her head back to the beach. None of the boys were calling her name—John was chasing Michael up the beach, Oxley laughing beside him. She turned her head back to the ocean.

"Wendy Darling . . ."

There was more than one voice now, female voices, trilling in cadence with the waves, an enchanting sound, like water trickling over bells. Wendy felt her skin tingle, the hairs on the back of her neck standing up. The enticing voice called out again. Wendy's mouth began to water, for what she wasn't sure, but she needed, she *had* to find out. She took a step deeper into the water, and then another. Slowly, she waded toward the voice.

"Wendy, come to us . . ." There were several voices singing now, their harmony piercing her eardrums, her skin crackling at music's most perfect sound. She waded in deeper. She could not turn from them, for the sound was lingering just under the water, and if she could get to it, she could wrap her arms around whatever called her and press her lips into the cool blue and drink in the sound. She would swallow the melody whole, and it would consume her, and then she would be a part of it forever. She took another step, the water caressing her waist, kissing her ribs, absorbed in the sound . . . the sound . . . She heard another sound rising beneath the luminous noise, a distracting yelling, so harsh and ugly against the music sweeping through her. She turned her head away from it. Nothing mattered but the music.

She felt the voices in the water, the water hands caressing up her thigh, the music a lullaby that cradled her in strong arms, forever comforted, never alone.

The music was all around her, everywhere, and she was in agony and ecstasy as arms tightened around her waist; for a moment, Wendy was confused at how music could feel so secure, so hard, like skin made of stone. She looked back to the beach, confused at how she gotten out so far, her skin still pulling her toward the sound, the voices reaching inside of her chest, strumming her soul. Oxley was running toward her, the water splashing around his ankles, his eyes wide with fear, his mouth open and screaming, and yet Wendy couldn't hear anything but the melody, a melody that coaxed forth everything inside of her that she had ever hidden.

Then she was yanked underwater without warning.

She flailed her arms above, suddenly terrified, reaching, reaching back for the sky that was rapidly becoming smaller. The surface of the water flew away from her grasp as she was pulled deeper and deeper into the depths and farther and farther out to sea. Her legs were twisting and kicking, and she tugged desperately at the stone arm wrapped around her waist. Wendy opened her mouth to scream, water rushing in and filling her lungs. She was so deep now, deeper and farther from shore, the water becoming a dark navy as the fathomless ocean opened up around her. She sucked in water again, flailing helplessly as the water around her had become luminescent, lighting up from within itself, a thousand diamonds in her vision. She ceased struggling when she heard the song begin again, a balm to her rising terror. Her body stopped fighting the water that poured into her lungs, and she turned to look at the arms that held her waist, the arms like stone, and the voice that called her out of herself.

A figure rose up in the water. She saw a swirl of green and blue hair, and then a face came out of the darkness, skin hard like white marble and just as pale. Translucent purple and blue lips shimmered like fish scales as they opened slightly in front of Wendy's face. The eyes opened, and Wendy tried in vain to scream as the stone arms pulled her lower still, a hand creeping over her mouth. From the surface, so far, far above, she heard a strange whistling sound, and a shadow passed overhead . . .

Peter Pan sliced through the water like a bird of prey.

The sea parted for him in a white line as he streamed downward toward her. Wendy fought to stay conscious. The stone arm gripped harder. Peter reached out for Wendy, and she struggled to free herself. Though the skin looked like cracked marble, it felt cool and soft as Wendy ripped at it with her fingernails. Peter raised his arm and with a snarl brought his golden sword slashing down; dark blood filled the water around them. The arm around her waist came free and floated down into the abyss. The lulling music in her ears dissolved into an unpleasant cacophony of high notes that resonated through the water, each one feeling as though it vibrated through her spine. The water tasted like blood. Wendy was drifting, spinning in the water. Her hair drifted past her eyes, and then she saw a face. At first she thought it was Booth, his brown hair curled in the waves, his blue eyes focused on her, but then she blinked and saw it was Peter, Peter's face that she hadn't even known she had missed until that moment, his green eyes widened, his bright red hair standing straight up in the water.

He reached out for her, and she saw that his arm was bleeding, his own spirals of blood falling down into the depths. The voices that had called to her were now screaming, and she clasped her hands to her ears as she struggled to kick to the surface. Peter looked backward and then back at her. He winked as he wrapped both of his arms around her.

Then they were flying. Up through the depths of the sea, the sunlight growing ever closer as the waves tossed it about. Together they exploded out of the ocean, straight into the sky, moving faster than Wendy ever dreamed possible, the water wicking off her skin in tiny droplets, up into the impossibly bright Neverland sky. She was coughing up water, gulping the air, of which there would never be enough. Peter cradled her against his body, taking them ever higher, until the beach and its sea seemed tiny beneath her feet, the boys barely visible on the beach, jumping and cheering and waving.

"Are you all right?" Peter gently turned Wendy in his arms so that she was facing him, even as he soared higher into the air. She was still coughing up water, suddenly aware of how miserable and unladylike she must appear at the moment. Her body was limp, her ears still ringing with the screams below the depths. Finally she found her voice.

"Peter! You saved me!" She reached a shaking hand toward his face. "Thank you, thank you!" She took a deep breath, trying to calm her thundering, fearful heart. Then she wrapped her body against his in a tight, grateful hug. She felt his body go straight with surprise and then mold against hers, his lips close to her ear.

"It's nothing."

"It isn't nothing, Peter! What is down there? What . . ." She shook her head at the terrifying memory of being pulled down, of the arm like marble, of the song that she still couldn't quite shake. Peter slowed his pace, circling gently in the air, always moving, even if only just in the slightest way.

"Was that a mermaid?" she gasped. "Why, I don't even remember why I went into the sea in the first place!"

Peter nodded. "The mermaids will call you out to sea with their irresistible song. They will call you down to them, then drown you, and use your virgin blood to feed their coral garden." Wendy shuddered.

"Queen Eryne, their leader, if you can even call it that, is a beautiful and wicked creature who loves to spew nonsense and spread her lies." That sounded truly terrible. How close she had been to death?! It terrified her to consider what would have happened if Peter hadn't been there. Peter continued, lazily circling a piece of her hair around his finger.

"The mermaids have been in Neverland even longer than I have. They are ancient beings, full of bitterness toward every living thing that experiences joy. Queen Eryne has hated men for as long as I can remember. They'll do anything to draw a virgin female down into the depths and claim her life. There aren't many young women around these parts. I imagine they were waiting for you."

Peter shifted his eyes downward, nervously, before resting his hand on Wendy's bare neck, his other arm still wrapped around her waist. Her heart began hammering at his closeness, at his skin that burned like fire against her freezing neck.

"Listen to me, Wendy—promise that you will never go close to the sea again—at least not without me."

She looked down at the turquoise waves lapping far below her, such a peaceful and mesmerizing sound.

"How can something so beautiful be so dangerous?" she murmured.

Peter raised his eyebrows and leaned his head forward. "There are places that the mermaids can't go, secret places within Neverland where the sea meets the land. I will take you there one day, I promise. And we can swim to our hearts' delight."

"Do you swim then? In the ocean?"

Peter grinned. "All the time! See, the mermaids don't care about boys. They don't want to be anywhere near boys. It isn't dangerous for us, but for you, the sea is the most dangerous place in Neverland."

Wendy shuddered against him, traumatized by how close she had come to death, but at the same time, loving how her very skin seemed to light up at his touch, at the way her heart was bursting with excitement. Was this what adventure felt like? An addicting rush of blood to the brain? She didn't know what to say. Instead, she turned her hazel eyes upon his green ones and whispered.

"Thank you, Peter, for saving my life."

A blush rose up from his cheeks, adorable beneath a smattering of freckles. "Ahem, shall we return to Pan Island and your brothers now? I'd love to see how they are getting along with that poor chap Oxley! He was swimming out to you when I arrived, but he never would have made it in time. It was a noble try though."

Peter spun in the air, and as they soared back toward the beach, Wendy looked with fear at the water below her, its dangerous song sparkling in the early afternoon light. There was a dark spot in the water, now churning with the fins of sharks. Wendy forced herself to look away.

CHAPTER NINE

AFTER STOPPING BY THE BEACH and reassuring Oxley that she was indeed okay, Peter finally returned Wendy to Centermost, setting her down with care on an outstretched deck. Her heart sank as his touch left her, as she felt the weight of her body against her feet. She wasn't sure which was more thrilling, the intoxication of flying or being clutched so closely to Peter's chest, feeling the hammering of his wild heart through her dampened shirt. When he stepped away from her, Wendy tried madly to contain her disappointment.

"Michael will be coming back from the water soon, I assume?"

Peter perched on the top of a wooden lantern. "Yes. The boys will meet us back here; there is no need to worry. I need to speak with the Generals, so he'll come up with Oxley. Don't worry. Ox is the most trustworthy boy on the island."

Wendy was busy tying back her wet hair into a braid, something Peter watched with fascination.

"And, the others? Abbott and . . ."

"Kitoko. Yes. Good boys, all of them. I can see John fitting in with them quite well. Abbott is my first General, and then Kitoko and Oxley. John can be number four."

Wendy nodded. "Where did they come from? Where do *all* the Lost Boys come from?"

Peter lowered his eyes. "The boys come from all over. Sad stories, unfortunately, something all the Lost Boys share. I found Abbott silently clutching the hand of his dead father just outside Berlin. His house had caught fire, both his parents killed, their bodies trapped inside of it. He was only about seven, staring up at the sky with dead eyes." He shook his head, and tiny droplets of water flecked onto Wendy's face. "Kitoko was an orphan, raised in a monastery along with a hundred other boys. One day, without warning, the government forced them to abandon their monastery in a matter of hours. Quiet as he is, no one noticed that Kitoko was missing, and he was locked in an empty garden and forgotten. He had been there three days when I found him, on the verge of starvation."

"And Oxley?"

Peter shook his head. "Oxley has a great story, but I should let him tell it—I won't do it justice. He makes me laugh."

"If you don't mind me asking—what does John have to do with any of those boys? He can't be . . . a General . . . he's a child. He doesn't know anything about battle or even about Neverland! He can't be involved in anything dangerous, Peter."

Peter chortled. "Don't worry, raiding the pirates, especially if Hook's not involved, isn't dangerous. It's . . . how do you say . . . like taking sweets from an infant."

Wendy laughed. "The saying is, 'taking candy from a baby.'"

"Ah, I knew it didn't sound right." Peter grinned, tossing his red hair back out of his face, and began drumming on the end of the lantern. "Are you worried that I'll corrupt your brother? John seems hardly naive. He's bright."

Wendy frowned. "No, he's not naive, and yes, he's actually quite intelligent, but he is somewhat fragile. Back home, he hasn't any friends." *Papa . . . London . . .* the thoughts were so foreign and distant. Wendy hadn't thought of them in what seemed like days. Peter rubbed his chin thoughtfully.

"And why is that?"

Because he's a prat, she thought, but she considered the more polite response.

"He fears being alone, I think. He wants to be included, wants people to listen to him. I think he uses his wit to deflect actual conversation. He's lonely."

She remembered the defeated look on his face when she had slapped him in the nursery, the way he had looked both betrayed and surprised. She felt ashamed, but also infuriated, remembering the things he had said to her about Booth. Looking at Peter, who was absentmindedly running his hands down his tan and lean arms, brushing the moisture off, she felt a sudden flush of shame at the thought of Booth. Why hadn't she thought of him more? Peter reached out his hand to her, and Booth was instantly forgotten.

"Shall we?"

With a shy smile, Wendy took his hand, and then they were soaring over several different huts and up through tree branches, past the large nests of bright exotic birds and a mosaic snake that slithered silently toward them. They landed on a platform several stories above the Teepee. Peter pushed back several dirty cloths that hung from a gnarled tree branch, covered with dense leaves. Behind them was a wooden door, with a small gold lock on the outside.

"Our camouflage." He shrugged. "It's not really necessary, but . . ." He popped the lock open with a tiny golden key, before pocketing it and turning his face to the sky. Then he crowed. Wendy only had to wait for a moment before she heard the loud sounds of the Generals, climbing up the branches, hand over foot, laughing as they went. As they emerged from the branches below, they looked around anxiously.

"Peter? Where are you?" Peter laughed as he mimed a woman's high voice, looking under a tiny leaf for himself. Abbott paced in a circle, twirling the spear that seemed to be always at his side. John frowned at Wendy.

"Why are you here?"

Peter chose that moment to leap playfully into the air, taking John's top hat right off his head. To Wendy's surprise, John laughed joyfully.

"Peter! I say, that's my father's hat!"

"Not anymore!" The boys laughed as Peter strutted back and forth on the roof, imitating Wendy, John, and Michael's father, smoking a branch pipe and rubbing his hands together. "Now see here, boys—and Wendy! You shall be in bed by 7 p.m., exactly! And no running or playing, or climbing trees, or flying, heavens no! In fact, do not behave like children at all! You shall be little adults, and we shall sit in banks and shops all day and discuss the most boring things we can possibly imagine!"

John laughed, a little too loudly. "That does sound like my father."

Wendy cast John a confused look.

"No, it doesn't."

Right? Wendy thought that sounded right. What had her father looked like again? She tried to summon his face, and instead there was just a blur, like looking through water. John shrugged nonchalantly. Peter tossed the hat back to John.

"I've a better hat for you. Abbott, bring me my red hat!"

Abbott, who had been standing silently by, arms crossed, glowering at Wendy, shook his head.

"He doesn't need it."

Peter raised his eyebrows at Abbott but continued talking. The General was taller than Peter by about a head. He had very sharp features that cumulated in a long nose that pointed straight out from his unfriendly face. Sun-streaked, cropped blond hair hung messily over his eyes, and his perpetual frown reminded Wendy of a disapproving crow. Abbott watched her with judgmental eyes as Peter strutted around above, still imitating their father. Finally, he plopped down exhausted onto the thatched roof.

"Okay, men, into the Battle Room. Oxley isn't here yet; he had some private business to take care," Peter wiggled his eyebrows. "Too much fruit, I think."

Abbott shook his head and pointed at Wendy. "She can't come in. She's a girl. There are rules."

John rubbed his mouth awkwardly. "I . . . somewhat agree."

"John!" Wendy's mouth fell open. Peter's eyes narrowed and Wendy noticed that his pupils seemed to be churning, tendrils of navy dripping into the bright emerald green, like spilled ink. Peter whirled on his tall General.

"It's true, Abbott, that is a rule. But let me ask you—who makes the rules?"

The boy looked down at the floor. "You do."

"Who controls this island?"

"You do."

"And then, who is the only person whose opinion counts on the matter?"

"Yours."

"Ah. And who do we protect?"

"Our own?"

"And who did I say the Darlings were?"

"Our own."

Just when Abbott started looking crestfallen, Peter reached out and pulled him close to his shoulder, in a brotherly fashion. "Abbott, we're going to let Wendy inside. But I can't tell you how nice it is to have someone who remembers the rules around here. That's why you are a General. I'm glad you're here, brother."

Abbott let a small, pleased smile creep across his face. "Fine. The girl can come inside." Then with an eye roll, he wagged his finger at Wendy and added, "But don't touch anything," as if her mere femininity would throw off the entire room.

She folded her arms, gave him a smug look, and ducked inside the Battle Room. Her first thought was that she had stumbled into a room made of gold. Gold was everywhere, from the medallions that dangled from the ceiling to the trinkets that adorned the walls and corners. Gemstones of bright violet and canary yellow sparkled in the light that filtered in through three small holes in the ceiling, none big enough for a man to get through. Rickety shelves, built from the familiar wood of the great tree, overflowed with richly adorned goblets, long strings of pearls, and golden bars the length and width of Wendy's fingers, strange hatch marks curling up their length. One large antique wooden chest in the corner—easily large enough for Michael to sleep in— overflowed with dozens of gold, silver, and copper coins. Wendy walked over to it and lifted the lid to get a better look. The lid of the chest was printed with raised lettering and a solitary symbol: a single tree, etched in black. With a rusty creak, the lid of the chest fell backward, and she looked down at an embarrassing amount of wealth. She turned back to the boys, who were all watching her with silent eyes.

"Where did you get this?"

Peter smiled naughtily. "Where do you think? From Hook. That's from the raid, what, a year ago?" He turned back to the Generals and began talking.

Wendy ran her fingers through the money, loving the calming way the coins flowed through her fingers, the light metallic sound of them rising and falling. Pushing her hands deeper and deeper into the coins, feeling their unique weight, Wendy flinched and shrieked when something burning hot brushed her fingers.

The boys stopped talking.

John rolled his eyes. "For goodness' sake, Wendy, what is it now?"

Wendy wrapped the edge of her shirt around her fingers and then reached in again, quickly finding the burning coin and pulling it out. She held it up to the light, ignoring the uncomfortable heat that was spreading to her fingers through the shirt. In addition to its radiating heat, the coin was heavy, and whereas the other coins were rather dirty, this one was shiny and clean, almost as if it had been created yesterday. She turned it over in her palm. One side was marked with a single tiny skull, with wings stretching out behind it. A jagged *X* then was etched across the entire side of the coin. On the other side, long spiraling lines circled the coin, with interspersed dots spotted randomly on the lines. Behind the lines was the faint outline of an arrow, a single arrow pointing north.

"How beautiful!" she murmured, turning it over again in her hand, ignoring the heat that was now burning a hole through her shirt. "What does it mean?"

Peter walked up beside her and popped her on the bottom of the hand. The coin flew up in the air, spinning as it went, and Peter leapt up to catch it.

"Fairy money. Very rare. You must be careful with it."

Abbott looked up at them. "Peter collects them. He thinks he has almost all of them."

The flying boy grinned. "Of course I do! But that doesn't stop us from looking for them on raids, ain't that right?"

Peter slowly floated back down to her and replaced the coin with a dazzling jeweled bracelet made of pear-shaped aqua stones and bright white pearls, each surrounded by gold trinkets of every shape: ships and fairies, trees, flowers and moons. He slipped it onto her wrist, his fingers lingering on her own. Wendy felt as if his gaze could peel the clothes from her body. She gave herself a tiny shake.

"Peter," she admonished, embarrassed, remembering that the Generals were all watching them.

Peter simply grinned. John rolled his eyes, and Abbott fidgeted nervously. Kitoko finally cleared his throat. It was the first sound she ever heard him make.

"Oh, all right. I suppose we should get back to the raid. Wendy, sit there." Peter pointed to a stump in the corner of the room. Wendy sat obediently, feeling quite awkward indeed. She fingered the bracelet on her wrist. Peter had given it to her as if it were nothing. Feeling undeserving, she quietly slipped it off her wrist and back into the treasure chest. She turned her attention back to the Battle Room. In the middle of the circle of boys, there was a table, and upon the table, besides several glasses filled with a deep red liquid, was a crinkled map of Neverland. It looked ancient, drawn with a whimsical hand. Dragons and mermaids danced on the bottom of the map, where the sea was drawn in curling strokes. In the left-hand corner of the map, there was an upside-down compass. Wendy watched with amazement as Peter carefully brushed the compass with his finger and the map changed before her eyes; north became south, west and east changed places.

"How . . ." John was breathless.

Peter grinned. "Fairy magic. It's still around here and there. And Neverland is not a place that wants to be mapped."

Wendy was bursting with questions but instead chose to listen as the boys laid out their plan for the next night. She had to sit on her hands to keep from being fidgety. Peter circled around the table, leaning forward to put a tiny black ship into the wide crook that was the Bay of Treasures.

"Here's where Hook will be tomorrow night. My spies in town say that he comes into Port Duette once every two weeks or so for food, drink, and of course, the tarts that grace Harlots Grove. He normally comes in on a Sunday night, the holy man that he is, but . . ." Peter laughed. "My spies deposited some rats into his cheese supply before he left for his last voyage. His men will be bellyaching for food. Hook will agree to go back to port a day early. He will land in the morning and will quickly dispatch his crew to get more cheese. Which means . . ."

Peter reached out and brought down another two tiny model ships onto the northern section of the map, far away from the first ship. "That the *Coral Plunder* and the *Vicious Seas* will be here, unguarded by the *Sudden Night* . . ." He turned to Wendy. "That's Hook's ship, an unholy black beast, built for the killing of Lost Boys."

He turned back to the table and brought the two ships down with the palm of his hand. "Unguarded by the *Sudden Night*, they are open to an attack. Now, we must remember to tell the troops that they are not looking for gold; no, rather, we are in need of replenishing our other treasure."

The other boys laughed as Peter raised his glass of red liquid. He turned to Kitoko. "You say this is the last of it?" The third General nodded. "Well, hell then, we better get some more."

Abbott was rocking back and forth on his toes. "What about the *Undertow* and *Viper's Strike*? Do we know where they will be?"

Peter nodded. "They should be out to sea on their usual rotation. Although who knows what *Viper's Strike* is doing. Hook doesn't even know." Peter gestured to two small ships that sat on the side of the table. "Those ships should have at least a few months' worth, wouldn't you say?"

Wendy saw John furrowing his brow, his forehead wrinkled.

"What say you, John?" Peter turned to him, noticing his silence. "Out with it! We value your thoughts here."

John flushed with pride before running his fingers over the map and the two downed ships. Then he ran his fingers inland, to where the ocean met a river that snaked around Neverland. He planted his finger on a large drawing of a skull with an *X* over it. He turned to Abbott, obviously trying to win the grumpy boy over.

"This is where Hook keeps his treasure, correct? The Vault? Isn't that what you told me?"

Abbott's eyes narrowed. "Yes, not that it's any of your business."

"Abbott. Answer him clearly," Peter ordered.

Abbott's eyes lingered angrily on Peter before he sighed and turned back to John. "Fine. I'll tell the whelp. Hook indeed keeps most of his treasure in the Vault, which is a huge cave at the mouth of this river. From there, the river leads out to the sea." He paused, his eyes narrowing as he brought up a painful memory.

"We tried to raid it before. A bunch of Lost Boys died." He looked up at Peter. "You can't be serious about trying again. They always have guards posted, which we can handle, but if we get trapped in the Vault, and then these two ships, plus the *Sudden Night*, come up the river like they did last time . . ." With two hands, he righted the downed ships and moved them to the *X*, following with the large model of the *Sudden Night*, painted black and three times the size of the other ships. "And they bear down on us with nowhere to go . . ." He shuddered. "It was a massacre. Eleven Lost Boys dead. Hook's dream, our nightmare. It's a trap. It's always been a trap. You remember. They have heavy guards, especially at night."

His icy blue eyes rested on Peter. Peter tilted his head and rubbed a hand through his red hair, then over his impossibly smooth cheeks. Wendy could see the gears in his head turning, how his green eyes lit up at the *X* on the map, how his skin quivered with excitement at the prospect.

"The problem is the ships. We could distract the ships, perhaps? Attack them while some others raid the Vault?" Peter thought out loud.

John frowned and tapped his lower lip. "What if they never had to know?"

"Who?"

"The pirates. What if they never even knew we were there?"

Peter's eyebrows arched. Wendy shot John a dirty look. He shouldn't even be involved in this.

"Aye, John, what are you thinking?" Peter asked.

John reached out, his eyes twinkling mischievously, and moved the two ships back to the ocean. "I've read in nautical journals that seasickness, even for seasoned sailors, is caused when a ship isn't in natural harmony with the waves." He rubbed his mouth, thinking. "What if a few flying Lost Boys quietly and silently pushed the ships sideward to the waves and held them there? Without alerting the pirates?"

Peter's eyes lit up. "I'm listening."

"They wouldn't even know we were there. While a few of us held the ships there, the rest of the Lost Boys could raid the Vault. If Hook's ship is in port, he would never make it back in time to the cave to stop us, especially if no one had any clue what was happening."

"And why wouldn't he?" Abbott asked, his voice tinged with resentment.

"Because, if everyone on these ships is seasick, then they will be very, very slow on the return. And if you do your job taking out the guards, they may not even have to return at all." A huge grin stretched across his face. "Think of it—we can be in and out without them even noticing! And even if they do find out, then they will have to vomit their way all the way up the river." He knocked over the model of the *Sudden Night*. "Whatever is in the Vault will be the main prize. Bottles are heavy—they would keep most of them there, rather than on a ship, wouldn't you say? And as for the attack—they'll expect us to come at night. Well, who says we have to go at night? I can't imagine they would think we would be so foolish as to attack during the day. But we just might have to be. We do the unexpected." John puffed out his chest.

Peter leapt into the air and spun around before lifting John up off the ground with a hearty shake. "Bravo!" he crowed. "This certainly sounds like a risky—but worthwhile—adventure!" He put John down. "This time we'll succeed, because we have you, my intellectual friend! Let's remind those pirates that they don't own the island, as they believe."

Abbott stepped forward and grabbed Peter's arm. "Peter! We've talked about this! The Vault is too dangerous. Do you want those ships bearing down on all the boys with no escape? Do you remember what we lost the first time? Eleven boys, eleven friends! Each of them now dangling from the Vault with a hook around their neck. This is reckless and foolish! We don't even know the layout of the inside of the Vault. You've heard of the fourteen doors. We could get lost, we could get trapped by the ships like last time."

Peter reached out and clasped both of his hands on Abbott's face with a smile. "Ah, my dear friend, my General. When did you lose your sense of adventure? When did you become such a nag? I have been so bored as of late, haven't you? We need a good adventure for our tales . . . for our souls. We will use John's plan. Aren't you that brave boy who once threw himself out a window in Port Duette with nothing below him, only hoping I might catch him? Be brave!"

Abbott's face grew red, and Wendy could see him trying to contain his anger, which seemed to deflate at Peter's funny memory, but which rose quickly when his eyes rested on Wendy.

"The cost is too high. Who exactly are you trying to impress?"

Peter's eyes flared navy, and suddenly Abbott was facedown on the ground, Peter's hand on the back of his neck, the boy floating parallel above his body, all his weight pressing Abbott's face into the floor. With his face inches above Abbott's head, contorted in anger, his voice hissed in his ear.

"You are my General, and at any time, I can take that away from you. In case you didn't remember, I saved your life, and what do I get? Disloyalty. This mission might be risky, but if you have a sudden phobia of adventure and danger, then maybe you shouldn't be here. Do you understand?"

Abbott nodded.

"Don't. Question. Me. Again."

"Sorry! Sorry, Peter."

Peter slowly floated away from Abbott as he pushed himself off the floor.

"Sorry, Peter," he mumbled again before sneering at John and stomping out of the Battle Room, his hands clenched tightly at his waist. Everyone was silent for a moment, John looking at the ceiling, Peter staring hard at the spot where Abbott had stood. Finally, Kitoko quietly raised his voice.

"Peter, this might actually be quite a *good* idea, but may I remind you that it's coming from a boy who until last night slept in a nursery. What does this boy know of pirates? Tell me, John, have you ever held a sword? A real sword, not a stick or one made of rubber?"

His voice was not unkind, and yet John's face flushed with embarrassment. "Well, I . . ."

"No," Kitoko answered. "Peter, if you insist, we can use his plan, since we can always adjust it at the last minute, but it will be too dangerous to take an amateur with us." Kitoko's voice, soft and yet assertive, spoke of experience. Wendy was hoping that Peter would agree with him. Her heart pained at the thought of either of her brothers being in real danger. Peter seemed to consider his thoughts for a moment and turned to Wendy.

"What do you think, Wendy? What say you to all this?" Wendy stood and looked at the three boys, each wanting something different from her. Her eyes focused on John, who looked at her pleadingly. She wanted him to feel included, and yet . . . his life was more important. What would her mother say if she were here? She tried to be magnanimous, but as soon as her words fell out, she knew John would hate her forever.

"I don't think John should go on the raid. It's too risky. Perhaps he can go over with the boys who are turning the ships? He has no experience with something like this. He's never held a sword or even been on a ship. Perhaps it's ultimately best if he stays behind. Please, Peter." She turned to John, who looked as if she had stabbed him. "I'm sorry. But it's true. Our parents aren't here, but if they were . . ."

"SHUT UP, WENDY!" he screamed, his face flushed and tears blurring his eyes behind his glasses. "Our parents aren't here, and in case you have forgotten, *you aren't our mother.* I'm going to go with Peter and have an adventure, and who are you to stop me?" He took a bold step toward her, his face contorted in anger. "Why are you so awful? Perhaps if you looked up from staring at him"—he gestured to Peter—"you would notice that we aren't in London anymore. So stop acting like the proper girl I know you aren't and let Michael and me do what we please, you stupid, silly girl!"

John stomped out of the hut, pushing over a box of gold coins as he went. Wendy was mortified, and she rushed after him. "John, wait!"

Peter caught her arm roughly. "Let him go. He'll calm down soon. I'll go talk to him."

Wendy peeked over his shoulder, but John was gone. She shook her head. "I didn't mean to make him upset, but he's my brother . . ."

Peter's eyes met hers. "But here in Neverland, he's not just your brother. He's a Lost Boy, and he's older than most of our boys. He's ready to be a General."

"But we just got here! You don't know anything about him!"

"I have already seen that John is smarter than the rest of the boys. His intellect is way above both Abbott's and Oxley's. They are loyal, and yes, with John that has yet to be proven, but he's smart." Peter tucked a piece of Wendy's hair back behind her ear, and she found herself breathless at his boldness. "All the Darling children, it seems, are very smart."

She smiled, in spite of her stomach churning at the look of betrayal she had just seen on John's face. "Michael?"

"Well," he laughed, "Michael is very funny."

Peter led her back to the table, and together they looked at the map. "What if John helps push the ships and comes nowhere near the Vault? He would be relatively safe from danger there."

Wendy's gaze lingered on Peter's hand that rested next to the small model of the *Sudden Night*, docked up against Port Duette.

Wendy sighed, abandoning her principles one tiny surrender at a time. "I guess it is a good plan."

"It is. And John seems very brave."

"John seems to have lost himself a little."

Peter leaned forward so that his mouth brushed her hair, his lips against her ear. "Everyone loses themselves a little in Neverland."

Wendy leapt up from the table, alarmed at the feelings coursing through her body. She looked up at Kitoko, who was still standing silently in the room, watching them, his face totally void of emotion. She straightened up her spine as a strange thought slithered up it. She wanted an adventure too.

"However, I have one condition: If one of my brothers is going, then I go as well. That is the compromise I am willing to make."

Peter grinned. "So you want a little adventure yourself? I like that. But you won't be going with John. You'll be staying with me. Only I can keep you safe here, remember?"

Kitoko leaned forward, balancing himself on his sword. "Peter . . . a girl?"

Peter looked up at him with a naughty grin. "Wait until Abbott hears about this! He'll have a fit! Oh, I hope I'm there to see it."

Kitoko simply shook his head, trying to restrain a small smile. Peter turned back to Wendy. "I'll need a few minutes with Kitoko alone. You, my darling, should probably rest up before the feast tonight."

Wendy could indeed feel the exhaustion pulling at the back of her eyelids, the tiredness that was seeping through her limbs. Between almost being drowned by mermaids or fighting with her brother . . . Wendy wasn't sure which was worse.

"Yes, that would be good. Perhaps just a short nap."

There was a rustling outside, and suddenly Oxley poked his head into the hut with a big grin.

"HELLO, ALL!"

If only he had been there the entire time, Wendy thought, *things might have gone much better.*

"Oxley, could you fly Wendy up to her hut for me?"

Wendy looked over at Peter with a surprised gasp. "Oxley can fly?"

Oxley looked over at Peter. "You didn't tell her?"

Peter shook his head. "I only have so many exciting things about myself that I have to dole them out slowly." He shrugged with an irresistibly naughty grin. "What can I say? I wanted to surprise her." Wendy blinked in confusion.

Peter's eyes twinkled as he looked over her face. "In Neverland, I can give flight to whom I choose, but only temporarily. It usually only lasts a few hours, which can make it very difficult—and dangerous. Only the Generals have really mastered how to use it best, and how to sense when their power is waning. It's unpredictable, which is why I only give it to them, and every once in a while, the Lost Boys. It's like a special treat."

An entire new world opened up before Wendy's eyes. Peter could give flight. How?

He laughed at her face. "Watch."

Her eyes widened as she watched Peter reach out to Oxley, putting both hands on his shoulders. Peter closed his eyes as his arms began to glow with a white light that snaked up his forearms, tracing his veins with forked tongues. Finally, the lights met each other, and a whirling sleeve of light encased his arms, flowing down into Oxley's shoulders, where it disappeared with a small sigh into his onyx muscles. Oxley leapt into the air, where he stayed suspended. With a hoot of delight, he swam backward, tipping his feet over his head before righting himself.

"Ah, now that's more like it!" He reached out to Wendy. "Ready?"

She nodded and put her hand in his large one. Peter tipped his head at Wendy. "I'll see you tonight at the feast. And afterward, stick around—there is someone very special I'd like you meet."

"You're introducing Wendy to *her* tonight?" Oxley asked with a surprised look. "Well, that will be something to see indeed."

Wendy's eyes widened. Peter winked at her. "Don't worry. I'll see you tonight. Wear your pretty dress for me?"

She had started to ask who she would be meeting, but then Oxley was whisking her up through the tree branches. There was a rush of warm air on her face, the vibrant green leaves swayed as they hummed past, and then she was in her hut. Oxley gently set her down inside her room before his normally joyful face clouded over with seriousness. He turned her to face him, her eyes lingering on his striking tribal markings.

"Wendy, listen to me. Peter thinks she's harmless, but if I were you, I would be very careful of what you say and do around her." Oxley looked around quickly to make sure no one was listening before leaning in close to Wendy's face. "She's very jealous of Peter, and you would be wise to stay away from him when she's around. Do you understand?"

Wendy nodded. "But . . . why? Who?"

Oxley shook his head. "None of the Lost Boys understand it, and Peter does not like talking about it. I wouldn't ask him."

The longer she was here, the more Wendy understood that Peter Pan seemed to be his own island of secrets.

"Ox, thank you for telling me." The General crouched on the edge of her hut.

"Remember what I said, Wendy. Stay away from Peter in her presence, as much as you can." He looked forward again. "It will be hard considering he's quite smitten with you. I've heard that fairies were once very powerful creatures. And Tink is, well, she isn't well. They have a very intense relationship."

Wendy gasped. "Did you say fairies?"

But Oxley had leapt out of her room already, and all Wendy was left with were a thousand questions dangling in the damp Neverland air. She couldn't quite believe what she had heard. *Fairies?* She tried to think of what her mother would say, but she couldn't even remember her face. She found herself caring less than she should and let the thread of guilt unspool in her mind for a few minutes before the rocking hammock, and her sleepiness, took over.

CHAPTER TEN

Wᴇɴᴅʏ ᴡᴏᴋᴇ ᴜᴘ ʜᴏᴜʀs ʟᴀᴛᴇʀ to a sticky face pressed next to hers. Dusk settled its hushed lull over them, and Wendy smiled, wrapping her arms around Michael, happy to breathe in his sweaty-little-boy smell.

"Hi, Wendy," he mumbled.

"Hi, Michael." They stayed in the hammock for maybe another ten minutes, sleeping on and off, enjoying the warmth of being snuggled up next to each other. Finally, Wendy gently pushed him off and began washing her face and hair in the large basket of steaming water that someone—Ox?—had somehow transported to her room. After looking around, she pulled off the trousers and lacy shirt that now reeked of salt and sea and washed her legs and arms, wishing for the proper bathtub back in . . . she shook her head. Back in . . . ? She turned to Michael.

"Michael, where did we live with our parents?"

Michael looked downright puzzled. "We lived in . . ." His face distorted. "We lived in . . ." His lip gave a quiver. "I don't know!"

He ran to Wendy, burying his face in her belly. "Wendy, I can't remember Papa's face!"

"I think it's something about Neverland that makes it hard to remember. It's okay. Do remember what Peter said, that when we get back, it will only have been a few minutes, and Mother and Father won't even know that we were gone."

"Wendy, you promise?"

She looked into his impossibly bright blue eyes. "Promise." Hoping to distract him, Wendy splashed some water on his face and rubbed hard with her hand, attempting to erase the dirt on his cheeks. He laughed and scampered away.

"No cleaning!" Her blue nightgown was draped over a rickety chair—the only actual chair she had seen on Pan Island—and when she picked it up, she was surprised that it had been cleaned. She pressed her nose to the fabric, smelling the aroma of herbs that even the best alchemist wouldn't recognize. She pulled it over her head and slipped her feet into her black shoes, still crunchy with sand. Her hair—well, the sea had made it curly, and there was no taming it back, and so she simply decided to let it cascade down her shoulders in messy waves. Michael was still wearing the tunic Oxley had given him, but someone had the good sense to cinch it at the waist, and when Wendy looked over, she noted with surprise that he had tied a maroon ribbon across his forehead and tucked some mauve leaves into it so they hung down over his ears. Wendy suppressed a giggle—he looked like a giant puppy. The poor kid.

"That's interesting. Here, let me fix it for you." She gently tucked the leaves so they were above his temples. Michael puffed out his chest.

"This is how Peter wants us to wear it. He showed me."

"Oh, did he? That was nice of him."

"Yup! He said that all the Lost Boys wear it this way the night before a raid. It shows their lawalty."

"Loyalty."

"Oh. Loyalty."

"Are you ready?"

Michael nodded. "And hungry."

"Me too. Now, how do we get down again?"

"Oh, Wendy." Michael giggled all the way over to the tree. "You know how." Michael climbed up onto her back, and Wendy stared at the trunk once again. Then, without a second thought, she wrapped her arms around the trunk and hurtled down toward the Teepee. Michael shrieked with delight. When she neared the landing, she hesitantly put her foot out to slow her speed, and it hit the landing with a hard thump, wrenching her off the trunk and onto her knees. She stood up flustered but proud. A smile broke open across her face. She was about to say something to Michael when the deafening noise of two hundred boys roared out of the open doors of the Table, a wild, blustery wave of voices. Wendy self-consciously gathered her hair to the side, knowing that all their eyes would be on her when she entered.

"Michael!" she hissed, approaching the outer doors.

"What?"

"Do you want me to hold your hand?" She was suddenly desperate to deflect the attention that would be put upon her. He looked at her with disgust.

"Not in front of them! I'm not a baby anymore, that's what Peter said!" he scoffed, before sauntering inside, as proud and mature as a five-year-old could be.

With a deep breath, Wendy quietly stepped inside the Table. Once inside, her eyes ate up everything around her; it was the strangest dining room she had ever seen. In the center of the room, there was an enormous round table, made of dark shiny wood, marked with a thousand tiny hatch marks. A chandelier made of broken wine bottles hung overhead, littered with half-burning candles, held up with a tattered rope that looked like it could give at any moment. Frayed ribbons dangled down from the broken bottle necks. One was on fire, a small smoldering flame licking its way up the ribbon to the glass top.

"Pretty great, isn't it?" Oxley asked, sneaking up behind her and yanking on her hair playfully.

Wendy looked around. "It's . . . something, indeed." The

circular center table was surrounded by dozens of tiny square tables that were heaped with piles of dirty dishes, stacks upon stacks of them.

"Who . . . washes the dishes?" Wendy asked cautiously, not wanting the job to be assigned to her.

"Oh, we just find the cleanest ones and wipe them down with our rags before we eat," Ox said, shrugging. Wendy must have made a face because he burst out laughing. "Things are different here, Miss Darling! This is Pan Island! We do not pretend to live like how grown-ups say we should live."

Wendy raised her head, standing on her tiptoes to see the center of the table, in which she could see people moving. At its radial core, there was a hole cut out in the middle where three young boys—Pips—stood, spooning out food and putting more on the table, where the ravenous Lost Boys constantly reached for more. The three servers were dripping with sweat, struggling to keep up with the demand. From where she stood, Wendy could see that under their feet were several layers of circular rooms connected by a spiraling ramp—and that was where the food was being brought up from, carried by a lean boy who moved impossibly fast, even when carrying what looked like a full turkey.

Awed by the sight of it all, Wendy breathed in too quickly and in return let out a loud cough when the smell of the sweat, the meat, and the dirty dishes became too much. All the eyes in the room turned toward her, and there was a moment of silence as they stared at the strange girl creature who had invaded their pit of gluttonous delights. Eyes narrowed, heads dipped, whispers rose. Willing herself to move, Wendy walked toward the table with her hands clenched, past the rows of judgmental eyes and twisted mouths. Peter was nowhere to be seen, and she felt as though she were wading through a den of hungry wolves. As she made her way around the circle, she was relieved to see John, ripping apart a turkey leg with his teeth, laughing at something another boy said.

She went to sit next to him and was surprised when he put his hand down in her way.

"Can't sit here. Sorry."

"John!" she snapped. "What are you doing? Let me sit!"

He looked up at her calmly. "I don't think so, Wendy. You'll have to find somewhere else to sit. Unfortunately, I don't think you are the most popular person in this room. Best of luck."

"John, if this is because of earlier, I'm sorry—I was just trying to protect you—"

But by then John had turned away and was chatting to the long-haired boy sitting next to him. She bit her lip.

"Fine, just see that Michael gets fed."

John gave the tiniest nod of his head before ignoring her completely. Turning away so that her brother would not see the tears that were stinging her eyes, Wendy moved toward the door. She was suffocating with all these eyes on her, the hungry looks of boys who hadn't seen a girl in years. The looks on their faces were either full of a ferocious desire that made her squirm or a seething hatred at her presence. Either way, Wendy wouldn't just stand here and be gawked at. Better to be hungry. Her stomach howled its discontent with her decision, but she still turned to leave before feeling a strong hand on her upper arm.

"Peter?"

A hope surged through her, but it was left unanswered when she turned to see Abbott. He looked at her with a frown.

"This is why bringing a girl to Pan Island was a terrible idea. Here."

He walked over to where two older boys were shoving some sort of black eel into their mouths. "MOVE!" he thundered, and the boys scampered aside, making more than enough room for Peter's General and Wendy.

She sat.

"Paran! Dimitri! Food!"

Two of the sticky boys in the circle immediately set to work preparing their meals, and soon, food was being shoved toward them across the smooth table, made that way by years of greasy meat being slung across it. A hunk of turkey meat landed in front of Wendy, along with a hardened roll, a piece of white cheese, and lastly, a huge plum, easily the size of a melon. A wooden goblet filled with wine sloshed over the food as it slid across the table. There were no plates or napkins.

"Are there, er, utensils?" Wendy asked delicately. Abbott stared at her for a moment before rolling his eyes and tearing into his piece of almost-raw fish. Wendy looked around the table, where all eyes seemed to rest on her. Abbott swallowed noisily.

"Eat, before it gets any worse. They need to see you are like them. Hurry." He gulped his wine down. Wendy reached for her turkey leg and hesitated for a moment, taking in its sinews and bloody stump. She closed her eyes and reached for her hunger, that need that was gnawing at the inside of her stomach. Then she ripped into the turkey leg, mashing the meat in between her teeth as Abbott had done. It was so delicious that she sighed with her mouth full, something she would have never done at home. Home, wherever that was—she couldn't be bothered to remember because there was just her and the turkey leg. The meat was spicy, seasoned with flavors that she had never even dreamed of—it was somehow buttery and tart, with a hint of bitterness and . . . onion? And yet, not onion. Whatever they had done to the meat, it was the most delicious thing she had ever eaten. The roll would not come apart easily, and so she banged it on the edge of the table until it broke open, showering her in crumbs. She tore the plum apart and spread some of the juices on the roll to soften it. The cheese went into her mouth whole, and she had no regrets.

The sounds of the boys eating rose around her: grunting, tearing, slurping . . . and after a few moments of watching Wendy eat, their gratified laughter rose back up through the Table, the giggling guffaws bursting from the mouths of the boys with abandon. The sound was wonderful, and Wendy quietly smiled to herself as she ate, trying very hard not to think about what she looked like at the moment. With ravenous bites, she tore into her turkey leg until it was nothing but the bone. Eating it that way was intoxicating, either that or her hunger had driven her a bit mad. She shoved the roll into her mouth, and then the remainder of the plum, until nothing was left except for her full glass of berry wine. Every few minutes, large jade leaves floated down from the mossy branches that curled their way under the roof of the Table. The ones that made it past the spitballs of the boys settled gently, as if the wind had loved them, on the glossy surface of the circular table.

Wendy took a final bite of her roll, and when she was finished, she pushed up from the table and grabbed one of the leaves. Abbott watched her with amused eyes as she folded it in half, and then half again, before raising the corner of the leaf to her mouth and wiping it daintily. After she was done, she set it down next to the abolished bone that had been her dinner. Abbott burst out laughing. She looked at him with a half smile.

"Just because I ate like a Lost Boy doesn't mean I'm not a lady."

"I can see that." He leaned over. "Well, just because your brother is smart doesn't mean he's a General."

The moment was broken. Wendy fell silent, not wanting to betray John again.

Abbott stood up. "I'll be skipping Peter's story in the Teepee tonight. Some of us have to actually prepare for the raid."

Wendy felt a panic rise in her chest as Abbott walked away, leaving her unguarded with all these boys, but she was relieved to notice that suddenly no one seemed to care. Their curiosity satiated, they were just gouging themselves on food, not even looking her way.

"I think they just realized that you eat just like the rest of these hungry wretches." Oxley slapped her hard on the back as he walked by her. "Peter's waiting for you in the Teepee."

Wendy had never heard such glad words and quickly brushed the crumbs off her lap before leaving the Table, happy to be away from prying eyes and the noises of hundreds of boys eating. She could feel John's jealous eyes burning into her back as she ducked her head under a string of glass bottles, each rocking in the warm air as she left the Table behind.

The night was perfect and still, and she watched in silence as hundreds of wooden lanterns along the walkways lit up from within, a white light pulsing out from their broken windows. Magic. It was alive here, in small ways, almost unnoticeable if you weren't watching. Wendy leaned her head back, taking in the evening sky, the wind that blew around her, somehow warm to the touch, like a loving caress. As she watched, Neverland spread its beautiful twilight in front of her; a sky the color of fresh thistle looked down from above, a finger trail of navy stretching across the firmament. The tangled trunks of Centermost wrapped around her, beckoning her to explore. Reaching above her, Wendy steadied her foot on a branch and began pulling herself upward toward a small hole in the branches, a tiny window to the stars. She pulled herself easily through the branches that were almost steps in their pattern, a relaxing climb. Without much effort, she made it to the top of Centermost, to a small break in the tree branches facing west. Wendy poked her head under a curtain of exotic, sharp-edged orange flowers and followed the branch outward toward the break in the leaves.

The view was worth the climb. Standing on top of the grainy texture of the tree that made Pan Island, she felt a breath catch in her throat as she looked out over not just Pan Island, but all of Neverland. The mysterious main island was quiet from here, a hulking giant slumbering on a silently pitching sea. Dark hills rose out from its watery base, impassive and beautiful, stretching miles beyond what she could see. The very dim lights of Port Duette and its small townships flickered in the shadows, the city dwarfed by the massive shadow of the mountain above it, a thin trail of smoke continually trickling out of the crest. Wendy let a surprised sob fall from her lips at the raw beauty that played out like a painting in front of her. The beauty of Neverland was almost too much, an assault on her senses, stripping all logical thought from her mind. She couldn't help but marvel at this magical place, this dream inside of her wildest imaginings. Even the air here moved differently. It caressed with its warmth, each breath filling you with the hope of adventure. The tree swayed in the breeze, thrumming out a peaceful rhythm against her feet. Wendy gave herself over to it all, to the rich beauty and the feel of Neverland. There was so much she couldn't remember or understand, but in that moment she knew that her heart was content, and she let the beauty soak into her skin like the sun. For a few minutes, she watched the dark horizon, and then, with a nervous heart, she turned back, happy with the knowledge that Peter was waiting for her.

The walkway between the Table and the Teepee was a long rope walkway, strung with tattered ribbons and more than a dozen hanging lanterns that danced like fireflies in the dusk, and it swayed and pitched with each step. Wendy held onto the rough frayed tassels that strung from end to end, proving, as she stumbled, to be completely useless. Her foot slipped on one of the boards, and suddenly her leg went crashing through, leaving Wendy with her shin dangling outside of the walkway, her heart hammering so loud it felt as though the entire island could hear it.

"This is so very unsafe," she mumbled, pulling herself back. Her shin was scraped and bloody, and she rubbed it quickly, trying to make the stinging pain disappear. Out of the darkness, she felt a breath wash over her face, smelling like sugar.

"You aren't very good at this, are you?"

The voice was female, the same voice that she had heard wailing on the wind when she had fallen asleep the night before. Wendy whipped her head around, but there was nothing there. She scrambled up to her knees and looked around.

As she stared at the night sky, she noticed something filtering down toward her in the moonlight, a glittering dust falling around her like rain. It shimmered and leapt in the light, its surface that of a multifaceted mirror that gleamed as it fell, gentle as a twisting snowflake. She reached out to touch it, but when she made contact, the dust vanished, leaving no trace on her fingertips. It fell onto her hair and on her eyelashes, Wendy caught in its glimmering cylinder. A strong gush of warm wind rushed through, blowing the dust up and over the rope walkway, and slowly the splendor waned, the night silent in its absence. There was another flutter in the air, and then Wendy felt a presence just behind her right shoulder.

She had barely turned her head when something shoved her roughly to her knees. Her knees hit the wood planks with a hard slam, but she had barely registered the pain coursing through her legs when something yanked her hair back, hard. A piercing whistle sliced through the warm air, its harsh sound causing Wendy to cover her ears momentarily and curl into herself. With a final loud tweet, the whistle ended. The silence that followed was even more terrifying. Wendy cautiously raised her head. The great tree seemed to let out a breath of relief as all the lanterns on Pan Island gave a shudder and then went dark. A wave of boy groans came out of the Table, far below where she was, suspended in the middle of a walkway hundreds of feet in the air.

Wendy held perfectly still, knowing that an incorrect step in the darkness could lead her off the walkway and down into the sharp tree branches below, right into the hungry mouth of death. Moving as slowly as she dared, she leaned over to clutch at the ropes with desperation, feeling the frayed ropes in her soft hands, her heart hammering at the knowledge that something—or someone—was there with her on the bridge. She could feel it. There was another whoosh of air above her head, and then more twinkles were cascading down around her, throwing tiny refractions of light across the bridge.

A whispered voice in her ear, "I know the walkways can be a little . . . unstable sometimes. They're really not a place for little girls to play. Especially in the dark. They can be very dangerous."

The voice was singsongy and sweet, though undercut with a seething hatred. Wendy had to swallow several times before finding her own voice.

"I'm not . . . a little girl. And I was invited here by Peter."

"You say his name like you know everything about him, but you DON'T!" The voice was rising in cadence now, angry and bitter, bouncing through the tree, louder than it had any right to be. "You have no business being here, Wendy Darling. Pan Island is for boys."

Wendy whirled her head around in the darkness, and she caught the slightest hint of—she stifled a gasp—a wing! Opaque with a lustrous glow, it had the same texture as a dragonfly wing, with delicate veins running up toward the tip. When the wing flapped, the luminous dust tumbled down from its highest edge. Then, as quickly as she had seen it, it was gone.

"But you aren't a boy either," Wendy said clearly to the black night, her shaky voice betraying her courage. "I had hoped that we may be friends, since we are both women. I would very much like to be friends."

"I would very much like to be friends." The fairy repeated her last phrase, mocking her with a sweet voice. "I have never heard something so laughable. If you had any sense in that pretty little head of yours, you would take your brothers and leave this island."

There was a hard thump that vibrated up the wooden bridge, and Wendy stared hard into the darkness, watching a glowing silhouette of wings, fluttering almost too quickly for her to see. Her sweaty hands grasped hard to the ropes at her side, and she planted her feet firmly.

"What do you think of Peter?" The voice laughed. "Do you think he thinks you're pretty? So plain, I told him, plain brown

hair, the color of dung, pale skin that has never seen the sun—
what could he possibly see in this plain girl from London? You
think you can come here and steal what is *mine*?"

Wendy cast her gaze down. "I don't know what Peter sees in
me, if anything. I did not come here with the intention of stealing
anything from you."

There was a long pause, then a hissing that sounded more
animal than human.

"I don't believe you." The bridge rocked hard to one side, and
then Wendy felt her presence growing closer, the glow of her
wings the only thing Wendy could see. "But we'll see."

She gave a low whistle, its sound melancholy and sad. At that,
all the lanterns on the island relit themselves, only this time they
flared brighter, so bright that Wendy found herself temporarily
blinded as the being walked toward her, only a slender shadow
in the blinding white light. The wooden bridge began to creak
and pitch uncontrollably, and Wendy let out a scream as she flew
to one side, almost skittering off into the darkness. She pulled
herself up to her knees, clutching hard a long piece of red fabric
that someone had tied to one of the handles, wrapping it several
times around her wrist, ready to plunge off the side of the walkway. As the fairy approached, Wendy felt a wave of heat coming
toward her, washing over her again and again, each time growing
in strength. The waves crept up her body, and suddenly there was
an uncontrollable burning sensation in her hands. Another wave
of heat washed over her face. It was as if her skin were blistering,
though her trembling fingers confirmed there was no outward
sign of it. She let out a moan as the invisible flames engulfed her
body. The fairy leaned closer, and Wendy, her body seemingly on
fire, emitted a curdling scream.

"Do you feel that? That is the feeling of magic, and it burns
white-hot. If you so much as touch my Peter . . ."

"**TINK!**" Wendy heard Peter's voice, and then a scuffle ensued.
She closed her eyes and heard their voices arguing. Something

hit the bridge with a loud thump, and then the heat disappeared, dissipating just as suddenly as it had washed over her.

"Wendy?" The voice was John's, coming from the end of the rope walkway, back toward the Table. Wendy raised her blurry eyes and looked behind her. John stood at the end of the bridge, his arms tight around Michael. When he saw that she was okay, he turned away with a shake of his head. Something in her chest unclenched itself, and she found herself grateful for her brother's concern, even if it was fleeting. She turned her head and looked up to see Peter's concerned face looking down at her. He gently helped her to her feet. She looked at her hands—they were perfect, no burns of any kind, and when she touched her face, she felt only her own flushed skin. Peter's face was contorted, his eyes vivid navy.

"Wendy, I'm so sorry! Are you all right? Oh, my darling, you must feel like everything in Neverland is trying to kill you."

Wendy brushed her hair out of her face before noticing that the ends were singed, her patience short. "Indeed, I do."

"Oh, poor Wendy, what can I say? Fairies are notoriously territorial." Peter wrapped his arms around her. "Tink wasn't trying to kill you. She was just trying to intimidate you. She can be quite jealous when she wants to be. I promise I'll take care of it."

Wendy leaned against him. "Peter, don't leave me again tonight."

He let out a happy breath at her invitation. "I won't. You will sit by my side in the Teepee." With a suppressed laugh, he touched the ends of her singed hair. "We will have to maybe find some scissors though. I'll ask Ox to bring some around."

Wendy sighed, and in spite of her thrumming heart, she dissolved into Peter's smile. "Neverland is an exciting place."

Peter slipped his hand around her hip, and Wendy straightened up, uncomfortable with his familiarity. "You have no idea."

"What is she?"

"She is the last fairy in Neverland, and I'm afraid she's a bit fond of me." He gave a lighthearted chuckle, as though Tink had just shoved past her at a gala, not tried to throw her off a bridge. Wendy narrowed her eyes in the murky night, looking for any sign of Tink.

"She's gone," Peter added. "I scared her off, I think."

Wendy whirled on him. "Where did she go? Does she live on the island?"

Peter laughed. "I would love nothing more than to tell you all about Tink . . ." He looked past her shoulder. "But we have about a hundred Lost Boys heading this way, and they are a fairly impatient bunch."

Wendy turned around. Peter was correct—a large stream of boys was coming out of the Table now, their loud voices carrying up the rope bridge and into the night. The bridge began to creak with their weight as they all headed up toward Wendy, their eyes lighting up when they saw Peter. Three little ones ran up the bridge toward him, each of them waving something in their outstretched hands.

"Peter! I found this!"

"Peter, look at this bone! I found it in the water."

Thomas, the young boy with the long blond hair who had been sitting by John, slowly poked his head around Wendy's dress.

"I picked this for you. I'm going to give you a flower *every* day."

With a blush, he handed over an exotic flower—its head a sunset orange with deep red spikes protruding from its slip. Wendy put it to her nose and inhaled its pungent scent. She grimaced.

"Thank you, Thomas, is it?"

He grinned, a lock of yellow hair falling into his eyes. He started running down the rope bridge, against the tide of boys that now swarmed around them like bees.

"Peter! I saw a silver fish today, just like the one you showed me!"

"Peter! Could you let me fly on the next raid, *please*?"

"Peter, Abbott said that I couldn't climb up to fetch the rainwater today because I spilled it yesterday."

"Peter . . ."

Peter looked over toward Wendy with a bemused face. His eyes twinkled mischievously, and she felt an uncontrollable blush rising in her cheeks as he reached for her hand, the throng of boys pushing around them. He wrapped his hand around her own, and she gave a small nod, and then they were flying up, up toward the Teepee. She enjoyed the wind on her face, cooling the parts of her that she felt were still warm from Tink's unholy blaze. Peter gently put her down on the wooden deck that extended outward from the base of the hut and leapt up into the air again.

"And here is the Teepee."

At least that name had some merit, Wendy thought. Stretching high overhead, this hut had a vertically slanted roof that came together at a sharp peak. Adorned with Peter's flag that flapped overhead, the sides of the Teepee came down, each decorated with leaves that draped from its steep roof. Ribbons blossomed out from its sides, each one tied to a nearby tree, giving the Teepee the look of standing in the middle of a rainbow sun. Wendy pushed open the wooden door and peeked inside. The room was empty, save a large wooden chair in the middle of the room, carved from the same bark as the tree that made up Pan Island. The back of it was a perfect circle, the same shape as the moon on the flags.

"That is Peter's chair," Oxley whispered over her shoulder. He had herded in a handful of boys. "No one touches it but him. It's where he tells us stories of his adventures."

Light filtered in through the holes in the roof.

"Come in, boys, sit down!"

Dozens of Lost Boys had already gathered on the floor around Peter's chair and now were shoving each other for closer proximity to Peter's throne. Boys continued to pour through the open doorway. Wendy silently took a seat close to the wall, leaning her head back against its muddy texture, and waited, knowing that any minute now her lap would be occupied by a certain five-year-old . . . and yes. Michael curled up on her legs and leaned his head against her shoulder. He reeked of turkey and spices, and Wendy could see in the fluttering lamplight that his face was smeared with berry jam. He gave a happy sigh against her.

"What happens now? I just followed all the other boys here." His happy face turned sour. "John didn't talk to me at dinner. I'm mad at him."

Wendy smiled, pushing his hair back from his face. "I'm mad at John too. But I think that Peter is going to tell us a story, and then we can head to bed."

Michael gave an exaggerated yawn. "Good, 'cause I'm tired."

Dominant footsteps echoed through the room as Kitoko, Abbott, and Oxley shooed the boys forward into a large circle. When they turned around to see Wendy, Ox winked in her direction, Kitoko kept his distance, and Abbott regarded her with a silent and menacing stare.

"Move forward," Abbott grumbled, tipping his head toward where the rest of the boys sat. Wendy brushed herself off, shuffled Michael off, stepped forward a few steps, and sat back down. She had barely settled when ten boys swarmed around her, the strong scent of their sweat overwhelming her sensitive nose. Some just stared at her with curious eyes, while others shyly reached out and just barely brushed their fingertips along the edge of her dress or her shoes. Wendy felt a sharp pain on the side of her head.

"OW!" She turned around to look at a tiny Asian boy, who sheepishly held a single strand of her hair in his hand. When she looked at him, tears gathered in his eyes.

"I wanted to smell it."

Wendy smiled in spite of herself. "It's okay. Just ask next time. What is your name?"

"Little Sun."

She reached out her hand, and he carefully took it. "Nice to meet you. I'm Wendy Darling."

The boy stared at her for a long moment and then sat behind her, leaning his head against the small of her back. She looked around at her group of boys, all piled around her like puppies, and realized that they were all very young, the youngest of the Lost Boys, and they watched her with sad, wishful eyes. A palpable longing filled the space, and Wendy wondered what they could possibly want from her. A small boy with glistening black skin was staring up at her face, and then she understood with a jolt. They missed their mothers. Questions flooded her mind. Who were these boys? Where did they come from? Did she have a mother? Where was her mother?

Peter jumped up, his toes barely brushing the seat of his moon throne. He gave a shrill trill of his lips before snapping, "Quiet now, settle down, boys!"

The excitement in the room boiled down to a rolling simmer, save the occasional shout that was quickly shushed by Abbott. Peter reached out his hand.

"My crown, Naji?"

A beautiful small boy, his skin the color of caramel, darted forward and handed Peter a crown of olive leaves that he proudly settled on his unruly red hair, tufts rising up and over the leaves. The moon rose over Pan Island, and the holes cut out of the thatched roof filled with moonlight. Peter snapped his fingers, and the lanterns that hung around the room dimmed until their light was barely a whisper. The wooden circle behind Peter was illuminated with moonlight, casting a dark shadow over Pan's face. Still, even in the dim room, Wendy could see his white teeth, his feral and charming smile.

"Boys. Generals." His eyes lingered on Wendy and Michael. "Honored guests. What tale should I spin this fine evening in celebration of our raid?"

The room erupted with suggestions, some boys leaping to their feet with excitement.

"The time you got lost in the Forsaken Garden!"

"When you sunk *Neptune's Plague!*"

"When you buried Piers on the great mountain!"

Peter floated up in the air until his toes touched the top of his throne. Stroking his chin, he walked up and down the edge of the circle, looking contemplative at each of the boys' suggestions.

"Why, yes, that is a good story! I had forgotten about that! Ha! The *Neptune's Plague* did sink quickly, didn't it, Waylan?"

Finally, he settled himself on the brim of the chair, folding his legs underneath him and leaning down over the crowd. He reminded Wendy of a stone gargoyle, perched on the buildings of . . . she frowned. Of . . . that place she lived once. That town, with its gray skies and stinking streets. *Why couldn't she remember its name?*

"Those are all good tales, surely. But I think, since the Darlings are here tonight, I will tell the best story I know . . . the story of how Hook lost his hand."

CHAPTER ELEVEN

THERE WAS A SHARP INTAKE OF BREATH in the room. Wendy
surmised that this was not a story Peter shared often—its impor-
tance had filled the space with sudden awe. Michael leaned
forward and put his hands on his cheeks with a sigh, the way he
always did when being read a story. Peter's green eyes glinted in
the moonlight as he began his tale.

"I've been here in Neverland for many, many years. Longer
than any of you have been alive. Imagine, if you will, a Neverland
untainted by the *Sudden Night*. Our beloved seas so clear and
open, all without the *Night* bringing horror to all who see it. It
was a different time. Port Duette was nothing more than a small
harbor where locals sold their fruits and the Pilvi Indian children ran shrieking through the street."

Wendy turned to Oxley, who was leaning against the wall next
to them, his eyes riveted on Peter. "Pilvi?" she whispered, remembering that Peter had off-handedly mentioned them before.

Without even looking down at her, he answered, "Pilvinuvo
Indians. The people of the earth and cloud. They used to be the
main inhabitants of Neverland."

"And now?"

He gave her an enigmatic look. "Gone."

"Where did they go?"

"Shhhhh!" hissed one of the Lost Boys near the back, and Peter's gaze came to rest on Wendy. She gave him a sheepish shrug and mouthed, "Sorry," at which he grinned, and she saw a faint blush creep up his cheeks. He continued.

"As I was saying, I spent most of my time exploring the corners of Pan Island with a small group of Lost Boys and trading goods with the Pilvi. I had a very close relationship with their princess, the beautiful Lomasi. And I tell you, boys, the rumors of her beauty are true: Her hair was as black as a raven's wing, but softer than the finest silk that you could find in Port Duette. Her eyes were the same color as rich chocolate, her skin like the bark of this tree, a warm cocoa that glowed in the sun. She was born in Neverland, the pride of her people, their ambassador . . ." he paused. "And my friend. My dearest friend."

Peter's eyes betrayed that he had seen her as more than a friend, and Wendy felt a surprising pang of jealousy in her chest. She immediately felt ashamed for it, for it was already clear that this story would not have a happy ending, not if the Pilvi tribe had gone missing. Peter took a moment to collect his thoughts, absentmindedly clenching his hands and giving his fists a shake before continuing. Wendy saw him blink back tears, wrestling with his sudden onset of emotion. The entire room was silent as they watched their leader struggle to find his words. Finally, Peter took a breath before adjusting his crown and moving on. Then he gave a quick twist of his head, as if he were physically shaking the memory loose.

"Forgive me, friends. I have not thought of Lomasi in a long time. I'll continue." He coughed into his hand and raised his head. "It was one of those days where the sun rose over our beautiful Neverland Sea, and everything in the world felt possible. I began my morning circling around Shadow Mountain—as I'm known to do. When you fly around the mountain counterclockwise, you can watch the sun hit each rock just perfectly, watch the shadows crawl away from their crevices and make their way to the peak. After I watched the sunrise, I spent the morning down in Port Duette, trading with some of the Pilvi children, eating a ripe pineapple, and—I must be honest—teasing some of the drunk pirates who were pouring out of the tavern after their nightly debauchery."

The crowd gave a chuckle at the idea of Peter pulling off the hats of drunken men and shoving them against each other, tweaking their noses and dropping items on their unsuspecting heads. Peter sighed, his red hair falling over his forehead.

"But that soon became boring, as it always does, and though I can't say exactly why, my intuition pulled me over to the dark corner of the island, the place where wicked men go to sneak a peek at bathing mermaids—Miath, The Gray Shore. The Darlings aren't familiar with Miath, so I'll quickly explain." Peter's gaze narrowed, and a shadow fell across his face as he dipped his chin. "Neverland lore says that if a man lays eyes on a mermaid that he will have good fortune the rest of his days, which we know isn't true. When a mere mortal sees a mermaid outside of the water, they lose their minds. Jealousy and lust overtake them, and half the time they will fight their companions to the death out of a perceived rivalry for a second look. But as we know here on Pan Island, the world of grown men is full of nothing but blithe idiots. Every year pirates flock to Miath from time to time to try and peek at the mermaids' beauty."

Peter shook his head with a barking laugh. "The fools. It doesn't affect us, does it, boys?"

The boys laughed and clapped, thankful for the youth that saved them. Peter grinned.

"Ah, it's good to be young! Back to the story—on that fateful day when Hook lost his hand, I decided that I would fly over Miath. When I arrived there, there wasn't the usual group of drunken pirates, gawking over some of the rocks that lie up the mountain from the mermaids . . ." Peter's eyes widened, and his voice dropped to a whisper. "No. There was only one man, his broken body lying on the great sea-glass rock that overlooks the Gray Shore. This is Sybella, the rock that the mermaids pulled from the bottom of the depths of the sea. As large as a table and filled with the skulls of their elders, the rock is pure evil."

Peter got a faraway look in his eyes. "To this day, I will never understand how the man got there. He had been stabbed with a single, thin blade, up through his ribs, and was slowly bleeding to death, his blood turning Sybella a terrible shade of auburn. His body was slowly calcifying, and green sores cracked at his lips, a combination of the salty air and the mermaids' poison that was slowly seeping up from the rock."

Peter shook his head.

"I did what I could to save him, but it was too late. I offered to carry him home, but he confided to me that he had no home, that the pirates had been his home, and they had betrayed him. I told him not to speak, to save his energy, but he kept whispering to me . . . three little words."

The entire room leaned forward as Peter bent over the moon throne, his eyes glittering with excitement. His mouth turned up in a serious smile, and he began whispering it again and again . . .

"'The *Sudden Night* . . . The *Sudden Night* . . . The *Sudden Night*.' I didn't understand what he was saying, but I was sure that he was calling out for death to take him. Those words had no meaning for me, not yet. I stayed beside him as he whispered these words, his body convulsing with each breath. Finally, his eyes went dim, and I saw the life snuffed out of him upon that green glassy rock." He closed his eyes. "Though he was heavy, I heaved his body off the sea-glass rock, where it would be a haven for Keel cats. It was only then that I saw the message that he had written in blood on the side of the rock. Scrawled in red were the numbers 42 and 73, and he had drawn some strange lines beside them. At first I wondered if these were the amounts of gold he had been promised, or the number of men he had left behind, but no. I remembered that many years ago, I had seen a nautical map, a tool of sailors, and had tossed it into the treasure room. The oceans of Neverland are vast, and pirates often end up circling in its tricky waters. I committed the numbers to memory and flew back to Pan Island. To say that I turned the treasure room upside down is a bit of an understatement."

He chuckled and took a breath. Wendy shifted, and when she moved, all the little Lost Boys moved with her. Michael clutched possessively to her hand, and she watched as members of the crowd kept their eyes riveted on Peter.

"Finally, at the bottom of a chest, under a bag of dresses, I found this map."

From his pocket, Peter pulled out a crumpled piece of paper and held it up to the lunar light. The crowd gasped at its beauty, but to Wendy, who had seen many maps, it seemed fairly plain.

"After a few minutes of figuring out how it worked, I learned that 42 and 73 were coordinates."

He paused for effect.

"And so, like a fool, I decided to fly there by myself. When I reached the coordinates, I kept rechecking the map, thinking that I had done it wrong, because there was nothing there. It was only the Teeth, those sharp white cliffs that rise out of the ocean on Neverland's east side—you know them well."

Wendy did remember them from their flight in: uninhabitable, sharp, deadly cliffs that jutted violently out of the surf.

"The water pounds so hard against the base of the Teeth that not even the mermaids dare to venture there. There was not a stitch of anything there, not a person, nor a glint of anything along those rocky crags. Until . . ."

He leapt off the top of the throne and settled down into the seat, his legs crossed, his body floating inches off the chair. *Showoff*, Wendy thought with a warm smile.

"Until I flew up to the sides of the cliffs, so close that I could brush their razor-sharp edges with my fingertips."

He trailed his fingers down through the air, and in that dark room, Wendy swore that she could almost feel the jaggedness of the cliffs.

"As I flew, I felt a strange, warm air brush my fingertips, so unlike the coolness that radiated off the Teeth. I turned back and followed the warm air upward a dozen feet. There, disguised by a crudely painted whitewood slab, was a . . . a hole."

The room gasped. A Pip with a jagged scar over his eye leapt to his feet, unable to control his excitement.

"What was in it, Peter? What was it?"

Peter grinned in his direction. "Would you like to know, Will?"

The boy was practically bouncing. "Yes! Yes!"

Peter turned to his adoring crowd.

"Would you all like to know?"

Shrieking pleas filled the Teepee. The boys were practically whipped into a frenzy. John was grinning from ear to ear, looking ridiculous. Only Michael seemed immune to Peter's charms, as he had fallen asleep on Wendy's lap. A large pool of drool had formed at the corner of his mouth, one arm outstretched over his head. Wendy looked up with a smile to see Peter's eyes trained on her, and she felt a flush of pleasure run over her skin. Peter began to walk about the room, his arms stretching wide as he continued the tale.

"I couldn't imagine what was inside the Teeth. An ancient burial ground? A monster? There was no way I could know, and so, with my sword clutched tightly, I entered. At first it was simply a wide cavern inside, the whitewashed walls of the cliffs surrounding me on every side. Seawater dripped down from several cracks in the wall. I had gone several feet when I heard a strange sort of chirping sound and looked up. Over my head were hundreds of white bats with their illuminated clear eyes, the kind I had seen when flying at night. This was their home, inside giant black nests that lined the walls and ceiling, the veins of the Teeth."

He gave a grimace.

"I walked a bit quieter after that, to tell you the truth. Those bats creeped me out a bit!"

He bent down to emphasize walking in the tunnel.

"A shallow trail of water trickled at my feet, making its way back to some unknown source. After about a mile or so, the cavern narrowed, and I began to hear a foreign sound—the sound of men. The sounds . . . of pirates."

The entire room hissed. Peter snapped his fingers, and the noise silenced immediately. He continued.

"It was also the sounds of labor: hammers, nails, clinks and clangs that echoed up through the cavern and out to where I was. Slowly, I crept closer, now on my stomach so as not to be seen, sliding along like a snake until the cavern opened itself up before me into an enormous white room, carved out of the Teeth themselves. The room, I tell you, was almost as wide as Pan Island, and deeper than any room I'd ever dreamed possible. The natural walls of the cave curved up and met in the middle, a cathedral of whitewashed stone. With fear in my throat, I looked down, and what I saw . . ."

He shook his head sadly, a red lock lingering on his forehead. Wendy's fingers twitched. She longed to brush it out of his eyes.

"What I saw chilled me to the bone. There were two ships sitting in the water in between the great white walls. Directly in front of me was a ship that I was very familiar with—Hook's ship, the *Jolly Rodger*. The *Jolly Rodger*, that old girl, a relic from another time, creaking in the soft waves that pushed it up and down inside the cave. You wouldn't have known it then, worn as she was, but the *Jolly Rodger* was a ship that had carried countless riches. From my perch, I could see the naked mermaid at her bow, a sparkling red gemstone glistening in her forehead, the cherry wood that flanked her sides. And below, the pirates, humming their familiar tune."

Peter tapped his chest and cleared his throat before letting out a gorgeous lilting tenor that filled the room, his rich sound swelling in the Teepee, filling Wendy. Slowly, gently, he sang:

> A-rovin over the sea
> Give me a career as a buccaneer
> it's the life of a pirate for me

Then, without a beat, he continued, "They were loading chests off of her deck and onto the white rocks below, a pearl necklace or a gold coin occasionally dropping down into the water with a plop. Honestly, there are probably untold riches in those waters." The smile on his face became more somber, his voice dropping. "The *Jolly Rodger* nestled up on one side of the cavern, and behind it a net, separating the ship from the black ribs of what must have once been a gigantic whale. I had to look at it for a few minutes to truly understand what I was seeing, for it was so large: Long timbers stretched out from their arches, the base of the ship. On the sides of the whale ribs were long pieces of wood, each sanded down and painted black, nailed into jagged rows to create the sides of the ship. To the side of the behemoth, all sorts of projects were being undertaken in the flickering light of sea and fire. I saw a man stringing a black net across two harpoons, then latching it to what looked like a rotating platform that was on some sort of rudimentary wheel. Another man was melting metal down for swords. When they were completed, he was mounting them on a long black board that ran the length of the ship. A string was drawn across them and pulled taut. When the man released the string, the swords leapt out vertically, so as to impale someone who was approaching from the water. When I saw that . . . I knew."

The room was silent as Peter wearily rubbed his face. "I knew what I was seeing, and I knew who had done this. Who would create such a monstrosity? Who could catch and kill a whale of such size, only to make a ship of its bones?"

"Hook," whispered one of the boys in the front, his face shining in awe at Peter.

"Yes. Hook," Peter whispered. "Hook and his men were building another ship."

He took a deep breath in, looking disturbed at the memory. "I didn't see it at the time for what it was. Hook has easily a dozen ships in his employ—what was another one? Still, I was fascinated. I watched the pirates for hours before I saw him. My lifelong enemy. Hook, striding up from somewhere below, his black boots clicking over the white stone, his navy blue jacket adorned with gold and silver medals, his famous sword always clutched tightly in his left hand. From my hiding spot, I could see the perpetual scowl on his worn face, those beady eyes that see malice in everyone and everything, his short-cropped gray hair. He was barking orders at his men, beating some when necessary, throwing one man into the frothy sea when he wasn't working fast enough. I watched him command the men to work harder, faster—a brutal slave driver. The look of greed and murder on his face was unmistakable, that famous sneer ticking as he walked along, always at that clipped pace, tick-tock, tick-tock. When he was directly underneath me, I pushed myself back up against the wall, my heart beating loudly in my chest. Hook looked around as if he could smell me, his lips curling up against that hideous face. He paused for a moment, blinked, and then kept walking, whistling his signature tune."

Peter shook his head with a laugh.

"That's when I, Peter Pan, made a colossal mistake. Lying on my stomach, I pulled myself back to the ledge and looked over, and when I did, I saw Hook's steely eyes bearing right into mine."

The room gasped, along with Wendy, whose heart was hammering, despite her attempts to quiet it. His story had captured her.

"The crafty bugger had *just pretended* to walk away. With a shout, he alerted everyone to my presence, and within seconds there were pirates swarming up the rocks toward where I was. Hook was among them, scaling the rocks, angry spittle flying from his mouth. I leapt out into the air above his head, barely fast enough—he caught hold of my tunic, and he came out into the air with me. I beat down at him with my sword, and he beat up at me with his, neither of us able to get a formidable strike. His weight was dragging me down, and I do believe that in that moment, I was saved by my tunic ripping. Hook tumbled down into the shallow water, and I surged upward. He climbed out of the water, screaming at the remaining pirates below, and they scattered for their weapons.

"From the air, I looked down upon the two ships and knew what I had to do, even though it might cost me my life. I had an opportunity that I would never have again. The ships were contained, not out on the ocean. Destroying the ships would ensure that you, my Lost Boys, would stay safe from harm, at least for a little while. My head spun as I looked down at the cavern. How could I destroy them with pirates swarming over the bows like ants? I certainly couldn't hack away at them with an axe. I flew as high as I possibly could, my head scraping the top of the cavern. The towering cavern ended in a haphazard stack of rocks and white dust where the pirates had blown their way in. That's when I spotted it: there was a low flame crackling on the side of one of the rocks, three forgotten fish cooking on top of it, their tails seared black. I careened down toward the flame, the cool sea air washing over my face.

"Hook screamed again, and then pirates were all clamoring down the rocks, each one with a sword drawn and his black teeth bared in my direction. To reach the fire, I had to fly dangerously low, well within the reach of Hook's henchmen. I took out the first one with a strike to the upper shoulder. He went down screaming onto the white rocks."

Peter was now pantomiming his performance, leaping and thrusting his sword out at invisible foes.

"The second and the third tried to cut at my chest, but I leapt behind them and slashed the backs of their knees open, ensuring that they would never walk again."

He chuckled.

"One grabbed my leg, and so I flew upward until he lost his grip. Sadly, I don't think that man lived much longer after that."

The room erupted with laughter, and Wendy found herself frowning. Death was hardly an amusing subject. Peter continued, leaping and flipping in the air, his sword flashing so fast that Wendy could barely make out the golden blade.

"I catapulted over their heads and grabbed a log from the flaming fire, waving them back. There were so many of them now, dozens around me, and I knew I had mere seconds to do what I needed to do. I leapt up into the air again. Unfortunately, an arrow pierced my shoulder here . . ." he pointed near the collar of his tunic, "and I was sent hurtling downward. I hit the black ribs of the ship and rolled a few paces. With a scream, I yanked the arrow out of my shoulder and looked around for my flaming log. It had landed right next to me and was flickering weakly. I crawled toward the flame, blood pouring from my shoulder, one hand over another, dragging myself toward it, thinking only of protecting the Lost Boys."

At this point, no one in the room was breathing, aside from Oxley, who Wendy noticed was looking mildly bored.

"I reached the flaming log and pushed myself up to my feet. Hook stood before me, the fire illuminating the murderous rage in his eyes. His sword hand was trembling, a smile on his face. Then he spoke."

Peter dropped his voice to imitate the pirate captain. "'I swear on the grave of my father—I live to see you buried, Peter Pan.' My sword was still in my belt, and I knew that if I reached for it, Hook would kill me. He may be many despicable things, but Hook has always been an excellent swordsman. In that moment, time seemed to stop. I looked deep into his eyes and flung the burning timber onto the deck of the *Jolly Rodger*. As luck would have it, it hit some empty burlap sacks that ignited instantly. Hook gave a scream and lunged toward his ship with his hand outstretched. At that moment, I pulled my sword from my belt, leapt up above him, and slashed at his wrist."

Peter turned in the air and brought his sword down with incredible speed. Wendy gasped at his sheer physical power.

"I saw Hook's hand fall from his wrist and the rush of dark blood that came with it. He grabbed his wrist and screamed my name, but I was already on my way up and out of the cavern, up toward the tunnel I had come from. I looked back one more time and saw that the *Jolly Rodger* had turned into a rapidly consuming flame. The fire had licked its way up the mast and down to the sea. As I watched, the flames reached the stores of the ship where gunpowder was kept, and a massive explosion ripped through its hull. The heat from the flame had turned the cavern into an oven, and pirates were leaping into the water to escape its raging heat. Hook was running away from the *Jolly Rodger* and toward the black whale bones, screaming to his men to protect her. The heat gave one final blast, so hot I felt it in my bones, and the *Jolly Rodger* gave a huge creak, as though she were surrendering, and began to sink into the water.

"I watched as her red eye disappeared underneath the black and red sea, the hands of burnt men grasping at her for one last moment before slipping underneath. The last thing I saw before flying up into the tunnel was the outline of Hook, fringed with fire, staring at me as blood dripped from his wrist, and the burning black and white flag of the *Jolly Rodger*. I knew then that I had started a new story, that Neverland was no longer his, but mine."

Peter took a breath and pushed back his crown. "I flew through the tunnel as fast as I could, my feet never touching the ground. I had never feared Hook's wrath as I did that day. As I flew, the white bats that were nesting on the roof of the tunnel stirred, and they began to attack me, their claws scraping my face and arms, their tiny teeth biting my ears. I barreled toward the entrance, fearing I would never make it there alive. Finally, I exploded through the painted wooden barrier and cartwheeled out into the beautiful Neverland sky. The bats flew out all around me, climbing as quickly as they dared toward the bright moon. From there, I could hear the sounds of Hook screaming my name, and I knew that his hunt for me would only intensify now that I had taken his hand and his father's beloved ship. I returned to Pan Island and told the boys what I had seen."

He shook his head. "Had I only known the cost then, who is to say that I would have done the same?"

Peter looked devastated, and he turned away from the boys, hiding his face. "Hook's retaliation was to take Lomasi from me, my princess and the light of her people. She disappeared the next night. I heard from the whores in Port Duette that Hook had thrown her overboard wrapped in chains, a red eye painted on her forehead, a message meant to wound my heart forever. I see her sometimes . . ." He struggled with his words.

"I see her in my dreams, fish flitting in and out of her black hair, pearls where her eyes should be."

Slowly, he regained his composure.

"After that, the entire Pilvi tribe disappeared, so great was their fear of Hook. I looked for them for weeks, but they haven't been seen since. They just disappeared."

The Lost Boys gasped. "And that wasn't all. The ship that I was forced to leave behind became the *Sudden Night*, that ship that has since plagued our existence. I had burned the *Jolly Rodger* to ash, but the *Sudden Night* rose out of those ashes, a nightmare that would one day appear on the Neverland Sea, a ship built to kill Lost Boys. A ship that can't be burned, due to some magical gloss that coats its surface. A ship created . . . to kill me."

There was a heavy silence in the room as the mood dimmed. Peter paused, understanding that this story had ended on a somber note. He stood perfectly still, his eyes lingering on each and every face. When they reached Wendy's, she found herself mesmerized by his unflinching gaze. Finally, after his long dramatic pause, Peter looked up with a naughty grin, his emerald eyes flashing in the moonlight.

"But at least I know that when Hook comes to take me, he will have to do it with a little bit less."

He raised one of his arms, his hand pulled back into his shirtsleeve, leaving nothing there. The room erupted with cheers and fractious laughter. Peter then gave an exaggerated bow, the leaf crown on his head shifting a bit. When he raised his head, his eyes were navy.

"And that, my Lost Boys, is the story of how Hook lost his hand."

The room erupted with cheers; the lanterns leapt to light with a new, golden energy. The boys swept around Peter, lifting him in the air on their shoulders, someone shoving a goblet of wine into his hand. The crowd carried him out of the door onto the open patio of the Teepee, their vigorous cheers echoing through the night.

That's when Wendy saw her. Sitting silently in the center of Peter's throne was a girl.

CHAPTER TWELVE

SHE WAS QUITE PETITE, just a bit shorter than Wendy, as narrow as a reed. A messy tangle of thick white-blond hair, matted at its core, was perched on the top of her head, shoved through with sticks, leaves, and dead flowers. She had very pale skin that stretched over immaculately carved cheekbones, her face perfectly symmetrical, flawless in its ethereal construction. Peachy pink and pearly lips that appeared to be just bitten pursed underneath a narrow nose. There were dark circles under her wide blue eyes, so deep that they appeared as bruises at first glance, giving her a hollowed look. Wendy had seen women who looked like this before, in a narrow alleyway on the dodgy end of her neighborhood, their empty eyes searing as they watched her scurry past. They were regulars in that alley, in that town, of that place, that place she used to live . . . Wendy shook her head and gave two long blinks.

"Trying to remember something?"

Her voice was high, like the tinkling of bells, though the dripping malice behind it was unmistakable. It was the same voice from the bridge, the same voice she had heard crying on the night of their arrival. Wendy was unsure of how to answer, and so she stayed silent, unmoving. The girl uncurled herself from Peter's chair and stepped toward Wendy, her features becoming sharper as she approached. Her clothes rustled as she walked, so bulky that they seemed to barely touch her frame. A faded brown dress wrapped around her shoulders and cascaded to the floor, strips of fabric sewn together without care—it was lumpy and unattractive. She had cinched the dress at the waist with a vine, but other than that, there was no color visible. Even with her drab clothing, it was impossible not to notice the shawl that was draped across her shoulders, so long that its ends were hooked around her thumbs, pulling the fabric taut across her back. The shawl was meant to conceal whatever massive feature lumped out of her back, a shape so large that she could as well have been concealing another small girl underneath it.

Then Wendy understood. *The wings.* She was concealing her wings. She silently approached Wendy on tiny feet, her steps making no sound, her arms and the shawl wrapped protectively around herself. Her lips up close were cracked and bruised, her dispirited face coming ever closer. When she breathed, her body seemed to give a small shudder, as though the act was painful for her. The word *broken* flickered through Wendy's mind as the girl drew up next to her. Without warning, the girl reached out to Wendy's face, her hand small and delicate, her head level with Wendy's nose. Wendy didn't move, not wanting to alarm this creature who had so terrified her on the bridge. The girl looked up into Wendy's eyes, and Wendy struggled to stifle a gasp. Inside of the fairy's eyes, resting on the bottom of her irises, small stars lit up and went dark again, one after another, flashes in the dark. *This,* Wendy thought, *is deep magic.* Even though the girl was small and slight, the hot power radiating out from her was palpable, and Wendy found herself frozen with fear.

"Nothing extraordinary," the girl whispered, running her small hand over Wendy's cheeks. "Normal face, boring muddy hair, strange purple flecks in the eyes." She clicked her tongue. "What does Peter see? Nothing I can see, not with my eyes."

Wendy didn't even breathe until the fairy stepped back from her, narrowing her eyes accusingly.

"I can't understand; what does he see in you?" She tilted her head sideways. "You're nothing but a silly, ugly little girl."

Wendy tried to remember how to speak, paralyzed as she was. Finally, she stuck out her hand, her voice shaking. "You must be Tink. I'm Wendy Darling. My brothers are John and Michael. I'm pleased to meet you. I've never met a fairy before."

The girl's eyes widened. "Yes, my name is Tink. It means heavenly sky, or . . ." she paused, "in other translations, torture. And no, you will never meet another fairy again," she snapped, turning her head away. "I am the last of my people, the sole fairy of Neverland."

"Then I am sorry for your loss," Wendy said sincerely.

Tink's head whipped around to gaze back at her. "What did you say?"

"I said I'm sorry. That you have no others of your kind. That must be very lonely."

There was confusion in Tink's starry eyes. "How dare you mock me?" She moved toward Wendy, but to Wendy's great relief, Peter landed back in the room with a resounding thud.

"Tink! Wendy! My girls! I'm so glad that you are getting to know one another!" Peter opened his arms wide, and Tink scurried into them, faster than Wendy had ever seen a mere human move.

"Peter!" she gushed. "Your story, it was magnificent! You were so brave! So handsome and so brave!"

Peter flushed. "Tink. That's enough. You've heard that story a thousand times."

She looked up at him with adoration, a pink blush rising in her pale cheeks. "Yes, but every time you tell it, it's like new. Only this time, there were bats!"

Peter's face tightened for a second before it dissolved into an uncomfortable smile. With a sigh, Peter reached down and tussled Tink's messy hair. "Are these zumeria blooms? That must be why you smell so nice."

Tink blushed. "I know you love that smell."

"I do." Tink laced her hand around Peter's and looked over at Wendy defiantly. "What shall we do tonight? I could make the trees sing for you. Shall we count the stars? We could go to our special place and watch the sea glow. You haven't been there in a long time. Peter. Peter?"

Peter was staring at Wendy, his green eyes unmoving from hers. Even as he embraced Tink emotionlessly, his eyes never left her face. Tink was getting agitated.

"Don't you remember what you said last time? Don't you remember?" She turned her head to stare up at him, the stars in her eyes brightening when he turned his face to look down at her. Her lips trembled. She reached out to stroke his cheekbone, and he made a disgusted sound. Then, with a grimace, he shrugged out of Tink's embrace and untangled his hand from her own.

"I was actually just about to fly Wendy up to her hut for the night. I'm sure the Lost Boys would love to hear you sing. They are down in the Table, probably eating the last of our cheese. Go find Oxley or Darby."

Tink's eyes overflowed with tears, which Wendy noted were also filled with small bursts of starry light. "But Peter, you promised! You said that . . ." Her voice rose to a whine. "You said that you would send them away. You said . . ." Her voice then dropped to a gentle whisper. "You said you didn't even like her."

Wendy's heart sank.

"I know what I said, Tink. Now go away, please. I'll find you tomorrow."

The fairy stomped her foot, sending bursts of light curling up her leg. Peter put his hands on his hips.

"Tink! Control yourself!"

She looked at Peter with teary eyes. "It's not fair! She is nothing. Just a plain, stupid, boring girl from London. She's nothing!"

London. That's where she had lived. Wendy repeated the word to herself again and again, hoping she wouldn't forget it. *London. London. London.* Peter whirled on Tink.

"I said leave. Now. Can't you see that you are upsetting Wendy?"

Out from behind Tink's wild hair, lines of curling white heat began to rise from the back of her neck. They lashed toward Wendy.

"Out!" Peter snapped, stomping his foot at her, as if he were shooing away a stray dog. With an angry cry, Tink sped across the room and leapt out into the darkness, leaving a small trail of glittery dust that lazily circled on the ground after she was gone. As Peter scuffed it toward the door with his foot, Wendy exhaled the breath she had been holding.

"Peter! Why did you say that to her? I wasn't upset. A bit intimidated, that's all."

Peter laughed hysterically. "Intimidated? By Tink? You would do better to be intimidated by a flower. She's harmless. Fairies are by nature flighty and silly creatures."

Wendy crossed the room, telling herself that it wasn't just to be nearer to Peter.

"She didn't seem harmless on the bridge."

His eyes watched her every step, taking in every inch of her. "She's been in love with me for as long as I can remember. I have done everything in my power to convince her otherwise, but once a fairy falls in love, it's for life. I try not to encourage it, but to be honest, it's exhausting." Peter stretched his arms over his head with a yawn. "Don't worry about Tink's jealousy. She would be jealous of Hook himself if I paid him too much attention. Are you afraid?"

Wendy shyly circled her fingers around her wrist. "Not afraid. I just don't want to upset anyone. And . . ." Wendy paused, the words heavy on her tongue.

"What is it?"

"Did she mean it? That you didn't like me?"

She immediately hated herself for asking but still raised her eyes to meet his own. Peter inched closer to her and took a tendril of Wendy's brown hair in his hand.

"Oh, Wendy Darling. Such a sweet, good girl. How was I so lucky to stumble across your window? Of all the stars in the sky, one must have led me straight to you."

Wendy stepped backward, unsure of what to do, untrusting of herself in the moment.

"Thank you, Peter, that's very kind."

A lock of red hair fell in front of his eyes. "One of these days, I will find a way through your wall of politeness and discover the girl within."

"Peter Pan!" Wendy blushed at the notion. "That was very familiar of you!" She stared at him; his eyes were unflinching and hungry as he gazed upon her. "While I would wish to stay and talk all night, you should probably take me back to my hut. I'm rather sleepy, and Michael is probably waiting for me."

"Ah, yes." Peter rubbed his chin with an aggravated sigh. "Michael. What an adorable little boy."

Wendy smiled. "Not always. Precocious and annoying and yes, adorable. Sometimes. And speaking of the boys, John seems to be fitting in quite well."

"Ah, yes, I've asked Oxley to take him under his wing. Abbott's not keen, but then again, Abbott doesn't really like anyone or anything."

"He does seem a bit wary."

"Ever since he was a little boy, he has had a jaded heart. Can you blame him?"

Peter laced his hand through Wendy's, and then they were both floating inches off the ground. "He's not like you, Wendy. You have a generous heart. I can see it. You will be good for Pan Island."

"But we won't be staying here forever, Peter. We have to go . . . home." As soon as she said the words, she realized how vague they sounded. Home—where was that?

He eyed her carefully, his green eyes swirling with navy. "Yes. Home. You can go home anytime you like. But I must know, do you like it here? With me?"

Wendy nodded her head, noting how Peter's hair moved ever so slightly even though there was no breeze. It was as if he were a part of the island himself, a creature of nature that moved with the whims of the environment around him. His very being seemed to hum with Neverland. With his eyes bearing down on her with so much intensity, Wendy suddenly felt very shy and unsure of herself in the moment.

"I should probably turn in for the night."

"Yes," Peter said, obviously not meaning it at all. "First, hold onto me."

Wendy wrapped her arm delicately around his waist, and then they were soaring up out of the hut and through the massive branches of the tree that made Pan Island. Golden-hued lanterns shimmered below their feet, and Wendy could vaguely make out the shape of the Lost Boys going to and from various huts, some finding their hammocks, others playing with swords through the tree branches. There was a boy swinging on a rope upside down below them, giggling to himself as he wound vines through his toes. Wendy smiled. There was no bedtime on Pan Island.

"Come," Peter whispered as they soared through the night air. "I want to show you something. It will be quick, I promise."

They soared upward, passing huts and tree branches, past Wendy's hut and Peter's, up and up until they reached the thatched roof where they had landed after their flight from . . . from . . . she couldn't remember. That place she was from. Peter's moon flag still fluttered in the air, and beside it, a Lost Boy stood as still as stone, his eyes on the main island, his face never moving—not even as Wendy and Peter flew over him. Then, without warning, he spun around and faced the opposite way.

"What is he doing?" Wendy whispered, not wanting to disturb the boy who looked like a marble carving of a solider.

"He's watching. We can never be too careful at night. Hook is a crafty man, not to mention all the vagrants, rapists, and thieves who live in Port Duette who would love to get their hands on our treasure—and on you. If anyone tried to attack Pan Island, we would see them from here before they ever made it to shore. Not that a ship could ever dock here. The roots are too high." He gestured to the boy. "This is the cost of being a Lost Boy. You take your watch every few weeks. If you fall asleep, well then . . ."

"What?"

Peter shrugged. "Then we find someone else to take the watch."

"What happens to them? The ones who fall asleep?"

"It's only happened twice."

His tone told Wendy that there would be no more questions. They circled around the flagged roof a few more times, the boy never taking his eyes from the sea, and then swirled down through the Neverland night to land with a bump on the floor of Wendy's hut. She looked around the dark room.

"I guess Michael is still with John."

"What a shame," Peter remarked with a smile. Wendy turned to him.

"Peter, I'm worried about my brother on the raid tomorrow. You must promise me that John won't be in any real danger."

Peter looked deep into her eyes.

"Wendy, what is life without adventure? It is meaningless, like being a piece of seaweed forever drifting."

Wendy could think of a dozen better metaphors than that one, but she refrained from correcting this wild boy with a beautiful mouth. Instead, she cautiously allowed an edge to come into her voice.

"Peter. His safety."

"I promise. John will be safe. After all, it's just a game, really! It's just a game! Honestly, I'm not sure why you like John anyway. He's not very nice to you."

"No, he isn't, but he's my brother. He just wants to find where he fits in, always has. Anyway, thank you for reassuring me." She gave him a friendly kiss on the cheek, and he involuntarily rose a few inches off the floor before he shook his head and returned to the ground. Wendy took a step toward her hammock, suddenly feeling very alone in a room full of shadows and dark corners. The fear she had felt on the bridge returned, the white heat of Tink's rage, the stone grip of the mermaid closing around her waist, the rush of blood spooling out into the water. She turned back to Peter, his green eyes glinting in the darkness.

"Would it be too much to ask . . . ?"

"Absolutely not," he said softly. "I'll stay here until you fall asleep."

"Thank you. Goodnight, Peter Pan."

"Goodnight, Wendy Darling."

Peter leapt out of the open door, the thin linen curtain blowing in his wake. She heard a thump on the roof and the sounds of Peter walking above. She heard him settle right above where her bed was. With a smile, she climbed into her hammock, pulling the thin blanket over her bare legs.

"Wendy?" Peter's voice came through the thatched roof.

"Yes?"

"I look forward to seeing you tomorrow."

She paused, her eyes growing heavy. "You as well."

Just when she was almost falling into unconsciousness, she heard beautiful music, climbing up and down an unknown scale. On the roof above her, Peter was playing a pipe of some sort, the sound bright and confident, a lilting melody drifting down and putting to ease all her fears. The music carried down from her hut, echoing throughout Centermost, and she imagined it flowing like liquid out through its branches, drifting down to the ears of the Lost Boys, who smiled at its reassuring sound as it fell around them like rain. Wendy felt her heart swell to match its lonely melody, felt her skin tingle. Wendy had played Dvořák and Strauss, but she had never heard a melody that was quite so beautiful and dangerous at once. The notes rose up before her like a swelling sea, pushing her further out than she had ever been, pushing her further and further toward Peter, until the music suddenly relented, crashing her like a wave at his feet. In its wake, it reminded her of someone, someone who had deeply loved her once. Someone who had wanted her to be brave. Without warning, she fell into the welcoming arms of sleep, her subconscious once again reaching desperately for the boy whose face was fading forever. Just before she fell asleep, she was sure she felt the touch of his fingers on her palm.

Chapter Thirteen

Wendy awoke to a pounding headache that thrummed against the inside of her head with relentless procession. *Wham! Wham! Wham!*

"Ughh . . ."

She moaned and pressed both hands up against her temples and rolled over in bed. Only she wasn't in a bed, she was in a hammock. The swinging bed flipped underneath her, and Wendy's knees hit the floor with a hard thump, followed by the rest of her body. She laid her face against the floor.

"Owwww. All right. Give yourself a moment."

Then she turned over on the floor, her body not willing to move. Instead, she sprawled out underneath the wildly swinging hammock, watching how the Neverland light reflected off the colored ribbons that brushed over her face with a gentle caress. The light refracted and bounced around the room, and Wendy thought that she caught the scent of breakfast wafting up from the Table below. She reached up her slender white arm to touch the light, watching it play over her pale fingers, reds and yellows filtered through the ribbons of her bed, purples and light blues through her linen curtains. Even the light here was different, she marveled—it was as if every particle of light had been brushed with gold, giving a hazy glow to everything it touched.

Wham! Wham! Wham!

The same drumming noise that she had thought came from inside of her head came barreling in through her open windows. What in God's name was that awful sound? She pushed herself off the floor and brushed off her nightgown, which was now filthier than she had ever seen it. She was practically a street urchin at this point. With a sad sigh, she untied one of the lapis ribbons from her hammock and pulled her hair into a neat bun, lacing the ribbon around her brown strands and tying it with a bow. Even though she didn't look like a lady, she didn't have to behave like she wasn't one. She splashed her face in the pot of water near the end of the bed. The morning was quiet without Michael scampering around her feet. She at once enjoyed the silence and missed him terribly. With more confidence than she had had the previous morning, she whistled her way down the tree branch, even leaping off it at the end with some grace. Oxley grinned at her from across a rope bridge when she landed, wiping her raw hands on her nightgown.

"You did that well, Wendy—no falling! Color me impressed! It must be a good omen for our raid day!"

Wham! Wham! Wham! Wendy turned her head away from the overbearing sound.

"Oxley—WHAT on EARTH is that?"

A huge grin stretched across his face. "Well, you aren't on Earth, so that may help explain it! Those are the drums of war. Should I show you?"

"Do you quite have to? Can't you just make them stop? It's absolutely horrible."

"I think you will want to see this." Oxley trotted over and grabbed her wrist, and then they were flying downward. "Peter gave me flight this morning. For the raid."

"Ah."

Flying with Oxley was so different than flying with Peter. Flying with Peter was intimate, a chance to be close to him, a chance for Wendy to feel that fire flush through her skin. Flying with Oxley was at the very least fun, but practical. When they landed with an "oof" on one of the lowest levels of the tree, he released her wrist and pushed aside some hanging maroon leaves, each of them covered with microscopic veiny black lizards. They scampered into the leaves at his touch, but one proceeded to run up his arm before sinking its teeth into him. Oxley flinched.

"Argh! Blood suckers!" He flung the tiny lizard off into the tree. "Watch out for those. Weird little buggers down here! Argh, follow me!"

Wendy quietly followed him out onto a small overlook that looked down through a thicket of roots below. Directly below them was a long leather drum, easily the length of several huts, large enough that probably thirty Lost Boys could stand on it. Right now, however, there were only two boys on it—and one of them was Michael. Once she saw him, she could hardly contain her laughter and burst out with loud giggles.

"Michael!" He looked up at her and grinned.

"Look at me, Wendy!"

She did. Michael was bouncing up and down on the drum, getting higher and higher with each slam of his feet, flipping forward and backward, landing on his knees the vast majority of the time and then leaping into the air again. *Wham! Wham! Wham!* The other boy, Thomas, with his long blond curls, was bouncing along with him, the boys occasionally running into each other midbounce and collapsing into a pile of giggles upon the drum.

"Keep jumping, boys!" Oxley called out. "Sound the troops awake!"

Michael bounced up again, his blond hair standing up straight in the air.

"Look at us, Wendy, we're making war!"

"Sounding the drums of war," Oxley corrected.

Michael just giggled. "Same."

Wendy was glad to see the big smile on his face as he and

Thomas linked hands, bouncing each other higher and higher. They seemed like easy friends. She turned to Oxley.

"Where is John? Did Michael sleep with him?"

Oxley shrugged. "The Lost Boys sleep where they want. He might have slept in a soup bowl for all I know."

Wendy frowned. Oxley grinned and linked her arm through his. "You must learn to relax, Miss Darling. There are no grown-ups here to tell you what you're doing wrong. Don't worry about Michael. He's doing just fine."

She nodded. "And John?"

"John is meeting with the other Generals in the treasure room. I'm actually heading there now. Will you walk with me there and I'll drop you at the Table?"

Wendy turned to him. "Why walk when you can fly?"

Oxley smiled. "Because sometimes it's good to feel your feet on the ground."

With a grin, she linked her arm through his. They walked together through the tree toward the Table, Oxley showing her various flora along the way and telling her hilarious stories of when the Lost Boys lost all their pants, or when they had to steal chickens from the mainland. The walk was too short, and they quickly arrived at the Table, where Wendy hoped there would be a suitable breakfast.

"I have one question before you go, Oxley—how exactly does one become a General?"

He looked down at her, his brown eyes glistening under his ebony skin.

"When you become a Lost Boy, you start at the bottom. You are a Pip, which means you have one of two duties: kitchen duties or chamber duties." That made sense—it was always younger boys who had been coming to fetch Wendy's mortifying toilet bowl. "Once you have put in your time as a Pip, you move up to a Lost Boy. That's the vast majority of the boys here. They go on occasional raids and live on the island doing various chores here and there, and they get to have a watch on the Moon Tower. You may be a Lost Boy for ten years before becoming a General. Only a General has the right to Peter's ear."

"And what makes someone worthy of being a General?"

Oxley's eyes focused on Wendy's face. "You arrive with a pretty sister?" The annoyance in his voice was palpable.

"I didn't tell Peter to do that. And John didn't have anything to do with that either."

He sighed. "You're right. I'm sorry. That was rude. Here." He plucked a small pink flower from an overhanging branch and handed it to her. "Forget that I said that! Okay? Please don't be cross."

She patted his arm. "I know, Oxley. You're the nicest person here. I could never be angry at you."

"In that case, where was I? Ah yes. Becoming a General. You must show extreme loyalty to Peter and not have any fear. When he feels you have mastered these things, you become a General. And then after General . . ."

"There is something above General?"

"Yes. Once you move up from General, then you become . . . a Swift."

"A Swift?"

"Peter is the only Swift. It means that you have flight, forever, always."

Wendy gasped. "That can happen?"

"No one knows how the gift is given. But once you move up from General, Peter gives you the gift. You become a Swift, like him."

"Has anyone become a Swift?"

Oxley nodded, pushing a leaf out of his way and into Wendy's face. "Felix. Felix became a Swift. But the night he got the gift from Peter, he flew too fast and plowed into the side of a mountain. He died there. That's why you must be a General for a very long time before becoming a Swift—it's a gift, but a dangerous one. Peter does not give it lightly." Oxley dropped his voice. "Felix was my friend."

Wendy gently placed her hand on his shoulder. "I'm sorry, Oxley. It must hurt to lose someone."

"An all-too-frequent occurrence, unfortunately."

"What do you mean by that?" The banging of the drums ceased suddenly, and then the sound of the moon bell clanged through the air. Oxley sighed.

"That's Pan, he's calling us to assemble. I was hoping to eat first. Mind seeing what's in here with me?" Wendy nodded, her own stomach growling. They scampered into the Table, scooping up piles of nuts, cheese, and berries that lay scattered on the table. Oxley grabbed a half-eaten egg left on the round table and slid it down his throat. Then he handed one to Wendy. She had to swallow a gag first but then did the same. She was hungry.

"Ready?" he asked, wiping a smear of yolk off his face. She nodded. He grabbed her wrist, and then they were soaring up out of the Table, up into the great jade canopy of the tree, climbing up past her hut, soaring past Peter's hut, up and up through a hole cut into the thick canopy at the tip of the tree. Wendy saw the branches around her thinning out, becoming short and brittle. The leaves of the tree gave way into small clumps of silverish gray berries that dotted the increasingly bare branches. Finally, Oxley pulled back, and they cleared a bramble of twigs, so thick that only the tiniest of creatures could slither inside. As they rounded the top of the bramble, easily ten feet high, Wendy gasped as a concave bowl as large as a building opened up underneath her feet, made entirely of intertwined fawn-colored branches. Dozens of Lost Boys were milling about underneath her, looking up as Oxley took her down to the base of the bowl, Peter's yellow moon marking its center. Wendy worried briefly about her nightgown and the boys underneath them, but she was thankfully distracted by the whimsical beauty around her. She had increasingly less time for modesty in this magical place.

"Where are we?"

Oxley gave a joyful grin. "Right above Centermost."

"Oh, oh!"

She had indeed seen this bowl before, but from below it only looked like an incredibly thick swatch of branched canopy. Oxley set her down gently on the branches.

"Welcome to the Nest!"

Wendy let out a girlish laugh, absolutely enchanted. It was indeed a nest, a giant bird's nest, only just the right size for the Lost Boys. The Nest was woven with thousands of different types of branches: white crackled branches with fingerlike knuckles, thin dark brown spindly branches that curled into elegant whorls, red branches that were marked with black pocks, seemingly unbending, one thousand branches forming a perfect circle. Tucked into its openings were thousands and thousands of tiny scraps of paper and pale blue scraps of linen. Wendy walked over to the side of the Nest (its walls towered at least ten feet over her head) and picked out one of the scraps of paper. She carefully unfolded it. Scrawled in messy writing was a tiny wish: "I wich Peter to make me a swuft." She smiled and put the note back, picking another right above it and unfolding it. "More meat at dinner & that Abbott would be nicer to me." The next paper made the hairs on her arm stand on end. "I wish that I could remember who I was before." She tucked it back, feeling guilty for reading the intimate wishes of the boys and alarmed by the uncomfortable feeling in the pit of her chest, which was threatening to take over her joy.

She followed the branched wall of notes until it stopped about halfway around the Nest, ending where the weapons began. Axes, bows, swords of every shape and color, wooden bats with jagged metal spikes, daggers, butter knives, and spears were stuck within the branchy tangle, jammed in between its crooked arms, the weapons looking so out of place in this natural wonder. A bounty of weapons, real *weapons,* Wendy noted with a shock. She reached out and touched a line of dried blood on the end of a sword, pulling back when crusted red dust came off on her finger. The quiet of the Nest was broken when the boys began cheering wildly.

Wendy's head jerked up. Peter was landing in the middle of the Nest, his adoring boys all around him. His wild beauty took Wendy's breath away, a violent tug on her heart. Gone were the forest-like clothes he had donned before; he was now wearing armor—if you could even call it that—over his white tunic, black pants, and short brown leather boots. The chest armor was made of tiny, glossy, mirror-like tiles that wrapped tightly to his muscular form, each meticulously sewed together so that the armor flowed with his movements. A black sash dashed across his shoulders and around his waist, holding his golden sword up against his hip. His red hair glittered with the same dust that had fallen around Wendy last night on the bridge. He had been with Tink. Flitting silver light darted in between his hair follicles and around his face, which was curved up in a naughty smile. As she gazed at him, he reminded Wendy of a fire on a cold winter evening—warm, radiant . . . and dangerous. A different sort of fire was burning its way through her chest as she looked at him, a desire to be close to his glistening skin, hoping that he would notice her. As she gazed upon Peter and he upon her, John entered the Nest through a small hidden ladder on the west side of the curved branches.

"John!" Wendy cried. He turned his head away from her and began talking to another Lost Boy who had picked up an axe.

"Don't ignore me, John!" She grabbed his arm. "John! Please! I just need a minute."

John rolled his eyes to the boy next to him and gave a snicker. "Women."

Wendy resisted the urge to slap the smile off his face and pulled him into a corner.

"John, I need you to promise me you'll be careful. Please! I'm sure there is nothing to worry about but . . ."

"I'm sure I'll be fine, Wendy. Go away."

"John! Why are you behaving this way?"

He gave an easy grin, tossing his dull brown hair off his dull face. "Because nothing you say matters here. I'm a General; you're not. I imagine once Peter tires of your frilly dresses and puerile charms, that you will be our cook . . . or nanny, perhaps?"

"What would our . . . our . . ." Wendy couldn't think at the cruelty of his words. She struggled to reprimand him. "Those people, the people who cared for us, what would they say if they heard you speak to me that way . . ."

What was she trying to say? John stared blankly at her and then turned to grab a sword off the wall. He considered his options for a moment before finally settling on a short, fat sword with an emerald pommel.

"I don't know what or who you are talking about."

Wendy felt a coil of anger unspool on her tongue. "You don't even know how to use that, John!"

John looked over his cloudy glasses at her. "You're trying to upset me before the raid. I have an important job to do, unlike you. Keep being oh-so lovely. It's what you are good at."

Wendy stepped back from him, disgusted at his words and attitude. Peter walked over and put his arm on Wendy's waist.

"Is everything okay here?"

She stepped away. "Peter, please, please don't let him go . . ."

"John may do as he likes here. He is an intelligent asset to our Generals."

"Or just an ass," Abbott remarked as he walked past the arguing siblings to grab a well-worn spear off the wall. John's eyes narrowed, but he said nothing, obviously intimidated by the other General. Abbott twirled the spear in his fingertips, flexing its tip. "Don't worry, Wendy, your dear brother is just pushing a ship to the side. That's all. There's no danger in that. Those who are going to steal bounty have a much more difficult job."

John's face flushed red as Abbott playfully nicked him behind the ear with the tip of his spear.

"Boys, Wendy, play nice." Peter chuckled.

"John, you take a seat here. Abbott, begin packing up for our departure. Wendy . . ." He looked her up and down, trying his best to figure out how to quench her growing frustration with John.

"Wendy . . . you're coming with us."

"What?" John practically jumped up from the bench. "She can't come! She's not a Lost Boy *or* a General! She's not even a boy at all!"

"And you weren't a General until you arrived and I gave you the privilege," Peter snapped, his eyes clouding navy and then returning to green. "If I say Wendy goes, then Wendy goes."

Abbott stared silently at both of them, his eyes darting to Wendy and then back again. He wisely decided to say nothing.

Peter cleared his throat.

Wendy stared hard at John and then looked back at Michael. "Michael . . ."

"Michael will stay here with the other Pips. He'll be safe. Thomas?"

The towheaded boy with bouncing ringlets scampered up next to Peter.

"Thomas! I have a very important job for you. Can you handle that?"

Thomas looked as though he was going to faint with excitement. "Yes, Peter. Of course, I mean, yes, sir, Peter, sir. Sir."

"Can you watch over Michael Darling while we are out on the raid? Can you keep him safe and out of trouble?"

Thomas nodded, his huge blue eyes exploding with pride. "Yes, SIR! I will!"

Peter turned away. "Then it's settled. Wendy comes with me."

The anger simmering in John's eyes could have set the Nest ablaze. He stared at his sister with unbridled contempt.

"You can take her, but she's not going to be much help unless you need some hair ribbons tied or a piano played."

Wendy shot daggers his direction and turned to Peter. "I'll go."

Peter leapt into the air, his mirrored armor sending shards of light all over the Nest as he pointed east. "Fantastic! Wendy, there are some extra clothes in the hut next to us, just past the Nest. Why don't you change and then join us back here."

It wasn't a question. Wendy nodded her head and walked away just as Peter clapped his hands and began instructing the boys on what they were doing and where they were going. She climbed down the rickety wooden ladder and onto a thin wooden platform that linked to the rest of the tree. Pan Island was silent outside of the Nest, an eerie sound that she had never experienced here. Without the constant ruckus of boys, wind hummed through the tree branches, and she could hear the light crashing of the waves far below. Insects buzzed and fluttered past her as she made her way quickly down the walkway. Ducking her head, she entered a dirty hut filled almost to the roof with piles and piles of boys' clothing, some clean, some dirty, all smelly. After a few minutes she found a semiclean long blue tunic and some loose gray pants that hit her at the shins and cinched with a white ribbon around her calves. She tied a purple scarf around her head to keep the hair out of her eyes. She jogged back to the Nest, where Peter was finishing up a grand speech.

"The pirates steal from the innocent people of Port Duette. They take from the Lost Boys, from the mermaids! Hook and his pirates are the withering disease of this island, and today we will strike a blow to them that will take the fun out of their frivolities. We will toast them as we toast ourselves! HA!"

His voice rose.

"Most importantly, without alcohol, we will hope that Hook's loyal soldiers will realize that he is a coward and a limbless freak."

He changed his voice into the signature growl of a pirate.

"And arrr, we will hope that by taking away their rum that we will slowly sow the seeds of a rebellion, deep into their thirsty veins! Now, let's go, you landlubbers!"

He did a little jig before dropping his voice back to his captivating tenor. The Lost Boys erupted into wild cheers. Peter grinned.

"All righty, boys—are you ready to go risk life and limb for a drink of wine? Then let's go have ourselves an adventure!"

The Nest filled with the wild chants of hundreds of boys. Peter rose slowly into the air, and the Lost Boys began reaching out their hands to him, raising them above their heads, their fingers splayed in worship. Peter rose higher, and the glittering dust around him seemed to be funneling down from his head to the tips of his fingers.

"More!" he whispered to the boys. "More."

The cheers of the boys rose to a deafening chant, John and Michael among them, screaming and shouting Peter's name. John had tears on his face, as did some of the younger boys, their cries reaching a fevered pitch. Peter's fingers began curling all the silver dust circled his forearms now, rushing up and down his arms, throbbing with each breath he took. It began to glow, a white heat that filled the Nest, until the shimmering dust pulsed with the same white glow that she had seen Peter give Oxley the day before. It ran up and down his veins, cracking through the pores of his skin.

Peter Pan was made of light.

The voices rang throughout the Nest as Peter's hands slowly opened. Then the voices fell silent, and after a moment, Peter forcefully clapped his hands out in front of him with a loud crack. The white light shot out through his hands and filled the Nest, pouring out in a single giant wave that rushed over every Lost Boy. It filled every corner of the Nest, racing from one end to another, a circle of light that crested before pouring out through the holes in the branches. Wendy felt it hit her body, felt the power of it rush through her, over her, around her. It filled her with its warmth, sinking into her cold bones, a warm feeling of sky and freedom, a comforting warmth, an exhilarating breath. Her eyes flitted around the room to find Michael.

Something at the edge of the Nest caught her eye. With a quick glance she saw Tink heave herself over the branches and let herself fall down into the tree. A trail of glittering silver dust ran up the side of the Nest, a splattered pattern of stars that stopped at the cusp of the branchy cup. The fairy had moved so fast that she was gone before Wendy had even blinked. She looked back up at Peter. He was grinning, laughing now, his hands clutched at his stomach, pointing at the Lost Boys who were now all rising off the floor, bouncing off the walls of the Nest with delight. Michael squealed as he turned over his feet and bumped into the thatched wall face-first.

"Wendy! Look at me! I'm flying!"

"I see you!"

She gave a careful push off her feet and then was soaring upward, up toward the burrowed, curved nest of branches overhead. Unable to control her excitement, she let out a squeal, grabbing hold of an outstretched branch to watch the others. Boys were everywhere around her, dirty feet in her face, hands reaching for something to hold, bumping into her. While some soared excellently, others threw up over the barrier of the Nest. From below she heard a disgusted "OY!" With envy, she watched as John flipped easily from corner to corner, using his force to propel other Lost Boys into a drifting circle. He twisted and turned in the air, learning quickly how to manipulate his body in flight. He tossed his new sword into the air, flipped over his feet, and then pushed off the ground, meeting the sword in the air, catching it expertly. Then he flipped again and flew backward toward the ground. He spun Michael around and left his brother circling in the air as he flew circles around him. Michael giggled.

"John! Stop it!" Wendy narrowed her eyes and let out a sigh as her hand continued to clutch the branch. Some things just came so naturally to him—mathematics, astronomy, and now flying. Of course. Of course John was good at flying. While she wasn't as bad as the boys who were stuck in the branches of the Nest, squawking for Peter to help them, she wasn't great either. She had a hard time turning her body in the direction she wanted it to go and often ended up whirling right when she meant to go left. Her feet were drifting upward, pulling the rest of her body up with them, when she felt familiar hands slide across her shoulders.

"You can fly by me," Peter said, laughing, his proud voice instantly making her smitten, even here while she drifted in a room of flying boys. As she twisted around to meet him, she felt a sharp pang of guilt in her heart. She couldn't imagine why as she gazed deep into his green eyes, lighting up at the sight of her. For a moment, it felt as if it were just them, drifting above the world, their eyes locked, boys floating silently by like stars in the sky. But then Michael flew up and grabbed Wendy's leg, giggling uncontrollably.

"Wendy! Watch this!" He pushed himself off her leg and managed to fly awkwardly across the Nest, his elated laughter filling the room as he unsuccessfully chased his toes.

Peter's eyes met hers. "Are you nervous to come?"

Wendy looked down and blushed. "Of course not. I'll be fine."

"Don't worry. I'll protect you," he whispered. "Between you and me, I don't actually think that there will be any fighting. We will take the liquor and get out. See, that's not very exciting, now is it? No reason to be nervous. I've always wanted to see the Vault, and I'm so excited to see it with you."

He let a finger brush carelessly across her cheek, and then he was off, soaring quickly to the front of the room, occasionally batting floating Lost Boys out of his way. Kitoko floated silently nearby, watching the boys and Wendy with observant eyes. Wendy floated up next to him.

"What should I do now?"

Kitoko looked over at her. "Whatever Peter tells us." He kindly pointed to the right. "In the meantime, I would take a weapon and then assemble over there. Then we fly."

His eyes then turned up at the corners. He was smiling. It was the first time Wendy had seen it. "Then we drink. I prefer reds." He gave Wendy a friendly pat on the shoulder.

A weapon? Such a task seemed intimidating. She pushed herself down to the wall of weapons, where the dangerous instruments sat. Wendy frowned as she looked at a huge silver sword, its hilt the open mouth of a dragon. She could hardly see herself swinging away with this sword, let alone any sword. She didn't even know the first thing about holding a sword. She pulled herself hand over hand toward the end of the line of weapons, carefully placing her fingers in between the thick branches that surrounded the Nest. When she reached the end of the line, she turned back with a sigh. Nothing. She pulled herself backward over the line of weapons, deciding that maybe nothing was a better option than something that would make her look, at best, quite idiotic. Her hands came to rest on an enormous golden bow, easily the largest weapon of the bunch. She was smiling at the thought of lugging this behemoth anywhere when something winked at her in the filtered light of the Nest, nestled in a thick tangle of branches behind the ostentatious bow.

Wendy's nimble fingers—the fingers of a piano player—skillfully untangled the bramble around the winking metal, thorny branches scraping under her nails. Finally, they reached into a leafy cluster and pulled out a petite dagger with an ivory handle. Intricate carvings marked the sides of the handle: ships at sea, tossed about by the waves; trees curled into patterned wings; a sun and moon connected by whorls of wind on opposite sides of the pommel. A small blue gemstone, the shape and size of a feather, marked the center of the hilt. The stone seemed to have a great depth to its blue, as if it were a portal to the deepest part of the sea. Wendy loved it immediately, turning it over in her hands, marveling at how it fit perfectly in her palm, how light and lovely it was. She blinked twice. Though it couldn't be possible, she was sure that for a moment she saw the leafy cluster that had once held the dagger give a shudder and curl back into itself. She looked again. Everything was still. Perhaps she had seen it because she was moving, slowly floating upward, which was what happened when she let go of anything grounding her. Shyly, unsure of where exactly one put a dagger, she tucked it into the waistband of her pants and prayed that she wouldn't accidentally stab herself. Even now, with the blade cool against her skin, Wendy felt like an imposter. She was not a warrior, or even a boy. Everything about holding this dagger was reminding her that she was a well-mannered lady who had no place here, and yet—she would rather be nowhere else. For a reason she couldn't fully explain to herself, she knew the dagger was her secret. Perhaps it was the thrill of a potential adventure working its way into her mind, thread by tiny thread. She felt a whoosh of air pass below her, and then Peter was beside her, pulling her down from the top of the Nest, his cheeks flushed with excitement.

"Shall we?"

She nodded. With that, the redheaded boy brought both hands up to his mouth and crowed at the top of his lungs. The Lost Boys all began circling around him, like a swarm of crows fluttering around a tree.

"It's time to leave the Nest!" he yelled, and then he signaled above him with both hands.

Wendy's breath caught in her throat as the canopy high above the Nest slowly began to inch open, pulled open by the willing hands of about a dozen Pips, each one tethering themselves to it with thick pieces of rope that attached to rusty pulleys above. The canopy separated in the center, cracking open like an egg, light exploding through the branches as the cloudy sky poured in above them. Peter looked down at Wendy and winked before shooting up into the sky. "Okay, Lost Boys, let's FLY!" With that command, fifty Lost Boys fluttered out into the open air in a rush of mad energy, birds released from a cage. John zoomed past Wendy without a second look as she struggled to keep up with the boys trailing into the sky, Peter the head of his flock. Wendy frowned and with great focus increased her speed, finally catching up to Peter, who was at a standstill, his eyes on the troops below him.

"John, Oxley: do you have your baker's dozen?"

John nodded with a confidence that Wendy could see was shaky at best. Her brother was nervous. *As he should be.*

"Take your boys, then. Remember what we planned: first the sky, then down against the sea once you are within eyesight. The clouds should hide you well. When you push against the ships, use a gentle hand, like you're touching a lady, boys!" Wendy blushed. Peter affectionately ruffled the hair of one of the Lost Boys, who positively glowed with the attention. "I look forward to many great stories of puking pirates. If we do the job right on our end, Hook's pirates won't even know that they were robbed until we are already gone. Perhaps they will think Blackbeard's ghost took their liquor!"

The boys broke into rowdy laughter. It occurred to a silent, nervous Wendy that this was a lot of work to steal some wine. Peter saluted John and Oxley, tapping his feet together as he rose into the air.

"All righty, boys, you have my blessing! See you on the other side of Neverland!"

With that command, John's group began to circle and rise slowly to the north, flying swiftly away from Peter's group—and John away from Wendy's protection. As she watched her brother's form fade slowly into the mist, she felt a painful tug in her chest but dismissed it as an overabundance of childlike sentimentality.

CHAPTER FOURTEEN

WENDY TURNED BACK, finding Peter beside her. He brushed her hair away from her ear.

"He'll be fine. It's just a silly game, Wendy. There is no need to fear. It's time for our great adventure to begin! Are you ready?"

She nodded.

"Then up we go!" Peter climbed upward, pulling them both high into the sky at a rapid pace with the two dozen older Lost Boys following behind, each one handpicked for this mission by Abbott, who served as the bookend for the group, looking unhappy as always as he soared quickly, cutting a line through the clouds. Wendy let her arms fall to her sides as she enjoyed the feeling of flying, slowly making her way through the endless sky, clumsy at best. The crawling lower mist of the morning thinned out the higher they went, and soon they were soaring across the miles that separated Pan Island from the main island, Peter twisting and swooping around Wendy, pulling her hair and tickling her foot as they flew, then disappearing into the mist that lazily embraced them in its folds.

The joy that was rising up in her chest overtook her, and she found herself laughing hysterically as she gained speed, plummeting through the clouds, the sensation of absolute freedom overtaking her. Wendy breathed in the cold air on her face, relished the rush of wind that pushed through her outstretched fingers. The air up here was clean and wet, the mist caressing her body as they whipped through its foamy gray, so thick she could almost hold it in her hand. She lost herself in the exhilaration, minutes passing before she felt Peter's absence, felt her own lack of direction in the churning sea of thick mist. Was she going the right way? Had they turned without her knowing? A grip of panic pulled at her stomach.

"Peter?" she whispered, before raising her voice. "Peter?"

She slowed down, suddenly very unsure of where she was going, looking up and then down. Which way was down again? She couldn't see anything. Where was she? Her heart rate increased as the lovely mist that had been her plaything moments ago became a choking fog. She turned over her feet and began flying downward (she hoped), crossing her fingers that she would come out over the turquoise waters separating Pan Island and the mainland. Up ahead, the clouds were clearing, and a sigh of relief escaped her lips. Something whooshed past her on the right, moving so fast that it sent her spinning in its wake. It passed again on the left. Wendy stopped moving completely, hovering silently in the air, her eyes alert. Peter's face appeared above her. Then he disappeared again into the mist. She laughed.

"Peter!" There was another brush of air, and he materialized underneath her, flying faceup, as if he were lounging in a stream. He winked at her and then sank below the clouds where she could not see him anymore.

"Peter! Stop this silly game! Stop it!"

She giggled in spite of herself, not meaning a word of it. After a moment, to her vast relief, Wendy was able to vaguely make out the voices of the Lost Boys behind her. She turned her head to see their dirty faces, but the mist hid them from view. Someone called her name, softly, like a whisper. When she turned her face back, the sharp wind carrying her hair all around her, numbing her cheeks and hands, Peter was there waiting for her. Her breath caught in her throat, her heart speeding up, thrumming so intensely that she felt it in her ribs. He was so close that his face was inches away from hers, and she could see the small navy flecks, lined with gold, that circled inside his green eyes.

His cool, clean smell, the smells of leaves and earth and magic, washed across her face as he trailed his fingers down her cheek and up into her wild hair. His body curled toward Wendy, his green eyes never pulling away from hers even though they were moving through the air, pulled by his momentum, downward, ever downward. Wendy forgot to breathe as he looked at her with wonder, his curious eyes tracing every line of her face with want.

"Wendy . . ."

Then he leaned forward and pressed his lips against her own with a palpable hunger. His lips were warm and woodsy. His hands traced her jawline and neck as they kissed, his tongue running over her own, his hands tangling in the hair that was standing straight up as they sank lower and lower through the mist. With a sigh, he buried his face in her neck before pulling back up to her lips and kissing her again, hungrily, his arms pulling her ever closer as they sank lower and lower.

There was mist and there was Peter, and Peter's lips, and Wendy felt herself falling, falling into him, falling down with Peter Pan, falling down *into* Peter Pan. She pressed herself firmly into his chest, wrapping her arms around his neck. They plunged downward, feet first, her blouse fluttering around them both, Peter's mouth drinking from her own, pulling away from her like water from a stone. They fell, their lips dancing and playing, the feel of his face against her own, soft skin over lean muscles. He ripped the scarf from her hair before lacing his fingers up in her thick curls as they fell ever downward, the wind cool around her body, Peter's heat warming her core. Finally, he pulled back from her lips with a regretful sigh and gave her a naughty grin.

"Wendy Darling, I could not wait another moment."

He shrugged, as if he couldn't help himself, and then launched himself away from her in a graceful backward swan dive, disappearing into the mist below her. She blinked twice, her hands touching her lips with shock. He had kissed her. Her mind flitted back and forth between ecstasy and guilt, but her need to follow closely behind him won out over both feelings as she followed him downward into the thinning mist, her lips on fire from where he had touched them. As they emerged from the clouds, Wendy gasped. She had become used to seeing the main island from Pan Island, where it appeared as an impassive bump on the distant horizon, but here it was below her, five hundred miles of foliage, white cliffs, and pristine beaches spread out like a tiny world below them, Shadow Mountain rising out of the mist like a green behemoth.

The mountain loomed ominously over the island, a thin stream of white mist trailing out from its open crater, its wide mouth forever watching over its rocky mass and jagged foothills. Peter appeared beside her once again, and the flock of Lost Boys began emerging from the mist, one by one, each looking relieved when they saw Peter's face on the other side. Peter waited patiently as they each plummeted down to meet him, some flying better than others, Kitoko flying down with incredible grace. He slapped Peter's hand as he passed, raising his eyebrows at Wendy in a way that suggested that he had been witness to their kiss. Wendy blushed and looked down, not wanting to meet his eyes. At the tail end of the boys, Abbott appeared in the clouds, holding onto a taller Lost Boy by the collar of his shirt, his face pale, a ring of sweat around his neck.

"We almost lost Alfonso in the fog." He looked over at Peter. "You were flying too fast."

Peter laughed, although Wendy saw a glint of annoyance cross his face. He flew up to meet Abbott and Alfonso, who was flushed with shame.

"Keep up next time." He swatted the back of the boy's head and then gave Abbott a playful grin. Abbott returned it with a forced smile before leveling his eyes at Kitoko and coming down from above. Peter turned back to the boys and Wendy, his feet hovering above the island like a god.

"From here on, whispers only. Understood? Hook has spies everywhere."

Not a word was spoken in reply. They flew low over the east end of the island, staying maybe twenty feet above the treetops and the rocky coast, which marked the island with its jagged gray rocks and pale sand. When they finally veered north, Wendy could see the edge of the white cliffs rising angrily out of the ocean, their peaks like razors.

"They are beautiful," she murmured.

"The Teeth," Peter whispered next to her. "That's where I burned the *Jolly Rodger*."

A minute passed, and then they were soaring above them, an endless stream of violent white, pockmarked with blue bird droppings and an occasional turquoise-green pool hidden in the deep grooves of the rock. Eventually the Teeth began to taper downward, towering peaks surrendering to sloping foothills that plummeted into the jungle, a tangle of waterfalls and rivers, twisted vines and green leaves the size of houses. The changes in Neverland's geography were just like its natural landscape: extreme and defiant, as if another country started at the exact line on a map, the greenery stopping right where it was supposed to.

From above, Wendy could perceive small marks of the hungry life below: a large bird's nest with robin blue eggs the size of her head, a green lizard with dazzling pink wings plodding its way across the canopy, an insect that resembled a gigantic dragonfly that followed them for a while before veering away to snatch up a yellow canary midflight with wide jaws that extended from a second mouth. Wendy gave a shiver as it spit out the yellow feathers and looked up at the unwelcome guests flying overhead. As they neared the end of the rolling hills of jungle, Wendy found her nerves tingling with fear when she saw the turquoise sea emerge once again on the horizon, realizing that they were close to their destination. She swallowed hard, for a moment forgetting the kiss. *It's going to be an adventure*, she reassured herself. *Just an adventure.*

The gentle creek that was winding its way like a snake beneath them opened up into a gaping river that ran upward to the middle of the island. They followed the river for a few minutes, seeing an occasional fin cut through the water. Peter pointed.

"Sharks. They love the river fish."

Finally, the lazy river gained speed, the water churning out over boulders as the land grew rockier, the jungle thicker. The river grinded angrily forward, falling downward in a series of small pools before it opened up into a gigantic waterfall that roared beneath them, the haze of spray rising up into the thick mist above them. From the base of the waterfall, a lazy stream, tired from its journey, wound its way quietly down to the ocean, the river bend making a sharp right turn before continuing out to the sea. Peter flew up beside her again and pointed to where the river bent away from its main stream.

"Do you see it, Wendy?"

She didn't, not at first, but then her eyes followed a small wisp of steam that trailed up from beyond the trees. *Steam*, she thought. *That's an odd thing to see in a jungle.* She would have easily missed it had Peter not pointed it out. The curling steam trailed up out of the trees and then dipped under a swaying green branch, massive in size, draping across a large rocky outcropping. Her eyes followed the serrated gray rocks down a slick tumble of stone, as if a giant had shoved over a mountain and then piled it back up again. There was a wooden stake that rose out of the peak of the stone pile, a huge cross that was turned sideways so that the arms of the cross pointed down into the peak. From there, a single white rope tethered to the cross wove its way down until it met the ground, its taut line disappearing under the rushing river water. Spaced evenly along the rope, each dangling in place by gigantic metal hooks, a line of broken skeletons blew in the wind, their bones rattling. The horrific sound whispered quietly out through the jungle and made Wendy long to clasp her hands over her ears, to block the memory out forever. A strong gust of the humid wind of the island rocked the skeletons simultaneously, and they all turned to face the sea, a macabre coordinated dance.

Large red birds, their brilliant feathers shimmering like ripe plums, reminiscent of distorted peacocks, nested in the ribs of each skeleton, looking from above like huge, beating hearts. The wind changed direction again, and the skeletons all twisted to look right at Wendy, and she saw the glittering black obsidian rocks that had been placed in their eyes. Her stomach lurched when she realized that the skeletons looked so terrifying not because of their red bird hearts or their coordinated turns in the wind, or even the metal hooks around their necks—the skeletons were uniquely terrible because they were *small*. Far too small to be grown men. These were the skeletons of children. These had been the eleven Lost Boys. Fear twisted Wendy's heart, over-whelming any lingering excitement that she felt.

This is a bad place. We should not be here. She looked up at Peter, whose eyes rested easily on her. She started to mouth the word "no" before he gave her a devilish grin and led the boys forward, banking hard in the air so that they silently came up above the jungle about a half mile from the Vault. Peter motioned to the jungle, and one by one the boys and Wendy dropped into the dense trees that grew beside the mountain of horrors. The jungle was deep and ill-behaved. Choking vines tangled around her, and the canopy slithered closed immediately after they slipped through, turning them all a sickly shade of green in its emerald light. Wendy watched with wide eyes as a hairy, scarlet spider made its way through Abbott's hair in front of her.

"Abbott!" she hissed quietly.

He rolled his eyes and batted it away without a second glance.

The spider gave a tiny cry as it fell through the jungle air. Peter motioned forward with silent hand gestures that Wendy didn't understand but didn't need to, as she just followed the rest of the boys, flitting from branch to branch, leaping through the air like apes, catching and swinging. Wendy was a bit more cautious as she went, carefully weighing which branch she would grab next, unable to swing so joyfully like the other boys. Peter laughed silently at her before giving her a wink. Her heart fluttered at the gesture. Through the trees they went, silently making their way toward the Vault. Finally they halted, and Wendy could see a small clearing through the dense mosaic of green, a peephole of misty gray light. They were here.

As she moved closer to the cave, hand over hand through the trees, Wendy began to understand that the pile of rocks she had seen from above was much more than a loose pile of boulders. What she had believed was the front of the cave was actually the side of a gigantic rock face, its discombobulated features assembling themselves at just the right point. Violently carved in shades of dust and bone, the menacing skull rose up out of the river, the main head composed of three enormous boulders clustered together. The face was made up of deep grooves carved into the rock face, each accented with stitches made of bones that crisscrossed over the eyes and nose. Dripping green condensation pooled at the bottom of the concave eyes and trickled down the face, angry tears to mar a horrified expression of fear. The mouth of the cave opened up underneath the pooling green, an unhinged jaw open in a perpetual scream, wide enough to swallow a man whole.

The river poured out of the mouth and onto the rocks below, foaming angrily underneath large wooden spikes that protruded out of the mouth like wicked teeth. On the other side of the skull's head, another line of children's skeletons rocked in the wind, their rib cages also filled with the red birds picking invisible scraps of meat off their bones. A gray mist of water and air and river poured over the skull, caressing the sides of the cave like a bridal veil. At the center of its forehead sat Peter's yellow moon, a painted third eye that seemed to watch their approach with an unwavering stare. The moon had been crossed out with what appeared to be blood in the shape of two hooks. The sun shifted, and suddenly the gigantic skull was encased in a dim light as Shadow Mountain cast its heavy shroud over it. The yellow moon glowed in the mist, the empty eyes weeping a luminescent green.

"Quite a sight, isn't it?" Peter whispered to the boys. "I can't wait to see the inside."

He rubbed his hands together greedily.

"Finally. The Vault. It's ours. Boys, this is going to be great."

Wendy thought quite the opposite as a panic rose within her. At the peak of the massive skull, a single guard stood watch, marching left and right, the tick-tock of a clock in his hand loud enough to hear from the silent trees, his eyes going from the sea to the land and back again. His lean muscled arms rested on the huge scabbard at his waist and the pistol in his other hand. At his feet sat a copper cannon that faced out to sea, its black string trailing between his legs.

"Idiot," Peter mumbled. He turned back to his troops, trailing silently behind him in the trees.

"It begins."

"Peter, no!" Wendy whispered as she reached out for him, hoping to try and convince him to reconsider this folly, but her arm fell into empty air.

"Peter?"

He was gone, and she watched in silent horror as he flew straight upward, out of the jungle, disappearing into the low clouds. She looked back at the pirate, who had turned toward the jungle, his hand twitching, his eyes narrowed.

She turned to Abbott. "But where . . ."

"Shut up, you stupid girl!" he hissed at her, and Wendy was reminded of why she thoroughly disliked him.

She turned her head back to the sky, and that's when she saw Peter. Nothing had prepared her, and she felt a cold hand of regret tighten around her throat. He plummeted downward through the clouds, feet first, the soles of his feet flexed out in front of him, his body hurtling down toward the guard with a staggering speed, a bullet in the air. Peter let out a happy crow, and the pirate turned his face up, raising his pistol in the air, but it was all for naught. Wendy watched in horror as Peter landed hard on the man with one foot on each shoulder, crumpling his body into the ground as if he were made of paper. Loud snaps filled the air as the man's bones broke one by one, his life snuffed out in seconds, his body contorting as it was ground down into the rock by Peter's speed.

The pirate's head snapped back hard against the roof of the cave, and then there was no sound, just the quiet cheering of the Lost Boys beside her. She covered her mouth with her hand as nausea rose up inside of her throat. Peter stood on the rock and waved happily toward them. Then, with a laugh, he kicked the pirate's body off the top of the skull. It fell a few feet before crumpling lifelessly against a large rock. Then, leaving a smear of blood on the rock, it rolled into the foamy river, where it turned over and floated faceup. With a whoop, Peter leapt down off the skull and flew toward the jungle, hovering above his troops.

"Come on, boys, the way is clear! Let's go!"

The Lost Boys grabbed their weapons and began flying down out of the trees, landing in a small patch of jungle that sat quietly at the edge of the Vault. Lost Boys swarmed down all around her, their swords and axes drawn as they quietly pulled themselves out of the jungle to float alongside Peter. Wendy willed herself to move and finally propelled herself down, landing gently on a tree branch. Following Kitoko's lead, she stayed low, her eyes on the thick jungle below, her mind swimming with the image of the pirate dying, again and again, a relentless battering memory. She

must have stopped moving for a moment, because suddenly Peter
was before her, a smile on his handsome face.

"Wendy! Are you all right?"

Wendy shook her head. Peter touched her face.

"Poor girl. That must have been the first time you've seen death.
It gets easier. And I promise, we'll talk later. But for now, I need
you to be brave."

His words shook something loose inside of her. A flood of
images whirled in her mind, jumbled and confusing. *She saw a
building of stone, a pile of books, suspenders, and a wool hat. A
hand pulling off a glove. A ladder.* She shook her head. *What was
happening?*

"Wendy!"

Peter was in front of her again, lovely Peter, his golden sword
drawn.

"Are you here?"

Her eyes found his face. There was a small spot of blood on his
ear, not his own.

"Yes, yes, Peter. I'm here."

The warm and wet jungle pressed around her on all sides.

"Good."

He cradled her cheeks, and Wendy remembered the way he
had kissed her, his warm, wanting mouth.

"Now, Wendy Darling, let's have ourselves a grand adventure!"

Peter flew up from her tree branch and flew down toward the
skull, landing in the river with a splash. He walked toward the
open mouth, the jagged teeth churning with angry white waves.
Peter's feet brushed the top of the river until he hovered in front
of the open mouth, which looked as though it wanted to swallow
him whole. For a moment, Wendy worried that it would. Peter
spun in the air until his feet were facing the sky and he could look
upside down through the wooden teeth, his body rocking ever so
slightly. The Lost Boys and Wendy held their breath. Then Peter
righted himself and curled his finger toward the jungle. *Come.*

The platoon of Lost Boys emerged from the jungle, flying silently up to Peter. Wendy stayed in the trees, still battling the barrage of images in her head—blue eyes, a dog barking at a window, the pirate's head exploding with a splat against the rocks.

Wendy felt an arm wrap around her elbow. It was Abbott.

"Come on, girl. You can't stay out here alone. Keel cats." Without warning, he flung her harmlessly into the air. She floated down to the ground and gave him a nasty stare.

"I think you are very rude."

He shook his head. "I couldn't care less. Stay out of the trees. Don't you Darlings ever think? God knows what your idiot brother is doing right now."

Wendy's voice caught in her throat at the thought of John doing something dangerous, so far from her protection. Her anger made her want to agree with Abbott, but her love for John, even though he *never* deserved it, won the battle for her tongue.

"John is very smart."

Abbott's voice lowered. "A lot of boys here were once very smart. Some of them are now swinging over there."

He nodded his head toward the hanging skeletons, now whipping back and forth in the wind. He gripped a spear in one hand and stepped out of the trees into the misty sunlight.

"Come on, girl, let's go. Stay by Kitoko or me. If something happens to you, we will never hear the end of it." He looked at Peter long and hard before shaking his head. "Honestly, you shouldn't even be here."

Following behind Abbott's filthy boots, Wendy flew up to the mouth of the cave where Peter waited. She tried not to look at the floating body of the dead pirate as she flew over him, his eyes and mouth widened in surprise, a tiny stream of blood trickling out from the corner of his mouth, water filling up the collapsed place where his rib cage had been broken. Up close, he looked no different than any other man. His face was clean underneath his black beard, and surprisingly young. Handsome even. He had not seen the death that came from the sky. He had not seen the boy who had crushed him into the ground like an insect. It was the first dead person Wendy had ever seen, and just for a minute she hoped that death was different in Neverland. That some sort of magic would rise out of his chest and that the man would be given another chance to become good.

The man stayed dead.

Abbott reached over and shut the man's eyes before pushing Wendy away from the body. Peter sloshed past Wendy with his sword drawn out in front of him.

"Lost Boys . . . forward! And remember, we are here for one thing only—if it won't make you drunk, don't carry it out! We've got plenty of treasure at home!"

The Lost Boys raised their weapons and began rushing toward the mouth of the hideout. Wendy followed behind them, her tiny dagger tucked underneath her shirt, practically useless, just like she felt. She ducked past the jagged wooden teeth that lined the entrance, wincing when she saw the bloodstains that dulled their sharp edges. The air changed, and she felt a shiver of terror run over her skin.

She was inside the Vault.

CHAPTER FIFTEEN

INSIDE THE HIDEOUT, the damp walls oozed with the same dark green condensation that dripped from the eyes, the sappy substance pooling with the river that pulled at their feet. The water was icy around Wendy's ankles, though her forehead dripped with sweat. It was all quite undignified, this adventure. Inside the open mouth, the rocky cavern narrowed, and a branch of the river poured down a slippery slope that hooked to the right.

"Come on!" Peter whispered, and they followed the hill downward, the river still at their ankles. At the bottom of the wet slope, a slight drop off the rocks led the water and the boys over a small waterfall that splashed onto flat rocks below. After the drop, which they all simply flew over, there was a sharp turn that led to an open archway, the walls decorated with tiny bones that made Wendy think of popcorn strings. Over the doorway, marked with a smear of blood that reminded Wendy deep in her brain of a very old story she had heard once, were the words *Turn away, turn away.* Peter flew underneath the arch, not even noticing the scrawl. Once through, he dropped to the ground.

"Incredible. Hooky, Hooky, what have we here?" Through the archway, an enormous narrow hallway stretched out before them, so deep that Wendy could barely make out the end of it. Dotting the hallway were roughly a dozen or so doors, each one marked with a hook symbol. They creaked and slammed in the warm, wet wind that rushed down from the mouth of the cave. Some doors were closed tight, others were open and slamming back and forth as the river water ran in and out of the rooms, one small wave playfully chasing another. From somewhere deep in the cave, Wendy could hear the faint mumble and laughter of friendly conversation, from pirates who were not yet aware that Peter Pan and his boys were in their midst.

Wendy counted fourteen doors, the hallway ending with one massive circular iron door that had a large metal wheeled lock as well as a dozen smaller ones that lined all sides of its hinges. *Ah*, she thought. *The Vault.* Peter looked at the door hungrily before crouching down and closing his eyes, sniffing the air. His fingers trailed in the water. Then he leapt up, his feet twitching, one hand held aloft for silence.

His whisper was sharp.

"Abbott, take your boys and search the back six doors, but go no farther. Listen for the pirates. Kitoko—go back outside to the rock and keep an eye out for any returning watches coming in from the jungle, or, God forbid, ships."

Kitoko nodded at Peter with a gentle smile. Peter raised his eyebrows.

"Keep your eyes on the sea, yeah? If John did his job, we should never see those ships turn our way."

Peter glanced over at Wendy with a hopeful look laced with expectations. *I hope John doesn't mess up*, Wendy thought.

"The rest of you, come with me, and we will check the first six doors. Wendy, you're with me." Wendy quietly walked over to Peter's side. He took her hand, and her heart skipped a beat.

"Are you feeling better?" he whispered, brushing aside a lock of her hair that was plastered against her forehead.

"Fine."

She wasn't, but there was no going back. Peter took her hand and they pushed through the water, a cluster of Lost Boys following behind them. They came up to the first door. It was unlocked, and opened with barely a touch from Peter's hand, water rushing up to push it open before him. The room was seemingly held up by broken logs and dilapidated pieces of driftwood. Clumsily arranged logs rose up to the ceiling, holding up a waterlogged set of pallets and branches. Across the logs, shaved-down tree branches functioned as shelves. Overflowing from the shelves and every possible surface were empty chests. Oak chests, with gaping mouths and sawdust handprints. Large chests, half the length of the room, marked by a hundred small drawers and petite maroon knobs. A silver chest that had eight different kinds of locks on it and inlaid rubies in the shape of a sun. There were chests shaped like suitcases. Bobbing up and down on the shallow river was an elaborate mirrored chest with a pale green top, the color of the Neverland Sea at sunrise. Red chests the color of blood, their tops wrenched open, seemed to beckon to the curious, and there were chests covered with pink seashells that flickered in the faint light. Wendy stared at the chests, fascinated, her ankles going numb in the river water that caressed around them. Peter turned away from the strange sight with an exasperated sigh.

"Boring. The wine isn't here. Next room!"

Wendy could have explored the chests for hours, but she followed Peter out of the room and back out into the narrow hallway. The next room had a half door that came down from the ceiling. Peter pushed it up into a narrow opening in the rock. They stepped inside, the Lost Boys at Peter's heels, the room striking them wide-eyed and silent. This room was much larger than the chest room and was designed for a specific purpose. It was a perfect cylinder on the inside, its white walls smooth and shiny, reminding Wendy of a waterworn pebble. Two dim lanterns flashed their light against the walls, where it crawled and jumped with a hypnotizing shadow that circled around them: the shadow of bars. The walls were scrawled with random words and discombobulated sentences, each written angrily in black soot, everything from the word *Pan*, written again and again, to a snippet of a John Donne sonnet: *Death, be not proud, though some have called thee.*

In the very center of the room was a hanging cage. Its shape reminded Wendy of a birdcage, only it was large enough for a full-grown man. Its domed roof was marked by iron locks that snapped over each hinge. At the crown of the roof, a single orange lily bent its head over the cage, its pollen drifting lazily down. The cage was empty, but its impact was haunting all the same; moved by a few gears and pulleys that hung down through a cylindrical opening at the peak of the room, the cage continually spun clockwise, making Wendy dizzy just watching it. Faster and faster it spun in that one direction until it seemed to slow down before spinning the opposite way, gaining speed again until the pattern repeated.

"What is it for?" she asked.

"Torture." Peter grinned, his eyes amused as he looked over the room without a hint of fear. "Particularly for someone who flies. It would disorient you, spin your internal axis." He leaned back and laughed, clutching his belly. "And it's all for me!" He kicked a splash of water toward the cage, completely unaffected by the jarring sight. He snorted.

"Hook thinks himself so creative with all his pulleys and inventions. As if he could hold Peter Pan. C'mon, the libations we're looking for aren't here anyway."

Wendy continued to watch the cage spin, fascinated by how it continued rotating this way and that, faster and faster, like a spindle. There was a seductive rhythm to it. Peter's fingers on her elbow finally pulled her out of the trance.

"Wendy?"

"Yes, I'm coming. Sorry." She shook her head. *Foolish girl.* Time was of the essence—any moment now, Kitoko could shout down that pirates had returned, or worse, that the ships had somehow been notified. Peter flew past Wendy and the boys, landing in the doorway of the third room.

"In this room, we have—" Peter stopped. Wendy saw his body go rigid and thought that they had finally found what they were looking for, but then Peter turned around, his eyes the darkest shade of navy that Wendy had ever seen. He struggled to control his voice.

"The wine isn't in here. Check the next room."

The Lost Boys stared at him until he narrowed his eyes.

"Now!"

Then they all trooped past him, on to the next room.

"This one's a privy!" one of the Lost Boys whispered, and then they all sloshed down to the next one, giggling as they went, as boys were known to do at the mention of a privy.

"Peter, look at this! Look at all this treasure!"

Peter darted toward the fifth door. Wendy quietly stepped into the third door, the one that had affected Peter so dramatically. She braced herself for the worst—bodies perhaps?—but found herself looking at a strangely familiar sight: instruments. Otherwise a bare room with elegant dark green walls piped with gold crowning, the room was piled high with haphazard stacks of instruments and sheet music, the piles sitting on a raised platform to keep them safe from the river lapping beneath them. In addition to the music, a broken harpsichord leaned up against the wall, its teeth askew. There was a lovely violin with tiny painted angels on the neck that rested on the broken harpsichord. A guitar, two brass horns, and one strange instrument involving animal skins, strings, and a corded bone also filled the space. The walls were adorned with flutes and clarinets and an ancient harp that looked like it once belonged to a lady of leisure. Wendy reached out to strum one of the strings of the harp, her fingers brushing it with a clean pluck. The sound rang out over the sound of the water around her feet, which were becoming quite cold.

A hand closed hard around her own.

Peter's.

She turned to face him, afraid that he would be angry with her. But the eyes that met hers weren't navy. They were the bright green that she adored so much, the color of trees and emeralds and life on Pan Island. He smiled gently at her.

"What are you doing in here?"

"I just wanted to see the room. I love music." She cleared her throat. "I'm sorry."

"Oh, you gentle girl," Peter murmured, his hand caressing her cheek. Wendy felt her heart quicken. "There is nothing to be sorry about."

Wendy turned and looked again at the instruments.

"Hook must be quite the musician. Strange, isn't it? A pirate musician."

Peter's brow furrowed, but only for a second. "I suppose. But I hear it's quite hard to be a musician with one hand." Then he laughed deeply before swiftly pulling Wendy out into the main hallway. Wendy watched as the Lost Boys went from one room to the next. Then it struck her.

"Peter!"

"Yes?"

"We're wasting our time! I know where the wine will be."

His eyes widened. "How?"

She laughed to herself. "I thought like John for a moment."

Peter still looked confused.

"The wine wouldn't be near the end of the hallway—it's too cold. It also wouldn't be near the mouth . . ."

Peter's eyes widened. "Because it's too warm!"

"So my guess would be . . ."

"Room seven?" Peter grabbed her hand with a smile, and Wendy flushed, feeling like a conspirator, the thrill of excitement overcoming any lingering doubts she had. So this was adventure. They flew quickly down the long hallway, landing with a splash in front of the seventh door. Peter took a deep breath and pushed against the door. Nothing happened. He shoved again.

"Locked," he mumbled. "The bastard. Of course he locks up his liquor. Darby!"

A kind Lost Boy who had spoken to Wendy a few times scampered over, carrying a small bag. The sandy-haired lad unfolded several strange metal tools and eyed them closely before picking up one.

"Stand back, boys!" He paused. "And ladies. Lady. You know."

They complied, and Darby began unfurling several tiny spirals from inside a glass tube. Finally, he selected a razor-thin pipe with a blossoming end that twirled in the dim light of the hideout. With a grin, he inserted the tube into the lock and began turning it.

"He was once a thief," Peter whispered to Wendy, giving her hand a squeeze.

"I can see that."

Darby listened to the door and turned the tube once, twice, and then a hard counterclockwise turn. Something clicked on the other side.

"Now . . ." he whispered.

Peter handed him a single match from the bag. Darby blew on the end of it, struck it on the rock wall, and as soon as the flame sparked, he shoved it inside the glass tube and covered the end with the palm of his hand. At first there was nothing, but then Wendy heard the slightest moan, as if the door itself were crying out. She felt Peter's arms circle around her waist and was about to object out of mortification when they were both blown silently off their feet, backward into the air. But as soon as the momentum pulled at her, Wendy felt herself stop. She wasn't falling. She wasn't slamming into the wall behind her. She was simply floating in the air, Peter behind her. She shook her head and floated back down to the ground, where the water swirled in angry waves, disturbed by the change in pressure. Silently and miraculously, the door had been pulled inside the room. Peter took her hand and led her inside, followed by his small army of boys.

"Beautifully done, Darbs!"

Darby grinned from ear to ear as Lost Boys patted him on the back and shoulder, congratulating him on his talents. Peter ruffled his hair affectionately as he walked past, and the boy practically burst with pride. Once Wendy passed the splintered wood that was once the door, she let a smile play across her face. The seventh room had been a good guess. Like the room with the giant birdcage, this room was also circular in shape, but it was narrow where the other one had been wide, a thin funnel that echoed outward. Naturally carved shelves of rock jutted out from the walls, and Wendy saw that the green condensation that graced the entrance also dripped down the walls here. Light came in from a small hole in the ceiling, barely big enough to fit a bottle through it, and bathed the room in a green, hazy light. And what bottles filled the room! Wendy gasped when her eyes traced up to the ceiling. Bottles of every shape and color surrounded her: blue bottles with naked mermaids carved into the sides, sea-glass bottles with clear liquids that sloshed around inside of them, as if moved by an invisible hand. Several clear bottles with bloodred wine and wooden corks sat on the topmost shelf. There were green bottles marked with tiny pocks that looked like stars. Black bottles with wide yellow stripes and elaborate jeweled tops sat next to tiny bottles that Wendy could fit into her pocket. There were hundreds upon hundreds of bottles, each one beautiful in the blazing vert light. How odd, she thought—this room of vice was somehow a place of tranquility in all the chaos. She cleared her throat.

"Are there so many versions of liquor?" she asked innocently.

Peter laughed. "This is but a small selection, my darling. But there . . ." He pointed to a bottle on the highest shelf, enclosed in a wavy glass case with a small lock on the side. "That is Hook's vice."

The bottle was thin, clear, and unremarkable in every way, marked only by an upside-down skull etched into the glass. Liquid the color of pure honey sat perfectly still inside of it, no more than would fill two glasses.

"Rum. The purest of its kind. It's made on one of the outer islands."

Peter looked at the boys lingering around, each one touching the bottles with a sort of intoxicated glee at their own success. He shook his head and frowned, his clever eyes darting around the room, calculating, measuring.

"This was almost too easy, wasn't it, Wendy Darling? Hm. Right." He clapped his hands once, and the boys silenced themselves. "All right, boys, load up! No one touch the rum!"

Everyone began grabbing liquor bottles and stuffing them into large sacks padded with blankets and clothing. Bottles clanged against each other as the boys shoved them roughly into the bags. The sound of chipping glass filled the air, sharp notes against the lulling sound of the lapping water at their feet.

"Careful!" Peter snapped. "Handle them gently!"

He turned to Wendy with a sigh.

"Boys."

Grinning, he flew up in the air and began rifling through an overflowing shelf, bottles rolling off the shelf and landing with a splash in the river. He pulled out a bottle and looked at the label.

"Aha! Yes!"

He flew back down to her.

"Lovely Wendy, you carry this one. This bottle can be just for you."

Wendy looked down at the bottle in his hands as guilt welled up inside of her. They were stealing. This was stealing. It was thrilling and terrible and wonderful all at once. She gave a small shake of her head, and Peter tilted his own toward her.

"But Peter—"

"They stole these from other people, you know. It's not really stealing if they stole it first." He shoved the bottle toward her, clear glass with a gold foil cap and a rose-colored liquid inside. "You can't steal from pirates."

Reluctantly, she took it. It wasn't just the liquor, it was all of it—the pirate outside, that John and Michael were away from her doing God knew what, how her body betrayed her misgivings by pulsing with excitement at the thrill of it all. Peter grinned at her.

"You have such a pure heart. I admire you for it. I—"

He fell silent, his head turning toward the door ever so slightly.

"Quiet!" Peter held up a finger. No one moved. Wendy's heart thundered inside of her chest so loud that she feared the other boys could hear it, her own red bird, furious inside of her lungs. Silently, Peter floated up into the air and peeked his head out the top of the doorway. His hand rested on his sword hilt, tracing the lines of the gold handle. Wendy heard nothing at first, but after a few seconds, she heard the faintest sound of a single pair of footsteps echoing down the Vault. Someone was running—and yelling. She heard the *shhhhinnnnng* of a drawn sword, the splashing of boots in the water, frantic cries, and the clanking of metal against wall—the sounds of men, men coming for them. The pirates had awoken, and they were coming for all of them.

A twisted jolt of fear mixed with delight shot through her fingertips as she reached for Peter.

"Leave them! Let's go!" Wendy urged.

He looked down at her as if he had never heard anything so ridiculous in his life. "Leave the liquor? Are you serious? This is what we came for." He laughed. "C'mon boys, pack it up!"

One by one, the boys plunged past Peter, each carrying their heavy bag full of bottles. Once they reached the doorway, they took off into the air, hovering just below the dripping peaked roof of the winding cavern. Peter was still flitting around the room, grabbing bottle after bottle and stuffing them into his pack.

"Peter! Let's go! Peter!" Wendy hissed, no longer amused. He made a silly face at Wendy in return. She used the stern voice that normally worked with the boys. "Peter Pan!"

He started laughing at her. She looked nervously back toward the door, where most of the Lost Boys were waiting for Peter, floating silently near the ceiling, the bottles in their bags clinking harmlessly together. The voices of the pirates grew louder, climbing ever upward, vibrating off the walls and into the room, into her brain.

"PETER!"

He had just turned to her when a deafening screech silenced them both. As they turned their heads toward the horrible noise, the piercing whine shook the walls, and the bottles began vibrating toward the edge of their shelves before plunging down, one after another. One smashed against Peter's face, and he tumbled downward to the floor before stopping himself. With an annoyed scowl, he wiped the blood off his face and turned to Wendy.

"I guess we should—"

He was cut off by the sound of the boys screaming outside the door, their proud boasts turned to the frantic cries of children. The high-pitched whine died with a whimper, and it was only then, in the deafening silence, that Wendy heard the mechanical turning of gears and the uneasy creaking of doors long shut. There were no voices of pirates now, only the thunderous turning, its voice grinding all other sounds to dust. Wendy looked at Peter with wild eyes.

"What is it?"

Peter opened his mouth to answer but was drowned out by a growing roar, its sound so distinctive, Wendy knew what it was even though she had never before in her life heard such a terrifying sound. The boys' screams grew, and she wondered if it would be the last sound she heard. Her feet seemed to be weights as she turned to run, Peter's name making it to the tip of her lips before her feet were swept out from under her in a violent rush of water. She hit the ground hard, the water sweeping her back into the room as it filled rapidly, her body tumbling head over feet. Her hands clutched uselessly at the floor, its hard rock surface scraping her delicate palms raw. Then the water pushed over her like a shroud, like a blanket over a child, and she was pulled underneath the river, the water filling her mouth with the taste of salty fish. Wendy righted herself and pushed off the ground, upward to where she could see light, crawling slowly to the surface, her feet so heavy in the churning water. With a gasp, she emerged through the foamy cloud.

"Peter!" she screamed, her flailing feet finding the wall behind her as she fought against the current that was swirling her ever backward, deeper into the beautiful room of green glass. Bottles of wine were all around her, being tossed in the rising waters, like ships on an angry sea. A red bottle of wine broke open against the wall next to her, sloshing its contents all around her, blood in the water. Her mouth tasted bittersweet, the tingling zing of wine mingling with the salty water. Something darted above her in the air.

"Peter!"

"Wendy!" Peter flew down toward her and grabbed her hand. "You can fly, remember?"

Wendy almost laughed in spite of herself. In her terror she had forgotten—*that's right*, she thought. *I can fly.* Willing herself upward, Wendy rose slowly up above the flood, water pouring from her body like raindrops. Several of the Lost Boys had been pushed back inside the room by the wave of water and began rising out of the river around her, their dirty hair parting the floating bottles like leviathans of nightmares. Their faces, however, betrayed them—they were only the faces of frightened boys. One of them was clawing the water, gurgling with a rising panic.

"Peter! I don't know how to swim! Peter!"

Peter ignored him, his eyes on the door. Abbott rose up from the water and grabbed the boy, tossing him into the air.

"Fly! Everyone, fly! Go, get out of here! Leave everything! Go back to Pan Island!" Abbott shouted.

Peter spun around, his eyes wild with excitement, his cheeks flushed. "Lost Boys, stop! Don't listen to him. Take your treasure—each boy with his own bag, or there will be dire consequences! Draw your weapons and head back to the top of the skull! Quickly! I'll meet you there!"

The boys began clustering at the door, heavily laden bags flung over their shoulders or wrapped around their backs. Abbott shot Peter a cutting look. The water was halfway up the doorway now and rising; the rock shelves around them croaked their dismay. Wendy drew herself along the walls and out into the hallway, Peter at her heels, the tiny bottle of rum tucked inside her blouse. The hallway was filling with water, the doors bouncing open and shut with the waves that were running up and down the corridor. Peter crawled along the ceiling behind Wendy.

"Darby!" he barked.

The boy flew up next to him like an eager pup, his hair dripping into his eyes.

"Yes, Peter?" His voice carried a nervous edge through the hallway.

"Darby, I need you to do something special for me—something only you can do. I only trust YOU."

Darby nodded. "Anything."

Peter pulled Darby's forehead against his own, Darby's body reaching toward Peter as if he were asking for a fatherly embrace.

"My good lad. Go back in there and get Hook's rum! You're the only one who can unlock it!"

Darby hesitated for just a moment before sputtering, "Yes, sir!" Then he gave Peter a nervous grin. With a deep breath, Darby ducked under the water and swam back through the seventh door, his body disappearing under the violently churning water, the same water that now was brushing the top of the door frame.

"Peter! He'll never make it!" Wendy yelled, but her words were drowned out with another mighty wave of water. She pressed herself against the ceiling, desperate to stay out of the water that threatened to swallow them all.

"Follow me!" Peter leapt ahead of her, his body curving quickly toward the mouth of the cave. Wendy looked back for Darby, but the doorway to the room was completely covered over with water, and she wasn't exactly sure anymore quite where the door was. Darby would make it, wouldn't he? From under the water, a hand reached out for her. Abbott rose up behind her, gesturing wildly to the boys flying past him, following Peter through the exit. The water was rising, more quickly than it had before. The tip of her pant leg brushed its hungry waves. Abbott screamed frantic directions to the other boys before turning on her.

"What are you still doing here? I'll get Darby. GO! NOW!"

Wendy nodded, and Abbott turned back toward the seventh door. He had gotten only a few feet from her when there was a screeching sound, as a pitched, mechanical whine filled the hall-way. It was so loud that Wendy clamped her hands over her ears, desperate to stop the sound that she was sure would split her in half. She watched in silent horror as a trapdoor, hidden in the arch of the doorway, slammed down, cutting them off from the room—and Darby

"That bottle was booby-trapped! Dammit, Peter!" Abbott yelled. He ducked under the water again, banging fruitlessly against the door. Wendy took a deep breath and followed behind Abbott, alternating between breathing and yanking desperately at the door handle. Darby's panicked cries reached her ears underwater, a muffled yell marked by desperate pounding on the doors. This time, when Wendy rose to take a breath, there was only a foot of space between her head and the roof of the cavern.

"Darby!" she yelled. "We have to get him out!"

Abbott looked at her, and then at the door, and back at her again. With heavy resignation, he turned away. "There's nothing we can do. Gods damn it, Peter!"

On the other side of the door, Darby's screams went silent, and Wendy's mind was assaulted with images of Darby drowning.

"Can't we . . ."

Abbott took her arm firmly, sputtering over the water. "The only person who could get into that room is inside of it. He belongs to Hook now. We have to go." Abbott shook his head. "Damn it! We'll be next if we don't hurry. Come on!"

Quickly they made their way toward the mouth of the cave, their bodies scraping the ceiling, scurrying like frantic spiders to safety as the water continued to rise. Eventually there was nothing to do but take a breath, latch arms, and let the current push them out toward the mouth of the skull. Wendy felt her feet twirling underneath the water, Abbott's hand jerking from her own, and her body sluicing through the narrow cavern as if she were inside of a pipe. She heard a strange pouring sound under the water just before her body slammed vertically against the teeth that marked the mouth of the Vault. She gave a muffled cry as she was caught between water pouring out over her and the wooden stakes that were gouging into her thighs and chest. With great difficulty, Wendy pulled her legs up to her chest before pushing herself out between the hanging sticks, water pouring out around her as she gasped for breath and struggled to free herself. Her elbow roughly dragged along the surface of a razor-sharp tooth as she kicked desperately forward. The river water was consuming her, streaming like a waterfall over her body, over her mouth, over her eyes. She twisted her torso and kicked, striving forward. Finally, her body pushed free of the teeth and she reached out into nothing as she fell forward. There was sky! And jungle! She let out an unladylike scream and pushed past the entrance to the Vault, her body spilling out into the foaming river below. Free! Free! Wendy hungrily gulped in the air, so clean and warm, filing her lungs greedily, all else forgotten for a few divine seconds.

Abbott landed with a splash behind her. She had barely caught her breath before he was yelling, "Fly! Up!"

Wendy leapt into the air, with Abbott following closely behind her. There were noises and shouts coming from the roof of the skull, and she briefly heard Abbott mutter curses under his breath before he was flying past her, his sword drawn menacingly. Wendy slowly rose up over the Vault, her heart dreading what she would—and did—find. In the middle of the horrific skull, tethered by the two laundry lines of skeletons, a dozen Lost Boys fought viciously against seven grown pirates. Seeing it from above gave the strangest perspective—like John's tiny toy soldiers, moving, somehow alive. Wendy drew closer, unsure of what to do. The fighting was quick and furious, swords and axes meeting and ricocheting off each other in the afternoon light, filling the air with the grating of metal and the sweat-drenched cries of young boys. There were three bodies on the ground, surrounded by blood, the bodies of pirates. Relief flooded her as Peter emerged from behind a pirate, a golden sword poking out from his chest and then disappearing. The pirate fell to the ground at Peter's feet. Lost Boys were launching off the skull into the air all around her, bags over their shoulders, tied around their waists. Peter was fighting four of the pirates as the Lost Boys around him struggled to contribute. On the corner of the rock, Kitoko was engaged in a fistfight that had come to desperate blows. Wendy reached for her dagger, but for some reason she couldn't bring herself to draw it. What exactly was she planning to do with it when she got there?

"Hallo, Wendy!" Peter gave a loud laugh as he leapt off the shoulders of one pirate, spinning in the air and planting his feet squarely into the face of another. The man flew backward, his sword landing beside him. Peter grabbed him and launched into the air, pulling the man up by his ankle. The man screamed as Peter rose higher and higher into the air before changing direction and flying back toward the crowning head of the Vault. He spun his body so that the man whipped toward the rocks, crushing two other pirates on his way down. They all rolled to a crumpled halt, their bodies entwined, one man's neck twisted at an unnatural angle. Peter picked up the man's sword and thrust it backward into the eye of a pirate who was choking a young Lost Boy. The boy sputtered before falling to the ground, his legs pumping uselessly. Peter patted him on the back, but not before grabbing a bottle from the boy's bag and breaking it open on the ground.

"Go!"

He launched himself off the ground and came back down hard again, driving the broken bottle onto the top of the pirate's head like a bloody crown. The man collapsed at Peter's feet. Another pirate snarled and threw himself at Peter, but unfortunately caught the edge of Peter's sword when he vaulted himself straight upward into the sky. The sword shoved up into the man through his ribs, impaling him. The pirate's body lifted off the ground a few feet along with Peter before he pushed him off his blade with a look of disgust. There was only one pirate left now, and he raced toward the cannon that faced the sea.

"Peter!" Wendy pointed, but it was too late. She was too high to do anything, but without thinking, she plunged down toward the fight. The pirate gave her a toothless grin and pulled a carved bone lever at the back of the cannon before aiming it right at her. As he gazed at her, a spear pushed out of the front of his neck, thrown by Abbott, who stood unsteadily behind him. There was a second of silence as she weighed her fate, but the cannon gave a roar that shook her bones before launching a yawning fountain of fire into the sky. The dozen red flares lit up against the misty clouds like the spark of a massive flame, a castle burning. A hundred shades of fire exploded in her vision, flares whirling like burning windmills, cartwheeling toward her, rendering her unable to move, to breathe. Finally, as she watched a tail of fire whip her way, she dove downward, narrowly avoiding the flames that licked her outstretched arm. Once the flares hit their peak, they burst into a brilliant explosion of gold and red light.

Wendy jerked her head toward the sea, where the two ships

rested on bucking waves. They did not move, hopefully because John had done his job and they were full of vomiting pirates, slow on the uptake. A breeze ruffled her hair, and a line of mist ran between her and the ships, concealing them from view. Wendy heard a scream below. Most of the Lost Boys had fled. The only ones left on the head of the Vault were Abbott, Kitoko, and Peter. Two new pirates were climbing up the Vault.

"Go!" she yelled, not understanding why the boys were not moving. Peter held his ground and watched the two pirates reach the top of the skull. What could she do? Without thinking, Wendy propelled herself down to the rock, landing hard, the tiny bottle falling out of her blouse and rolling down the side of the skull. Peter was staring at one of the pirates with a palpable hunger as he pointed his sword in his direction.

"Smith!" he hissed. "So good to see you. I hope you can give Hook my regards, perhaps in the form of a disembodied head?"

The man he had spoken to let out a gruff laugh. He was twice the size of Peter, with curly black hair slick with oil and thick eyebrows, his forearms as large as grapefruits and covered with tattoos of angels and demons. A banshee leered at her from just behind his elbow. Suddenly, all of the boys seemed very much like children. This man was most certainly not a child, and Wendy felt the toxic chill of fear fill her bloodstream.

"The Captain wouldn't have your regards, not even in that form, you blistering pustule!"

"Stay back, girl!" the other pirate hissed at her, a bloody knife in his hands. "Don't move."

"Don't touch her," Peter snapped. "Do it, and I'll kill you twice."

The man named Smith raised his eyebrows. "Peter Pan has a little girlfriend, does he? I know someone who might be very interested in this revelation. What is this, the second one you've ever had? Do you even know what to do with this pretty girl, Peter? If you don't, I'll show yah."

"Don't talk about her," Peter growled. "You stupid oaf."

The man shrugged. Wendy could see a fierce intelligence dancing behind the man's eyes as he looked at Peter and then back at Abbott and Kitoko. Smith's fingers were twitching.

"So, who feels like dying in this tired dance today?"

Peter's gaze was steady. "Abbott, you can take him."

The second pirate was creeping closer to Wendy. Peter leapt into the air, flinging himself between them. Abbott looked over at Peter with dead eyes, before turning back and lunging at Smith. He was too late. The pirate leapt back before pulling a hidden pistol out of his coat, shooting it not toward Abbott, but right into the middle of their group. They scattered, and the man ran hard toward Kitoko, who was on the edge of the skull. Abbott knelt to the ground before throwing his spear toward the pirate's back. It bounced harmlessly off his shoulder armor before he grabbed Kitoko roughly, bringing a serrated knife up to his throat. He turned to Peter.

"Now . . . here's what's going to happen, little boys. You are going to give us back all the bottles you took from us. Peter Pan is going to call back the rest of the boys, and we will get every last bottle, or so help me God, I will slit this boy's throat. No one touches our booze."

Kitoko's eyes were wide with fear as he tried desperately to untangle the man's arm from around his neck. His mouth formed the word "Peter" again and again as he looked at Peter, terrified. Wendy's heart was hammering so fast that she clutched at her chest.

"Peter! Give him the bottles! Call them back!"

Peter looked, panicked, at Wendy, then at the pirate and back at Kitoko again.

"It's too risky. To bring the boys back. They'll kill us all! It's a trap!"

The man straightened up and pointed his knife at Peter. "I'm not playing you, little boy! Have them drop the bottles in the river, and your friend will live."

Peter's gaze never wavered. "I cannot risk the lives of all my boys for one. He'll kill us, I'm telling you! Kitoko, you understand . . ."

Kitoko nodded at Peter before closing his eyes. Abbott reached for his spear, yelling Kitoko's name. Wendy opened her mouth to scream, but it was too late. With a terrible grin, the man opened up Kitoko's throat, pushing his dagger in before tearing across his collar. There was a rush of bright red blood, and Kitoko fell facedown on the rock, his body becoming nothing more than a loose rag doll. Wendy heard nothing after that, as a fog of shock surrounded her. Peter was yelling, his face afraid and his arms strong around her. Abbott was pointing as they rose into the air. There was a loud bang, and the hair on the right side of her head felt whipped away, the smell of gunpowder on her cheek. Wendy looked out to the sea, to the two ships bearing down on the Vault, to the men swarming off the sides of the ship, so many, climbing over the river like ants, waving weapons and screaming. So many. She felt Peter's body tighten his hold around her as they climbed into the mist. Behind the two ships, a black shape was appearing, twice their height and wider than both the ships together. The hulking mass growing closer, the fog slowly pulling away. Something in the blackness winked at her—a mirror?

"GO!" Peter screamed. "It's the *Night*!"

And suddenly they were climbing up into the sky, far away from the bloodied chaos below, far from where Kitoko was lying on the rock bed, all alone as the pirates ran over his body. Wendy rested her head against Peter's thundering heart. Up, up, up.

CHAPTER SIXTEEN

WENDY DIDN'T REMEMBER FLYING HOME. She remembered the heat of Peter as they rose through the mist, the blood that soaked through his shirt and pressed against her cheek, warm and sticky. She remembered Kitoko's face. When they landed on the thatched roof, the Pan flag flapping in the wind, there was a great rush of boys. Peter set her down gently onto the wooden walkway that linked the Moon Tower to the rest of the tree. She blinked in the afternoon light.

"Peter . . . Kitoko."

"I know," he said gently. "That went differently than I expected it to." His face was honest, bewildered, and a bit distraught. He tilted his head as he looked at Wendy with curious eyes. "Was the blood too much?" She nodded weakly, her stomach churning inside of her. She wondered if she was going to be sick. She heard the shouts of voices as hundreds of Lost Boys ran toward Peter, their laughter such a foreign sound after what she had seen. The boys that had been with them began unloading the wine, bags and bags of bottles, giving the bags to the younger boys. Peter leapt up.

"Oy! Take those to the Table and store them in the back. No one opens the wine until we've mourned Kitoko and Darby!"

The Lost Boys froze. A skinny boy with caramel skin and tousled brown hair stepped forward.

"Kitoko is . . . dead?"

Peter nodded sadly before climbing up onto the ledge. Wendy remembered the first time she had seen Peter talk to the boys, preening and triumphant. Now he was solemn, his hands crossed in front of him, reverent and sad.

"Kitoko gave his life for the Lost Boys you see beside me. Smith wanted them to return, and Kitoko stood his ground. He died for his brothers. He died being a General, and in his last moments, he confirmed why I picked him for General. Kitoko was brave, intelligent, and selfless. And though he wasn't the type to share much of anything"—the boys gave a soft, sad chuckle—"I think he wouldn't mind if I told you that he had become a Swift. Three days ago, Kitoko was given the gift of permanent flight. He wasn't ready to share yet, being as shy as he was, but we had spoken of it last night, that it was time for him to take his place beside me, publicly."

Peter's eyes filled with tears. "Pan Island is not going to be the same place without Kitoko. Or Darby. I grieve alongside my other Generals—Oxley, Abbott, John."

John. Wendy's head jerked up and she found her brother, standing smugly at the back of the boys, arms crossed, trying hard to not look pleased at his inclusion in Peter's speech. Wendy felt a weight lift off her chest. *He is safe. Thank God. The little git.* From here he looked so much older than the last time she had seen him. Perhaps it was the confidence that radiated out from him, and for a moment she was glad for him. Her brother, finally accepted by his peers, finally proud of something he had done. Perhaps the bitterness would melt from his personality. He looked over at Wendy, and she weakly raised her hand. He rolled his eyes and turned his gaze back to Peter. Perhaps not. Peter was going on about Kitoko now, where he had found him, and his early exploits as a Pip. The crowd was both laughing and crying, except for Oxley, who was sobbing openly into his hands at the back of the room. Michael was holding onto the bottom of his shirt. A blinding pain shot past Wendy's eyes, and she winced. Peter's voice carried out over the boys, a wave of comfort, cradling them all in his confidence.

"Where do we go from here? Well, even I'm not sure. From here we mourn our loss, and when we are done mourning, our grief will turn to anger, and soon the tears will be those of Hook's men, the men who did this. We will have our vengeance, and as we take it, we will whisper their names . . ." Peter's voice dropped low as he whispered, "Kitoko. Darby."

The boys joined in, whispering their names again and again. When their whispers grew loud enough, Peter drew his golden sword and pointed through the tree. "Grab your lanterns and head to the beach, to mourn our beloved General and our friend! And then we will feast!" Wendy watched silently as the train of boys began to snake its way down to the beach, a moving cloud of dust that quickly became one with the dark leaves around them. Suddenly, the island felt very empty, and as she looked down from the huts, she was struck by how sinister a place could seem without the laughter of boys. She stepped softly behind them all, lost in her thoughts, ignoring the headache that pressed against her temples. The boys were out of sight now, and she stumbled over her feet, unable to forget what had happened at the Vault. Barely thinking, she made her way to the side of one of the platforms, winding her way through the rope walkways until the sounds of the Lost Boys and Peter's stirring speech faded into a dull buzz. She stumbled, her mind flitting between Kitoko's face, Peter's emerald eyes, and the fountain of impossibly red blood that had sprayed from Kitoko's throat. Wendy was on her hands and knees now, dry heaving, clutching at wooden planks outside of one of the Lost Boys' huts until she was finally able to rest, pushing her sweaty head against her hands. There was a soft flutter in the air above her, and then there was the silvery glittering dust falling all around her. She lifted her head up and saw dainty bare feet in front of her.

"Tink? I beg you, please leave me alone. I'm not feeling well."

"Kitoko's gone," Tink whispered. "And you're to blame." Her bright blue eyes flared with pure hatred.

Then she kicked Wendy off the walkway.

Wendy felt herself falling, falling over the edge. She saw the great green plume of Centermost poke up far below her, the spindly crossed branches that would not stop her fall as she plummeted to her death. Her hands clutched at the air as her body tightened, her muscles tense and ready to spring to life, ready to fight. She blinked. The branches didn't rush toward her, their grand arms staying perfectly still where they were. The ground didn't rush to meet her. She was floating. Relief swept through her. Of course, she still had flight. She turned her head up to look at Tink, a litany of formidable words forming on her tongue, as Tink stared down at her from the bridge.

"Lucky guess." The fairy shrugged, and with a flutter of gossamer wings, she was gone in a second, heading down toward the beach, where Peter's loud voice rang through the tree. Wendy cautiously flew down to the nearest hut, relishing the feeling of her feet on the wooden planks. Righteous anger at Tink burned through her, though she wasn't able to maintain it for very long. Tink looked so lost and sad, truly a miserable creature if Wendy had ever seen one. She was undoubtedly powerful, but there was a trembling beneath those bruised eyes, an undercurrent of vulnerability that reminded Wendy of a frightened child. Her blazing jealousy of Wendy, the way she clutched so desperately to Peter—Tink seemed more childish than the youngest Lost Boy, while at the same time seeming as ancient as the warm wind that pulsed around the island. Wendy walked to the edge of the walkway around the hut, pausing to push aside some branches and take in the turquoise sea crashing beneath her; the comforting sound of waves pulsing against the island calmed her thundering heart. Bright pink flowers above her head draped and winked in the sea breeze, tiny pieces of translucent dust spiraling down from their lips. With a deep breath, her mind trying to stay off of what had transpired at the Vault, Wendy turned toward the beach. Taking each step slower than normal, her stomach tightening with dread with each pad of her foot, she reluctantly made her way down, her eyes constantly looking up to make sure that Tink didn't return. She didn't.

When Wendy emerged at the beach, the Lost Boys were all standing linked together, their hands wrapped around each other's wrists, their bright faces turning out toward the sea. The line of them stretched the entire south side of Pan Island, water lapping at their feet. Peter was out over the water, his pointed feet hovering just over the surface, a white lotus flower in his outstretched hands. When he saw Wendy, he nodded to her, and the Lost Boys fell silent.

"We begin," he murmured.

The Lost Boys began humming, a sound so low and quiet that it reminded Wendy of the flutter of a bee's wings. The low hum echoed out over the water, reaching Peter and beyond, out into the depths of the dark water, out to the sea, out to other worlds, probably. Peter slowly lifted the flower over his head, and Wendy could see the snaking white tendrils of flight flowing slowly from his forearms into the flower. The lotus began to glow, unearthly, pulsating with pure white light, its beating heart at the center of its petals, thrumming to the sound of the Lost Boys' hums. Peter held it for a minute over his head before gently unfolding his hands in a circular motion. The flower rose up into the air, spinning as it went. As it went higher, the Lost Boys raised their hands with it, the slow line of arms moving upward as their hums turned into the quiet chant of Kitoko's and Darby's names to all who would hear. The lotus climbed swiftly upward, a sparrow of light, until eventually it became one with the heavy rain clouds that were quickly darkening the Neverland sky. It disappeared into the lowest of the clouds, its light winking through the cluster like a faraway star. Peter turned back to the boys, tears spilling down his ruddy cheeks.

"And now Kitoko and Darby watch over us all, Lost Boys no more. They are found." He choked on his words, coughing to cover his sob.

The boys repeated it quietly to themselves.

"They are found, they are found."

Wendy mouthed the words, unable to make sound escape her lips, so heavy was her heart. *They are dead.* Wendy caught a shimmering wink from the outskirts of the beach. Squinting, she spotted Tink, the fairy perched as still as a statue, her chest resting on a rocky outcropping that overlooked the beach. Tink's gaunt face was stoic, her body curled in on itself as she stared blindly out to sea. Pain radiated out from her, even at this distance, and Wendy could see that her skin seemed to glow with a dull blue hue. Wendy looked away, suddenly feeling voyeuristic to Tink's unhappiness.

The line of boys had quietly turned away from the beach, and they were hoisting themselves up the sheer rock face, back to their huts. Oxley, John, and Abbott remained on the beach. Oxley was still crying, big sobs that wracked his shoulders. Abbott's face remained stern, his emotions unreadable. John stood awkwardly beside them both, fidgeting the way he always did. Peter gave Wendy a small smile as he made his way back to the Generals. Abbott unexpectedly reached out and pulled Peter into a hug. Oxley joined them. John eventually joined in as well. The Generals stayed like that for several minutes while Wendy looked out over the ocean, something unseen pulling at the back of her mind, like the beginnings of a thread unraveling a sweater. Peter eventually withdrew himself from the Generals and flew toward her, his white shirt flapping in the ocean wind. He gently rested both hands on her shoulders.

"Are you all right?"

Wendy nodded, feeling stronger in the crisp, clear weather.

"It's going to rain," she murmured. Peter didn't seem to hear her, his mind somewhere else, but he nodded anyway. Then he looked down at her, his bright green eyes looking deeply into hers. The thread stopped pulling as she fell deep into his scent, the feeling of his hands on her shoulders.

"Wendy Darling, I promise tonight will be a night you will never forget."

His fingers trailed her cheek, and Wendy suddenly turned away, embarrassed at the public affection of it all. Abbott and John were staring at them, Abbott's eyebrows furrowed, his eyes calculating. John looked simply disgusted. Peter tilted his head.

"Why don't you go lie down for a few minutes? You look tired. Then in a few hours, you can join us for the wine feast. Does that sound pleasing to you?"

Wendy looked back at him. "Kitoko and Darby are dead, Peter. You can't have a feast tonight."

He kissed her forehead.

"Life is for the living, Wendy. And I plan on living a very, very long time."

With that, Peter Pan flew off into the tree, and Wendy felt the beginning of raindrops on her face, dripping off her chin and mingling with her tears, the differences between them rendered obsolete as they made their way to the sea.

CHAPTER SEVENTEEN

AFTER THE NAP PETER HAD SUGGESTED, which did turn out to be sorely needed, Wendy moaned as she peeled off her sticky shirt and pants, soaked with sweat and flicked with blood. Kitoko's blood. The air rushed around her skin as she washed herself with the bowl of water, longing for soap that she highly doubted existed anywhere on Pan Island. There were a few dresses that had been laid out for her by some Pip earlier in the day, and Wendy decided on a simple white nightgown, pale pink stitched flowers dotting the neck, the cut of the gown a bit lower than her liking, no doubt a sleep frock that once belonged to a pirate's mistress. She slipped on her black shoes and tied up her hair with a light blue ribbon that she untied from the hammock. She gradually made her way down to the Table, not even flinching as she slid down the trunk this time, her legs wrapped around it like some sort of primate, feeling miles away from the lady she once was. She was still very far from the Table when she started hearing their voices, the feral shouts and insults of the boys, like a roar through the tree, unhinged in all their maleness. With a sigh of resignation, she continued on her way, eager to spend some time with Michael and—dare she hope for it?—Peter.

Hundreds and hundreds of candles flickered and leapt as she walked toward the Table, following the funnel of noise that seemed to circle around her the closer she got. Before she even entered the room, she smelled the feast, and to her dismay, her mouth began watering. The aroma of mushrooms and cream, butter-soaked beef, and pungent berries swirled in her nostrils. As she ducked into the hot room, filled to the brim with scream-ing and laughing boys, her eyes took in the enormous piles of food that covered the circular table. Pips were racing up from down below, covered in sweat and carrying the food with their bare hands before plopping it down messily in front of the rav-enous boys who tore at it like animals. Plump shrimp dusted with herbs and piles of white corn disappeared into hundreds of mouths, each one noshing the food, crunching and talking as they reveled in the stories of the day.

"Here!"

A Lost Boy handed her a hunk of meat, charred and crusted in all the right places. Wendy's stomach betrayed her emotions, and she found herself biting at the edges before she could stop herself. The meat was tender and perfectly cooked, and she was barely aware of the juice dripping off her chin until she had polished off most of it. Wiping her hand on the back of her dress, Wendy grabbed a piece of dark brown bread before making her way toward a towering pile of wine bottles, stacked haphazardly on a rickety table and adorned with hundreds of daisies.

She reached out, her fingers trailing along each raised glass, red, white, sea glass, all filled to the brim, all waiting for the ravenously hungry boys to descend. Her eyes filled with tears, looking at the bottles, remembering what the cost of this tower of debauchery had been. She remembered how the pirate's hand didn't shake as he drew the knife across Kitoko's throat. She remembered the growing desperation of Darby's cries. Wendy stared up at the bottles, a whisper in her mind encouraging her to break them all. Instead she started to turn away, until a smaller bottle at the base of the pile caught her eye. It had a small tag on it that read *Wendy*. Her hand curled around it as her mouth fell open in shock—it was the same small rose-colored bottle that Peter had given her, the same bottle that she had left at the Vault. When had he had time to grab it? He must have gone while she was sleeping. The nerve of that boy—and the romance of him. It took her breath away.

She turned it over in her hand. Such a lovely little thing couldn't hurt, she mused, and it was so pretty. Closing her eyes, she willfully pushed the violent memories of the day away and uncorked the bottle, taking a huge swig without thinking. It was strong, like taking a sip of sweet fire. The honeyed liquid filled her mouth, a sharply pleasant burn traveling down her throat and into her belly. It warmed her from within. Wendy gave a small laugh. She hadn't expected it to be so . . . good. Without thinking, she took another drink, feeling reckless and buzzy all at once, like a very grown-up girl indeed. A shadow passed overhead, and she looked up to find Peter hovering above her, delicately fingering a lock of her hair.

"Such a pretty color, like a newborn fawn."

Wendy smiled up at him. "Some may say dirt."

Peter's eyes grew serious. "You could never be as plain as dirt. Just look at your face." He cradled her cheek, and Wendy turned away, a blush creeping over her face as she remembered their passionate kiss in the mist. It seemed now like a hundred years ago, though it had only been that morning. So much had happened since then. The irresponsible thrum in her heart fluttered away as she remembered the two boys who hadn't returned home with them. Peter landed softly beside her and took her elbow gently with his hands.

"After the feast, I want to take you somewhere. Somewhere special."

Wendy blushed at the thought, but at the same time, she felt a twinge of betrayal in her chest. *But why?* She couldn't think of a single reason why this should make her feel anything but giddy.

When she tried to pinpoint the feeling, all she could see were the rapidly turning pages of a book.

"Peter, it's so odd but . . ." She was about to describe the strange image when the sound of the bell high atop of Pan Island began to ring loudly. Peter's eyes twinkled, and he leapt into the air, floating backward away from her.

"It's almost time!" He clapped his hands together, and for a moment, Wendy saw the boy he must have been when he was younger. Dirty, excitable, quick. The boy who looked down on her now was still that boy, only the look in his eyes when he gazed at her—no, there was nothing youthful about the fire in his adoring eyes, the way they swallowed her up in a consuming blaze. Wendy swallowed nervously. Peter pointed up to the alcove above the table, a wooden outcropping that she hadn't noticed before.

"That's where the Generals eat. And tonight, where we will drink! You'll be welcome up there with us."

"And Michael?" Wendy had finally spied her brother making his way across the Table, no interest whatsoever in the bottles before him as he chased a small mouse that was bolting for its life across the room. Peter's mouth twitched.

"I'm sorry, Wendy, Michael can't come. He's not a General, so you can imagine how that would make the other boys feel. It would be unfair." Peter waved his hand dismissively in Michael's direction. "He'll be fine."

Michael narrowly missed the mouse, which had darted out of the open door and into the night. Michael collapsed into belly laughs after his breathless chase, resting his hands on his knees.

"Wendy, I think that Mr. Mouse likes me!"

Wendy grinned. "I can see that. He must!" It was then that John pushed rudely past her, on his merry way to the alcove. "John! Excuse you!"

John was snide. "Yes, excuse me, your royal highness."

"John!"

Her brother spun on Michael. "And don't be silly, Michael, that mouse doesn't care about you one way or another."

"John, why are you being so cruel?" Wendy demanded.

He ignored her reprimand and without another word, leapt into the air with Oxley, both Generals then settling smugly in the alcove overlooking the Table. Wendy pursed her lips in a tight line. *Ah, so that's how they got up there.* John gave her a smug shrug from the alcove before turning away. Who was this boy? His change of behavior turned her stomach. *Sodding git.* She turned to Peter.

"I'll stay down here with the other boys, I think. Thank you for inviting me."

Peter gave her a hard smile, the corners of his mouth turning down a smidge, like a pout, which she found herself wanting to kiss off his face. Then she shook her head. The thoughts this boy made her think!

Wendy pulled out a chair from under the table and made herself comfortable, crossing her legs at the ankle as the chair creaked underneath her. Everything on Pan Island was like that: one hard movement away from collapse, an entire world made of breakables. She pulled Michael onto her lap, inhaling her younger brother's golden hair, a mix of rich ferns, notes of citrus, and a heap of sweaty dirt. He snuggled happily with Wendy for a few blissful moments before scampering away with Thomas. The boys were flooding the room now, their bellies full, the whooping and calling growing ever louder, their jovial boyishness filling the room like a balloon. Shouts rang out as they tore into the bottles, each one feigning some liquor expertise as they ultimately chose the bottle they had laid eyes on when they entered. A fight quickly broke out over a particularly large bottle with black liquid inside of it and a puzzle of crossbones etched into its casing.

"'Tis mine!" cried a chubby Indian boy, a red tunic his only clothes, as he yanked the bottle away from a smaller boy, whose dark chocolate skin and deep-set iris eyes were almost blindingly beautiful.

"No, it's mine, Eence! Don't touch it again, or I'll slit your throat!" Wendy flinched at their harsh words. Punches were thrown as the argument took a serious turn, and soon the two were wrestling on the ground, biting and hitting, throwing dirt in each other's faces and mouths. The bottle was forgotten as their fight escalated, one boy pushing another into the side of the table, which shuddered and spun with the impact. Hunks of meat and piles of fruits went flying to the filthy ground. Eence was on top of the smaller boy now, his hands covering the boy's face, pushing him down into the dirt.

"You want it? Well, you can't have it! Peter said I could have it! He said!"

"No, he didn't! It's mine because I touched it first." Blood was flowing from both their noses, dripping onto the dusty ground, mingling with spilled liquor and bits of food. Wendy looked up toward the alcove, but Peter wasn't even watching the fight. He and the other Generals were laughing and toasting, Abbott's arm casually around Peter's shoulder. John stood awkwardly beside them, swirling a glass of wine in one hand and trying to look as though he fit in perfectly and that drinking wine was something he did nightly. Wendy turned back to the fight and the large circle that had formed around them; Lost Boys were six deep, some sitting on the shoulders of others, one frantically pushing past the bigger boys to see.

"Eence is going to kill him, I think!"

Another boy shook his head. "My bet's on Ahmeh."

The boys started chanting, "Kill, kill, kill!" as the cloud of dirt around the boys settled into an uncomfortable stillness. With her heartbeats thundering in her head, Wendy pushed through the boys, who parted upon seeing who moved through them.

"Excuse me, boys, excuse me!" Exasperated, she finally snapped, "Out of my way, PLEASE!" Finally, she had made her way to the front, where the two boys were so covered in blood and dirt that they were now almost indiscernible from each other. The wine bottle they had so coveted had been smashed, its contents soaking into the ground, although one shoeless boy was scraping it into his mouth. Wendy stomped her foot.

"Stop it! I said, stop it!" The two boys kept wrestling, and Wendy finally grabbed the nearest one by the back of his neck, now using a maternal voice that she had heard someone use once upon a time, somewhere.

"I said, stop it! Right now, or you'll both be sent to bed without your suppers! And I'll make you say a hundred Hail Marys in front of me before I let you go to sleep!"

All eyes turned to her, and the two boys froze, their arms in choke holds around each other's necks.

"What's a Haley Marie?" Eence asked, before the other one punched him squarely in the mouth.

"Oh, for goodness' sake, stop acting like animals! Stand up!"

The two boys rose slowly to their feet. Wendy turned back to look at Peter, who was watching her with amusement, his glass held aloft like a king.

"It's a Hail Mary, and I don't think one hundred would even suffice for this lot." She pointed to the bottle. "Who started this?"

"He did!" the boys answered in unison.

"Of course," Wendy said. "Neither of you. Well, here is what you are going to do. You are going to pick up these broken pieces of glass and dispose of them. Then you are both going to your hammocks for the night and staying there while you think about what you've done. You've wasted an entire bottle of wine due to your . . ." her words were coming faster, "irresponsible behavior. Kitoko and Darby gave their lives so that you could have this!" She gestured to the table, now glittering with far fewer bottles than it had before. "And you have wasted it."

She shook her head. "I'm ashamed of both of you."

Both the boys stared up at her with wide eyes. She waited for

the group to laugh or push her aside to continue with their bac-
chanalian feast, but they didn't. Their lips quivered, and then
they were wrapping themselves around her waist, their hot tears
soaking her hips.

"We're sorry, Wendy! We won't do it again! Please don't send
us to our hammocks!"

Wendy felt a rush of affection for them both and laid her hands
atop their heads, feeling their dirt-laden locks.

"Don't do it again, boys. I don't want to hear any more about
your fighting. Eence, go get your Lost Brother a drink."

Eence nodded and scampered off, pulling a green bottle off
the table. "C'mon, Ahmeh." With a grin, they patted each other
roughly on the shoulder and slouched off to a dark corner to
drink more wine than any boys their age should. The rest of the
Lost Boys were swarming around Wendy now, reaching for her.

"Do it again! Tell me about the Mrs. Hale Marie! Will you yell
at me? I'll go to my hammock! Please, Miss Wendy!"

She laughed gaily as Michael buried himself in the folds of her
dress, at once needy and possessive of his older sister.

"Not tonight. But be on your best behavior!" The boys nodded
and scampered off. She sat back down at the table and continued
to sip on her warm rose liquid as the feasting continued. More
large oak platters of food were brought up by the Pips, through
the center of the table—bright yellow cheeses and buckets of berries, leafy greens and . . . Wendy poked a strange-looking fruit,
bright green with a gaping red mouth. The bug wiggled off her
plate, and she sat back, repulsed. An older Lost Boy plopped
down next to her, effortlessly scooping it into his mouth with
one hand.

"You don't know what you are missing," he said between sharp
crunches. Wendy laughed and dove into the berries, smearing
them on a hunk of bread. As the night went on, the boys got
more rowdy, the bottles of wine whittling down steadily until
there were only about twenty left. Wendy, on the other hand, just

sipped her bottle slowly, taking it all in: the Table now full of boys lying around, swinging their bottles in the air, breaking them against the ground and then crying, arguing belligerently with each other one minute only to be best friends the next, wrapping their arms around each other with profound declarations of love. Peter had given a few of them temporary flight before the feast, and they were drifting lazily through the air, bumping into the perfectly round walls of the Table, then drifting downward, reminding Wendy of kites, their pants like tails lazily spinning behind them. Three Lost Boys were lying under the table at her feet, batting her shoes every once in a while as they slurred tearful memories:

"Remember when we raided the Vault? Peter was so brave. He killed a pirate with his feet. I saw it."

"That was a long time ago."

"That was today, I think!"

"I heard Peter killed them with a bottle!"

"No, it was his feet!"

"How many pirates were there?"

"A thousand thousands!"

Then a silence.

"I will miss Kitoko."

Then giggles turned to sobs, and before she could even adjust to the sad sound of little boys crying, they were giggling again, poking each other.

"Your tears are fat!"

"They aren't even real!"

"Crocodile tears!"

There was a boy quietly throwing up in the corner, and though Wendy longed to comfort him, she also longed to not get vomit on her dress. Besides, he was the first, but he certainly wouldn't be the last that night. She began passing around some large wooden bowls that she found stacked behind the wall, just so that when the time came, the boys wouldn't be throwing up willy-nilly all over the place. From the General's alcove, she could hear Peter laughing hysterically at something Abbott had said, and she heard John and Oxley attempting to sing some form of a pirate song.

"Yo ho ho . . ."

Wendy herself felt dreamy and full, though when she closed her eyes, she had the strangest visions: a finger pointing to the stars, blood, books, a veil blowing in the wind. The smell of rain. Instead, she chose to keep her eyes open, and she kept her eyes on Peter. She watched the way his gray tunic rode up around his arms, showing the tan muscles, his skin the color of ripe honey, the texture of a smooth pebble. She watched the way he laughed easily with the Generals and the way the Lost Boys looked at him with desperation for his approval, which was given often and generously. Peter saw her watching him and gave a friendly wave in her direction; Wendy flushed and raised her hand to wave back. A small, delicate hand wrapped around her own, and Wendy felt a rush of heat gather and pool in her palm, felt its power dripping through her fingers. She turned with a grimace. Tink was standing behind her, her hand wrapped tightly around Wendy's.

"May I sit?"

Wendy thought that she would rather keep company with a tiger but decided to be polite.

"Of course."

Tink shrugged and sat beside her. "Quite a sight, isn't it? All these boys, all this wine. It will be quite the night."

Wendy stared at Tink as the fairy easily twirled the tip of a wooden fork on her finger, watching the way subtle streaks of liquid gold rippled across her hair when she turned her head.

"Tell me something, Wendy Darling . . ."

Tink reached out and curled one of Wendy's hairs around her finger. Wendy watched as the stars in Tink's eyes exploded and shrank, Tink's cosmic beauty overpowering her own, even now, when Tink was dressed in rags, her wings hidden underneath the brown shroud. Glitter sprinkled the ground at Wendy's feet.

"Tell me, was it worth it?"

"Was what worth it?"

Tink nodded to the bottles.

Wendy shook her head. "No. No, it wasn't. It wasn't worth Kitoko and Darby's lives for this night of fun."

Then Tink shook her head. "That's where you are wrong." The fairy looked around at all the boys tumbling around them, shrieking and laughing, wine spilling everywhere. Two of them thundered past Tink, stopping to kiss her cheek. She patted them affectionately on their heads, and they scampered off into the tree.

"This life with these boys, without adventures, would crumble like old toast. Bored boys, in a great number, could be very harmful to our way of life. I believe where you come from, they call those wars."

Wendy stared straight ahead. "You play at war here. Death is death, and I'm not sure I see the difference. Wars are fought for freedom. Kitoko and Darby died for wine."

"Wars are also fought for treasure. Why am I even talking to you? You couldn't possibly understand," Tink snapped before closing her eyes. "Sorry. I am sharp edges." She took a minute before responding in a much friendlier voice.

"Men where you come from have died for much sillier reasons than wine, I'm sure. Besides, as long as Peter stayed safe, isn't that all that matters?" Her voice rose when she mentioned Peter's name, her eyes drifting up to the Generals' booth. "He is the sun and the moon and everything in between." She looked at him longingly before turning her eyes back to Wendy.

"I'm sorry for the way I've acted since you arrived. I'm sorry about earlier today." She twisted up her glittery pink lips. "I knew you still had flight. I would never . . ." She looked down, a hint of sadness trembling her features. "It can be quite lonely, you see, being the only one of your kind left in Neverland."

Wendy's fingers traced a small circle on the table, feeling the splintering wood beneath her palm.

"What happened to your kind?" Tink blinked back tears, looking surprised. Wendy waved her hand.

"I'm sorry, I shouldn't have asked—you don't have to tell me."

Tink regained control of her features and began scratching her head, pulling out leaves from her blond bun.

"I am not used to being asked."

Her voice dropped to a whisper so that the drunken boys dancing past them in a conga line wouldn't hear. She choked out her words, her hands splayed on the table.

"I was just a young child when the darkness came. I had been sleeping, nestled deep in the dreams and consciousness of our people. It crept down from the mountain, like a black fog. They welcomed it, but their welcome songs turned to screams." A sob rose in her throat. "Such a cacophony of sounds, the screaming and the singing. There were blasts of white heat, and a singeing black cold, like a burn. I remember the last sound I heard of my people, their voices lifting together before there was a ripping sound, and then there were wings, shredded wings, falling like snowflakes through the air. Bodies falling to the ground, hitting it hard, staying still. I ran and ran, and I hid in a grove of trees, burying myself in some muddy leaves. I was so young and so terrified. I could hear the darkness roaring after me, tearing the trees apart to find me. Our King, Qaralius of the Great Acorn, appeared above me to fight, attempting to draw the darkness away from the last of his race. He was . . . glorious."

Tink looked down at the ground.

"He fought valiantly, but I heard his cries as it ripped him apart."

Tink shook her head and turned away, grabbing a bottle of wine from the seat next to her. Wendy felt her eyes swell with tears for this pathetic girl who had seen so much death.

"Then Peter came. He came with his sword, and he fought the darkness, and he won. He found me, picked me up, and took me here. He saved my life. He was just a boy then, and we grew up together, bound forever, closer than siblings, closer than you could ever *dream*."

Wendy shivered at the word, imagining Peter and Tink, tangled up in each other, the hungry eyes of the jungle all around them. Tink turned back to Wendy, a smile upon her face.

"But things change. I hope you can forgive what I've done to you. I can be . . . jealous of Peter, but who am I to stand in his way? If his desire is for someone else, then I must give him what he wants."

She reached for Wendy's glass, sloshing out a dark red wine into her cup. Then she poured her own glass.

"We'll drink tonight, to new friends." Her eyes clouded over. "To Wendy-bird. May she fly forever."

Wendy grasped the cup, her eyes on Tink. An uncomfortable chill was spreading through her chest. She looked up, and Peter's eyes were on them both, a confused smile on his face. He leapt off the alcove and landed hard beside Tink.

"Tink. What are you doing here?"

She turned to him with a desperate smile.

"I'm doing what you asked," she whined. "I'm making friends with Wendy."

Peter gently ran his hand under her chin, turning her face up toward him. "Good. I'm glad. I would really like for you both to be friends."

Tink looked from side to side, nervously.

"Peter, you should go celebrate with the boys. We are just making lady talk here, nothing that would interest you."

Peter nodded before stretching out, making himself at home on the chair beside Wendy.

"I'll stay, I think. What exactly are you two talking about?"

Wendy looked over at Tink.

"Tink was just telling me about the day you saved her life."

Peter looked hard at Tink before taking Wendy's hand in his own. The fairy turned away, but not before Wendy saw a star-filled tear drop down her cheek. Wendy shook her hand loose from Peter, though she missed its warmth immediately.

"Actually, I was just thinking that I might head to bed for the night. It's been a very long—" She was interrupted when a Lost Boy tumbled across her lap in a misguided attempt at a hug. It was Thomas, his dirty blond curls draping over her legs. Michael followed behind him. Peter looked annoyed.

"Boys, get off her."

Wendy helped Thomas to his feet. He giggled and with a blush held his hands behind his back.

"Michael and I have something for you!"

Wendy turned her head and smiled.

"Oh? It's not a lizard, is it? Because I already got one of those tonight."

Thomas shook his head.

"Nope. Here!" He produced a stunning flower, a huge lavender bloom, adorned with spiky yellow fringe on the tips of its fluttery petals. The petals opened and closed of their own accord, teasingly showing a glimpse of a deep scarlet center.

"Oh, boys, it's beautiful!"

Thomas reached over her. "It needs a drink!"

Before Wendy could stop him, Thomas plopped the flower into her wine glass.

"Thomas! That's not the same as water." At their disappointed faces, she shrugged. "I suppose it's fine."

She leaned over and gave Thomas a peck on the cheek. He blushed and moved aside. Wendy went to give Michael a kiss as well, and he pulled away from her.

"Yuck, Wendy, I'm too big for that now!"

Wendy felt a tiny pang in her heart at his words but ruffled his hair. Then, in a swirl of dust and feet, the boys were gone. Wendy turned back to Peter and Tink, hoping that the tension between them had dissipated, but instead she found Peter, wide-eyed and shocked, staring at the table. She had never seen true shock play across his face and was taken aback by how young he looked in that moment, just like a little boy. He opened his mouth and, in a voice that seemed to cut through all of Pan Island, bellowed.

"TINK!!!"

Tink leaned in quickly toward Wendy, her mouth trembling in fear.

"Pull the veil," she whispered.

"What?" Wendy asked, bewildered, but the fairy was already moving. In the blink of an eye, Tink was rushing toward the open doorway of the Table. She pulled back the brown shroud from her shoulders as she ran, and Wendy watched in awe as with each step, each foot of her wings unfurled behind her, translucent webbing pulsing with life, sparking silver dust raining down from the tips. Then a blast of heat shot through the room, and Tink was gone, hurtling herself off the platform into the open air. Peter thundered down right behind her, and before they disappeared from sight, Wendy saw him catch her heel, angrily cursing her name. Then they were both gone, lost to the night. Wendy blinked.

"Peter?"

She turned at the sudden silence. The Table was silent, all the Lost Boys staring at her with somber expressions.

"What . . ."

She raised her eyes and looked up toward the Generals. John was staring down at her, his face flushed with anger. With a raised eyebrow, he gestured to the table in front of her. Wendy turned her head. The flower that Thomas had given her was withered and black, its inky petals scattered below where it sat perched in Wendy's wine glass. A faint smell of sulfur filled the air, and Wendy watched in horror as the flower curled in on itself, shuddered, and then disintegrated into black soot. The poison had done its job. Wendy grabbed at her throat. Michael tugged her hand.

"Wendy, you didn't drink that, did you?" Her throat constricted at the thought, and suddenly she was light-headed.

"No, no, Michael, I didn't drink it."

Michael reached for the cup to peer inside of it.

"Stop!"

Abbott pushed past him and grabbed the cup with some loose leaves, careful not to touch the base, which was beginning to leak.

"I'll get rid of this." He looked over at Wendy, his lanky build towering over her. "Go back to your hut." Then he shook his head and made a disgusted sound. "Women."

Chapter Eighteen

Two hours passed, and Wendy was hanging her feet off the edge of her balcony when Peter came for her. Trying to ignore the beginnings of a headache that seemed to emanate out from the middle of her brain, she kicked her feet out over the drop from her hut, watching a black and white bird flit about the leaves below, catching large ants and gargling them down its enormous throat. Wendy noticed a shape swimming up out of the dark leaves below, becoming clearer and clearer, flying with impressive precision and speed. Peter. She smiled.

He flew up past her feet, landing behind her in a whoosh of air that sent her white nightgown swirling around her. He yanked her to her feet. Wendy crossed her arms in front of her chest and peered at him. "Tink?" Peter shook his head. "She's fine. She's . . ." He shook his head again and reached for her hand. "Honestly, the last thing I want to talk about tonight is Tink—is that all right? I'm sorry for what she did to you, and I swear on my life that nothing like this will ever happen again. I promise. I'm so angry at her." He leaned in and pushed his nose up against her hair, clutching her desperately. "I can't imagine anything happening to you."

Wendy smiled shyly, loving the feel of his warm breath on her face. "Well then, you can thank Thomas later. He saved my life by giving me that flower." *She almost killed me.* The thought kept bouncing around her head.

"I will. I'll make Thomas a General for it."

"Well, you don't have to go that far."

They both laughed nervously. Peter pulled away from her, and it was as if she knew what he was going to say before he said it. "Wendy, will you come somewhere with me tonight?"

Without a word, she put her hand into his. His green eyes stared at her, unabashedly worshipful. Wendy felt the blush rising up her cheeks, but something else rose with it—a strange twinge of betrayal, a tiny needle in her heart, and the quickest of sharp regret. What was wrong with her? There probably wasn't a girl in the world who wouldn't be burning alive with the way he looked at her now. Peter took her hand and spun her around and then covered her eyes with a blindfold. "Do you trust me?" There it was again, the pinprick of guilt in her chest, but when she felt the brush of his lips on her cheek, she could do nothing but nod.

Then there was the wind on her face, and she knew they were flying, lifting up and out of her hut and into Pan Island's canopy of branches. Seconds passed, and then the air was clean and warm, and she knew that they had left the branches of Pan Island and were now flying up and above the island, heading to . . . somewhere. She laid her head on Peter's shoulder and felt the whipping air on her cheeks, the strong muscles of his arms that held her, content and excited.

They flew for a few minutes before she felt Peter begin his descent on the other side of the island. His flight slowed carefully, and she felt the sudden lack of wind on her skin, only the radiating heat of his hand around her waist. They landed on a hard floor that bucked and swayed underneath her feet. Wendy grinned underneath her blindfold as her feet struggled with the pitch of the ground.

"Peter, where are we? I can't stand straight." She giggled

foolishly. Almost drinking poison had made her giddy and reck-less, and Peter was having that same effect on her.

The ground rocked beneath her again, and she finally pulled back her blindfold and gasped. At first she wasn't sure where she was, or what she was in. Tall panes of green-blue sea glass surrounded her on every side, square vertical panes that ran from floor to ceiling. The glass was etched with subtle lines and patterns—squares, crescents, and arrows. She brushed her fingers across the glass, feeling the raised design like hard bubbles underneath her fingers. Her mouth fell open at the beauty of the craftsmanship. She raised her head. The tall single panes of dark teal glass then tilted inward on an iron bar and ran up toward a pointed ceiling. Where the ceiling came to a point, the glass on every singular pane ended at different lengths, their smooth tips capped off by iron. The tip of the ceiling was a deliberate pattern that opened up to the sky above—a star made to gaze at the beauty of the stars, and large enough to fly through. So that's how they had come in. There was a small door in one of the glass panes, marked only by a small black latch and otherwise invis-ible. After all this time in round huts, being inside of a physical structure was incredible, and Wendy found that she had missed hard architectural lines. She spun around, taking it all in. It was the most beautiful place she had ever been.

"Why, Peter . . . it's . . . it's . . . we're inside of . . . a lantern?"

He put his hands on his hips and laughed. "That it is! You're sharp, Wendy. This is a fairy lantern, one of the last, and the only one on Pan Island."

The ground moved slightly underneath her again, and she understood instantly: the lantern was hanging. Cautiously she crawled on her knees and pushed opened the latch on the door, letting it swing open in the wind. She poked her head out, the wind whipping her hair in all directions. Below her was only sea. Craning her neck, she looked up and saw that the lantern was attached on an outstretched branch that had curled itself out over the water, the farthest eastern point of Pan Island. The lantern gave another rock, and Wendy pulled the door shut again, not wanting to fall into the sea, so far below. She looked up again, taking in the stars that shone through the star-shaped portal.

"Peter." She turned, suddenly feeling very shy. "This is lovely, but we probably shouldn't be here so late." She gulped and added, "Alone."

Peter tucked a piece of her hair, curling from the humidity, behind her ear. "Why wouldn't we want that? You are so innocent and good, Wendy. It's made it so hard to be near you—I am drawn to you, you must know."

Wendy blushed. "I do know. I . . . feel similar." She paused. "But I don't feel like I know anything about you. I want to *know you*, Peter." She touched a hand gently to his face before he turned away. "What question do you want to know? Ask me anything." He seemed unsure of himself in this moment, disarmed by curiosity.

Wendy thought for a moment. "Where did you come from? When did you get to Neverland. HOW did you get to Neverland?"

Peter laughed. "That's three questions." He frowned quickly. "It was so long ago, I hardly remember myself. The details are spotty."

Wendy smiled reassuringly at him. "I'll take anything. I feel you know everything about us, and yet, we know nothing about you."

He took a deep breath and looked up at the pointed ceiling. "I grew up on a farm in Wick. Wick was in Scotland."

Scotland. Wendy tried to remember if that was near the place she had lived, which was . . . which was . . .

" I was the youngest of seven children. We were very poor. A family like you Darlings would have scoffed at us, or perhaps taken pity on us. There was never enough to eat, only herring and bread on the good days. We would sometimes play at Vikings, or Norse Gods, but there was always the fear that tomorrow would bring an empty plate, and so we fished, all day, every day. No time for play, or dreaming, just an endless stretch of nothing and backbreaking work." His voice grew angry with emotion, his eyes flashing navy. "There was nothing, nothing on that godforsaken island, just endless green and craggy rocks, a cold, angry sea, and bitter winters! My family lived in the long shadow of Old Man Wick, the castle on the sea, our Lord of the Manor, and we his pitiful serfs and slaves! The landowner was cruel, taxing us to death, helping himself to all we had, even though he had everything. And though we hated him, we dreamt of living there, in Old Man Wick, buried amongst such riches, such food, such wealth!

"My father, a selfish coward, drank himself to death when I was very young. I barely remember him, a useless waste of expanding flesh, but I remember seeing him beat my older siblings, and in turn, they beat on me. My mother had no interest in being a mother. When she could bother to feed us, she would slap down some food, remind us of what she could have been if it hadn't been for us wretches, and leave, a new baby always on her hip, one that she would later resent and stave. It was a paltry existence, but sometimes late at night I would untangle myself from my brothers and sisters and sneak out of our tiny cottage of mud and rock, just to gaze up at the stars, so bright there at the edge of the world. I knew I was bound for something different. Something better. I was meant to rule the stars, not gaze at them from under our poverty. Every night for years, I watched the sky, asking whoever was up there for something more."

He took a deep breath and turned away from Wendy so she could not see his face. "I was thirteen years old when my older brother pushed me into the River Wick, after I had the gall to suggest keeping the fish I had just caught."

"Oh, Peter." Wendy's eyes filled with tears.

"It had already been a strange night. The sea next to our town was violent and angry, and a full harvest moon rose over Wick, its orange light bathing the town red. I fell into the river and was pulled under. My body was dragged down deep, deep into a crag that lay under the river, deeper than a river should be. It was bottomless, like the ocean. I sank down, lower and lower, as the water grew dark around me. I passed deep into what seemed like an endless current, and then I remember seeing blue and lavender lights swirling under the water, the same lights you passed through when we came here through the portal. The next thing I knew I was swimming upward, and I came out of the sea just beyond the beach of Pan Island. I swam to shore, instantly fell asleep, and I woke a day later to a beautiful Neverland morning—and quite a bad sunburn!"

Wendy giggled. Peter turned and faced her. "I've never looked back. I am not that child, and that was never my life. I never speak of it, because it has no relevance to who I am now." Peter looked down at her, his emerald eyes shining as he took in her face. "Everything I have ever wanted is here. Especially now."

Wendy looked at the darkening green walls of glass; the directness of Peter's gaze made her uneasy. "Thank you for telling me."

Peter flew to the top of the lantern and poked his head out through the open star. "Ooooh. It's starting." He flew down and stood beside her, shyly taking her hand. "Wendy, I wanted to take you here to show you something extraordinary. Something you would never see in that other world. Darling, you haven't seen anything yet of Neverland. I will show you every treasure, every secret pocket of this land. There are so many beautiful things here."

He reached out and brushed her cheek with the edge of his finger. "Such beauty. Now, sit . . . here." He settled Wendy down on a stack of blankets that was piled on the floor. "Just wait. And while we wait . . ."

He reached deep into the pocket of his long coat, patterned with autumn leaves and cobwebs, and his hand emerged holding an exquisite set of pan pipes, etched with golden vines. With a coy smile, he began playing a melody that seemed to weave its way right through her skin—low and lilting and penetrating, the music was a soft caress of notes that she felt in every part of her. The strange trill of the pipes, like reeds weeping in rain, filled the lantern up with its forlorn sound. She felt as if she were floating above herself. Her headache subsided, and any thoughts of doubt or guilt disappeared into the wholeness of the music, Peter rendering her into nothingness with just his gaze.

As Peter continued playing, the room filled with light. Wendy gasped as the sea-glass floor of the lantern lit up with a thousand tiny stars. The light from below projected around the glass, and she was suddenly swimming in fragments of blue-green light, each one the shape of a tiny star. She reached up her hand and let the lights play over her splayed fingers. "What magic . . ."

Peter stopped playing and laughed. "It's not magic. Look." Wendy opened the tiny door and looked out over the ocean. Below the lantern, for perhaps just the length and width of a mile, the sea glowed with stars. Peter leaned over her, his arm around her waist. "They are starfish, and this time of year they illuminate their limbs in hopes of attracting a mate. It happens every night around this time for a couple of weeks; then once they have found their mates, they disappear back into the sea, back into the night."

The ocean surface swayed over the starfish, but their light pulsed on, steady and bright, their stars hopeful of the perfect mate, their light beaming up through the waves that battered around them. Wendy raised her eyes to Peter, his eyes looking out over the water, so happy and so lovely, and it was then that she knew she would lose herself here, to him, to this place. He looked back at her.

"Wendy . . ." He clasped her against him, and then they were floating up into the lantern, the light of a thousand stars all around them, the green glass around them dancing with reflections.

Peter's face was shadowed by the light as he bent to kiss her.

Wendy felt a twinge of guilt sneaking its way back into her heart, but she chose to ignore it this time, and without thinking, she threw herself into his arms and pressed her lips against his with abandon, so unlike her, so brave. Their lips were salty with the ocean air, the warmth of his mouth and tongue brushing over her own, driving her mad. Wendy gasped with desire, and Peter pressed against her again, harder this time, his arms crushing around her waist, his mouth on her own.

The fire inside of her felt like it would consume them both, and yet she wasn't able to keep the nagging guilt down. It pressed harder and harder against her heart as she pushed herself further and further into Peter. Peter was kissing her hair, her neck, his hands roaming up and down her sides, Wendy dizzy as she lost herself in his mouth. They were circling slowly in the empty room now, the room glowing with the light of a thousand stars, his boyish face so beautiful that she could hardly breathe. She couldn't breathe. The guilt was so present now that it was practically thumping against her chest, bursting, crying to be let out. She couldn't breathe.

"Peter," she cried. "Peter! I'm sorry, this is improper; we must slow down."

"Never," Peter mumbled, wrapping her waist in his arms and diving back in for another kiss, drinking in everything about her. He was like a current—just when she got her feet underneath her, he pulled again and she was lost, drifting, Peter encompassing every breath. Now he was pulling them downward in the lantern, toward the blankets that sat on the ground, and Wendy put a cautionary hand up against him, trying at once to control her own passion and understand why she was suddenly so nauseated and unhappy.

As Peter continued kissing her, a face appeared in her mind, hazy, particles of a face, discombobulated. Blue eyes. A strong mouth. Brown hair, straight and dripping with rain. Wendy's teeth clamped shut and she pushed Peter back, her body mourning the loss of his heat, his embrace. She realized in that second that he was away from her that if she let herself go with him, she would never be able to reclaim her innocence. Not ever.

"Peter, please, slow down. Something is happening to me . . . my mind . . . I think there is . . ." Peter pulled her roughly down onto his lap and kissed her hard again. "Ignore it. It's probably the weather," he whispered frantically, tugging at her dress.

Wendy was flustered and embarrassed, unsure what to do, trying to keep her passion at bay, trying to piece together the puzzle that was tearing her apart. Her heart and mind wanted one thing, her body another. She felt ripped to shreds, as if she could howl at the moon and curl up in a ball, all at once.

"No, please, stop. Peter, I'm not ready. Peter . . ."

"Shhhh . . ." he pressed his lips against hers roughly. Her fingers trailed down his neck as she kissed him harder, harder, tumbling down into Peter Pan, feeling the light of the starfish pulsing from somewhere inside her. Her fingers found his collarbone, the place where his muscles became chest. His skin was smooth and clean under her fingertips, so warm and welcoming. Wendy leaned back from him, breathless.

"Your scar?"

Peter pulled back from her, his eyes narrowed. "What?"

"Your scar? From Hook? Where is it?" She gently ran her fingertips over his collarbone. "It was your shoulder, right?"

Peter pulled his collar back angrily. "Don't worry about it, Wendy." Then, with a growl, he buried himself in her neck and was kissing her harder and harder.

Something inside of Wendy broke open, gushing forward like a broken dam, the pressing on her chest becoming unbearable and painful. She didn't know what the word meant, or who it was, but she could only hear one word, pounding against the inside of her head: *Booth. Booth.* The word rushed through her veins, calming the fire that was consuming her judgment. *Booth.*

The word echoed in her mind, again and again. She was outside herself, inside the word; it was all that mattered. *Booth.* "Peter, no."

Peter pulled back, flushed and annoyed. "What? What is wrong with you?"

Wendy pushed herself back from him and stood. "I'm sorry, Peter, no. I can't do this. I'm so sorry."

"Whatever do you mean?"

Wendy backed away from him. "I should have never let it get this far. I'm sorry, Peter. I didn't mean to lead you astray."

Peter's face seemed to change from disappointment to anger. His eyes clouded over with navy, but when he blinked, they were green again. The green she had adored so much, before . . . before the word came. *Booth.* Wendy needed to be alone. Her stomach was churning, and her mind was breaking apart. She would be mortified if she got sick in front of him. Peter's face began to crumple, much to Wendy's horror.

"But, Wendy! Why?"

She picked up her shoe that had slipped off during their kiss. "Peter, please take me back. I'm not feeling very well."

He angrily slammed his foot against the glass floor of the lantern, which gave an unhappy shudder, and his voice rose to a desperate shout. "But I love you! I love you, Wendy."

Wendy looked down, unsure of what to say. "I'm sorry, Peter. I can't explain it. I just can't be with you—not like that. Perhaps for now we can just be . . . friends." She could see immediately that it was not the right thing to say.

"A friend?" Peter repeated with a dead voice. "A friend. I see. Not because I have plenty of friends already." He turned away from her, his shoulders shaking in anger as he buttoned the top button of his shirt.

"Peter, please. I can't explain it."

He whirled on her. "YOU'RE MINE, AND SO YOU NEED TO TRY!" he screamed at the top of his lungs. Then he was silent again, but Wendy had stepped back, terrified. "I'm sorry. That was . . . not right to yell at you like that. I'll take you back."

As if there had been an unspoken agreement under the depths of the sea, the starfish below them all gave a shudder and then went dark. The lantern swayed in the wind. Wendy's pulse quickened, and she suddenly felt very afraid, unsure of why her mind was telling her to flee. Her eyes couldn't adjust to the lack of light, and Peter's voice was steady and firm in the darkness, just over her shoulder, closer than he should be, his hand tracing over her hip.

"At least tell me why, Wendy Darling. Why can't you love me?"

Wendy reached out for him, to comfort him, but her hand only swept darkness. "I think there might be someone else. I can't explain it, but I know it. My heart knows it. My love is spoken for. I didn't . . ." She cleared her throat. "I didn't remember before. I don't really remember now, but I . . . I need to figure things out before anything else happens. Can you understand?" Her breath was calming now; all she felt was the desperate need to be alone. "I just need some time." Her eyes searched for Peter in the dark, feeling the enchantment of him return. She shook her head. No. *Booth.*

Peter turned away from her and wiped his eyes. When he turned back, his voice was cool and collected. "Whatever you desire, Wendy Darling. I can give you time." Without feeling, he grabbed her hand, and they flew up and out of the lantern. As she looked back, she saw a flutter of white wings enter the lantern from above and heard an anguished cry rise up from inside. She turned to Peter with a horrified gasp.

"Is that where Tink lives? We were in Tink's house?"

Peter gave an angry shrug. "So? Tink doesn't own Pan Island."

The rest of the flight back to her hut was spent in awkward silence. She could feel an angry heat blazing through Peter's hand. He deposited her roughly inside her doorway and turned to go. With his back to her, he spoke slow, careful words: "I'll wait for you, Wendy Darling. I can be patient for your heart. I can be. I will be."

Wendy dropped her eyes to the floor and gently placed her hand on his back. His body shuddered at her touch. "Peter. I don't know what to say. I'm sorry."

He turned around, his eyes clouding darkest navy. "Say that you will love me. Say it. Say that you're mine."

Wendy shook her head. "I can't. Not right now." Suddenly she was wracked with a violent lurch in her stomach. She fell to her knees, trying her best to not lose her supper. "Peter . . ." When she looked up, he was gone, and her head split wide open.

The pain in her head was overcoming her senses now, and patches of blackness swirled in her mind. She blinked. She was in a nursery. No, she was on Pan Island. There was a book, a book open to a letter. She saw Peter's hand stretching toward her. Blood on the rock. She shook her head. What was happening? Was she losing her mind? Was she dying? She fought to focus, struggling to stay conscious.

Wendy had barely made it inside the door when there was a physical pull from inside her skin, as if her center of gravity had shifted. Wendy waited a moment to see if the pain in her head subsided. There was a pause, and she raised her hands to push on her temples. Oh, Lord, was it gone? Then the blinding pain returned, roaring this time, pressing on her brain like someone was smothering her skull. With a gasp, she fell to her knees as the pain ricocheted around her head and behind her eyes. She crawled, hand over hand toward her hammock, sweat dripping off her forehead. Wendy wretched and wretched again as her head felt as if it were being torn in two. She clasped her hands over her ears and screamed, a funny thought bursting through the pain that this was all so improper. If Peter saw her now, what would he think? Tears dripped down her cheeks as she pulled herself along the floor. If she could just make it to the hammock, if she could just sleep forever, the pain would go away. If this was death, then it would be a release, a relief, from the pain that was setting her skull ablaze. Her white hand clutched at the floor as the pain overtook her, her fingernails making grooves in the wood as splinters shredded her fingertips.

She didn't make it to the hammock. The images cascaded around her, drowning her mind. A teddy bear. A man pointing at the stars. Tea on a tray. A soft blanket wrapped around her shoulders. A dog's silky fur. A woman embracing her. The chant of prayers and the smell of incense. Wendy rolled onto her back and surrendered to whatever blackness was calling her, sweat dripping down the sides of her face. *Goodnight, goodnight.* She hurtled herself toward unconsciousness.

When she woke up, it was the middle of the night, and Pan Island was still. Her mind was foggy. Somehow she was on the other side of the room, and her clothing was drenched through with sweat. Wendy rolled over, pushing herself off the ground and sitting up on her knees. Her hands delicately traced her forehead. The pain was gone. What had it been?

Staggering like a drunk, she made her way to the door and looked out at Pan Island. The remnants of a pink sunset still striped across the sky, the rosy light giving the stars a pastel playground. A cool breeze was whipping through the island, rustling the leaves around her hut, bringing the scent of the hibiscus flowers into her nostrils. Below, she could see the line of the beach that marked each end of Pan Island.

She saw something wink out of the corner of her eye, and Wendy turned her head. It was the lotus flower, still spinning in the air over the water, illuminated with light, honoring Kitoko and Darby in its soft white glow. It was beautiful, and Wendy closed her eyes, hoping to honor the fallen Lost Boys, but instead seeing Kitoko's very dead, much-opened throat. She saw it all again. The look of fear on his face as he looked at Peter. The way the pirate had scowled in grim determination, not looking entirely pleased as he pulled his knife through the tendons of Kitoko's neck. The blood. So much blood.

Her vision blurred, and Wendy braced herself for another onslaught of the pain that had ripped her brain in half, but none came. She took a breath, and the air around her changed. She blinked twice and opened her eyes. It was then that she realized that she was still dreaming—she looked down and saw herself lying on the floor of the hut, her hands clutched around her head.

Wendy turned away, and as she did, a filmy gray veil fell over her sight. The veil fluttered in the Neverland breeze, transparent, and yet she couldn't see behind it. *Pull the veil.* Wendy reached out her hand, her fingers gently parting the veil, aware somewhere inside of her that this was certainly happening in her mind. Her pointer finger parted the veil ever so softly, and behind it she felt a crisp, damp air and a woolen glove on her hand. She closed her eyes. The smell coming through the parted slit of the veil consumed her, the smell of wet cobblestones, Earl Grey tea, and musty books. It smelled familiar, like the smell of home.

Wendy took one step closer, and the curtain blew across her face, its silky gossamer fabric brushing her cheeks and hairline, the caress of a lover. She pulled her hand back out of the fold and was struck by a sudden emptiness. Then she understood. *Something was waiting for her on the other side. Love. Wet cobblestones.* She reached out her hands, and the images began flooding her mind, this time no threat, this time like coming home, like leaping into a familiar lake. The memories came, one by one. Hands on a book, hands on a glove, hands held by another, hands reaching for the stars. Wendy instantly understood. The choice was hers to make, but there really was no choice. Wendy took a deep breath, and with both hands, she pulled the veil down forcefully.

The memories fell upon her like a crumpling building, violent, sudden, and overwhelming. She saw her mother's eyes looking down at her in her bed, as Wendy cried over a bloodied knee. She saw her father's study, his kind blue eyes as he picked up an astronomy book, settling his girl child in his lap. She saw Michael as a baby, so tiny in her arms, his blue eyes watching her as she sang softly to him, Nana sitting protectively at Wendy's feet. She saw herself passing John a bowl of soup when he was sick with fever, wiping his forehead as her mother prayed at the window. She saw the acolytes carrying the candles at Mass, her father's hand strong on her shoulder as he repeated lengthy prayers with annoyance.

Every single memory returned to her. The letter tucked in the book. John's face, filled with anger as they fought. Michael curling against her as she slept. The nursery window melting, the arrival of Peter. Wendy fell to her knees, taking the veil with her. Her memories continued to fall around her. When they had all come, she knelt down, waiting for the memory of him, him.

Finally, the bookseller's son came. Booth. His memory was the sweetest, a painful cut across her heart, a delicious guilt that was both wonderful and devastating. *Booth.* Booth, the name that had rested on her lips when she slept, the face that had haunted her dreams here on Pan Island. Wendy raised her hand and traced through the air as she remembered the strong line of his cheekbones, his bright blue eyes that looked out with such kindness, such intelligence. She remembered how he had kissed her, his breath quaking as it washed over her lips. She remembered the way he had cautiously pulled the glove off her hand. Oh, Booth. "Be brave, Wendy." He had told her to be brave, and she had betrayed him.

Wendy buried her head in her hands and began sobbing. What had she done? Why had she forgotten who she was? Had she been responsible for this? She frantically wiped the tears from her eyes. She had forgotten her parents. The Darlings. Oh God, her parents. Did they know that their children were gone? Were they holding each other right now, fearing the worst? Had she broken her parents' hearts? She had a vision of them kneeling at the nursery window, her mother looking at the ground below that was suddenly so tempting, her father suspiciously eyeing the stars.

Peter had said that time was different in London than it was in Neverland, that her parents would never even know that they had gone. Was he lying? She prayed that he wasn't and that some-where, past the morning stars, her parents were still laughing at the party, her father swirling his brandy glass, her mother talking much too loud. Her lips clenched at the memory of them, of the love that rose up inside of her. The hollow of her heart that she had ignored since she arrived here was full, brimming over with happy memories, with love for her parents, with love for Booth.

Wendy pulled her arms back from the veil. No. That wasn't right. She felt the wood under her fingers. She was still lying on the floor. There was no veil in her hands. It had all been in her mind. But Wendy remembered. Every moment of her life, she remembered. She was Wendy Darling of No. 14 Kensington Park Gardens, and she was whole again.

And they needed to go home.

CHAPTER NINETEEN

THE NEXT MORNING, Wendy stayed quietly in her room, rocking silently in the hammock, slowly drinking in all of her memories, precious jewels, each one of them treasured and tucked away. She would never lose them again. She turned over as the hammock swayed underneath her and watched the shadows play across the room.

Wendy couldn't even remember when she had started forgetting. Had it been right when they had left London? Was it when she saw Neverland for the first time? Had Peter known that she couldn't remember? He must have. Tink had known Wendy was forgetting, had known about the veil. Wendy considered, not for the first time that morning, that maybe her memory loss was connected to Peter's presence. When he was near her, she was rendered into blind passion, disarmed by his charm. He made her forget who she was.

Wendy frowned as she sat up, resting her forehead on her knees. Her feelings for Peter were complicated, complicated even more now that she remembered Booth. Had she led Peter on? Perhaps. She experienced overwhelming guilt when she remembered how she had felt when they had kissed in the mist and then again in the lantern. It had felt so right at the moment, and yet, she knew that Booth's kiss was right in a different way. Booth's kiss was earned—somehow that made it more real.

Even now, though her heart was nestling happily into the memory of Booth, she still felt a pull toward Peter, toward his magnetic smile. Peter made her skin flush, made her heart hammer, but what was he expecting would happen? That she would live here on Pan Island with him forever? No, that couldn't happen. Wendy shook her head and then remembered the rush of fear that she had felt with Peter last night in the lantern. He hadn't seemed entirely in control when he had looked at her, in the way he had clutched at her so desperately—as if he were a drowning man and she were the shore—how quickly his hand had inched up her skirt. No, they couldn't stay here. They had to go home. Leaving this magical island of delights and adventure would be hard, but the Darlings belonged in London, with their parents. With Booth.

Wendy climbed out of the hammock, anxiously tying her hair back in a ponytail before washing her face in the basin. She ravenously consumed the bread and cheese that had been left out for her, batting away a few flies from the food beforehand, something she would have never dreamed of doing a few weeks ago. *How long had they been here in Neverland anyway? Weeks? Days?* The time here seemed to slip away, falling down into some rabbit hole where hours, days, and years blended together.

After she had eaten her fill and then some, Wendy slipped on her tiny black slippers (given to her as a Christmas present from her mother, wrapped in a mink shawl that was still hanging in the nursery closet—each memory was now a perfect little gift to unwrap) and then made her way down the tree, easily slipping down the trunk like she had been born on Pan Island. The island was almost empty, with all the Lost Boys down at the beach, fishing and playing, walking off their headaches from the night before. As she wandered through the branches of Centermost, picking up stray bottles here and there and putting them into a cloth bag—*Boys! So messy!*—she felt a pang of sadness at the thought of leaving Pan Island. Perhaps they could return? Maybe every year to visit Peter and the boys, to have a little adventure?

Then she remembered Kitoko's throat and the very real consequences of adventure. She shook her head. No, she could not let the boys return. And Peter . . . the effect he had on her was too potent, like a drug. No, there could be no returning to this magical place.

She paused to push some branches aside and to look out at the turquoise sea beneath her, the comforting sound of its waves pulsing against the island, lulling her senses. Far on the horizon, she could make out the main island, the white Teeth rising aggressively up out of the turquoise waters. Wendy closed her eyes. She would miss this island of enchantment, and the feeling that anything could happen here. But then she saw her mother's eyes filled with tears, and suddenly the water wasn't so blue. With a sad smile, she stepped back, letting the leaves fall in front of her eyes.

Each soft pad of her steps filled her heart with dread as she made her way down to the beach. Lost Boys shrieked when they saw her emerge from the tree. "Wendy, watch this!" "Wendy, look at this shell!" As she made her way closer to the beach, she stopped to observe a small circle of boys sharpening sticks in the sand.

"What are you doing?" Wendy asked a boy named Little Sun, who batted his long black eyelashes at her under a tangle of thick black hair.

"Preparing."

"For what?"

"For war on the pirates." He lifted up a spear that was larger than he was. "I'm going to shove this through Hook's eye!"

Wendy raised her eyebrows before moving on. A dozen Lost Boys were splashing and laughing in the ocean, spraying each other with conch shells. John was one of them, and Wendy watched in fascination as her brother tackled another boy into the water and they both emerged sputtering and laughing, splashing each other in the salty waves. John leaned his head back and looked at the sky, spitting the ocean water up into the air as his brown curls floated around his face. The other boys began singing a joyful tune, and John joined in for a few seconds, surprising Wendy with his perfect pitch. With a grin, he put his feet down and shook the sand out of his hair before running to the shore.

He looked so *free* there, laughing with the boys in a way that she had never seen him laugh before. Wendy's chest seemed to collapse on itself, and she was filled with a sudden dread. He looked up and saw her, the joy falling from his face. Wendy motioned to him, and he begrudgingly made his way over to her.

"What?"

"I need to speak with you. It's not okay to be rude, John."

He shrugged. "We can speak here. What do you need?"

"No. We cannot speak here."

"Then I'm not going."

Wendy pounced on him. "Oh, John, for heaven's sake. Stop acting like a pouty child. Could you please just come with me?"

He sighed, as if Wendy was putting him out. "All right. Where's Michael?"

Wendy looked over John's shoulder. Michael and Thomas were skipping stones on the beach, their gray pebbles flitting out into the ocean as if they had wings. Wendy watched as an older Lost Boy picked up Michael and put him on his shoulders and Michael began happily drumming on the boy's head. She turned back to John. "He'll be fine. Please, John, don't put up a fight, don't argue, just come with me."

John shrugged. "Fine. I know someplace we can go."

Using the pulleys and ropes, they lifted themselves off the beach on the cliff side, climbing up until they were at the base of the great tree. John motioned for her to follow him, and soon they were twisting through thick tree branches, climbing over and under the maze of gigantic roots that supported Pan

Island. Wendy had never been to this part of Pan Island before. Hammocks were everywhere, brushing her hair as she walked past them, their ribbons trailing to the ground, a labyrinth of colors.

"There are so many."

"This is where the Pips sleep," John muttered. "I'm surprised that Peter hasn't showed you this. He's always going on about taking you visiting around Neverland."

"Well, he hasn't. I'm sure he plans to."

John ducked under some huge tropical leaves, their offshoots easily the size of a carriage horse, trailed by rubbery purple vines that dragged behind him as he made his way through a green tunnel of foliage. He leapt down a cascading stairway of rocks as Wendy took her time making her way down their rickety turns. At the bottom was a small circular clearing. A thicket ringed the borders, hung with the dirty tunics of boys, their bright shirts and pants hanging from every exposed thorn. In the center of the clearing, a small pool of turquoise water bubbled and steamed.

"Laundry," said John with a jerk of his head. Wendy recognized her blue dress, set apart from the boys' clothes, blowing faintly in the wind. It was somehow mortifying to see it hanging there for all to see, and she ripped it down, tucking it under her arm.

John leapt up on a thick branch and walked down its wide length. "Here, it's just up this way." He ducked behind a patch of dead branches, not bothering to leave them pulled back for Wendy. They whipped back and caught her squarely in the face.

"John!" But he was gone. Wendy frowned at his rapidly diminishing manners and pushed out to the opening. It was a small ledge, no more than six feet across, made of branches and thatched felt that looked out onto the east side of Pan Island. Below them stretched miles of ocean, the turquoise waves rising, their crests glinting like pearls in the sunlight. Above them, the huts of Pan Island hovered, their squat bottoms a black spot in the tree above.

"I come here to think. Peter showed it to me. It's his own special spot, but he lets me come here too." John turned to her. "What is it that you need so urgently to talk about?"

"John." Wendy reached out her hand and gently took his in her own. John looked repulsed. "John, listen to me. We need to go home."

He jerked his hand away. "Home? Home? Is this what you've come to ask me? I should have known as much."

Wendy kept her voice steady. "John, what do you remember about our life before we came to Neverland?"

John's eyes scrunched together. "I remember enough to know that this is where we belong."

"Please, be specific. What do you remember?"

John brushed his hair out of his eyes with a flourish, the same way that Peter did. "I remember we had parents. And we lived in a . . . city?" He shrugged. "All that matters is that I remember that we are much better off here than we were there."

"No, John, that's wrong. We are not better off here. Our parents, George and Mary Darling, they miss us. They might think we are dead! Doesn't that concern you? Our father might think you are dead, John! And Michael . . ." She gestured behind them to the single, filthy tub that cleansed hundreds of boys. "Michael can't grow up here, living like a wild animal! Do you really think that this is the best place for him?"

John turned away from her, his eyes on the sea. "I knew you wouldn't understand it here. I knew the minute we arrived, when you looked out at the Lost Boys with such horror, that one day you would make us leave. They don't fit into your pretty world. You don't belong here, but Michael and I do."

Wendy tried to calm her voice so that she wasn't yelling. John wouldn't respond to her growing desperation. "John, I love it here. There is no prettier place than Neverland. But John, boys die here. Darby—and Kitoko died. I watched his blood spill on the rock." Her voice caught in her throat, unable to control the sob shaking up it. She saw it again. "You weren't there; you don't know how horrible it was."

John spun on her, and Wendy was caught off guard by the fact that he was almost as tall as she was. "I do know. I do know you're a girl and you don't understand. There are risks to adventure. This is war . . ."

"This isn't war!" she erupted. "This is a game! Don't you see?"

John's hazel eyes narrowed. "And Peter? Are you ready to leave Peter?"

Wendy was silent as she considered the question. No. No, she didn't want to leave Peter. In fact, at the sound of his name, her skin flushed. When she remembered their kiss in the mist, she wanted to stay. And yet . . . Booth. A feeling pressed on her chest, an uncomfortable shifting. She wanted Peter, but not in the same way that she needed Booth.

The sea crashed underneath them, showering their shins with a salty spray. The bright Neverland sun bore down, rays of golden light washing over them, turning even an argument between siblings into a beautiful moment. John gestured to the scene in front of them. "How could you want to leave this, Wendy? It's the only place we've ever belonged."

Wendy tried to reach for him, but he shrugged away. "John, that's not true. We belonged at home."

He turned to her with cold eyes. "You're free to go anytime you please."

Wendy thought of what the look on her parents' faces would be if she returned without one of her brothers. "John, don't be ridiculous. I could never leave without you or Michael."

John scoffed. "Why do you care now what I do? Why do you care if I stay or not? You never cared about me before, never wanted me to have anything good."

Wendy reeled. "What are you talking about?"

"You told Peter that I was too young and too inexperienced to lead the raid. You betrayed me to him. You could have lost everything for me." He shook his head. "I will never forget it."

Wendy didn't know what to say. John looked so deeply hurt. Could he have truly been so wounded by her words? What had gotten into him? "John? That was nothing! It was nothing. It didn't mean anything. I didn't want you to get hurt! I said it because I care about you. You're my brother; of course I want you to be safe. That's what family does. Don't you see? Our parents need us; our place is in London with them, in our home. What if we have broken their hearts, John? What if they are waiting by the nursery window, clutching each other? You can't live here forever, just being a wild boy and killing pirates."

John whirled on her, his face crumpled and cold. "Why not?" Wendy didn't know what to say and stared at her brother in bewilderment. "Wendy, the truth is, *you* need our parents because you're the good girl. You always do the right thing; always the center of attention. Even here, in this place that is everything I've ever dreamed of, you have somehow made it about you, you and Peter. We should be fighting pirates and planning battles to win this war, and you're in the corner, with your stupid bows and dresses, and all Peter can focus on is you—you, Wendy! You've thrown off the balance of this world, all because you're pretty!" His lips curled up in a mean sneer. "But prettiness fades. Adventure is forever. Glory is eternal."

Wendy threw up her hands. "Listen to yourself! What are you saying? What are you even talking about? John, this world isn't real!"

"You're wrong. The life I have here is much better than any life I was living back in London. I can't understand why you would want to go back."

"You don't understand because you don't remember our London life. You choose not to remember. I don't know how it works, but something about this place puts a veil over your memories, John. You aren't yourself here!"

He looked away from her, his eyes steely and hard. "I'm more myself here than I have ever been. See, I remember some things. I may not remember our so-called parents, but I remember how I felt there: bitter, quiet, jealous, invisible. If you truly love me, you would never ask me to choose a boring life over being here, being alive. What is so great in London that it would be worth leaving this for?" He raised his hands above him, as if to sweep in all of Pan Island.

Wendy grabbed his hand and shook him. "John! Do you not understand what Neverland does to you? The enchantment of it . . . yes, it's beautiful and perfect here, but it's also violent and dark. You didn't see what I saw at the Vault. You didn't see the death that is waiting for you. The pirates aren't imaginary, John! They are grown men, and they have real swords and real pistols, and they hate Lost Boys, especially Generals. And you aren't a General, John! You are John Darling, the child of George and Mary Darling, my brother! You love the stars, and you love reading twisted stories of the North! You aren't even whole here! You don't know who you are without your memories. John, please, our parents are waiting for us!"

She was getting desperate, her voice rising over the crash of the pale green sea below. She fell to her knees, throwing aside her righteous anger and any shred of pride to reason with him. She clutched at his hands. "Please, John, I'm begging you! Please listen to me! Michael can't grow up without parents!"

John shook her off in disgust. "Michael has parents. Peter can be his father. You can be his mother. His family is here, with the Lost Boys." John yanked her to her feet and pulled her close, whispering in her face. "Does Peter know that you want to leave? He can't know. You can't leave Peter—he'll be angry. Even if Michael and I stay here."

Wendy jerked back from him. "I will not leave without you both. John, I watched Kitoko die! Do you not see that there is no one older than Abbott here? That's because Lost Boys, particularly Generals, die!"

John gave snort. "Wendy, you are such a woman with your hysterical dramatics. It's just a game."

That was it. Wendy lost all sense of decorum, driven mad by her brother, something that happened so easily between them, and always had. Wendy lunged toward him, pushing him down easily. John scuffled up to his feet, his hand against his shoulder. "Wendy! Stop! What's gotten into you? You're acting mad!"

Tears blurred her eyes. "How could you not want to grow up in our house, with our parents who keep us safe, who love us? Do you remember Nana?"

John looked stunned. Finally, she had hit a chord. John's face changed, his eyes blurring over with confusion as a memory stirred. He blinked twice.

"Do you remember the way Nana sleeps beside you? The way she follows you to school and waits beside the school gate until you are done? Do you remember holding her as a puppy, when she would lick our faces until we collapsed and Father had to push her away? Do you remember when she had her puppies, and you sat up with her all night, putting a warm water bottle on her back?"

John's eyes filled with tears before he spun away from her. "Go away, Wendy."

Wendy leaned over him. "Do you remember when Nana almost died because of that rat poison? Do you remember how you sobbed into our mother's arms and how we prayed all night on our knees that she would live?"

John let out a small cry before grabbing Wendy roughly by the back of the neck and thrusting her out over the drop, so that she looked down to the rocky sea below. A huge wave crested up on the rocks, splashing her face. When had he grown stronger than her?

"John! John!" She gasped. "What are you doing? Let me go!" He did, throwing her roughly backward toward the branches.

"Sorry, Wendy. Please just go away. And don't talk to me like that, ever again! I don't want to hear any more about London or Nana! You may go home anytime you choose, but Michael stays here with me. In fact, I think that would be best. You don't belong here." He took a deep breath in, breathing in the sea. "This is a place for people who want adventure."

Wendy stared at this stranger who was once her brother, barely recognizable as the sun set ablaze his shadowed form. Her heart still hammered from his sudden threatening manner, but she dared one last time, in a small, pleading voice, quivering, "John, we have to go home."

He turned to her, and in his eyes she saw that it was no use. There was a finality there that she had never seen before. "Neverland is my home."

CHAPTER TWENTY

Wendy didn't remember making her way back to the Teepee, or into the tangle of branches that lay behind it. Hours passed as she walked quickly, wiping hot, angry tears off her face, her anger at John boiling up from her heavy heart. Who was that, back there? John had always been a brat—that she knew before they had come to Neverland—but who had that been, that tall boy who held her over a drop, whose glasses were fogged with humid air, who didn't care about his family? His feelings had poured out all around her, drowning her logic.

Beneath her anger thrummed a very obvious problem: she couldn't leave without the boys. She couldn't. Even if she took just Michael, how would she explain to her grieving mother, and her papa—oh God, her papa, who doted on John, who looked at him with such admiration and pride—how could she explain that she came back without him because *he didn't want to*? It was inconceivable. They were a family. They would leave together. Wendy wasn't so easily put aside, as John conveniently forgot. She might be a girl who preferred dresses to playing with swords, but she wasn't leaving this world without John. She would try again tomorrow and the next day, and the day after that, until she wore him down.

Three Lost Boys stampeded past her, leaving a flurry of dust in their wake. Wendy coughed and wiped her face off. Not that she knew how to get home from Neverland. That was fine though, because Peter would know. He knew everything. Maybe he would even convince John for her. Yes, that would be good. John worshipped Peter—he could perhaps get through that thick skull.

Wendy sniffed loudly as she walked, wiping her tears on the corner of her hand. Crying wouldn't do any good, not now, and certainly not with John. Emotionally exhausted and somewhat turned around, Wendy decided to nestle up against a massive wooden branch and just close her eyes for moment, just a moment to catch her breath . . .

Suddenly, she awoke to a rustling in the branches above her.
"Peter?"

"Wendy Darling." His voice surrounded her in the small grove that she had stumbled into. The branches were short and squat here, dangling with heavy yellow orbs that emitted soft curls of scent when the wind rustled their leaves. Peter landed in front of her, his feet barely brushing the ground as he reached out and swiped his long fingers through the bush, pulling off one of the yellow orbs. With a devilish grin, he brought it to her lips.

"They taste like sugar. Here, taste it." All she could think was how completely inappropriate this was, and yet, she opened her mouth and closed it on the strange fruit. The fuzzy texture thickened on her tongue, becoming a bit like the rock candy that Michael was so fond of. It fizzed and then dissolved against one of her back teeth, giving her a rush of energy.

She gasped. "Magic?"

Peter shook his head, his red curls falling charmingly over his face. "Neverland."

He reached out for her hand. She pulled it back, shaking her head. "Peter, I need to talk to you about something."

His brow furrowed. "Something serious, I'm guessing."

"Quite. Peter, it's just that . . ."

The playful look on his face became serious as his mouth sharpened into a grimace. "You want to go home."

Wendy's head jerked up. "Why, yes, how did you know?"

Peter shrugged. "There are very few secrets on Pan Island. This island has ears."

Wendy looked away from the quiet betrayal on his face. "Peter . . . you must know . . ." She looked up to meet his eyes, but he had stepped backward.

"Let's not do this. No sad goodbyes, no speeches, no promises. I knew that I had you for borrowed time, and that time is almost up. Tick-tock." He said it sadly. "I'm sure you will want to make sure you are back in time to beat your parents home from their ball. It's understandable, Wendy. You have a family."

A wave of relief washed over Wendy. "Oh, Peter, yes! That would be wonderful. I'm so relieved to hear you say that. I keep having these visions of them crying at the nursery window."

Peter waved his hand at her. "They don't even know you are gone." He turned to her and smiled with his small white teeth. "I promise."

A dozen Lost Boys ran past them, looking at each other with smug smiles when they saw Peter and Wendy alone together. "I see those looks, boys. Keep moving!" Peter snapped. They scampered past, making their way down through the tree.

"Where are they going?"

Peter pushed his red curls back. "Fishing. They are taking the boats out. I told them whoever caught the most fish would get flight given to him every morning for the next three days."

Wendy laughed. "You are very good at keeping them motivated."

"We need to eat."

There was a moment of silence as they stared at each other. "I'm sad to leave," she finally said. "I'm sad to leave you, but it's the right thing to do. You are quite an adventure, Peter Pan." Wendy stood up slowly, and after a moment's hesitation, she wrapped Peter in a friendly hug. "Thank you," she breathed over his neck. "Thank you for everything." She felt his hand hovering above her waist, and then he was wrapping her against him, curling Wendy into himself. She could smell him, like fresh wood and wine, the smell of sun upon skin, and she could feel herself falling into him with each breath. She pushed herself gently away with a blush.

"Peter. Now, I have one question for you, and that is—"

He gave a naughty grin, a flush on his face, his body seeming to quiver with want before her. "How do you get home?"

Wendy laughed, pushing her brown curls away from her face. "Yes! How do we begin to get home?"

He ran a few feet until he perched out on a branch that hung out underneath the open sky. "Second star to the right and straight—" He laughed joyfully. "Well, why don't I just show you, Wendy Darling?"

She smiled and held out her hand to him, so relieved at his cavalier humor. Everything was going to be fine. Peter would convince John to come home, and soon they would be lying in the nursery, retelling tales of Neverland to entertain them on winter nights as the wet London snow slapped the pavement. Peter slowly reached out and took her hand. She would see Booth's face again very soon. Peter was looking down at her, ever so dashing. "Come. You'll understand." She slipped her hand into his, and then they were flying up through the tree branches, a sensation that was so thrilling and yet familiar. They lifted up and off Pan Island. As they pulled upward, Wendy looked down and saw a dozen fishing boats, crawling with boys, on the north side of the island. As they rose, the boys became ants, the boats like tiny nutshells rocking in a gutter.

Up and up, Peter flew, his arms cradled around Wendy. She reached out her hand and watched the air move it up and down, the brisk wind caressing the skin in between her fingers. They rose. In between the layered clouds, she could make out the main island, a giant crest of sharp green hills that climbed up out of the water. Whorls of black smoke rose up out of the northern corner of Port Duette—there had been a fire there.

"Peter, do you see the smoke?"

He nodded, his eyes not moving as they flew upward. "Probably drunk pirates, burning down another one of their taverns. Idiots." They were flying slightly south now, still climbing, and Peter looked on steadily, his hand tightening and loosening on her waist, as if he were trying to knead her.

"Are we almost there?" she yelled. The air was becoming thinner, sharper.

"Almost!" he yelled back. "The passage is very high!"

Wendy nodded, remembering how high they had been when they had come into Neverland. "When can we come back with the boys?"

"Soon," Peter answered, soaring upward, faster, faster. Wendy leaned back against him, trying to place the memory of flying with Peter Pan deep into her brain, like sealing a treasure in a locked room. She never wanted to forget this moment, the joy and freedom of flight. Goosebumps had begun tracing up her arm when Peter finally slowed. Wendy looked up into the endless sky with a shiver. She remembered coming through the passage, the purple light, the swirling fragments like glass . . .

"Peter—can you not see the passage in the daytime?"

Peter looked down at her for a moment, his face sorrowful as he pulled her away from his body and held her out at arm's length, almost as if they were dancing. Wendy looked above her. "Is there some trick? I don't understand . . ."

"Wendy."

She looked at him in alarm. Her body tightened with fear, the malice in his voice unmistakable. She looked up at the boy who had kissed her and barely recognized him. His red curls swirled around his face in the wind, and the charming face was hard, like stone. His eyes were navy, his jaw clenched.

"Peter?" The fear had crept into her voice now.

"Wendy, Wendy . . ." He shook his head. "There's no trick. You see, you will never be going back to London, because there is no passage without my consent. There is no going home, but there is no reason to even try, because Neverland is your home. Forever, your home." His eyes narrowed. "Forever with me."

Wendy instinctively shrunk back, but Peter clutched her hands and pulled her closer. "Wendy, listen to me—I love you. You were meant to be mine. We were meant to be together, forever."

Her heart was closing in on itself, and suddenly, she found it very hard to breathe as terror tingled across her skin, worming its way through her chest. "Peter . . ."

"There's nothing you can say," he snapped. "Here are the facts, Wendy. You and I will be together. I will be the father of the Lost Boys, and you will be their mother. We will raise up Pan Island, and once I kill Hook, eventually we will rule over the main island. The King and Queen of Neverland."

Wendy let out a sob. "Peter! No, I can't, I . . ."

He whipped both of his arms forward, bringing Wendy back against his chest. She shuddered as he ran his fingers aggressively through her hair, a move that once drove her mad now so repulsive. "Shhh . . . it's okay. You will *learn* to love me. I know it. I'll give you as much time as you need. But have no doubt about it, you will be mine in every way possible. My little London doll, my darling." Then he kissed her on the lips, hard. Wendy pushed him backward; with one hand clutching his arm, she slapped him hard with the other one.

At her actions, he gave a naughty grin. "There's your fire. Up until now I thought it was just under your dress all this time."

"How dare you?" she cried.

His smile vanished. "How dare I?" A scream rose out of his throat. "How dare I? You led me to believe that you loved me! And I know about him, about Booth!"

Wendy froze. "But how . . . how do you know about him?" She closed her eyes. "John. Of course."

Peter huffed. "Do you not think I found out everything about you before John lost his memory? He was all too happy to betray you, of course. You Darlings certainly have some sibling rivalry issues to work out, that's for sure." He laughed, a cruel, shallow cough. "Now, the question is . . . Wendy, do you believe you could love me? In time?" He shook his head. "For so long I have been alone on this island, alone in a sea of boys who don't understand me. I want a girl, someone to lie beside me at night, someone to wipe the blood from my face and care for my needs. I can't be all alone forever here, I can't. Hook grows only stronger, and a war is coming. I need you. The boys need a mother. I can't . . . I can't live without you. Don't you understand?"

Angry tears filled his eyes, and she was struck by how much Peter resembled Michael at that moment, a boy having a tantrum over a toy. But she was not his toy. Wendy looked at Peter anew, seeing for the first time someone terrifying and unhinged. *Insane.* She remembered how he had killed the pirate by stomping him into the ground like an insect. How could she not have seen? Was his glamour so enchanting?

He grabbed her chin roughly, a sad look coming over his face. "I know that this is probably very hard for you, but soon, you will see that I was right and we were meant to be together. Our souls are entwined, Wendy. We have a bond. Your lips, your curls . . ." He tilted her face to the sun to see it more clearly. "Your perfect face, it was meant to be only mine. You will be my Neverland bride."

Wendy's hazel eyes opened wide. "Peter, I can't make myself love someone! I'm already spoken for! And we must go home, our parents . . ."

Peter snapped, "Your parents already think you're dead. Everyone thinks you're dead." Clouds drifted lazily past them as Peter's hand tightened on her wrist. "There is nothing for you to return to. And this Booth, well . . ." He shrugged. "He's nothing compared to Peter Pan. Who could hold a candle to this?" He looked out over Neverland. "I have a kingdom."

With that, he pulled her close to him, and Wendy let out a gasp as Peter pushed his lips over hers, but she was afraid to move. He breathed a sigh of disappointment as she stayed frozen. "So that's how it will be, you stubborn girl. There's something else." He pulled her body against his, the smell of him now making her nauseated, the sharp notes of sweat infiltrating her nostrils against her will. He breathed once before whispering in her ear. "If you don't learn to love me . . . I'll kill your brothers. Slowly. And I'll make you watch."

He pulled back with a friendly smile. "Well, Wendy, what do you say?"

She stared at him, tears running down her face, her hands shaking. "Why are you doing this?"

Peter shrugged. "Love makes you do crazy things."

Then he dropped her.

She felt the heat of Peter's sweaty hand fall away from hers and the biting air that rushed into her palm, stretching through the veins to her fingertips. She dropped away from him. She saw the icy stare, the cruel hint of a smile as she dropped down to his chest, then his feet, reaching out, desperately, for any part of him. With death so close, she hurtled herself toward whatever could save her in that moment, even if it was Peter Pan. But she didn't catch him, not an inch of his pant, the tip of his shoe. Instead she fell forward, grasping and clawing at the open air, nothing below her, the horror inside of her reaching outside her mouth in a terrified hysterical scream.

For a moment, all she could see were clouds, clouds rushing past her at an unthinkable speed; her hands tried to grab at them, but they filtered through her fingers, no more substantial than a dream. Her body twisted in the air, rolling in on itself, her legs thrashing as she fell, past the cloud bank now. The main island rushed into view, the fall more horrifying now that she could see the water below her; blue, green, and gray tumbled together as she spiraled in the air, her feet tumbling over her head, until she flipped headfirst, unable to see anything but the ocean below her, so far below her. She screamed again, and the realization that she was falling to her death finally came upon her.

The ocean was rushing up quickly now and Wendy commanded her brain to connect, to understand: she was going to die. She was going to die. The wind rushed around her, parting so fast underneath her that she felt like a ship breaking a wave. Wendy looked up, trying to take in her last view of sky and sun, the smell of the salty air, and yet there was only terror, her heart thundering in panic, feeling like it would explode out of her chest at any moment. Her hands flailed frantically for her neck, grasping for anything, anything to hold, anything to bring comfort, even her own skin. As she plunged downward, Wendy Darling closed her eyes, realizing that the violent gasps of ricocheting air that had been exploding in her ears were bursting out of her lungs, pathetic cries, desperate breaths. Her eyes closed out the blur of land and sky, the speed at which she was falling. She desperately searched her mind for images of comfort: Michael's impossibly long eyelashes. Her mother's tea. The gilded angels that hung above the altar at Mass. Booth, reading a book in a slant of sunlight. Her lips repeated prayers, ingrained so deep within her that even the fear of imminent death couldn't erase them. She fell, faster and faster, her body soaring toward the water. "I'm sorry!" she screamed, "I'm sorry!" Sorry to her parents, sorry to Booth, sorry that she had come to this nightmarish, magical place.

The ocean was so close now that she could hear the rushing waves beneath her. Her body flipped in the air again, her side facing the sea. Wendy wondered if it would hurt, dying. Would her body simply disintegrate upon impact? Would she drown, trapped inside of broken bones? "Oh, God, Oh, God, no!" It was close now, the salt on her skin, the water that she knew would be as hard as rock. She opened her eyes for one more glance at the world, seeing only the sea rush up to meet her. She took her last panicked breath.

There was a rush underneath her and she felt a hand wrap hard around her wrist.

She stopped falling. There was no violent jerk, no swing through the air. Once Peter touched her, she was weightless. The fall stopped. Wendy looked down as a gigantic wave rolled underneath her, the break of the water splashing her legs. Peter looked down at her, but this time he was the gargoyle perched atop a building, so devious his smile, so wicked the satisfaction that glowered down from his face.

Wendy was hollowed. She silently let Peter pull her back up to him, her body dangling limp in his arms as he flew them back toward Pan Island. She was numb as they flew over the lanterns that flickered in the early twilight, over the Lost Boys who waved happily as they passed overhead. She was a ragdoll, shocked to the point where she wasn't sure whether she had died. Was this the beyond? Was this her way of escaping death? Was she floating lifelessly under the waves now, a bobbing piece of flesh as fish fed on her bones? Had he only saved her in her mind, the boy who she had once wanted so much? Wendy didn't understand that it was real until Peter dropped her roughly onto the beach, both of her knees slamming hard into the gray pebbles that lined the shore. She finally took a breath, and then another, her hair falling into her face as she knelt on the sand, never so happy to feel land beneath her fingers, her nails curling into the damp earth.

Peter spat down in front of her. "Look at me." Wendy weakly raised her head, tears streaming down her face. She hated herself for being so weak, so terrified of his power, but the fall . . . she couldn't even breathe when she thought of it. She looked at him. The wicked Peter seemed to rescind into his face, and he curled his mouth empathetically. "I'm sorry I had to do that. I just had to teach you, I had to remind you, what you have to lose here. And I can do it anytime I want." He landed softly beside her and reached out to stroke under her chin. "That must have been very scary. But you see, I was trying to help you. I'm trying to protect you, because I'm the only one who can keep you safe here in Neverland. You were meant to be with me, Wendy." His voice choked up inside of him. "You have to love me. And if you do, I'll take care of you, I won't hurt you."

He spun around to face out to the sea, which raged against the beach. "I shouldn't have done that, I know I shouldn't have!" Then with a disturbing calmness, he pulled his fist back and struck himself hard in the face with it, his knuckles leaving a short, jagged cut across his perfect cheek. He sank to his knees beside her, his face twisted up in pain. "Can you forgive me, Wendy, please?"

She looked into his eyes, unable to process anything, anything at all. Her hand clutched her heart, feeling each beat as it hammered inside of her. She was so grateful for her heartbeat, so thankful . . . "I need some time," she whispered, staring into his red-rimmed eyes. It was all she could manage.

He hopped up to his feet. "Of course. Of course. Women need time. It's called courting, I believe."

Wendy bit her lip, drawing blood. She had never wanted anything so desperately as she wanted to be away from him, except maybe to have lived. Still, she considered flinging herself into the ocean, just to put distance between them. Peter took a step away from her. Then, leaning over her kneeling form, he drew a heart in the sand with his finger that stretched all the way around her. Wendy, trapped in Peter's heart.

"I remember the way you kissed me." He stood before her, whispering out to the sea. "I know you can love me. I know you can want me. You have your brothers to think about." He bent over her and gently planted his lips on her forehead. Wendy whimpered, digging her hands into the sand, one hand closing around a rock, but then he was gone, up into the air, back into the deep folds of Pan Island.

Wendy lay down flat on the sand, sobbing loud enough that she was sure even the coming stars could hear her, great gasping sobs. She cried for herself, for her brothers, for her parents, for Booth. The sobs were violent, a ripping of herself, so cathartic and so cruel. She had no idea how long she cried, but she knew that it was a nightmare of reliving the fall, of clouds and water, of Peter's face again and again.

Time passed. Wendy finally pushed herself up on the beach with a gasp, brushing granules of sand off of her cheek. The Neverland night was still, water lapping mere feet from where her collapse had left a curled form in the sand. She stood up, brushing off the sand from her tattered dress. Then she began walking on the edge of Pan Island. Ten miles, Peter had said once, ten miles around, a jagged circle.

She climbed over boulders, ducked under branches, making sure that her feet never touched the water. She didn't think. She just walked, clutching at her chest, feeling the breaths leave her body, breathing in the air of life again. When her mind tried to connect with what had happened, she would give her head a hard shake, pushing the image of Peter leering over her far from her mind. She just walked, kept moving, for her sanity, for hours, just walking until the sun began its languid rise over the horizon, the deep green of the main island made florescent by the harsh orange light. Wendy saw Neverland wake itself up in a blaze of peaches and deep reds, topped by an impossibly violet sky. Insects buzzed, and velvety moon flowers gave a shake to raise their heads to the light.

The sun shook Wendy awake too, and she began paying attention to where she was walking. Finally, she made it back to where Peter had left her, the heart he had drawn in the sand around her still there, its very deep groove surrounding the imprint of her knees, her body. Wendy looked down at the heart and then raised her eyes to Pan Island, her head leaning back to take in its great height, from the sea at her feet to Peter's flag at its highest tip. Fear began to slip back into a recessive corner of her mind, and her eyes narrowed. With her chin raised, Wendy reached out and scuffed the heart back into the sand with her foot, slowly at first, and then feverishly, until there was just an explosion of sand where the heart had been. Her spine straightened, and she felt her resolve become cold. She would not be his. She did not love him, would never love him. He did not own her.

And yet, when she looked up, her piercing fear of the sky remained.

CHAPTER TWENTY-ONE

WENDY MADE HER WAY UP TO HER HUT, wanting to change out of her clothes. Peter had touched them. She wanted to burn her skin off. Lost Boys chatted happily with her on the way, and Wendy acknowledged them but kept moving, her mind elsewhere, her smiles shallow and meaningless. Once she stepped inside the hut, a change in the air was immediate. Someone had been here. The small hand mirror that Oxley had given her was broken in the center, and everything was a bit askew. More than that, it was the palpable heat that filled the room. On the floor was a smattering of dully sparkling dust that trailed across the room and out the window. The sheer curtain was still blowing in her breeze.

"Tink?" In her fear, Wendy had totally forgotten about Tink. All this time, and she had thought Tink was the worst thing to fear. Wendy ran across the room, momentarily forgetting about her hut with its meaningless trinkets. "Tink! Wait!" She climbed out of the window, balancing her feet carefully on a thick branch that ran away from her hut, a trail of dust splashed across it. A large lizard slowly trailed his violet tail through its path.

"Dammit, Tink!" Her father would be ashamed of her for cursing, but Wendy felt she had earned it. Balancing as carefully as she could, Wendy made her way across the branch, grasping at the vines atop her head for balance. The branch spiraled downward before leaping up into a thick brush of thin sticks, rocking back and forth in the slightest breeze, a reedy sound rising out of their throats. Wendy paused for a minute, holding her breath. Directly below her, there was a tiny sound, like the peeping of a new chick. Wendy lowered herself to her knees, her belly across the branch. Below her sat the reedy nest, easily a ten-foot drop. And what was below it? The dimensions of Pan Island were hard to guess. It could be solid ground underneath it—it could be nothing but air.

Wendy heard the sound again, and without thinking, she let go of the branch and dropped feet first into the vertical reeds. It was time for answers. The soft reeds broke her fall, though her body pushed through them easily. She heard a crackling sound, and then there was nothing but air and . . . Wendy was submerged. Water rose up over her head. She felt her feet bounce off a shallow bottom, and she pushed up, kicking and pulling for the surface, which wasn't far. Sputtering, she emerged, fresh water running over her face. Her dress was a cloud of blue sky around her. With water dripping from her hair and hands, she waded out of the shallow pond, pushing her hair out of her face, scolding herself for being so impulsive.

Above her, reeds silently closed around the body-shaped hole she had left. Wendy looked around her. She was in the middle of a shallow pond, maybe only twenty feet across. The water was perfectly clear—she could see her toenails under the water, being surrounded by curious tiny black fish flecked with silver. She looked up, noting that in fact, everything around her was flecked with silver—the branches, the reeds, the grasses that grew out of the pond, the base of the pond. Wading through the water, Wendy came up to a narrow sandbar made entirely of silver flakes. She moved slowly, her hand outstretched, for Tink was curled upon it, staring silently at Wendy, tears filled with stars leaking out of her eyes and down her cheeks. Her ratty brown shroud was wrapped tightly around her, and her eyes were still as she watched Wendy slowly move toward her.

"Tink?" Wendy tried to keep her voice as low as possible. "Tink, are you quite all right?"

"Are you?" the fairy asked, her head buried in her knees. Then she sniffed.

Moving slowly, like she was approaching a rabid dog, Wendy climbed out of the pond to sit beside the fairy. The silver flakes of the shore crinkled when she touched them, breaking apart like wafers in tea.

Tink hesitated for a moment before turning her face away with a sob. "Go away, you silly girl!"

Wendy didn't move—instead, ever so slowly and ever so gently, she brushed a piece of Tink's impossibly golden hair back to look at her face. Tink's skin was white-hot to the touch, and underneath its porcelain exterior, Wendy could see the glowing tendrils of flight, tracing off her pores like wisps of fog. When Tink finally turned her face to the light, Wendy let out a cry. Her left eye had a deep swollen bruise underneath it, the size of a quail's egg. Purple and yellow bruising stretched out from the mark, marred by a deep cut that ran from the side of her nose down to the curl of her lip. On the other side of her perfectly sharp face, an angry red cut protruded from the side of her forehead. Dried blood and sparkling silver dust mingled together.

Wendy felt tears of empathy fill her eyes. "He did this to you. Peter."

Tink turned her head. "I deserved it. I tried to poison you."

Wendy uttered a sob. "Yes, you did. But no one deserves this. Not ever." She reached down and tore a huge strip of fabric off her dress, then walked over to dip it into the edge of the pond, wringing it out the way she had seen her mother do a dozen times for the boys' endless injuries. As she walked back toward Tink, the fairy flinched. "Don't be afraid. I won't hurt you," said Wendy softly.

Settling beside the girl, Wendy carefully reached out and began wrapping the cool bandage around Tink's head. She winced and whimpered. "It hurts."

"I know, I know." Humming a gentle Christmas tune, she began carefully tending to each of Tink's wounds: wrapping the bruises in the cool cloth, splinting the arm that Peter had wrenched, wrapping the legs that had been kicked again and again. When Wendy finally raised her head to wipe the sweat off her face, she saw that Tink was staring at her with tears running down her pale cheeks, tears filled with bursting stars.

"Why are you doing this?" She let out a strangled sob. "I tried to poison you! I kicked you off the walkway!" She took a deep, labored breath. "I hate you!"

Wendy shook her head. "It's not me that you hate."

Tink scoffed and then winced at the effort. "I love Peter. More than anything. He is the moon and the stars and everything in between."

Wendy blinked. "I believe that you think you love him. But love and fear aren't the same thing."

Tink sneered as Wendy smeared some mud on a bruise. "He doesn't love you, you know. He only thinks he does. Because you're his shiny new toy."

Wendy remembered falling. "Then Peter has a strange way of treating his toys." She gently touched the bruises on Tink's shoulder. The fairy shuddered, her shrouded wings giving a shake of dust.

"I messed everything up. He did this because I tried to poison you. It was me. Stupid, stupid Tink!" Tink reached out and struck herself hard before Wendy grabbed her hand.

"Stop that! Right now! Peter does not have a right to hurt you, do you understand? Ever."

Tink dropped her eyes. "You don't understand anything."

Wendy let out a sigh. "I'm tired of being told that. Tell me. What do I need to understand?"

Tink looked around and then bent to the ground. A creamy flower with drooping lips leaned (*leaned!*) toward her. Tink whispered something to the flower and then turned her head to hear a soundless reply. Then she turned back to Wendy with wide eyes. "Peter and I are linked, forever. My power is his, and his is mine. You can never come between us, not ever. I can never be extracted from him, not while I live." Her eyes narrowed. "He loves me. I belong to him."

Wendy looked over at Tink, her heart breaking for this sad creature, a piece of herself, forever shattered. "You belong to no one. He cannot own you."

Tink shook her head. "All I want him to do is love me. We are going to be together forever, he and I, my Peter Pan."

Wendy let her fingers cinch a knotted bandage on Tink's ankle, swollen and bruised. She thought about how Booth looked at her, so worshipful and respectful all at once. "You should believe me because I've known real love. And it doesn't come with bruises." Wendy remembered the fury in Peter's face when she had rejected him. She had thought Peter was a consuming fire, but it turns out he was just the flame, turning her skin to ash. She was so afraid of him. "Here, let me help you." Tink lifted her arms, and Wendy managed to drag her to the edge of the pond, silver shale slipping down the small bank. She dipped Tink's swollen ankles under the water, then used her palms to wash the dried blood off Tink's arms, legs, and face.

Tink began crying. "I can't understand why you are helping me."

Wendy leaned forward and kissed her white-hot burning forehead, her lips feeling that same wave of heat that she had on the bridge. Remembering the powerful Tink and seeing this pathetic, broken creature who clutched at her arm tore at Wendy's heart and hardened her growing hatred for Peter.

"I do it because that's what my mother taught me to do. I forgive you for the poison and the walkway."

At those words, a bit of the angry Tink returned, jerking her head back. "I don't need your forgiveness. Who are you to forgive me? I am a fairy, one of the oldest creatures in Neverland. The flowers and the trees bow to my song. In fact, you shouldn't even be here. This is where I come with Peter."

Wendy nodded. *Peter.* "Tink, I need you to tell me something."

Her eyes narrowed. "What?"

"How do I get home?"

Tink shook her head. "I can't tell you, I'm sorry. Only Peter can open the passage voluntarily. Otherwise, it opens every thirty years. You'll have to ask him."

Wendy remembered falling through the air. "I did. And it didn't go entirely well."

"Wendy . . ." Tink said hesitantly.

The pond gave a jolt, as ripples of water began parting and rolling toward Tink's ankles. The two women watched as tiny ripples of water crinkled down the pond, previously so lovely and still. Then they heard the drums. Tink turned her head. "Oh, no. Not again."

Wendy leapt up to her feet. "What is that for?"

"Peter must be readying the boys for another raid. Or an attack."

"So soon?"

Tink turned her starry eyes upon Wendy's face. "What did you do?" She began wringing her hands. "The boys, we can't lose more of them. Kitoko, Darby . . ."

Wendy stood up. "I have to go, I'm sorry. I'll come back."

"Wendy." Tink was suddenly beside her, her feet brushing the ground. She leaned in close to Wendy, her breath grazing her face, her voice pleading and fractured, confused and discombobulated. "Listen to me. He'll kill you if you try to leave. He will. Please, you have to believe me. You don't know him . . ."

Wendy looked Tink straight in the eye. "I know him now."

Tink turned away from her, her ear tilted to the ground. Then she whirled on Wendy, her voice returning to its normal razor edge. "Get out of here then! You've spoiled my haven and my pond with your selfish pity."

Wendy stared after Tink for a moment before pushing her way

past the reeds. Everyone here was insane. To Wendy's surprise, she ended up stumbling into a cluster of branches that hovered a few hundred feet above the Table. Pan Island was a labyrinth, an elaborate maze of winding branches and concave spaces. She didn't understand it completely, but she had the feeling that it had to do with the same sort of memory loss that had come upon her once she was in Neverland.

The Lost Boys were gathered in a large circle at the base of Centermost, a teeming heap of sun-kissed skin, sweat, and dirty clothes. Peter was at the front. Wendy could barely bring herself to look at him, though she felt the weight of his eyes on her, pushing her down into the ground. Peter started strutting back and forth.

"Boys, I've decided it's time. It's time for a change in our way of life." The boys fell silent, a relentless tapping of some boy's foot the only noise in the hushed crowd. "Since Kitoko's death, I have been doing some soul-searching. I've come to realize that taking the pirates' wine wasn't enough. It wasn't enough of a lesson. The pirates, they kill us. That's what they do. We raid their treasure, and they kill us, or we sometimes kill them, right, boys?"

The boys cheered, one boy yelling out, "I love you, Peter!" Peter grinned down at him, but his eyes stayed on Wendy.

"Well, I've decided that we need more than wine. We need more than treasure. We need provisions."

Confusion broke out among the boys. "What does that word mean?" asked one of the boys.

Peter smiled with a glint of malice in his eyes. "It means . . ." He gestured behind him. "Bring 'em up, boys!" Four larger boys were struggling to carry a large linen sack, the length and size of a body. Wendy's breath caught in her throat, fearing the worst, but when the boys dropped the bag down, there was a distinctly metallic sound. The Lost Boys were climbing over each other to get a look at the package.

With a dramatic flourish, Peter knelt down and flung back the linen corners of the bag and reached inside. He held the musket above his head. "Boys, we have guns!"

The thundering of the cheers shook Pan Island. "But Peter, how?" came another shout from the crowd.

Peter laughed at their excitement. "I visited Hook's armory late last night. I took the guns and left the rest smoldering, along with a handful of deader-than-dead pirates." He looked straight at Wendy, daring her to reveal why.

"Yeah! Guns! Guns! Guns!" The boys were chanting. Peter kept his eyes on Wendy.

"Here, John, why don't you be the first to try one out?" John flushed happily and walked to the front, pushing his glasses up. He took the musket in his hands, turning it over, wondering at the bayonet, his fingers brushing the lock. Wendy could see his brain figuring out how the gun worked, no doubt something he had studied back in London. Wendy saw a small smile brush his face. Then, without warning, he whirled around and aimed it at one of the thick limbs that branched off Centermost. The branch exploded into a thousand pieces, showering delighted boys with splinters of wood.

"Right shot, John!" Peter yelled, looking impressed. John had never looked happier. Peter raised his eyebrows at Wendy over the crowd. She held his gaze. "Now, you may be wondering—why the guns? Sure, we will have fun with them, but are they necessary?" At this, he knelt down as if telling the boys a secret, his voice dropping to a dramatic whisper. "Yes, they are. For you see, our days of playing games with Hook are over. There will come a time very soon when our battles will turn into all-out war. I grow weary of our small adventures. Beginning now, we will raise up our army. I'll bring more boys and find more guns! And when Hook least expects it, we will strike. Once the pirates are defeated, we will be truly free, and all of Neverland will bow to us. Wendy and Peter, the King and Queen of Neverland."

The surprised eyes of the Lost Boys all turned to Wendy, who stood at the back, her hands clenching with anger as she gazed at Peter. Hatred burned through her chest as he looked at her, claiming her as his own in front of all the boys. "She'll be our mother?" one asked.

"Yes." Peter smiled. "She knows the cost." He looked down at Michael, who was reaching for one of the muskets. Wendy looked up and forced a smile upon her face. John was looking at her now with confusion playing across his face, his head tilted, his glasses almost sliding off his nose. He was unsure, and she was glad. Thankfully, John reached down and tugged Michael away from the guns. "Awwww!" Michael flailed in his grasp, and Peter laughed.

"Don't stop him! We have enough for all of us! Every boy to a gun!" There was a wild clamor for the front, and Wendy watched with relief as John took a musket in one hand and Michael's hand in the other before walking swiftly away from the crowd. John was stubborn, he was utterly unlikable and completely under Peter's spell, but at least he was smart. At least there was that.

Wendy turned away from the boys and walked quietly into the tree. A cacophony of gunshots followed her, and she cringed at each one, waiting for a bullet to tear through her wounded heart. It didn't come. Instead, she wove deep through the great tree until she began making her way upward, climbing through the branches, step by cautious step. Slowly, a plan was forming in her mind. There was a soft thud behind her, and she knew what it was without even turning. "Peter."

"Wendy." When she turned back, he stood proudly, his legs splayed wide, a gigantic musket in his arms. "Do you like my new toy? I'm thinking of calling it the Wendy-bird. John had to show me how to use it, can you believe it?"

Wendy saw herself step outside of her body and make her way over to the tree branches in the distance. *Pretend he is Booth. Think of Michael.* Wendy turned to Peter. "It's lovely, Peter."

His face registered surprise. He was obviously not expecting her to be so kind to him. "Yes, well, it's a start. We'll need many more if we are to try and overthrow Hook."

"I imagine you will." Wendy shyly pushed the hair out of her face. Peter's eyes lit up, lingering on the line of her neck. Even now, when his presence made her want to bathe in scalding water, she could feel her body pulling toward him, feel her skin flush at his gaze. "Peter, I've been thinking. And I do need some time, but I do believe, I do believe that I could love you. I was just scared, you see. What I feel for you is confusing." At least now she wasn't lying. "I fear losing myself in you. It's not something I'm familiar with, and it frightened me."

Peter's face darkened. "I understand, Wendy, but when will you be ready? I have waited long enough, I feel. I'm losing my patience, waiting for you to sort out your womanly feelings." He stepped menacingly toward her. "We need to take our place as King and Queen of Pan Island, and soon. Who knows, perhaps we should even think about children to carry on our legacy?" At Wendy's horrified look, Peter laughed. "Not soon, of course. After the great war has ended."

Wendy felt frantic and trapped, like an animal in a cage, wishing more than anything that she could bury her head in her father's chest and he would take care of this wicked boy once and for all. But there were no grown-ups, no rules; there was no order here. There was just Peter, looking at her hungrily, and Wendy, hands shaking as she tried to maintain her composure in utter despair. She raised her head to look up at the sky, at the darkening clouds that dotted the distant horizon above the sea. She couldn't wait any longer.

"Tonight." She turned to him. "Tonight. Meet me by the branch that holds the lantern, long after the boys have gone to sleep. I'll be waiting for you." Peter was so excited by this that he fumbled, dropping the musket, for once out of control, belying the maniacal god-child she knew he was. But then he was back, calmly picking up the musket and walking up to Wendy. The smell of him, once so seductive, was now repulsive. Instead of leaves and spice, he smelled now like muddy earth, decay, and death.

She raised her eyes to meet his. "Tonight. And make yourself ready for me as well." She could tell by the look on his face that he wasn't sure what that meant. Good. She reached up, kissing his cheek softly, her teeth clenched so hard that she felt a shot of pain bounce off her jaw. "Everything must be perfect."

"I will. It will be perfect." He kissed her hard on the lips, and she stayed perfectly still, furious at the way her lips rose underneath his, the way her skin tingled with fire. *Booth. Booth.* She repeated the words in her mind as Peter kissed her. Finally, he pulled away, his boyish face elated. She bit her tongue to keep from crying and clutched her shaking fists. "I'll go. And I'll be waiting for you. My darling. I can't wait for you to be all mine." He turned away from her. "And it looks like there will be a storm. I'll bring extra blankets."

"Thank you."

He soared up and away from her, and soon she heard the happy notes of his pan pipe flitting through the tree. Wendy began making her way back to her hut. She had much to do and very little time to do it in.

Dusk came quickly, as if it were also trying to outrun the storm that courted its nightly turn-in. Wendy's body shuddered as a huge thunderclap shook the leaves above her. She peeked her head out of her hut to look up toward the sky. Huge heavy clouds, their billowy breasts flashing with green bursts of lightning, were rolling toward Pan Island. Rain clouds. Her father had not taught her as much about the weather as he had John, but she knew this: those clouds held rain, and lots of it. *Perfect.* The gray sky above her was thick with moisture, and she felt the first drop of light drizzling rain upon her cheek.

For a moment, she stood, looking out at the sea, and then her head turned west, toward the main island. How far could it be? Peter had said eighteen miles, but was that true? *Was anything he ever said true?* The sky answered with a clap of thunder so loud that it seemed to echo and bounce around inside her bones. The rain began to pour, warm and wet and drenching. Two Lost Boys ran past her hut, holding giant leaves over their heads for shelter. "Big storm! Get inside!" one of them shouted at Wendy before disappearing into the shady grove beyond. She nodded silently. *These boys.* She looked down at the tiny boy footprints they had left in the muddy ground, now filling with rainwater, now drowned out and disappearing under a small puddle that turned their footprints into a widening lake. It wasn't a question anymore. It was time to act.

Hours later, she stood up and forced herself to take a jagged breath. She had rested an d planned, until her path lay clear before her. She had tried to channel the strength of her mother, her strong hands and unwavering protectiveness. She had tried to channel the intelligence of her father, of his steady heart and quick mind, and finally Booth: his compassion, his kindness, and what he believed she was—brave. Wendy turned and went back into her hut, which she had totally ransacked. The small overturned table had been broken. The linen curtains were shredded. Food and ribbons were strewn everywhere. The water basin dripped over the floor. There were deep grooves in the wall where Wendy had raked a table leg with violent, heavy slashes. Wendy reached down, grabbing the burlap sack that she had packed earlier with a few dresses, shoes, apples, and her small dagger. For her last step, she turned over the small wooden chair that Michael was fond of, and with a careful stomp of her foot, she broke off one of the legs. She held up the jagged end, turning it over in the waning light of the storm. Yes, that would work just dandy.

Wendy stood up to survey the room, to take it in one last time. She watched the hammock rock in the wind, the way that the ribbons draped across the floor, a shuffling melody filling the space, a room she had once loved. She watched her shredded curtains blowing in the quickening breeze. It was the loveliest of prisons. Wendy pulled a single lavender ribbon off the hammock and tied it around her ponytail, smoothing the hair away from her flushed cheeks. She straightened her blue dress and slipped on her sensible black shoes. Through her window, she could see the mainlaind, a slumbering, green leviathan, lit up with jagged, angry bursts of heat lightning that peppered the island like an attack.

Wendy tightened her fists and recalled the memory of falling, of twisting and plummeting, of her panicked thoughts. She remembered the way Peter had drawn the line in the sand around her, the way he had kissed her as if she were his to claim. She let the memories rise up inside her like bile, filling her body with potent fear. Her breaths became ragged as she remembered it all. She turned to the small mirror hanging above the broken table. She looked back at herself, her hazel eyes rimmed with red. Her lips parted as she spoke quietly to herself. "Be brave, Wendy." The wind roared its approval outside.

Moving quickly now, she grabbed the wooden leg of the chair and shoved the tip of it into the burning torch outside her hut. She watched as the fire seduced its way into the wood, lighting it from within until the piece flared and sparked. Wendy ran back inside with the flaming stick and laid it down, ever so gently, on the hammock. Within seconds, it caught fire. She sprinted to the doorway, kicking over another torch on her way out. Smoke began to fill the hut. Without stopping, Wendy leapt out onto the tree, wrapping her legs around it the way Oxley had taught her.

Her body hurtled downward, the levels of Pan Island flying by as she dropped. When the main platform appeared below her, she hugged her thighs together, slowing her momentum so that she could leap off onto the rope walkway. She landed on her knees, falling forward, scraping her face on the disintegrating wood panels. With a small cry, she pushed herself up to her feet and ran toward the Table, where she knew the boys were probably eating dinner. Shouts rose in the distance, and she glanced up. Her hut was now billowing black smoke into the stormy sky. Thunder cracked as she cleared the side of the rope walkway and pressed her back against the side of the Table.

A small boy named Alexander was relieving himself off the edge of the walkway, laughing as he peed into the branches below. "Alexander!" Wendy barked. He turned around, a blush spreading up his cheeks. Wendy pretended not to notice. She raised her voice to a hysterical pitch. "Fire! Fire! My hut! The pirates! The pirates! They are attacking us!" She pointed up frantically. The boy's mouth dropped open, and he sprinted inside the Table, half-elated to be able to share the news, half-frenzied.

"PIRATES! FIRE!" There was silence inside the Table. "PIRATES! FIRE! WE'RE UNDER ATTACK!" Suddenly, the Table seemed to explode with noise as everyone was pushing up and running for the door. "Grab the guns!" someone screamed. Wendy silently tucked herself back against a wall. No one noticed her. A hundred boys were pouring out of the Table now, and an alarm bell had begun ringing. "Fire!" one of the littlest boys screamed when he stepped outside, unable to keep the smile off his face. "It's a FIRE! A REAL FIRE!"

The boys were everywhere now, each of them sprinting toward the walkway, grabbing buckets or swords or both. "Where is Peter?" someone screamed. "Has no one seen Peter?" A small boy began shooting arrows at the burning hut. Wendy watched them all silently, studying each face with careful eyes. The sounds of chaos rose up through the tree, shouts and screams. The fire had grown now to engulf her hut completely, a blazing inferno against the gray sky. Wendy looked at the clouds above. The rain had begun coming down harder now—thankfully, there was no danger of the fire spreading. She ducked inside the Table. A breath of relief pressed out of her. Michael was lying on the floor with his feet in the air, watching a bright green caterpillar crawl through his toes. Tears rolled down his cheeks onto the dirt floor.

"Michael!" she hissed.

"Wendy!" He turned over. "Where have you been? You left me alone!"

"I'm sorry, Michael. Something happened to me."

He turned his head sideways, his blue eyes tracing her face. "Something with Peter? Something bad?"

Wendy nodded.

"You left me!" he cried, dissolving into unhappy tears. "I'm tired! I stayed up all night and still no one would play with me! Peter told them not to play with me because I'm a baby."

He struck her in that five-year-old way, more adorable than painful. She cradled his hand. "We don't hit people, Michael. Ever." *Or drop them. Or threaten them*, she thought.

He looked down sheepishly. "I'm sorry, Wendy. I feel different here."

Wendy lowered her face to his and looked into his eyes. "I know exactly what you mean. Michael, we don't have a lot of time. We have to leave, and I'll explain later, but we have to go now. Do you understand? Peter . . ." She shook her head. "Peter is not a very nice person, and we have to go. Do you understand?"

Michael's eyes widened. "I want to go with you, Wendy." His small hands rested on her cheeks, and he leaned against her, his sweaty forehead pressed against her own. "Don't leave me."

She wrapped him up in her arms. "Never. I will never leave you. But I need you to be very quiet, do you understand? I need you to be silent, to keep us safe. And for the next two hours, I need you to be *very* brave. Can you do that?"

Michael nodded and raised his fingers to his lips. She looked down at him. "It's time to go." Wendy wrapped her arms around him and hoisted him up onto her hip. Then she ran. She ran out of the Table, turning down and down again, weaving her way over walkways and under branches.

"We need to get down to where the Pips sleep," she whispered to Michael, and soon he was pointing over her shoulder as they wove deeper and lower into the island, stepping on branches and curling under thick hedges of tropical leaves, an endless maze of curves and turns that were as natural to him as the hallways in their home. Wendy could hear the shouts of the Lost Boys far above them, their panicked cries as they tried to put the fire out. She poked her head out underneath a rubbery-tongued flower, sending a spray of water to her feet as rain poured down all around her. The sky opened up for a moment, and she could see the hut. The fire was much smaller now, a yawning black hole of smoke and smoldering flame. A shadow was circling around the roof, its movement quick and agitated. Peter.

The cold knife of fear twisted inside of her, and she turned back, running faster, Michael bouncing with each step. His tiny finger pointed again, and she turned, grateful to find a thin trail twisting underneath her feet, like a snake making its way to the beach. They ran under the perch where she had argued with John. She could feel the memory like a hot scar across her mind, at the way his face twisted in disgust at her, at his blind loyalty to Peter. She would come back for him. She would not leave Neverland without both of her brothers, but since John couldn't be carried, he would have to wait. Peter wouldn't hurt him—he needed John. She wiped away a tear as the sea came into view ahead of them through a thicket of vines, its waves peppered with a hard rain. The guilt at leaving John settled in the back of her brain like a cancer.

"Wendy!" Michael tugged hard on her shoulder and let out a whimper. "Stop!"

A figure stood in the darkened tunnel ahead of them, his tall form blocking the way, the rippling sea churning at his back. Wendy put Michael down and stood in front of him. With shaking hands, she drew the dagger out of her bag and stepped closer. "Peter . . ."

The figure stepped into the light. It was Abbott, soaked to the bone, his sword drawn but dangling at his side. Water dripped from the tip, mingling with the puddle at his feet. Lightning flashed, and Wendy saw the determined look in his eyes, the way he stared right through her. He raised his sword, and Wendy raised the dagger. "Please, Abbott, he's just a child . . ." He tilted his head to the side and looked at the dagger, and with a roll of his eyes he gave a soft shake of his head. Then he pointed the sword to the right, pointing to a small hole in the bushes, barely noticeable. Without a word, he gestured again with the sword. Wendy blinked and raised her eyes to his. He gave a barely discernible nod.

Wendy didn't have time to think. She pushed Michael through the small hole, just the perfect size for Pips. The hole opened up into another trail, this one covered by a canopy of white flowers, their mouths shuttered shut against the storm, a perfect cover from above. Clutching Michael's hand tightly in her own, they sprinted through the canopy before it spilled them out, without much warning, onto the rocky shore.

"Wendy!" Michael shouted, pointing past a large boulder. "Look!" Wendy turned her head. The boats that she had seen with Peter were still tied in groups, rocking violently just on the other side of a rocky outcrop. She had found them, thank God. They were right there. She raised her head to look up to the top of Pan Island. The fire was out, only a burning husk remaining. A strange horn blast rang out through the island.

"Run, Michael!" she screamed. "Go!" They ran toward the boats, both frequently stumbling and rising again, knees and shins leaking blood, leaving trails on the jagged peaks of rock that led to the sea. Wendy made it to the makeshift wooden dock, a thin piece of rotted plywood painted yellow, the water of the sea sloshing around her ankles, pulsating up over the dock. The boats were rising and falling on the angry waves, slamming into each other with violent cracks. She carefully picked up Michael as she made her way over the planks. Rain poured down all around them, heavy drops that blinded the eyes and made clattering sounds upon hitting the boats. Wendy could barely make out twenty feet in front of her. She plucked Michael up and set him down hard in one of the boats.

"Throw out everything!"

Michael began dumping the fish baskets and reed poles, each piece disappearing silently beneath an angry wave. She began untying the group of boats, her fingers shaking, making clumsy mistakes in her haste as she pulled one knot out only to make another.

"Dammit!" she screamed.

Michael stared at her. "WENDY!"

"WHAT?"

"You can't say that!"

"I know, I know, sorry!" She looked back at the rope, her brain finally connecting what she was seeing. She pulled one end of the rope after looping it through another. The knot dissolved, and the boats began pulling away from each other. Wendy leapt off the dock, landing hard next to Michael. He handed her an oar. Wendy stared at it, trying to remember how Booth had paddled the one day that they had rented a small boat on Buttermere. With a shake of her head, she grabbed the oar and began pushing the other boats out of their way as they paddled out of the tide pool and into the open sea.

Michael curled against her as she pushed the wooden oar into the water and back out, their boat rocking wildly as the angry sea curled around them. A wave crashed behind them, spinning the boat outward from the shore, Wendy losing control of the direction as the turquoise water flexed its muscles around the hull. The wind whipped the water into sharply crested waves, the salt spray splattering them both. She pushed again, harder this time, sweat dripping from her forehead, mingling with the drenching rain.

"I can't see!" Michael cried.

The small rowboat battled against the waves, occasionally churning in a circle as swirling crests around them roared with unchecked fury. The boat finally pitched and rocked forward, striving out to sea as if the waves themselves were carrying it. Wendy felt her arms clench as she drove the paddle into the water again and again, her hard determination inching them forward, her teeth grinding against each other. Michael was sobbing beside her, clutching the boat with one hand and her dress in the other. Finally, the boat seemed to pass some sort of barrier; the angry waves determined to hurtle themselves against the rock turned into waves that rose only to disappear again without the resulting foamy splash.

The paddle went in again and again. Wendy, soaked to the bone, her hands bloodied and splintered, began to hope. A full white moon rose over Neverland, and even through the pouring rain, she could make out its pocked surface. At first, it brought her comfort, this moon with all its history, the moon that she had watched out of her nursery window, just a girl gazing at the stars. Then she remembered that this wasn't the same moon, and that these weren't the same stars. She was a world away from her parents in the most devastating of ways. A prayer fell from her lips into the open ocean, out over the waves, into the pouring rain.

Her paddling slowed but kept its soothing rhythm: splash, pull, pivot, rise. Pan Island rose up behind them, fading now into the misty shroud that wrapped the island, barely discernible through the fat raindrops that were filling the boat. There was a moment of quiet before Michael began screaming. Wendy looked up to see a figure plunging toward them through the air, hurtling down toward the boat with unthinkable speed. Wendy stood up and held the oar out, trying to keep her feet steady as the boat pitched underneath her. Thunder crackled across the sky as gray clouds swirled in a tumult of stormy air, the sea and the sky becoming one. Wendy braced herself, the oar across her chest.

"Leave us alone!" she screamed into the wind. "If you love me, then you will leave us alone!"

Peter's voice swirled down from above, moving so fast, Wendy couldn't be sure exactly where it was coming from. "You know

I can't do that." There was laughter, rising into hysterics. "You thought . . . you thought that you could escape me?"

A funnel of air pushed past her face. He was close. "Michael, lie down in the boat and cover your eyes. Do as I say," she whispered. The waves around the boat were growing larger now, each one more powerful than the next, coming from some unknown shift in their pattern. They began spilling over the side, sloshing the hull, filling the bottom. The boat was pitching from side to side, pitiless gravity taking its toll, the small boat lingering on each pitch before violently bursting upward. Wendy stumbled, falling to her knees before righting herself and pushing her soaked hair out of her eyes.

"COME ON!" she screamed into the air, tired of waiting, tired of being afraid, anger rolling off her with beads of rain. "I'm RIGHT HERE!"

But there wasn't a sound, except for the rain, which finally slowed to a drizzle.

"COME AND GET ME, PETER PAN!" she screamed, her legs straddling her little brother, who was curled at her feet, the water lapping at his face as he cried with his hands covering his eyes. She waited a moment, watching as the waves grew larger, engulfing the tip of the boat, unrelenting as they pounded the wood. It hadn't occurred to her that they might drown. Michael's sobs were becoming hysterical, and without looking down, she knelt, reaching out one hand to touch his hair.

Lightning flashed, and she saw him, lunging for her, the handsome boy with the emerald eyes. She swung the oar as hard as she could, and it caught him on the side of the head. He tumbled into the water with a roar. Wendy looked over the side, and that's when the boat overturned, flipping so fast that there was only water, and Wendy knew they were dead.

She could feel the saltwater rushing into her lungs, all around her, salt in her eyes, the callous crashing of the waves pounding and spinning her under the surface. Lightning cracked above and she saw the flash of a fin underneath her, the flick of a sharp tail. She gasped and kicked, her arm,s clawing, her dress all around her, drowning her. With a loud scream, she broke the surface.

"MICHAEL! MICHAEL! MICHAEL!" She couldn't see anything but she was screaming, screaming his name, hoping that the water would take her before she would see her brother drown. A head slowly rose up in the water before her, dripping red hair, bloodred in the night, wide eyes that streamed navy tears. Terrifying, a monster. Peter stared silently at her for a moment before his hands wrapped around her throat.

"Peter! Please!" She struggled to breathe.

He began sobbing. "I love you! Why are you doing this? Why can't you love me? It could be . . . so . . . easy."

Her ragged breaths were being choked out of her as she struggled to free his hands from her throat. "Peter . . . I can't breathe."

"Nor can I," he whispered. "Not without you." His hands tightened.

Stars exploded in her vision, but just before she caved to the darkness, she saw a flash of blond hair in the water. Michael. She brought both of her legs up and slammed them hard into Peter's stomach. He gasped, and his grip loosened. There was a loud rush of water, and suddenly, a rogue wave flung the boat hard into them both, cracking against both of their heads and pushing them underwater, momentarily freeing Wendy from Peter's grasp. A strange sound filled the water, a throbbing pulse, the hum of something that came from above. The waves were violent now, folding in on themselves again and again as they pitched Wendy about, her body churning in the waves like a feather.

A small pale hand brushed Wendy's leg, and she grabbed onto Michael, yanking him up and into her arms. Kicking as hard as she could, Wendy sputtered to the surface again. Just as she emerged, she looked up in horror to see a large wave crowning before her, higher than she had seen before, and a huge black shape riding its crest. There was nothing to do but wait, to breathe in for a moment. Loud cannons echoed through the night, and Wendy heard the screams of men. Her arms clutched desperately to her brother, who wasn't moving; he wasn't moving. The rowboat was flung out to sea, far beyond their reach, and Michael wasn't moving. Wendy pulled his head up, turning his face toward her. His lips were blue, his eyes closed.

"MICHAEL!" She barely had time to scream his name before the giant wave crashed down around them, pulling them close to something that pulled them down, down into an undertow, the taste of the sea so salty in her mouth, in her lungs. She cradled her brother as the water swirled around her, unsure of which way was up or down, sea and sky and death all one shade of deepest black. She felt something sharp and hard press against her leg and tried not to imagine teeth, the flesh of a shark.

Whatever was touching them was everywhere now, all around, and she held her brother's body close to her as it pushed them together and then began tearing—no, pulling, pulling at their skin—as they rose out of the water. Wendy greedily gulped the air as they came up out of the sea. Lightning cracked against the sky, and she could see black wood, so much glossy black wood, windows and harpoons and jagged barbs, black figures that watched silently from an open deck. There were black sails snapping in the wind above them, and the voices of men, men yelling, and they were still rising up and up, out of the depths, into the air, held by—what, a net? Wendy's fingers curled around the black netting, silver fish flapping all around them, a small shark gasping for breath beside her, its eyes rolling back in its head, its bloody mouth snapping for air. She turned to Michael, who was still and blue and cold.

"MICHAEL!" She screamed his name and slapped his face, pressing her mouth against his own, thinking she could pour all her breath, all her life into him. "MICHAEL, PLEASE!" She blew into his mouth, pushing the air into his lungs, slapping his back, beating her hands at his heart, breathing, breathing, and sobbing as she cradled him, pressing him against her, breathing into his mouth, praying for his lungs to rise, crying and screaming, vaguely aware that they were no longer in the air but being settled onto a hard wooden surface. There was the sound of boots around her, the sound of shouts, and then an eerie quiet as she stared down at her brother, so blue and so cold. She began shaking him, desperately slapping and pounding on his chest as she cried his name.

"MICHAEL! MICHAEL! Please, oh, God, please, I'll do anything, please, take me instead . . ." She held his body curled into her chest, his still face against her own, her cries raking the air around her as she prayed that death would be quick because Michael was gone. Michael was gone, and there was nothing else.

She thought of her mother and father, how they had cradled his tiny body at birth, how they had handed him to her, wrapped in a soft blue blanket. "This is your brother Michael. You're going to take care of him, aren't you?" Wendy had been afraid to touch him at first, so tiny and so weak, and yet, when she had held him, she knew he would be a part of her forever. "Yes, Mama, always," Wendy had said.

She held his lifeless body against her own now, a whisper escaping her lips. "Oh, God . . ." she cried. "Please . . . forgive me, Mama." She touched his face softly, taking in his still eyelashes, his perfect blue lips, his pale chubby cheeks, the limp legs that splayed out on her lap. She had leaned her cheeks against his own, trying to pour her own life into his, her tears splashing over his face, when her brother sputtered and coughed. Wendy let out of cry and flipped him over, hitting him hard on the back until water poured out of his mouth, dark and green, splashing over her nightgown and feet.

Michael took a few deep breaths and began wailing, the happiest sound Wendy had ever heard. He clutched Wendy, his voice hysterical. "I want to go HOME!" She sobbed happy tears as she pulled Michael against her, noticing for the first time that they were on a deck, a black deck, with a black net settled all around them, gathered in folds. Wendy looked up to the sky as her arms tightened around Michael's shivering form. There, silhouetted against the white moon, she saw Peter's shape, watching, waiting, and then he was gone, out into the dark night, once a prince, now a creature of her nightmares. Wendy shivered and pulled Michael close to her, burying her face in his wet hair. She was afraid, she was hunted, and yet this was all she could do—hold onto the only family she had left and pray that someday the Darlings would all be together again, one family among these unflinching stars.

Wendy closed her eyes, Michael clutched to her, when she heard the click of boots, the sharp sound of leather and heel making its way to her, each practical step hard and unforgiving. The boots came to rest in front of her face: black leather, etched with swirls of smoke and water and tiny skulls. The voice rang out over the storm, the outer fringes of adulthood captured in its deep clip. Wendy raised her head, unable to see the figure clearly through the now-battering rain.

A large silver hook reached out and caressed its way across her cheek, the metal bone cold.

"Welcome aboard the *Sudden Night*, Miss Darling."

Wendy's story will continue in Volume Two:

✳ SEAS ✳

Acknowledgments

All the world is made of faith, and trust, and pixie dust.

—J.M. Barrie, Peter Pan

THERE ARE SO MANY INDIVIDUALS that made this magical little novel possible, without whom it would not be the same, nor would my career be where it is without them. I am indebted to you. Thank you.

To my beloved, Ryan Oakes, who not only believes in me, as a writer, as a wife, and a mother, but who always has just the right ideas when plot holes present themselves: Thank you for your masterful theological brain, which lent itself to this novel and the ones that will follow, very heavily.

To Maine, thank you for being the joy that propelled me to write a book overflowing with the wonder of childhood. I am privileged to surrender my adult years into your tiny hands. I love who you are.

To Mom, Dad, and Denise McCulley: Thank you for your support, your time, and your many hours of babysitting. Your overflowing love for your grandchild reminds me that you still have things to teach me.

To Cynthia, thank you for making my heart light.

Thank you to my dear friends and family, who smiles and

encouragement are the ideal sustenance of writers: Kimberly Stein, Cassandra Splittgerber, Nicole London, Elizabeth Wagner, Karen Groves, Katie Hall, Sarah Glover, Katie Blumhorst, Butch and Lynette Oakes, Emily Kiebel, Terri Miller, Amanda Sanders, Wendy Marie, Erin Burt, and Erin Chan.

To Mason: I'm eternally grateful for our writing partnership and our friendship. My words are infinitely better because of you. O Captain, my captain?

Thank you to my remarkable test readers, who brought me so many important questions, their suggestions like flashes of stars: Heather Erickson, Amanda Sanders, Jen Lehmann, Patty Jones, Jenna Czaplewski, and Katie Hall.

To Erin, my story editor: At this point, you know my writing better than maybe anyone. My work loves snuggling into your capable hands.

To my Sparkpress Team: The incredible Crystal Patriarche, whose name conveys the power she wields, whose unstinting enthusiasm for my work still bewilders me. Janay Lampkin, Christelle Lujan, Julie Metz, Brooke Warner, Lauren Wise, and Megan Connor—what a brilliant group you are. To my agent, Jen Unter—I'm so glad you are on my team. We're going to do big things. Thank you to the editors: Wayne Parrish, Lauren Wise, Barrett Briske, and Pamela Long, for their hard work and keen eyes.

To J.M. Barrie. Thank you for writing a book that has enthralled children around the world for over a hundred years. You taught us to dream.

And finally, to the original charmer David Hall: We miss you. We love you. We'll see you soon.

Author Bio

© Colleen Oakes

COLLEEN OAKES is the author of books for both teens and adults, including the Elly in Bloom Series, the Queen of Hearts Saga (HarperCollins 2016), and the Wendy Darling Saga. She lives in North Denver with her husband and son and surrounds herself with the most lovely family and friends imaginable. When not writing or plotting new books, Colleen can be found swimming, traveling, blogging, or totally immersing herself in nerdy pop culture. She is currently at work on the final Elly novel and another YA fantasy series.

CPSIA information can be obtained at www.ICGtesting.com
Printed in the USA
BVOW08s0604231215

430862BV00003B/8/P